FLYING WITH KITES

Alan Reynolds

Fisher King Publishing

Flying With Kites

ISBN 978-1-913170-25-7

First published in 2010

This is a work of fiction. Names, characters,
businesses, places, events and incidents are either
the products of the author's imagination or used
in a fictitious manner. Any resemblance to actual
persons, living or dead, or actual events is purely
coincidental.

Published by Fisher King Publishing
The Studio
Arthington Lane
Pool in Wharfedale
LS21 1JZ
England

Also by Alan Reynolds

Breaking The Bank

Exfil

Smoke Screen

Taskers End

The Coat

The Sixth Pillar

The Tinker

Twelve

Valley Of The Serpent

While all characters and events in this work are fictitious, the incidents relating to the Kosovan War are based on fact and news reporting at the time from a variety of sources.

The author wishes to express thanks to Fatmire Halili-Bunjaku for her assistance in translating various phrases within this book.

'Evil is the absence of empathy'

Nuremburg War Trials 1947 –
psychological conclusion

Chapter One

March 1999

The road from Pristina was deserted. Snowmelt trickled down the gulleys either side from the roadside drifts which encased the single track. The local school where Katya Gjikolli taught was closed, derelict, devoid of life and laughter; just the ghosts of former pupils remain. Swings in the playground dangled from their ropes, swaying in the cold early-spring morning, bouncing only to the whims of the passage of air. Bullet holes peppered the walls.

Katya pressed on with a sadness that enveloped her, but she had become used to the feeling; now, there was only numbness.

Three years earlier, Katya had graduated from The University of Pristina with a degree in English. The University had a history of dissidence, a hot-bed of radicalism according to the Serb authorities, but she had stayed out of politics, and religion for that matter, indoctrination served no purpose in her life; she was a free thinker. After completing her education, Katya had been approached to work for the local administration as a translator and interpreter, but she had declined. Various inducements had been offered – this lecturer post, that headship; all would be available should she so choose after she had served her time. She also refused to sign the loyalty pledge to the Serbian regime, which, as an ethnic Albanian, she was required to do.

Her decision meant that she had been excluded from the best jobs, the fast-tracks that would ensure a comfortable ride for her and her family. But she had no regrets, her little school suited her; politicians had always let her down. First the Serbs and now the Kosovan Liberation Army, she wanted no part of the struggle;

everywhere she looked, all she saw was misery and death.

Ever since she was a child, Katya had wanted to be a teacher, she loved the innocence of children – so uncomplicated, but in the last two years her life had dramatically changed.

She had met her husband Ibrahim, known to everyone as Ibi, at the University and they married just after her graduation. Unlike Katya, he was an idealist and joined the Kosovan Liberation Army in late 1997. They had been married for less than a year when he was sent at short notice to support the offensive at Glogovac. Initially, she had had the occasional scribbled notes from him which had been delivered by a local policeman who was sympathetic to the cause, but then it went quiet. She had heard nothing of his whereabouts or well-being for over three months, and she had no address to write back. Hours had been spent looking aimlessly from her window hoping to see him striding homeward.

Katya stopped momentarily. Had she heard a sound? Her heartbeat increased. She looked back... nothing. Fear plays tricks on the senses.

The breeze tugged at the brown scarf, which pinned back her blonde hair, her baby son safely asleep facing her in the papoose sling which she had strung snug across her chest. Picking up the pace once more, she anxiously made her way along the road, although that description was euphemistic; it was more a track where tractors and other vehicles had carved out ruts in what was once tarmac. On she went towards the cottage, slush clawing at her worn-out shoes like icy hands, hampering her progress and freezing her feet to the bone.

These were dark times.

She thought of Ibi and that day three months earlier when she answered a knock on her door. It was a bitter, snow-swept morning, two days before Christmas – not that anyone was celebrating. She could remember the event as if it were yesterday. It was just after breakfast; she was in the kitchen washing-up when there was a knock on the front door. Not an urgent knock that would have caused alarm; there were few visitors to the cottage, but an authoritative, business-like knock.

She dropped her dish-cloth into the lukewarm water. "Ibi...?"

Katya hurriedly made her way through the living room and slowly opened the door. She was confronted by a stranger, unkempt in a grubby military uniform. Her heart sank.

"Are you Katya?" he asked. They spoke in Albanian, their native tongue.

"I am Major Qazim Kraniqi, I am commander of the local K.L.A unit.

As she trudged slowly onwards, her head bent forward against the biting wind, her breath visible in the cold air, she recalled she had asked him in and made him a drink. In her mind, as if it were yesterday, she could see his dishevelled appearance, his soulless eyes staring at the grounds of coffee as they revolved around the top of the steamy liquid like a whirlpool, watching as they dissolved to nothing.

He appeared at first struck dumb with fright, fear, or just fatigue, lost in his own world, tired, drawn and beaten. Then, as he sat at their dining table, he started to talk in a faltering, trembling voice, an intensity of emotion that Katya had never witnessed before.

"Yesterday..." he paused and took a breath. "We were outside a village not far from Poljanci, when we were... ambushed by Serb militia, twenty, maybe thirty enemy. We fought them off for a while, but I had lost many men." He paused again; his voice laboured and filled with emotion. "Ibi and me... we managed to hide in a cottage, but we were discovered. Ibi told me to go... kept shouting... 'Go... get out; I will hold them off...' He said that if I made it, I must come and find you and tell you he loves you."

Katya continued her journey towards the cottage, the familiarity of her surroundings reviving the flashback. She remembered the major holding his coffee, tears rolling down his cheeks, before continuing his story. "I made it through a back door just before the Serbs stormed the refuge and later I saw them drag Ibi from the building and put him in a truck. He was... seemed, unconscious but it was difficult to tell; I was many metres away..." He paused again and took another sip of coffee; he kept repeating, "I am so sorry, I am so sorry; he was a brave, brave man."

He wiped away a tear with a grimy stubby finger. It had taken all night for the commander to deliver that promise, but he owed Ibi his life.

The news had stunned her and, recounting the event, Katya felt the pain again like a knife through her heart. Given the Serbs' reputation, she knew that survival in their prisons, if he had made it that far, was unlikely; but she had made a pact with herself that she would keep. She knew she had to be strong for their baby son. Melos had been born less than four months ago and was conceived the very night before Ibi had left. It grieved her even more that Ibi did not know he had a son.

It had been hard coping with her confinement on her own, but right up to the birth her fellow teachers had been a great comfort and support. Her mother visited when she could but, living an hour away, she had to rely on her neighbour for occasional lifts in his old tractor; there was no public transport.

Katya had kept working eight months into her pregnancy which meant she had earned enough to feed and clothe herself and put something by in case of emergencies. She had only taken two weeks off before returning to work, but after just a couple of days the school closed; it was too dangerous. Almost six months ago, how everything had changed in such a short time.

Katya checked the road again... nothing. The school had disappeared from view behind her; not far now. She whispered a silent prayer to anyone who would listen. "Please keep us safe; please, please keep us safe."

She could hear the rustling of the bare branches of the trees clacking against each other like some manic timpani. A cold shiver ran down her spine, nothing to do with the penetrating wind... utter, petrifying fear. Once again uneasily, she glanced behind her... still nothing.

Kosovo was a dangerous place and she and her son were both in peril if she were to be captured by the Serbs. Rumours were rife that they made little distinction when it came to slaughtering ethnic Kosovans, particularly those with apparent KLA connections.

"I have to be strong; I have to be strong." It was like a mantra, she kept repeating it to herself.

After the devastating news of Ibi's capture, she was eventually persuaded to leave her cottage in Lapugovac and stay with her mother in Lapusnic, a small community some ten miles away from. She had only stayed home in case Ibi had returned. At the cottage, there were simply too many reminders of family life with her husband. She realised it was time to move for her son's sake and had taken just a change of clothes for her and Melos.

Katya was an only child and was close to her mother. Maria Vitija had lived with her husband Josef for over thirty years but had been widowed five years earlier. Josef had gone into Pristina for some supplies and did not return home. He turned up in the morgue three days later. Maria had been given no details of how he died or in what circumstances.

For over two months during the harshest period of the Kosovan winter, Katya had felt relatively safe in her mother's cottage. They were reasonably stocked with food and neighbours supported each other; there was a great sense of community. But with each day, the war drew closer to their door. News came that the Serbian forces were seen in the next village pillaging for supplies. Stories of brutalities spread among the local population and Katya knew she would be in extreme danger. It was time to escape and join the countess other refugees who were fleeing the country. She pleaded with her mother to go with her, but Katya knew it would be in vain. "I was born here, and I will die here," her mother declared, unequivocally.

So Katya was embarking on the dangerous trip back to her

home that morning to collect what belongings she could carry and anything else she might need before making her escape. Her mother pleaded with her. "Where will you go?" Katya couldn't answer. She had no real plan, no arranged itinerary. She just knew she had to get away.

Katya managed to beg a lift from Afrim, a neighbouring farmer and family friend who, somewhat reluctantly, agreed to drive her back to the cottage on his wreck of a tractor. They set off just after dawn and Katya had to drag herself away from her mother's grasp as she cried out. "Katya, Katya, please... do not leave me," she implored one last time.

It took all Katya's mental strength, but she knew she had to go and, as she looked back from the seat of the tractor, she could see her mother collapsed in the doorway of her cottage overwhelmed with grief. Tears wouldn't come, she was beyond that. Katya was cried out.

The weather was still very cold in the early morning, but at least the snow was almost gone; just the drifts in the verges where it had been piled high to clear the way for the occasional traffic. The tractor made slow progress, the huge tyres struggling to maintain traction on the treacherous surface. The noise of the ancient Lanz Bulldog's engine was loud enough to wake the dead, certainly sufficient to arouse the interest of any nearby Serb patrols.

Eventually, after an hour, his nerve failed him and Afrim stopped at a junction, still some two miles from the village. He looked left and right; then behind him, anxiety etched on his face. The farmer turned to Katya. "I am sorry Katya, I cannot go any further, it is too dangerous."

Katya looked at him with a mixture of surprise and disappointment and nodded. "It is ok; I understand; we will manage."

She grabbed her bag and descended the steps of the tractor, clutching her son. She would have to walk the rest of the way.

Lapugovac was a small village of fewer than two hundred

inhabitants. There was one shop, a general store where villagers could usually buy what they needed, and the school where Katya earned a living. With her teacher's salary and the money Ibi earned from the local garage where he was a mechanic, it meant they were comfortable compared to others.

Their home was a modest house with a small garden at the front and in the middle of a group of three detached two-bedroomed cottages. Ibi had taken their ten-year-old Volkswagen which had been donated to the KLA. So, without any other obvious forms of transport, a long walk looked likely. Although the weather was inching into spring, it was still cold, particularly at night and early morning with the inevitable frost of a Balkan winter; but if they wrapped up well, she reasoned, it was comfortable enough.

She was close now as she approached the brow of a hill and squatted low to create as small a silhouette as possible. She could see the three cottages clearly, about a hundred metres ahead. Like the rest of the village, they looked deserted. She had been away for over two months and in that time, the neighbours had fled - or had been forcibly removed; there was no way she could be certain. Tentatively, she walked towards the house, looking left and right as if crossing a busy freeway. She reached the front door, then stopped.

"Booby traps; always check for booby traps." That's what Ibi had said. Katya had always thought it was alarmist, but this was different. Rumours were rife that Serbs were carrying out all manner of atrocities. There was no sign of forced entry; the door appeared intact. Perhaps she had been lucky.

She looked at the door frame, not really knowing what to look for. No sign of wires or anything obviously out of place. She moved closer and peered through the frosted glass which was surprisingly unbroken. There was no movement in the blurred background, nothing. She took the chance and placed the key in the lock and slowly turned it.

Click, the key turned, she heard the lock fall reassuringly.

She pushed against the door, carefully increasing the pressure until a gap appeared. Further... gently. She peered through and opened the door a shade more.

That's when it hit her... the smell, like rotting meat. She gagged. Quickly, holding her scarf to her nose and mouth, she moved inside. It was dark, but the curtains, not fully closed, allowed a shard of light into the room. She gasped in horror; only her hand across her mouth prevented a scream.

He was highlighted by the sun's hazy rays, like a music-hall performer in a spotlight, his eyes vacant staring at the wall as if appreciating some old masterpiece. His mouth was open, his face twisted by the pain of his final death throes and the all too vivid tracks of blood from a gaping hole in his chest was clearly visible.

Katya retched.

"Ibi?"

It was her initial thought, but straight away she could see it was an older man in what seemed to be the remnants of a military uniform. She didn't immediately recognise him. Then she remembered; it was Major Kraniqi. But what was he doing here and, more importantly, how did he get here?

Her heart was pounding as she moved through the house into the kitchen and found the back door had been forced. There were bloodied footprints leading to the living room and to the table where the body now sat. He must have been shot somewhere close by and made his way to the back door from the woods; that was a possibility Katya thought. He knew the house and would have been looking for help. Instead, he had bled to death at her dining table where only a few weeks earlier he had told her of Ibi's capture.

This was no place for any detailed scrutiny, there was no time; the Serbs could be close. Quickly now, her mind racing, her pulse sprinting off the scale, she went upstairs. Melos began to cry; he had been asleep for the last hour. He would need a change and feed soon but not here; he would have to wait a little longer.

Trying desperately to think logically, her nerves shot to pieces, her emotions in shreds, she went through her cupboards. She had her passport, papers and a small amount of money, about fifty Deutschmarks - the currency of choice in Kosovo, and a gift from her mother. She carried them in a small purse which was attached to a belt around her waist. She went upstairs and lay Melos on the bed.

Her hands shaking, she managed to take the photo of her and Ibi from its frame, which still stood on the bedside table. She put it into a rucksack together with a change of clothes, some baby things, a blanket, disposable nappies, moist wipes and a few jars of baby food.

Must keep focused, must keep focused, she repeated to herself.

In her mind, she was making an inventory, trying to salvage some sense of order in the chaos that surrounded her. A couple of minutes passed or was it seconds, it was difficult to tell, just a blur. That's it, any heavier and it would slow her down and she couldn't afford to hang around.

Got to hurry, got to hurry.

Then she heard it; some distance away but definitely coming closer, the low rumble of a truck. She wanted to pee.

Katya listened fearfully to the crunching of gears as the driver made allowances for the incline towards the cottages. She crouched at the window and cautiously looked through, peering just above the lower edge of the frame and saw the vehicle. It stopped. Six soldiers, Serbs, got out. Four of them immediately started to urinate against the tree next to the first house. Katya froze; Melos continued to wail, his cries getting louder and louder.

"Sshhh!" she whispered abruptly. Whether the sense of danger or just the tone of urgency in Katya's voice had passed to the child, she would never know, but at that moment Melos, looking startled, was silent.

Katya could hear her own breathing. She tried inhaling slowly to regulate her heart rate, but her level of concentration was being driven by her mechanism for survival. She exhaled counting to five – a trick she had learned to use to control her nerves at college, but this was no end-of-term presentation. She knew she was in grave danger... but what should she do?

Decisions, possibilities.

Should she try to make a break for it which would almost certainly start Melos crying again, or keep down and hope they would simply drive away?

Her mind was made up for her. From the next building she heard the breaking of glass and automatic gunfire. A cry went out to the driver, "*benzin!*" and she saw him go to the back of the vehicle and bring out a large jerry-can. They disappeared from view, but she guessed what was happening.

Now or never...

She picked up Melos from the bed and put him in his sling. Then she took the rucksack, wrapped the straps around her shoulders and fastened it securely onto her back, her legs barely able to obey the orders from her brain. The sudden movement started Melos crying again.

Noise... too much noise.

Quickly down the stairs, into the kitchen, she stopped only to grab a small carving knife from the drawer by the sink. She dropped it into the opening of the rucksack. Then out through the back door, tramping over the small vegetable patch that had sustained them in recent years. As the cold air hit her, she remembered she had left her gloves on the dressing table in the bedroom... too late.

She reached the chain-link fence at the end of the garden and pushed it with her foot. It gave way and she leapt the half-metre obstacle while holding her child tight to her chest. It was probably two hundred metres to the protection of the woods across an open field of rough marsh-grass freckled with lying snow. Running was almost impossible but run she did, keeping her head down as low as she could as she headed towards the distant trees. Melos was screaming from his cocoon.

Hope was hanging by a thread. If the Serbs were preoccupied with their looting or whatever they were doing next door, then she may have a chance... her only chance.

Katya struggled across the field; one minute her feet were landing on the tops of the mounds of grass, the next they disappeared into a hollow of snow. She was clenching her toes to avoid losing her shoes which would render her immobile; frostbite was still a possibility.

One hundred metres, her eyes played tricks on her. Despite her efforts, the tree-line seemed even further away. She dared not look behind her, worried about what she might see. Fifty metres, twenty, ten, then into darkness as the forest enveloped her. She raced further into the trees, not stopping to look back, half-running, half-walking, desperately trying to increase the distance between her and the danger not far behind. The further in she went, the denser and darker became the forest, the pines no more than two metres apart. After what seemed to be an eternity, she stopped, totally disorientated.

She leant against a tree, her chest almost exploding with the pressure of blood being pumped around her body. Melos, in his sling, moved up and down to the rhythm. She looked around and realised she was hopelessly lost; a feeling of sheer desolation enveloped her. She tried to catch her breath but, with no time to lose and no choice, she carried on further and further into the gloom. The loneliness was beginning to eat away at her strength like some unseen parasite; panic lay just below the surface.

After the arbitrary tracks, mostly made by animals, she eventually picked up a more obvious trail, but had no idea where she was or in which direction she should go. Although she had lived nearby for almost two years, she had steered clear of the forest. She found it frightening; it reminded her of the Brothers Grimm fairy tales her mother used to read to her as a child.

North, she thought, would take her towards Glogovac. Katya

knew she must stay away from there at all costs. She remembered there was a train station at Klina which was where the main line from the south to Pec joined the line west from Pristina. Klina would be about fifteen miles away as the crow flies but nearer twenty across country. The terrain was mountainous, and she would need to follow the contours of the valleys. She recalled visiting the town as a young girl, in happier times. From there, she could possibly catch a train and reach the border with Montenegro; then, who knows. But at this moment she had no concept of the points of a compass. There were no landmarks; she couldn't even see the sky, just the canopy of the tall firs.

Melos was crying again; she would have to see to him soon. For the first time, she looked back in the direction she had travelled and saw no movement. The darkness of the trees cloaked around her like a shroud. In the distance, for a moment, she thought she saw a pall of smoke but couldn't be certain. She was safe, for now. She quickly saw to her son, cleaning him with wipes and replacing his soiled nappy which she then buried under some pine needles to ensure no trace.

Again, it was decision time. She chose the path to the right, concluding logically it appeared to be heading away from Lapugovac. She followed the track for probably an hour without seeing a soul, Melos had mercifully gone back to sleep. All she could hear was the wind struggling to break through the trees. Progress was slow and the weight of the rucksack on her back was beginning to tell. It felt as if it were getting heavier by the minute, the straps cutting into her shoulders. She continually blew into her hands to warm them and aid circulation.

After a while, the track widened, and she suddenly came out of the eerie gloom of the trees into a clearing. The weak sunlight after the darkness made her blink, and she shielded her eyes with her hand. In the corner, she could see an old building, a hut of some kind. It reminded her of the woodman's cottage from Hansel and Gretel. It looked deserted, but she wasn't taking any chances. Slowly, keeping to the tree line, she carefully approached the shack.

As she got nearer, she could see it was made from logs with one open window cut into the middle on the side facing her, not particularly robust, but it would provide shelter while she fed her son and took stock. She needed to rest; she had been walking for two hours. Reaching the entrance, there was no door, she could see it was a shelter of some kind designed to provide the woodsmen with a place to eat their lunch or have a smoke out of the wind.

Anxiously, she slowly peered inside. It was dark and gloomy, the small window not really providing sufficient light. She could see evidence of previous visitors - discarded beer cans, cigarette stubs. She could also see in the corner the source of the rancid smell; it was also someone's lavatory.

Steering clear of the mess she found a spot which was reasonably clean and put her rucksack down on the bare earth floor. Lifting Melos from his carrier, he woke up and, clearly hungry, started crying again. Without water or heat, she did what she had to do, she unbuttoned her shirt and pulled down her bra connecting her son to her right nipple. He suckled gratefully. For the first time she started to relax; so far, so good.

She completed her feeding and placed Melos on a blanket to change his nappy. Her back was to the door, but instinct told her something was wrong. The light had changed; it had gone dark. She turned to see a shape in the doorway blocking the hazy brightness. Silhouetted against the opening was a man in a military uniform, carrying the obligatory AK 47. She inhaled sharply as her survival reflexes took over. She heard the voice of another man, so there were at least two, and she was trapped. There was no escape, no way out. Once again, her heart raced.

"Hello, what have we got here? What is your name, my lovely?" said the man.

It was Serbo–Croat, not her native Albanian, but she understood. It was not a greeting.

"K... K... Katya... Gjikolli," she managed to stutter.

"And where are you going?"

She told him where she was heading. "Klina."

She heard the other man's voice. "Who is it?"

"She says her name is Katya... She is very pretty, too, for a Kosovan."

He took two steps forward, slowly, eying up the girl. Immediately his gaze was drawn to her open shirt and half exposed breast. Melos was still on his back on his blanket, legs pounding in the air, gurgling happily, totally oblivious to the danger. Katya quickly clasped her shirt to protect her modesty and started to button up.

"Ne, ne...!" He motioned with his weapon for her to drop her hands.

She was still on her knees and turned her back to the soldier. Her hands moved to the floor and she leant forward on all fours protecting her son. She felt hands grasping her ankles and pulling sharply. The momentum caused her to fall flat on her stomach, instinctively she kicked out at the soldier. Her skirt rode further up her legs, exposing her thighs to her attacker. Her knees dragged across the rough ground, grazing them; she felt nothing. Still on her stomach, she screamed, a totally futile gesture. She heard the click of the safety catch of the AK 47 being released. She turned over and gasped in horror as she saw the soldier pointing the automatic rifle at her son. She was almost convulsing with fright.

"Ne...!Ne...!" she screamed.

The second voice called out. "What is happening?"

"Stay outside and keep guard. This one is mine," said the aggressor.

The second soldier obeyed; a question of rank and knowing his turn would come. She was still on the floor and recognised her situation was hopeless. She faced the soldier, her hands held up in submission. Whether it was the inevitability of the situation or some inner strength that had taken over, she would never know, but somehow a calmness took hold of her.

There was a voice in her head. 'Be strong. I must be strong,' it was saying.

Sitting up, she lifted her skirt and slowly pulled down her pants. Her situation was desperate, she knew resistance was pointless and would surely mean the death of her and her son. At least she may be spared a beating. The soldier placed the gun down on the ground beside him and started unbuttoning his trousers revealing urine-stained underpants. Katya caught her breath, bracing herself for what was to come.

He fell on top of her and she let out a deep breath as his weight pressed her to the dirt. She felt his hardness enter her. It was rough and painful. She had not had a man inside her for a long time, not since that final night with Ibi. Tears fell from her eyes as the man pumped into her. She was angry, sad, terrified, but somehow, paradoxically, she suddenly sensed control had moved in her favour. She stopped crying; this violation was not of her seeking. 'Be strong. I must be strong'.

His breath smelt of stale cigarettes and he was beginning to sweat profusely. It was all over in a matter of seconds and, as she felt the stream of his orgasm shoot into her, he collapsed on top of her, totally spent.

She wanted to be sick.

His weight was pinning her to the floor, no chance of escape. She turned her head and saw Melos still on the blanket playing with his toes. But between her and her son, within touching distance, was the open rucksack. She slowly moved her hand and carefully felt inside the bag. The man was still catching his breath. She found what she was looking for as she touched the hard handle of the knife with her shaking fingers. In one movement she swung her arm around and plunged the blade into her assailant's back with all the strength she could muster.

Blood oozed from the wound and he screamed a piercing shriek like a stuck pig, both hands grasping for the knife that was out of his reach. She pushed him off and grabbed the rifle just as the second soldier, alerted by the scream, appeared in the doorway. Still seated on the floor, she blindly aimed and pulled the trigger. The recoil sent her backwards, missing Melos by a matter of inches.

Daylight streamed through the gap; the blockage having slumped to the ground... lifeless.

Melos started crying again, frightened by the sudden noise and commotion. She slowly moved towards the door and the motionless body blocking the entrance. Turning him over, she could see the bullet had hit him in the face which was now unrecognisable as that of a human being.

She threw up what was left of her meagre breakfast.

Struggling to remain in control, she recognised she was still in danger; other militia could be close by. She quickly dressed, grabbed her rucksack, zipped it up, wrapped it around her shoulders and heaved it onto her back once more. She lifted Melos into her arms and into his papoose.

Suddenly, she heard a moaning noise behind her. It was the first soldier, her attacker, still alive. He knew her name and could obviously recognise her again. She had no alternative. Without a hint of hesitation or conscience, she stared into the eyes of her attacker as she raised the rifle to his head and pulled the trigger. The groaning stopped. She pulled the knife from his back, wiped it clean of blood on his jacket and put it back in the rucksack.

Melos screamed.

She dragged the second soldier into the hut away from inquisitive eyes.

She had to move fast.

Chapter Two

The track away from the clearing had widened, designed to take logs and equipment to the main road. The gradient was steep, sloping down the side of a large hill. Katya went for the cover of the trees, walking parallel to the track, keeping out of the line of sight of anyone responding to the ruckus she had just left. Walking was difficult, the downward terrain pulling at her leg muscles; the straps of her rucksack once again pressing into her shoulders. She was wary of going too far into the forest for fear of getting totally lost with the risk of walking in circles.

It was mid-afternoon and the weak sun had been replaced by a rolling mist coming down from the mountains. Visibility was less than a hundred metres; this could be a blessing. She knew she had left the evidence, the bodies of two dead Serb militiamen, and was all too aware of the consequences, for her and her son, if she were captured. She also knew it wouldn't be long before her attackers were missed, and a search launched. She must keep moving. She could hear the sound of aircraft overhead and in the distance, the report of explosions rumbling like thunder. The fear and anxiety she felt following her ordeal had been overtaken by her need to survive.

"Be strong. I must be strong." The sound of her whispers was being borne away on the breeze.

She talked to Melos to keep him occupied and calm, at least he was quiet for the moment. After a couple of miles, she reached the end of the tree line and a tarmac road crossed in front of her. At the lower level, the fog had lifted, and hazy sunlight again filled the landscape. She did not recognise the road; nor were there any signposts. She crouched in the shadow of the trees listening and watching. Right or left? She chose right for no particular reason, just an intuitive decision. The blacktop continued downhill, the pot-holed tarmac making the going easier, and for the first time since the attack, she started to think about her own well-being. She had had nothing to eat since breakfast, and most of that had been returned. Her legs, back and shoulders were aching, and she was sore. She had put up with the dampness which followed her rape, but it felt uncomfortable; she was desperate to wash.

She walked on. Then, after another half an hour, she could see she was approaching a village. The anxiety returned. Although she was well away from the site of her earlier ordeal, she was still vulnerable. She had a choice, cut back through the forest or take a chance. She decided to continue.

As she got closer, she could see no signs of life, the houses that were still standing looked deserted. The first cottage she came to bore the evidence of war, it had been burned out and bullet holes pock-marked the outside walls in crazy patterns. Melos started to grizzle again. He had been so good, asleep most of the time, but he was used to a lot of attention and not being cooped up in the sling for hours on end.

When he had been awake Katya talked to him and he seemed to take in the sounds of the forest; woodpeckers hammering for insects, the wind rustling through the trees. It also kept Katya focused. Now it was quiet, very quiet; even the birds had left this place to its fate. She passed more houses, still no-one. More dereliction. Just ahead she could see the road joined another wider road that came in from the left, and then she saw a familiar sight.

Now she recognised where she was; it was Balince. She had passed through the village a couple of times in the past and remembered she had once stopped at the local general store to buy a sandwich. This must be the main road from Lapusnic to Pec; but not as she recalled it. She felt her confidence growing, buoyed by the familiarity but it still did not ease their plight.

Sure enough, as she reached the T-junction, she could see the village store ahead.

To the right, the road continued towards Pec. Like the rest of the village it had been looted; the front window had been smashed. She reached the building and peered in. There were empty cartons and discarded cans everywhere littering the customer space. The shelves were empty, and the shop door hung at a crazy angle blocking the entrance. The thought of shelter and a place to rest had drawn her to it; a hidey-hole to gather her thoughts and strength until she was ready to move again after dark. It gave her a brief sense of security. She was about to push open the broken door to get inside when suddenly something caught her eye, a movement. She jumped back with a jolt as if she had had an electric shock. Melos bounced up and down in his papoose.

It was a cat.

She stood back as it crawled through the open space at the foot of the door.

Then the world turned upside down. The force of the explosion knocked Katya off her feet and into the road and dust and debris clattered around her. She looked down to see if Melos was alright. He seemed none the worse, as far as she could tell, protected by his covering. As fortune would have it, she had been blown backwards and not on top of him; her rucksack had broken her fall.

A booby trap, a grenade probably, not enough to kill unless you were standing on top of it, or you were a cat, but enough to seriously injure any unsuspecting guest. Unsteadily, she got to her feet, thankful for their lucky escape. She checked herself over; she could feel blood trickling from a cut above her eye caused by flying debris; otherwise, she seemed ok. The wound stung as she dabbed it with the back of her sleeve. She breathed a sigh of relief; it could have been a lot worse.

She started shaking. The shock was setting in, but there was no time to wait around. She had to move on before someone decided to investigate the noise.

She walked to the other side of the road. With the trees

immediately in the background, it was more sheltered, although there was still no actual cover, just more broken buildings. Given her recent experience, she was not about to seek shelter in one of them.

Quickly she pressed on in the direction of Pec. For a quarter of a mile still more abandoned cottages dotted the roadside, forlorn like some deserted township from an exhausted gold rush, and then she was out of the village.

Another mile or so passed and more fir trees lined the road which gave her some concealment, and then a deep ravine, probably a hundred metres or more, dropped away to her left as a stream cut its way through the mountain. There was a sharp bend in the road to the right to accommodate the bridge which traversed the water. Katya crossed the maelstrom, which cascaded noisily in a torrent, swelled by the melting snow. She turned the corner and froze.

A convoy of three trucks was heading towards her. It was too late to hide; she had already been seen. The leading vehicle braked hard and stopped less than a metre in front of her. Katya was traumatised – fight, flight or freeze? It had been involuntary. The driver got out and approached her. She didn't recognise the uniform; it wasn't Serb militia or KLA that she could tell, and then she noticed the blue flag and the white letters, 'NATO', painted on the front of the truck.

Then she collapsed.

Katya had no idea how long she had been unconscious but, as her eyes started to focus, she realised she was lying down with a drip, connected to her, arm hanging next to her. The clock on the wall said seven-thirty. It was almost dark outside, and the room was bathed in electric light.

"Melos! Melos!"

"Hello," a soft voice whispered from behind her head. "Do you speak English?"

"Yes," replied Katya.

"You are quite safe, and so is your son. I will take you to him later. You need to rest for a while and get your strength back."

"*Ku jam*...? Sorry, where am I?"

"You are at a NATO post, outside Pec. I'm Doctor Anna Henricksson attached to the Hærens Jegerkommando - Norwegian Special Forces. You've been through quite an ordeal judging by the cut over your eye and the stains on your skirt."

"How did I get here?"

"You were picked up by one of our aid convoys and brought here. I need to ask you a few questions and our intelligence officer will want to speak to you later."

Katya didn't answer.

"How do you feel?"

"My head, it aches, and I feel sore..." She paused and turned her head away from her inquisitor. "I was... attacked... earlier."

"You probably have a mild concussion. I've stitched the cut over your eye and put some antiseptic on your grazes. How did you get hurt?"

"There was an explosion, a booby trap I think, I was looking for somewhere to stay."

"You say you were attacked... who attacked you?"

Katya turned her head again and made eye contact. "Two soldiers... Serb militia."

"They... abused you, you say... sexually?"

"Yes, one of them raped me." Katya started to shake at the recollection.

"It's ok, you're safe here." The doctor's voice was soft and comforting.

"You were lucky they don't normally let women go."

"They didn't... I killed them," said Katya defiantly, her words spitting out.

She recounted the details of her nightmare to the doctor, sobbing in deep heaves, her body trembling with emotion at the recollection.

The doctor let her calm down before speaking again.

"Ok, here's what we're going to do." Her voice had a calming authority about it. "I'm going to take some blood and get it analysed for HIV and other infections. Then we're going to get you cleaned up; we have hot water and showers. Oh, and I'll give you a pill to make sure you won't get pregnant." The doctor smiled and placed a comforting hand on Katya's forehead.

"Thank you, you are very kind, when can I see my son?"

"I'll take you to him very soon, once we've finished here. What's his name?"

"Melos."

"That's a good strong name," said the doctor.

"Yes, he was named after his grandfather."

"You have a husband?" asked the doctor as she helped Katya sit up and removed the drip from her arm.

"Yes... Ibi."

"Where is he?"

"Captured by the Serbs... dead now I think." Katya looked down and played anxiously with her fingers in her lap.

"I'm so sorry. I can't begin to imagine what you've been through," said the doctor as she rolled up Katya's sleeve.

The doctor tapped the crook of her arm to expose a vein and inserted a hypodermic. Katya winced at the sharp pain.

"Sorry, won't be a moment."

The doctor drew the blood then wiped down Katya's arm and covered the puncture mark with sticking plaster to stem the bleeding.

"You speak very good English."

"Thank you." Katya gave the doctor a potted history describing her time at University and her job as a teacher. Being able to converse with another intelligent human being felt somehow therapeutic.

"What about you? Where did you learn to speak English?"

The doctor sat on the bed. "My father was a surgeon before he retired; he'd spent ten years at a hospital in London. I was born in Norway but spent most of my childhood in England.

Went to school there - English was my first language. Have you been to England?"

"I was supposed to go to a language school in..." Katya paused to think for a moment. "Er... Bournemouth? Yes, Bournemouth I think it was called, part of my degree course, but no visas were being issued and we couldn't afford it anyway; it was very expensive, so I watched a lot of American films on TV... Why did you join the army?"

The doctor checked Katya's pulse again. "I studied in Oslo after I qualified, I wanted to specialise in field medicine. I thought it was more interesting dealing with wounds than diseases, and there are not so many people who have the expertise. I answered an advertisement in the newspaper about two years ago, and here I am."

Katya felt at ease with her provider.

"Now, what about that shower? Have you a change of clothes?"

"There's a spare blouse and skirt in my rucksack."

The doctor lifted the rucksack from the chair beside the bed and rummaged inside. "There are some clothes in here, but I don't know how clean they are."

"They will have to do for now."

Anna pulled out the blouse from the bag, the picture of Katya and Ibi fell onto the bed.

"Is that your husband?" asked the doctor, picking up the photo and looking at it.

"Yes, that is Ibi."

"He's very handsome. You must miss him."

"Yes, very much... I think about him all the time." Katya placed the picture back in the bag.

Anna helped Katya off the bed. Her legs nearly gave way; her calves had stiffened, and she was still sore.

"I'll give you some antiseptic cream for the soreness. I use it for abrasions, and it should ease the discomfort... Oh, you may need this." She handed Katya a plastic bottle of shampoo and a large bath towel.

Katya's eyes widened. "Thank you, thank you so much, I can never repay you."

"That's not necessary."

The doctor showed Katya the way to the shower room just along the corridor. Katya walked past a couple of empty rooms which were furnished with small desks and chairs. There were children's paintings on the walls, a school, how ironic. She went in and turned the key in the lock.

The shower area was a sports changing room. There was an alcove with four showerheads and a place to change with lockers. All the doors hung from their hinges, vandalised. In the corner were three reasonably clean toilet cubicles. She removed her scarf, her blouse, her skirt and finally, a little self-consciously, her underclothes. She placed them on the shelf below the lockers. She stood for a moment, naked, examining the cuts and abrasions that crisscrossed her body. Her knees were badly grazed but were smeared by the cream that had been applied by the doctor. She went into one of the cubicles and started to pee. There was a painful stinging sensation.

She flushed the toilet, then went to the shower area and turned on one of the taps. A stream of water gushed down and slowly, Katya entered the flow. The temperature was tepid at first, but it gradually got warmer as steam started to make its way to the ceiling. Katya let the soothing water wash over her body. She took the shampoo bottle from the floor and squirted it into her hand. A blob splat out and she inhaled the wonderful fragrance before massaging it slowly into her hair. She looked at the bottle... Clairol. Cost a fortune in Pristina; if you could get it.

"Arghhh," she winced as the shampoo reached the cut above her eye. She ignored the pain and luxuriated in the bubbles, gradually letting them fall down her body. She was quite tall, around five feet seven inches with a slim physique, but because she was still feeding Melos, her breasts were at least two cup sizes larger than normal; she liked her new shape.

In one of the soap trays, there was a bar of soap which she used to good effect. The detritus of the rape had congealed into a flaky crust and there was dried blood on her inner thighs. She scrubbed vigorously trying to eradicate every last trace. She didn't know if she would ever feel properly clean again. Removing it from her mind would take more than soap and water.

She stayed there until she felt the temperature starting to cool and then turned off the tap. She wrapped herself in the towel and dried off. Taking her change of clothes from the rucksack she shook them out, dust flying in all directions, until they were at least wearable. She put on her fresh underwear and skirt; her jumper was old and worn, but fashion wasn't a priority at this moment. She looked at her shoes. There had been no room in her rucksack to put in another pair. They were badly scuffed and still wet; the soles were beginning to wear out. They would have to do.

Katya made her way back to the treatment room where the doctor was washing the plastic sheet covering the bed where Katya had laid.

"Thank you... I didn't think I would ever be clean again," said Katya handing back the toiletries.

"You will get over this if you keep strong. The wounds to your body will heal, but in your mind... it could take some time."

Katya looked down at the floor, the desperation clear.

The doctor spoke again. "I've spoken to the Intelligence Officer; he'll need to talk to you in the morning, and we'll try to get you on some transport. You can't stay here; it's too dangerous. It's officially a war zone."

"I didn't think you were fighting."

"We're not, not yet anyway; we're trying to keep the peace, but from what I've heard, it's only a matter of time."

"But where will we go?"

"We'll discuss it tomorrow, but for now you have a son who'll need feeding. He's with some other people we picked up this morning. Refugees are fleeing everywhere, most seem to be heading for Albania, but some are crossing into Montenegro, some into Macedonia."

Katya thanked the doctor again and hugged her.

"Come on, I'll show you where he is."

Further down the corridor, past the shower area, there was a larger room, the school sports hall, which had been set out with a few tables in the middle and bedding against the walls. Children were crying, several others, older, were running around playing catch-me. One of the women looked up as Katya and the doctor entered.

"Hello, are you looking for your son?" She spoke in Albanian.

"Yes, Melos," Katya confirmed.

The woman pointed to a carry-cot next to her. Katya walked over and looked inside at Melos, who was sound asleep. Katya put her hands together as if in prayer and started to cry. Then she hugged the woman.

"I am Hava Goranovic from the village of Kacanic."

"Katya, Katya Gjikolli," replied Katya, letting go of her new acquaintance.

Katya looked at Melos; she wanted to pick up her son and hold him close, but it was better he slept. She could see he had been fed and changed.

Hava described her story. Like Katya, she was lucky to escape. She spoke animatedly, the staccato Albanian phrases sounding like machine guns.

"The Serbs were going from house to house. They took away all the men to the town square and just shot them... one by one, without any provocation." She paused and looked down in despair. "My father was one of them... Then they built a big fire and put the bodies on it."

The look of abject nihilism was reflected in her eyes. A look of despair and complete helplessness; a look Katya would experience again and again.

Hava continued. "I waited until dark before I escaped with Ardian... That's him over there." She pointed to a young boy running around.

"How old is he?"

"He's five…. We just fled with just what I could carry."

She made no mention of a husband and Katya did not want to ask.

Hava continued. "As we walked through the town, I could see bodies of women and children lying in the street…" She paused again… "It was dreadful… dreadful." Her voice trailed off.

Katya placed a comforting arm around the woman's shoulder and hugged her. Hava continued. "We had been walking for two days until we were picked up by a NATO convoy… We had had no food and only a small bottle of water, most of which I had given to Ardian. They looked after us and brought us here this morning."

As Hava was relating her story, so other women came to join them, all anxious to share their stories too. After a few minutes, Hava, who was obviously in charge, cleared the women away.

"Have you eaten?" she asked.

Katya had not felt hungry until now. "Not since this morning."

Hava got up and took Katya next door to a small kitchen where there was a large urn of soup warming on an old kitchen stove; it smelt delicious. She took a ladle, scooped up a portion of the aromatic liquid and poured it into a bowl. There were some loaves of bread on the worktop near the sink, Hava cut off two thick slices and handed the feast to Katya. She thanked the woman again.

Katya went back to the hall, picked up the carrycot and sat at a table in a corner while she ate her meal, not really wanting to talk to anyone. When she had finished, Katya fetched an old mattress from the small pile in the corner of the room and laid it on the floor next to the table beside her son. The room was beginning to quieten as the children gradually settled. Katya pulled the old blanket from her rucksack, wrapped it around her and thankfully, overcome with exhaustion, fell asleep.

It was early when she heard Melos starting to grizzle; time for breakfast. Katya went to the kitchen and warmed some water in a saucepan and dropped in one of the jars of baby food. A couple of other women were heating tins of beans ready for hungry mouths.

By seven o'clock, the room was a hive of activity. Katya had eaten some soup and had her first cup of coffee for weeks; her mother didn't drink it. Katya thought about her; she was missing her now.

Half an hour later, a smart-looking officer in a NATO uniform entered the hall.

"Katya Gjikolli," he called out. He asked again in English.

Katya stood and identified herself. He motioned for her to follow him. She picked up Melos and put him in the carry-cot; Hava indicated she would keep an eye on him. Katya left the room, walking behind the officer.

They entered a small room to the right, just after the shower area. There was a desk with a chair on either side. Maps and an information board with notes and writing on it were fixed to the wall directly behind the desk. The man sat down.

"I understand you speak good English." He spoke in an accent that could have come straight from the British military school, Sandhurst.

Tall, with angular features, Katya guessed he would be in his mid-thirties. He had dark hair and there was an intimidating presence about him.

"Yes," said Katya, anxiously.

"This won't take long; just need to tidy up some loose ends. Take a seat."

Katya sat down opposite him. She looked at the man as he rustled some papers on his desk. He picked up a pen and started writing; it seemed slow and deliberate. Then he looked at Katya.

"My name is Captain Janssen, Intelligence officer with the Norwegian Special forces." He didn't proffer a first name.

Katya looked at him nervously.

"I understand you were heading for Klina. Why there?"

"Er… to catch a train… to try to get out of the country."

"Lucky you didn't make it. It was attacked by the Serbs a couple of weeks ago, many dead. Not much there now... certainly no trains." He made a note, then looked up again. "The doctor tells me you ran into some bad types up in the woods. Can you show me where on the map?" He indicated behind him. "We've had several reports of gangs of renegade Serbs doing all measure of nasty things in the area. Want to see if we can round them up."

"They are dead," she riposted without any emotion.

"Realise that old girl, the doctor told me about your attack, but pick up the bodies and we could get some ID, you know the thing."

"I'll try."

"Good girl," said the captain as he got up and stood at the map behind him. Katya joined him and examined the cartography of the area she had been through in detail, trying to make some sense out of it.

"We picked you up about here," said the captain pointing to the road outside Balince.

Katya traced the road back to the logging track which led into the forest. She recognised it. "About here, I think." Janssen put a cross on the map with a marker pen.

"You know you were extremely lucky. The Serbs have laid thousands of land mines right across that area. We found a ten-year-old girl yesterday not far from where you were picked up with her foot blown off, terrible mess."

Katya grimaced in horror at the thought.

"Anyway, thanks for that… just need to take a few more details."

He got a form out from one of the desk drawers. "So, your name is Katya Gjikolli," he began filling in the form. "How do you spell that?"

Katya spelt it out.

"Address?"

She gave him her address.

"Date of birth?"

"September 14, 1974."

"Name of Spouse... er husband?"

"Ibrahim."

"Ah yes, Ibrahim... tell me about him." His tone had changed. "In the KLA I understand?"

The doctor had obviously told him everything.

"Yes."

"And you supported him joining these... how can I put this delicately, terrorists?"

"They are not terrorists!" she exclaimed, almost shouting, "They are trying to save our country."

"Ah yes, so you say, but that's where I have a problem you see; they're not recognised by anyone as representing ordinary Kosovans."

Katya was getting angry. "The Serbs are butchers! You have seen what they have done, to me, to all the women here. We have been raped, abused. Our houses have been destroyed; our property violated."

Janssen cut her off in mid-flow. "Ah yes, but the KLA have also committed war crimes. We have reports of indiscriminate murders of Serbs in retribution, a blood bath in fact. A few weeks ago they shot the Mayor of Pec."

"They deserve everything they get... What about Račak?" Katya was in her stride.

"And what do you know about Račak?"

"The Serbs massacred almost seventy Albanians, slaughtered, in cold blood."

"And how do you know about it?"

"It was what I was told."

The captain paused; the atmosphere was tense. "Hmm... You see my problem, Katya. How do I know you're not a terrorist? NATO is neutral here, trying to secure peace. We must be even-handed."

Katya was worried now.

"I have never been involved in politics... I am a teacher. I refused to work for the government... I had the chance."

"But your husband was involved. And you supported him," he countered.

"And what good did it do...? He is DEAD!" Katya shouted the last word and then burst into tears.

There was a long silence, broken only by Katya's sobbing.

The Captain looked at her for a moment, making an assessment.

"Ok, I think that's enough for now... You can go back to the hall, but we may need to talk again later."

Janssen got up and opened the door. Katya left the room and made her way back to the hall still sobbing.

Hava greeted her and could see straight away that Katya was upset.

"Katya... are you alright?"

Katya walked towards the table next to where she had slept and checked her son asleep in the carry-cot. She turned to Hava.

"Why do they treat us like this?" Her face was filled with anger.

"It's ok, we have all been questioned. The NATO soldiers, they just need to make sure there are no spies or war criminals trying to escape. That is all... It will be fine."

"Do we look like war criminals?" Katya looked at the bedraggled flotsam of humankind around her.

Hava left Katya in a reflective mood and walked back to the group.

Melos woke and started crying. Katya picked him up and held him until he stopped. She sat down in the corner considering her latest ordeal; the boy was on her lap. Gradually her mood relaxed and one or two of the children came over to see Melos and started playing with him. Then at about eleven o'clock, a soldier came into the hall holding a clipboard in his hand.

"The following people must pick up their belongings and

make their way to the front of the building." He spoke in heavily accented English. Katya translated for them.

He started calling out names in family groups. Six or seven names had been called and then "Hava Goranovic and Ardian Goranovic."

Hava looked at Katya and held out her hand. "*Ne...! Ne...!*"

"It's ok, you go. I'll be fine." Katya waved for her to go with the officer.

About fifteen names were called and then, "Katya Gjikolli and Melos Gjikolli."

Katya picked up the carry-cot, which she had now acquired through squatter's rights, and followed the other women and children along the corridor, past the shower room, past the interrogation suite and Anna's surgery. The door was open, and the doctor saw Katya go by. She got up from her desk, where she was writing some notes, and rushed to the door.

"Katya...! Katya...!"

Katya was a good few yards away; she turned around and saw the doctor. She had mixed feelings, part of her thought she had been betrayed, but she owed Anna a great deal.

Anna walked up to Katya. "How are you this morning?"

"I am not sure after the interrogation earlier."

The doctor held Katya's arm affectionately. "Look, don't worry about the captain; he's just doing what he has to do. He has a very difficult job you know."

"Yes, ok, I guess so... but I don't know how he could think we are terrorists, we barely escaped with our lives."

"Don't be concerned anymore, Katya, the important thing now is to get you all to safety."

Katya relaxed. "Do you know where we are going?"

"Yes, it is too dangerous for you to stay in Kosovo, so we are taking you across the border to a refugee centre in Vratnica."

"But that's in Macedonia."

"Yes, but it's ok, you'll be safe there, and they have the facilities to look after you properly. There's a huge evacuation going on; many countries are involved. We have a bus which will take you there, and you will have an escort to the border."

The doctor was holding a plastic bag in her hand. "Here you may need these," and she handed it to Katya who looked inside; there was a packet of pain killers, antiseptic cream and another bottle of shampoo.

"One more thing," Anna looked around to make sure she wasn't being overheard. "In case you were wondering, I got rid of the knife that was in your rucksack." Katya had forgotten all about it. "Don't want any evidence, do we?"

Katya looked down, then up, and smiled. "Thank you, thank you for everything."

She continued along the corridor holding Melos in the carrycot with Anna following close by carrying Katya's things. Once outside, Katya was able to see the school building now in more detail. It was larger than she had thought; probably built in the sixties judging by the bleak concrete and glass. Several military trucks were parked along the side of the main block, and further around she could see what seemed to be classrooms that had been converted into barracks. A dozen or so soldiers were unloading from a truck. She could see weapons of every description being moved into the store.

"Have you got your passport?" Anna asked.

"Yes, it's in my rucksack, thank you."

"Good luck Katya... I hope you find some peace." The doctor looked in the carrycot at Melos. "And you, little one."

"You too doctor," and they hugged each other warmly.

"I think my war is just about to start," replied Anna portentously.

Katya noticed Captain Janssen at one of the windows staring at the group as if sizing them up one by one. Katya looked away, not wishing to make any eye-contact with her former interrogator.

A couple of minutes later, the bus arrived through the school gates and into the square followed by an armoured car with a long antenna on the back. The NATO flag was tied to it.

"We are going to Macedonia in that?!" exclaimed Katya, pointing to the ancient vehicle posing as a bus.

Anna started grinning. "Don't worry, it's all downhill. " They both started to laugh.

Their names were called again by the same soldier from earlier. He dutifully compared their passports and papers as they got on the bus with the list on his clipboard.

Katya gave Anna another hug and got on the bus holding the carry-cot in front of her. She found a seat, took off her rucksack and placed it on the overhead rack. She put the carry-cot next to her. Melos looked up to her and smiled.

Hava was in the seat in front of her. She turned to Katya.

"Where are we going, do you know?"

"To Macedonia," replied Katya.

"Macedonia?!" exclaimed Hava.

The bus slowly moved off; almost one hundred and fifty kilometres to go. Katya's life was about to take another turn and change forever.

Chapter Three

The old bus made heavy weather of the road, the driver, a rather morose Albanian called Perparim, but known as Pepe, constantly wrestled with the gear stick as it struggled up the mountain roads. He had to double de-clutch every gear change. Downhill it was even worse; the brakes squealing as it struggled to resist the pull of gravity. Katya looked anxiously out of the window, wondering if the old bus would reach its destination. A soldier in NATO uniform sat in the front seat next to the driver and stared ahead. It was dry in the main but with every incline that took them into the hills, the rolling mist surrounded them like a blanket.

Katya had Melos on her lap talking to him and playing with his hands. Most of the passengers were asleep. One or two of the children had been boisterous at first, buoyed with the excitement of the journey, but even they were now quiet. They had been on the road for about two hours and needed a stop. Katya got out of her seat and spoke to the soldier. As the only English speaker, she had now unwittingly taken over as leader. All the NATO soldiers seem to speak English.

"Is there any chance of a stop? The children are very hungry and desperate for the toilet."

He got out a folded map from his blouson and checked the route which had been highlighted in red.

Sure enough, he replied in an accented English voice. "Yes, we should be in Dakovica in less than half an hour. We can stop there for a few minutes. I think Pepe could do with a smoke." He indicated towards the driver. "He's done nothing but curse since we left the compound."

Katya smiled. The soldier spoke to the driver in Albanian; he gave a toothy grin and nodded in acknowledgement. Katya was impressed by the officer's language skills. He picked up a walkie-talkie from the dashboard and spoke into it. He turned to Katya. "Just telling the jeep."

Katya went back along the bus explaining what was happening to the passengers.

It was almost two o'clock when the coach reached the outskirts of the town. Katya viewed the devastation. This was a large town, a place of over a hundred and fifty thousand people in normal times. But these were not normal times and it was almost deserted. She put Melos in his cot and went to talk to the soldier.

"Where are all the people?" said Katya.

"Gone," replied the man. "First Serbs, then police and Yugoslav military... then the KLA... much fighting here; the people... they have gone."

Shops were burned out and there was evidence of looting everywhere. A couple of tractors chugged in the opposite direction, the drivers staring straight ahead oblivious to, or just ignoring, the bus. One or two people, old men mainly, alerted by the noise of the vehicles, came out to see what was happening. The bus reached the town square and the armoured car came to a halt, the bus pulling in behind it. The air brakes hissed violently. Pepe opened the door which let in a blast of cool air. He walked around to the front of the bus, removed the radiator grill and looked knowledgeably at the engine.

Katya rummaged in the rucksack and pulled out the papoose sling. She put it around her shoulders and dropped Melos in the gap in the front, snug against her chest. One by one, the passengers got out stretching their arms and legs. Children started running about like uncoiled springs venting their pent up energy. "Keep close to the bus," the soldier shouted. Katya shouted a translation and the children moved back to the pavement with their mothers.

Across the square, there was a small cafe with a couple of old men seated outside drinking what looked like coffee, and the small group headed towards it. Katya looked back and saw Pepe drawing urgently on a cigarette. The officer was talking to the driver of the armoured car.

He looked up and shouted. "We must leave in fifteen minutes."

Katya translated to the group.

They reached the cafe and went inside. Various breads and cakes were on sale and there was meat cooking on a spit. There were some pallets of fruit in varying degrees of decay. The women queued and ordered their needs and the proprietor quickly fulfilled their requests. Children fussed around, waiting for any treat.

Katya's turn came. "What do you want?" asked the proprietor gruffly.

She ordered some bread, dried pressed meat and some very strong coffee, which he poured into a paper cup. She picked up a half-litre bottle of water from a stack by the front door. She gave the man a ten deutschmark note, and he held it up to the light. He put it in his till; there would be no change. Katya looked in disapproval but said nothing.

Katya asked for the toilet. The proprietor indicated across the street on the right.

Katya put the food and water into the rucksack and sipped her coffee as she walked in the direction of the toilets.

Some of the women had already made their way there, and some were walking back, grimacing, having completed their ablutions. Sure enough, the facilities were filthy and smelled foul. However, it was either this or by the side of the road; it was a case of grin and bear it. Naturally, there was no running water, so Katya used a baby wipe to clean herself off. The soreness had thankfully disappeared and there was no stinging sensation; she felt better for that.

Back at the bus, Pepe was topping up the radiator with water ready for the next stage of the journey. Katya approached the soldier and he smiled. "What is your name?"

"Georghi," he replied.

"You are Greek?"

"Yes, I am sergeant in Greek Army from Thessaloniki attached to the NATO forces."

"You speak English <u>and</u> Albanian?"

"Yes, my mother she comes from Tirana and my father runs a bar in a village on the coast about ten kilometres outside Thessaloniki, so with the tourists we had to learn. I can speak a little German and French also."

"That must be useful."

"Sometimes."

"Where to now?" asked Katya.

"Prizren. It is not as bad as this. I was there two days ago, not much fighting there, mainly demonstrations... more people around; some refugees have gone there also. NATO have a small base just outside the city. We will be able to stop and get some more food."

Katya had been to Prizren before but a long time ago, and she had difficulty bringing it to mind.

Georghi ushered the passengers back inside the bus making sure there was no one left behind. Pepe started the engine and it rasped into life once more. Then, seemingly from nowhere, a truck appeared. It raced around the square and stopped in front of the armoured car blocking its path while half a dozen heavily-armed soldiers got out surrounding the bus and escort, Kalashnikovs raised. Georghi instinctively went for the sidearm in his holster which was on a leather belt around his waist but thought better of it. He went down the steps of the bus and confronted the leading militiaman.

A heated exchange took place. Katya strained to try to hear what was happening. The rest of the passengers cowed behind their seats. Then Georghi stepped back on the bus and collected his clipboard and gave it to the soldier. The man-made a gesture with his gun. Georghi stood aside and the soldier climbed on the bus. Slowly he worked his way down the aisle looking first at the list of names and then staring intently at the faces of the passengers.

Melos was back in his carrycot but was starting to cry again. "Sshhh!" whispered Katya. The soldier reached Katya's row and she looked at him. She immediately recognised the uniform – KLA, the same as the major who had called to tell her of Ibi's capture and who later died in her sitting room. Katya shivered at the association.

He moved down the bus completing his audit, looking at each passenger in turn until he reached a scruffy-looking man, about nineteen years old, who seemed to be trying to hide under the seat in front of him. There was an angry tirade which Katya could not make out and the KLA man raised his weapon and called out. The passengers were still cowering in their seats, covering their faces, children started crying as another two KLA soldiers got on the bus and joined their colleague. Further exchanges and the youth was grabbed and pulled forcibly over the seat by his hair and dragged the length of the bus kicking and screaming expletives. It was not Albanian but Serbo-Croat.

The soldiers shoved the passenger out onto the pavement and started kicking him violently. The KLA officer got back on the bus and had a final look down the row of frightened people. He gave a suspicious look at Pepe, then jumped off and spoke to the NATO officer. The soldiers lowered their rifles and dragged their unconscious prisoner into their truck and left. Georghi got back on board.

It was eerily silent. Trauma had enveloped the group; fear once more replacing the fragile sense of security the old bus had given them. Children whimpered pathetically as their mothers stared blankly, momentarily in a paralysis of hopelessness.

Katya got up and sat behind the Greek officer as the armoured car moved away. Pepe pulled out close behind.

"What was that all about?" asked Katya.

"KLA, looking for Serbs. They have been infiltrating refugee columns trying to escape."

"What will happen to that boy?"

"Who knows?" He shrugged his shoulders. "But there's

nothing I could do. You saw the numbers... many men, and NATO has no authority here. We are supposed to be peace-keepers, but not for much longer, I think. They have started to bomb Belgrade. Did you know?"

"Who have?" asked Katya.

"NATO," replied Georghi. "But for now we are not permitted to open fire on anyone unless we are attacked, so, how you say? Our hands are tied up. Let's hope we don't run into any Serbs; it could be very different."

That did little to reassure Katya, but a bombing campaign might just bring the Serbs to press for peace. At least someone was doing something.

She went back to her seat and explained to Hava and the other women what had happened, which went some way to change the mood on board. It was possible to hope.

Katya tried to sleep. It was three o'clock, mid-afternoon, and it would be another three hours before they reached Prizren.

Kilometre after kilometre, the bus crunched its way up the hills and freewheeled down the other side, Pepe managing to coax the engine into sufficient horsepower to keep moving. He seemed to be talking incessantly, occasionally cursing, sometimes pleading. Forests swept down the slopes of the mountains like avalanches.

After an hour or so since leaving Dakovica there was a short stop at a lay-by, the result of water and coffee. With no toilets, the women had to stoop behind the trees. Pepe lit up a cigarette and sucked in so deeply his cheeks almost met inside his mouth. As a predominantly Muslim country, one or two women had taken out prayer mats and knelt down to face Mecca. They said whatever it was they had to say and got back on the bus. The children were not allowed to run around the road, such as it was, mainly potholes and gravel, no tarmac. It was narrow with barely enough room for two vehicles to pass and while they had only seen a few tractors and the occasional truck, it was still dangerous. Fortunately, there was no obvious military activity.

Prizren is Kosovo's third city and lies on the slopes of the Šar Mountains. It is also close to the Albanian and Macedonian borders. In peacetime it has a population of over a hundred and seventy thousand, but, with all the refugees and military personnel, it was now more like two-hundred thousand.

As they entered the city, it was clear that the buildings were in much better shape, there didn't appear to be any visible damage from the main road. Many minarets dotted the horizon, sitting comfortably with orthodox churches. The terrain was flat with the mountains in the distance like sleeping giants rising above the plain. People jostled in the busy market; how different to Dakovica.

They crossed a bridge over a small river and immediately turned ninety-degrees right. Pepe struggled with the steering wheel before the road straightened and ran parallel to the river three or four kilometres before the bus made a left turn. The signpost said 'Štrpce - 65 kilometres'. It would take at least another two and a half to three hours through the mountains.

It was now ten-to-six and the sun had set; it would be getting dark soon. After about another three kilometres, a sports stadium appeared ahead of them with floodlight towers at its corners. The armoured car turned right off the main road and along a short drive and through the entrance. Two NATO flags hung from the walls. The bus followed the escort into a courtyard in front of the main building and stopped outside the ticket office. Georghi shouted for everyone to stay in their seats, Katya translated. Pepe got out and lit up.

Ten minutes went by and the passengers were starting to get restless; there was much disgruntled murmuring on the coach before Georghi returned and spoke to Katya.

"We will stop here for tonight; you will be quite safe. The mountain roads are too dangerous to cross at night. But do not worry, there is food here and you can wash. There are enough beds. We will leave in the morning."

Katya translated to the passengers.

They had been on the road for almost seven hours and it was a chance to recover from the journey. The passengers seemed very happy with these plans and followed the officer to the makeshift accommodation block.

Katya, carrying the carry-cot and Hava holding her son's hand, led the group and followed Georghi to the sleeping quarters where they stowed their gear or what little they had. Katya took off her rucksack and placed it beside the carry-cot next to one of the beds. They were fairly basic with metal frames, topped with a bare mattress. There was a pile of blankets in the corner which were quickly grabbed. Once settled the group were led to the dining area.

The children seemed bewildered at yet another upheaval, but the mood soon changed once they saw the food that had been laid on for them. Big urns of stew, dumplings and bread with some potatoes and carrots were lined up on trestle-tables. There were also some containers with ice cream. Three local women stood behind the tables with big serving spoons and started dishing out portions to the waiting group.

Considering the circumstances, it was remarkably orderly; the refugees just waited patiently in line to be served. Smaller tables with chairs had been provided for the refugees to sit and eat.

When it was her turn, Katya took enough for her and Melos, then sat at one of the tables with the food. There was a highchair in the corner which she manoeuvred next to her and lifted Melos from the carry-cot and placed him in it. She put a small portion of stew on a plate and some ice cream on another and started to feed him.

Katya had forgotten what it was like to feel full. She had eaten very little for over twenty-four hours and her clothes were starting to hang off her.

Satiated, the group left the dining hall and made their way back to the sleeping quarters. By this time, it was almost eight o'clock but already Katya felt tired and decided to try to get some sleep. Despite the number of people, it was remarkably quiet. Voices talked in whispers and children drew pictures or read comics which had been thoughtfully provided for them by their hosts.

Katya slept fitfully, the nightmares of rough soldiers haunted her - staring eyes, bloodied clothing, shouting, rifles, and the pain. She woke with a start several times when the dreams had reached the surface and threatened to suffocate her. Melos slept on, thankfully unaware of the events of the last couple of days.

She was in a deep slumber when Georghi entered the room and announced that breakfast would be in half an hour. It was six o'clock. Bleary-eyed, the women got their stuff together and made their way to the washrooms. By seven o'clock, after a breakfast of toast and cereals with real milk and coffee, the refugees made their way to the bus. Pepe had filled it up with diesel courtesy of the NATO store and was checking the oil and water. He seemed satisfied, still talking to his vehicle like it was a woman. He lit his third cigarette of the morning.

Georghi took a roll-call as everyone got on the bus; all present and correct. He spoke to another officer who was standing next to the bus, saluted and got on. Pepe threw his cigarette out of the window and seemed to say a prayer as he turned the ignition key. The engine coughed into life once more and they pulled away in a cloud of diesel smoke behind the escort.

The early morning was grey, and mist shrouded the distant mountains as Pepe manoeuvred the bus out of the gates and back on the main road to Štrpce. Once out of the town the road deteriorated with potholes and no barriers to prevent vehicles from plunging two hundred metres into sweeping ravines which would appear at regular intervals. Wrecks of old cars that hadn't made it were clearly visible from the road. Thank goodness they had not tried this in the dark, thought Katya. Pepe guided the bus around every corner - talking, pleading, cajoling, before Štrpce eventually appeared below them in the distance. It had taken nearly two hours.

There was a long steep hill approaching the town and Pepe crashed through the gears to keep it from gathering too much speed. The brakes just about held but the distinctive smell of burning rubber permeated into the bus. There were looks of concern among the passengers.

Štrpce is a small town set in a valley, popular with skiers in the winter. Virtually cut off from the rest of Kosovo by the mountains, it is an enclave and predominantly Serb. Katya had heard of the place but never visited, and she was aware that there could be potential dangers. She went to sit behind Georghi leaving Melos on the seat in his carrycot.

"What happens now?" she asked.

"I have spoken to the driver of the jeep and we are going to go straight through to save any possible, how you say...? Complications."

"But we could do with a break."

"We will stop outside the town as soon as we can," responded Georghi.

The bus entered the town, keeping a steady speed. There were a few people about, but they didn't seem to take much notice. A couple of trucks passed in the opposite direction and a tractor crossed the road in front of them pulling an empty trailer from a side road causing the bus to slow down, but apart from that, there were no problems and Katya breathed a sigh of relief as they left the town behind them. The last signpost said 'Skopje, 61 kilometres,' so the border would be half of that, less than an hour away.

It was a steep climb away from Štrpce, with Pepe continuing to eke every ounce of power from the old bus. It took about twenty minutes until they reached the top of the mountain pass and the Albanian exhaled loudly as he eased the vehicle into a lay-by. The driver jumped out and immediately opened the radiator grill to let the engine cool. Then he lit up and leant against the bus. The passengers got off and stretched their legs and once more had to find a convenient tree. Katya nibbled on some bread she had stowed in her rucksack which she had saved from breakfast. Others did the same.

Katya caught up with Georghi who had been in discussion with the jeep driver. "How much further?" she asked.

"Not too far now," said Georghi. "Probably about half an hour if Pepe can keep the bus going."

"How far is it to the camp from the border?"

"Only about ten kilometres; not far."

After about fifteen minutes, Georghi asked everyone to get back on board and they headed off. They reached the Macedonian border at about half-past ten and were ordered off the bus and through a checkpoint. Their passports were presented and stamped without too much bureaucracy and they re-joined the bus in another country. Katya breathed a sigh of relief and hugged Melos.

The bus went through the checkpoint, but the jeep remained behind having no jurisdiction in Macedonia and the passengers climbed back on board for the final leg of the journey. Katya watched the military escort turn around and head back. After about another twenty minutes they arrived at the camp in Vratnica.

They entered through what was basically a gap in a hedge monitored by a control post. A NATO flag flew from a pole adjacent to it, giving the only indication of its purpose. The guard on duty waved the bus through. Katya couldn't believe the sight that stretched out in front of her

It looked more like a scout jamboree; an enormous field, probably over half a mile square, with row upon row of tents, burning campfires and mud; mud everywhere. There was no road as such, just a worn track where other vehicles had passed. The bus stopped at a large Portakabin with another NATO flag flying above it. Georghi got out and went inside. After a few minutes, he returned to the bus and spoke to Katya.

"Someone will be out to see you in a minute. You will all be... how you say? Processed; and allocated a tent."

Katya looked at Georghi and then the rows of tents. This was not what she had expected.

The passengers were ordered off the bus. They collected their belongings and just stood there next to the vehicle that had been their security for the last day or so, staring, taking in their surroundings.

Georghi spoke to Katya. "I hope everything works out for you. Good luck."

Katya shook his hand. "Thank you," she replied, and the officer got back on board the transport for the long return journey.

Katya watched the old vehicle shudder as it tried to grip the slippery surface. Mud flew up from the wheels as it struggled to gain traction. Pepe wrestled with the steering wheel negotiating a three-sixty degree turn, then it slowly headed away and out of the gates before disappearing from view. She wanted to thank the Albanian but had forgotten in the melee. The group of new arrivals were stood in a huddle, looking dazed and confused.

Just then they were approached by a smart-looking man in military fatigues accompanied by a woman in a white coat. "Hello, does anyone speak English?"

Katya stepped forward. "Yes, I do."

"Ah, good... Name's Drury, Captain Drury, in charge of things, welcome to Vratnica camp." He was stood erect, as if at attention. "Officially, I work for NATO, but I also act as the liaison officer for the Red Cross." He looked across at the woman. "This is Doctor Bernadette Flaherty in charge of our medical facilities."

"I am Katya, Katya Gjikolli." She shook hands with the captain. "How many people are here?"

He looked around at the sea of tents. "At the moment...? Around ten thousand, but we're shipping out as many as we can... Italy, Albania mainly, but we've recently had offers to take people from other countries; Norway, Turkey, US, Germany,

Canada and Australia and we're also liaising with the government in the UK. The response has been quite amazing really."

He looked at Katya who was still trying to take in the scene. "It's a massive operation and not without its problems. Just last week we had to take in over three-thousand from the camp at Blace which was being overrun. We had buses turning up every few minutes. It's been a very difficult time."

You don't know the half of it, thought Katya.

"Mind you, this is only one camp, there's another at Stenkovec about twenty miles from here; they've got around fourteen-hundred tents," he added. He looked down, trying to ignore the look of despair on Katya's face. "You and your people need to go over there." He pointed to a large marquee about a hundred metres away.

"We have to process everyone... You know, sort out the administration, names, addresses, those sorts of things, then we'll get you allocated to a tent. We've had some new ones arrive today from the Red Cross. Some of my men are putting them up as we speak."

He continued. "Once the paperwork's been done, we'll hand you over to the doctor and her medical team, then we can get you some food."

Katya was trying to be sanguine about it all, appreciating that a lot of effort was being made to help them, but it was hard. She picked up the carry-cot and rucksack, Melos was back in the papoose, and she joined the women from the bus. She translated the captain's instructions to them. There were worried looks among the group. The once-boisterous children were clinging to their mothers for comfort and reassurance. Hava told Katya that she wished she had stayed in Kosovo and had taken her chances.

The administration took over an hour, and then the passengers were taken to the medical centre, which was basically another large tent not far from the main gate. Katya counted six nurses on duty, grossly inadequate for the numbers of refugees. There were lines of people waiting to be seen.

The group from the bus had been allocated a senior nurse who came from Hungary, Katya learned, and were examined in turn. They were asked various questions about their health, but apart from some general under-nourishment, they were in reasonably good shape, physically at least. The mental scars were another matter and would take years to heal. Some children were clearly struggling with the effects of their experiences, uncommunicative, involuntary shaking, bed-wetting and so on. One child was totally dumb having seen his father shot on the front doorstep by Serbian Police.

Katya and Melos were examined and were declared in good health. She told the nurse about the assault in the woods and her injury in the explosions. The nurse examined the stitches and was happy with the healing; she would take them out in a couple of days. She also promised to contact Doctor Henricksson at the Pec centre for the results of the blood test.

Once the medical examination was over, they were led by one of the assistants, a Rumanian called Iuliana, further down the field to a group of newly-erected tents. They were like large wigwams and reminded Katya of those she used to see in Wild West films as a child. There was no heating. The weather, fortunately, had got a little warmer since they had left Pec; so, at least they would not freeze to death. The smell, however, was something else.

They reached the first tent and Katya looked inside. There were wooden floorboards over the bare earth and sleeping bags lined up on the floor. Katya counted fifteen and sure enough, fifteen names were called, including hers, to stay in this tent.

Katya looked at the assistant in horror. "But this tent is not big enough for that many."

"You very lucky, in Blace many sleeping, thirty and more, in a tent like this," replied Iuliana in fractured English. "Some sleep in fields, no tent... Some people died."

Katya was horrified, and certainly did not feel particularly lucky, however, with no alternative, she had to accept the situation for now and hope that things would improve.

"What about washing?" She was almost afraid to ask.

"No water here... There is only bottles," replied the assistant.

"But how will we clean ourselves?"

Iuliana shrugged her shoulders. "You will... how you say? Make the do. Hope only for short time."

Katya hadn't asked about the toilet facilities but Iuliana told them anyway. There was a line of chemical loos, similar to those you see at rock festivals, in the far distance at the top of the field. There were more murmurs among the women.

"In Blace they had no toilet, just... er." She tried to find the right word. "Holes... yes, in the ground."

Katya just looked in horror.

Before she left the group to sort themselves out, the assistant pointed out the catering area close to the medical tent.

"You go there for food," she instructed.

Hava came up to Katya complaining vigorously. "I want to speak to the person in charge... It is terrible; they treat us like dogs."

According to the Refugee Council, the humanitarian daily rations, known as HDRs in military terms, are meatless and contain foods like rice, lentil stew, crackers and fruit bars. They are designed to be acceptable to refugees of any religion or ethnic background, and suitable for people who have been without food for a long time. The UN was shipping plane-loads at a time to the camps in Macedonia from Boston in the United States.

The catering area, as Iuliana had called it, was another tent piled high with HDRs being distributed by NATO soldiers. Like at the medical centre, a long line of people waited their turn.

When she eventually reached the front of the queue, Katya received her allowance and asked for baby food for Melos. Although she could still breastfeed, she was trying to keep Melos on solids to help his development. There were tins of powdered baby milk and a selection of baby food in jars donated by one of the big drug companies. Katya chose three, her ration, at random and left to go back to the tent.

That night as she lay shivering in her sleeping bag, Katya thought of different times when she and Ibi were together. The walks, the meals she cooked for him, and for the first time in a while, she remembered the tenderness of their love-making. Then suddenly her mind flipped, and the ghosts of the woods came to haunt her. The brutality, the degradation she felt, and the violation. For a moment, she was racked with guilt and wrestled with her conscience. She was trying not to blame herself for killing her attackers; it was self-defence after all. But, surely, taking another human being's life must be wrong under any circumstances. She lay there in turmoil wishing the comfort of sleep would take her away to another world, away from the reality of this one.

Dawn, Vratnica Refugee Camp, Macedonia; a weak sun glimmered on the horizon almost mockingly. A mist hovered at ground level rising from the cold earth; a deathly silence engulfed the camp. It was broken by a dog barking from the security compound. Birds were vainly trying to add melody to brighten the scene, but to those inhabiting the tents, the notes were discordant and jarring, rudely awaking them to face the misery of another day.

Katya had slept in her clothes in the sleeping bag to keep warm and was disturbed by Melos wanting to be fed. Other children in the tent grizzled and cried; they were cold and hungry.

Katya got up and opened the tent flap and peered out. She could see the queue for the toilets in the distance which stretched for maybe a hundred metres. It was such that many didn't bother and sought their privacy where they could. Others didn't have the same inhibitions and just did what they had to do in full view of others without a hint of shame. The result was a recipe for disaster; cholera and other diseases caused by unsanitary conditions had not broken out in the camp yet, but at this rate, it was only a matter of time.

Katya picked up Melos and put him in his sling. She left the tent and walked towards the Portakabin to complain to someone. She reached the marquee housing the medical centre and decided to see if there was anyone in authority she could speak to. As she entered the tent, she reeled at the sight. Two women were giving birth in adjoining beds being attended to by what looked like relatives. The only available nurse flitted from one to the other like a butterfly on a flower, checking and moving on, backwards and forwards. Katya was transfixed at the mayhem being played out in front of her. This was not the time to voice a complaint and she left the tent with a feeling of total helplessness.

Then she spotted Captain Drury walking towards her on his way back from the catering area. She confronted him.

"Why aren't you doing something?" Katya asked.

"About what?" replied the captain.

"About this," exclaimed Katya, her hand sweeping the vista.

"We are doing all we can."

"I want to go back to Kosovo." Katya's frustration was boiling over.

"Listen, I understand how difficult it is, but as I said, we are doing all we can."

"There must be something more!" riposted Katya.

"Look, what's your name again?" said Drury.

"Katya... Katya Gjikolli."

"Miss Gjikolli," said the captain.

"It's Mrs!" she corrected.

"Sorry, Mrs Gjikolli... Look, you speak good English. You could help a great deal as a translator. As you can see, we have a lot of frightened people here and we cannot communicate with them. What about it?"

"Yes, anything I can do... of course."

So for the next three weeks, Katya reported each morning to Captain Drury for duty. She had her daily HDR's and Melos was reasonably well looked after. Working for the captain had its advantages. She had the occasional cup of coffee and was privy to what was going on. She was also able to use the executive washroom as he jokingly called the adjoining Portakabin designated for NATO personnel.

Major challenges were facing the refugees and those trying to look after them. A couple of days after Katya had started working for the captain, the Yugoslavs closed the border with Macedonia which meant there would be no more people entering the camp. That was the good news. The bad news was the Macedonian Government were starting to put pressure on NATO to remove refugees still on their soil, so a major evacuation was underway.

Katya quickly impressed Captain Drury with her organisation and people skills and, with the enormous pressure of the logistics of this scale of operation, she was co-opted to help look after the administration.

Katya thrived in the role and despite the dire conditions in the camp, her mental state improved dramatically as she helped Captain Drury and the rest of his staff to manage the evacuation.

It was a Sunday in late April, and Katya had some news. First, on a visit to the medical centre, she was told her blood test results had come back from Pec as negative, no infection, which was a relief. Then Captain Drury asked her to come to his office. She sat down.

"I've got some news, Katya, which I thought you might be interested in." She was wondering where this was leading.

"I've just heard we've been allocated a hundred and fifty seats on a plane going to England. I can get you on if you're interested... although of course I'll miss you here," he quickly added.

She looked at the captain. "But I really want to go home?"

"Yes, I understand, but it's still not safe. We're continuing to get reports of Serbian action in reprisals for the bombing campaign all across Kosovo, but particularly around Pristina.

You can stay here of course but the conditions are not much better than when you arrived."

Katya was thinking. "How long will we have to stay?"

"Difficult to say, but from what I know, the initial visa would last for up to a year and then you will have the option of applying for permanent residency."

"I don't know what to say. When would we leave?"

"This morning... the bus will be here in about an hour which is why I have mentioned this now. I need a decision."

"Thank you..." She paused. "Ok... thank you, yes, I will go. I have always wanted to see London."

"No... it is I who should be thanking you Katya, for all your help."

Katya strangely felt a twinge of sadness. She had enjoyed working for the Captain despite the awful conditions. She got up and left the office and headed back to her tent to collect her things. Melos was tucked safely in his papoose. She had given the carry-cot to one of the new mothers.

She went to find Hava who was in another tent to say goodbye. Hava hugged her and wished her good luck. She told Katya that she had decided to stay at the camp until it was safe to return. She only spoke Albanian and would feel even more isolated away from her people.

Captain Drury was supervising the embarkation helped by Nadia, another one of his assistants, as Katya reached the waiting transport. It was a modern coach, much better than the battered old bus in which Pepe had earlier negotiated the road from Pec. The assistant checked the names off a list she had on a clipboard.

The captain approached Katya and shook her hand. "Katya, I don't know how we'll manage without you. Your help has been invaluable... Safe journey... and good luck."

"Thank you," said Katya and she got on the coach with her rucksack around her shoulders with Melos in his papoose.

She found a seat near the front and waved to the women from the original group who had come to see her leave. After the driver had loaded up the rest of the gear in the hold beneath the seats, Nadia jumped on board and sat on the seat at the front next to him. The coach moved slowly away along the muddy track, through the camp entrance and onto the main road towards Skopje.

Skopje is the capital of Macedonia and has been almost completely rebuilt since the devastating earthquake of 1963. The airport lies about eight kilometres to the east of the city and the journey by coach took under an hour. Being a Sunday, there was less traffic than normal. As they entered the road which approached the main building, Katya sighed in despair, more chaos. There were military trucks everywhere, local police cars, coaches and buses of every description, and people, hundreds and hundreds milling around, most looking bemused. Children were crying in pushchairs or being dragged along by their mothers, old men shuffling along pushing tattered luggage on trolleys. There were very few younger men.

The coach came to a stop outside the departure gate. The driver opened the front door and an official-looking man got on and spoke to Nadia. He then addressed the group from the front of the bus. The passengers looked on with a degree of uncertainty.

"Good morning, my name is Geoffrey Bywater from the Refugee Council and I'm looking after your flight to the UK. I just wanted to say 'hello' and let you know that we will deal with all the paperwork, so you won't be hanging around for too long. We have a plane especially chartered from the UK to take you to England."

Katya reflected on this for a moment now realising the enormity of her decision to leave her homeland. The rest of the passengers looked on confused, not understanding a word. Katya interpreted for them.

"Thank goodness," said the man, looking at Katya. "Can you help translate the rest of the instructions?"

"Of course," said Katya.

Bywater addressed the passengers explaining the departure process, with Katya providing the Albanian translation.

"In a minute, you will leave the bus and make your way to a special departure gate just over there." He pointed to an entrance at the far end of the departure building. Your luggage will be checked-in and your passports will be stamped. Don't worry, there are a couple of my assistants there who will help you... The plane is due to take-off at around half-past two, so you won't have too long to wait. There will be refugees from three other camps here in Macedonia, about a hundred and sixty in total." His tone was very authoritative.

What a nightmare, thought Katya as she interpreted for the man. Then they all got off, collected their belongings and left the bus to follow the official. Melos was starting to become fractious at being disturbed again and Katya tried to soothe him.

"We're going on a long journey, won't that be exciting?" she whispered to him, though more to convince herself.

There was a line of about fifty people when they reached the check-in desk, a pitiful sight. They looked like the displaced from the Second World War newsreel films, bedraggled, dirty, unkempt and very afraid. Katya took her place with them in the queue, carrying her rucksack; Melos was in his papoose. They waited.

After about half an hour, Katya reached the front and the airline assistant, in an immaculate uniform, neat hair and make-up looked at her. Her long, manicured fingers reached for Katya's passport. She made no eye-contact; just checked the details against the passenger records. Katya felt almost ashamed at her condition. Her nails were grimed and eaten back. She had not had a proper shower for three weeks since Pec and had had to make do with wash downs with bottled water and baby wipes. She was conscious she might smell. She had washed her clothes fairly regularly but with only one change and no washing powder, they were starting to look extremely shabby. Her shoes were in an even worse state, scuffed and caked with mud.

The assistant eventually looked up and handed back Katya's passport with a boarding pass. She smiled, a rehearsed smile, probably more in pity. "That's your boarding pass. You'll need to hand that in at the gate," she added, showing Katya the document.

"How long before we get to London?" asked Katya.

The clerk looked surprised at the question, and the fact that Katya spoke English.

"Oh, you're not going to London."

"But I thought we were going to England."

"You are," said the girl. "To Leeds/Bradford."

"Leeds/Bradford...?" Katya responded somewhat confused. "Where is that?"

"It's in the north somewhere, I've heard it's quite nice... Next please."

The check-in assistant looked over Katya's shoulder to the next passenger, leaving Katya perplexed.

Another aid worker ushered her into the departure lounge.

At just before two o'clock their flight number was called, and Katya and the rest of the passengers made their way to the boarding gate. After a few minutes she approached the plane and at the top of the steps to the cabin she stopped and took one last look at Macedonia.

Chapter Four

They arrived in England at about half-past three local time, allowing for the two-hour time difference. It was Katya's first experience of flying and had been a mixture of excitement and nervousness. She gripped the armrest of her seat as the plane's wheels bounced on the tarmac as it landed.

It made a turn off the runway towards the arrival stand; rain was lashing down. Katya peered out of the small window, trying to take everything in and noticed how green everything looked. During the flight, the cabin crew had been friendly and attentive and had provided the refugees with sandwiches and hot drinks, but the atmosphere had been subdued, the passengers anxious at what lay ahead.

As the plane came to a stop, she picked up Melos and put him in his papoose. He had been asleep on the vacant seat next to her in a makeshift bed made from blankets which one of the flight attendants had given her. She took her rucksack, her only belongings, from the overhead compartment and joined the rest of the group slowly filtering out of the aircraft. Down onto the tarmac, the rain and gloom seemed to match the disposition of the bedraggled refugees as they traipsed forlornly towards the airport building. Katya took a last look at the plane that had carried them and noticed it had been supplied by Bulgarian Airlines; it had been a real international effort.

They were led to the arrival terminal and, as they walked through the gates, Katya stopped in her tracks. She thought a pop star was about to land such was the media frenzy. There had been a few reporters at Skopje airport; one from the BBC even riding with them on the bus from the terminal building to the plane, but nothing like this. There were vans with satellite dishes, reporters doing pieces to camera and journalists everywhere trying to get interviews.

Like Katya, everyone from the flight seemed dazed and confused. The cameras seemed to pay a particular interest in a small girl, about four-years-old who was being pushed in a wheelchair. She was frightened rigid by all the attention. The passengers were ushered by an assistant into a makeshift medical centre for a brief examination and as they waited, in turn, to be seen. Katya noticed one family with two children being interviewed by a woman with heavy makeup; bright lights lit up the scene. Katya couldn't help hearing the questions which were being translated by an interpreter.

"How do like being in the UK?"

"What do you think of the aid effort?"

"What were things like in the camp?"

"How do you feel about leaving loved ones back home?"

Katya wanted to scream; they had no idea.

Once they had been 'processed' - that word again, by immigration officials, they were guided to five coaches waiting outside the front of the building. A posse of journalists and cameras followed their every move. Melos blinked as a camera light flashed in his eyes and he immediately started to cry.

Katya boarded the second coach and found a seat; Melos was on her lap, still crying. Cameras were snapping away at the windows, flashlights burst like fireworks lighting up the inside of the coach. Once it was full, two smartly-dressed women got on. One of them explained they were being taken to two former nursing homes in Leeds; the other lady translated for them.

Melos had been good on the journey, but the attention and commotion had upset him, and it took Katya a few minutes to get him calm again. She was feeling more refreshed having managed to snatch a short nap on the plane, but a sense of anxiety was creeping over her again, like the one she experienced when they had arrived at the Macedonian camp.

The trip from the airport took about forty minutes. On the journey, Katya noticed the rows of houses with green lawns in the front. There were trees and parks, Katya hadn't really thought about what to expect, but it wasn't this. The traffic was relentless; she had never seen so many cars, buses, vans, trucks. Even before the war, Pristina was never like this. She was particularly intrigued by the double-decker buses which she had never seen before.

The bus turned through a gateway and approached a large brick-built house. In front of the entrance, there was a wide gravel parking area. The coach stopped, the door opened, and another woman got on. Matronly-looking and wearing a two-piece suit, she was also accompanied by an interpreter. She spoke like a head teacher addressing an assembly.

"Hello and welcome to the UK. My name is Mrs King and I am from the Refugee Council. My role is to make sure you are comfortable after your long journey." The interpreter passed on the information.

"You will stay here for a few days at this reception centre and then you will be resettled to a more permanent residence in due course. Each family will be allocated a room, and a meal will be ready for you once you have settled in. There will be fresh clothes for everyone... Can you follow me, please?"

The message was translated and, rather cautiously, the passengers started to exit the coach.

The anxiety of uncertainty returned as the refugees slowly filed through the tiled entrance hall and into a large open area. Three trestle-tables had been set up, manned by volunteers and the arrivals were asked to report to register and receive their keys. Small queues formed at each table and a great deal of activity ensued as the administrative procedures were carried out.

Katya reached her turn and gave her name which was checked off a list. She was given her keys and directed to the first floor.

She couldn't believe her eyes when she opened the door to her new accommodation; a bed with clean sheets and blankets, a chair, a washbasin and a bathroom and toilet next door. There was a range of toiletries including soap, shampoo, toilet paper and clean towels which Katya cuddled like a baby with a toy, feeling the softness next to her skin. A cot had been provided for Melos.

Once she had settled in, Katya made her way to the dining area with Melos back in his papoose.

Others from the group were already eating. Katya joined them and she had her first proper hot meal for almost three weeks. Chicken, potatoes, vegetables; after a diet of HDR's it felt like a feast. One of the assistants produced a highchair and she was able to feed Melos from a selection of baby foods.

After dinner, the refugees were shown to another large room. There were armchairs and sofas and on the tables, books in English and Albanian. They had also provided toys for the children and, in the corner, there was a TV, larger than Katya had ever seen. Volunteers again were on hand to provide assistance. The group were given the opportunity to speak to another representative from the Refugee Council individually.

Katya's name was eventually called out and she was introduced to a lady called Rachel. She handed Melos to one of the staff who was looking after the children and followed Rachel down a corridor to a small interview room away from the main lounge area. Rachel was already aware of Katya's relative fluency in English and had dispensed with the on-hand interpreter.

There was a desk and two chairs and for a moment Katya's interrogation experience in Pec flashed through her mind. She suddenly felt nervous.

"Take a seat," said Rachel. "This won't take long; I just need to take a few details. I'd like to hear more about your escape from Kosovo?"

Her voice was calm and reassuring and any worries that Katya might have had were quickly dispelled.

Katya recounted her story, including the incident in the woods; Rachel was busy taking notes. She told Katya they were taking a particular interest in violations and cataloguing full details for any future action that might be taken against the Serbs. There were some harrowing tales.

"What about relatives?" asked Rachel.

Katya gave her mother's address in Lapusnic.

"We're trying to make contact with as many relatives as possible to let them know their loved ones are safe," she explained.

"But she doesn't have a telephone."

"That's ok, we will send the information to our centre in Pristina and they'll try to make contact. We'll let you know if we hear anything."

Katya then told her about Ibi and his capture. "He is dead now, I think." She dropped her head in sadness.

"I am so sorry," said Rachel.

There was a pause while Katya composed herself. She raised her head again and Rachel continued.

"Well, we're in touch with the Serbian authorities, so we will make some enquiries. But I do need to warn you that communication at the moment is extremely difficult. As you can imagine, there's a lot of confusion just now and with the bombing campaign, not surprisingly, the Serbs are being somewhat uncooperative, particularly when it comes to prisoners of war."

Rachel concluded her interview; she had written several pages of notes. She put her papers to one side and explained the asylum process. "You'll be allowed to stay in the UK for at least a year and you're free to look for work. You'll be entitled to the same benefits as everyone else."

"Thank you, that's very kind," said Katya.

"That's the system. You'll also get a small amount of money to tide you over until you get settled in."

Rachel stood up.

"Oh, one other thing before you go. There's been a major relief campaign here in the UK. People have been donating money and all kinds of things and in the morning you'll be able to choose a new set of clothes and other bits and pieces you might need."

Katya appeared overwhelmed. "Thank you," was all she could say.

"Come on," said Rachel. "I'll take you back to the others."

That night, after luxuriating in the warm bath for what seemed to be hours, Katya slept soundly. She felt safe and warm, although a long way from home. For the first time in a long while the demons stayed away.

The following day after breakfast, Katya joined twelve other families in the common-room. One of the representatives came in and took them to another room where a selection of clothes had been laid out. They took no time in sorting through them.

One of the assistants looked after Melos and the rest of the children while the families went through the clothes. Katya chose a blouse with a floral print, a grey skirt and a new scarf. The clothes were second-hand but there were a couple of boxes containing brand new underwear courtesy of a major chain store. Katya didn't understand the measurements and had to ask one of the assistants for help in getting the right sizes. Then shoes, heaven! There must have been two or three hundred pairs, all donated by the people of Leeds. She found a pair of flat shoes that looked like they would fit and tried them on. They were brown leather with thick soles and looked like they had never been worn. Katya walked up and down the room, they were a little tight but would soon give.

"You can choose another pair if you like; we have plenty in your size," said another assistant who appeared to be supervising the melee. Katya found a pair of black shoes and a pair of trainers. Like a child in a sweet shop, this had been a joyous occasion and Katya was beginning to put all her troubles behind her and relax for the first time in months.

Katya collected Melos and went back to her room. She put him down on the floor where he was kicking his legs in the air. Katya could see he was growing and would soon be crawling about. She took off her old clothes and put on her underwear then tried on the blouse and skirt and looked in the mirror. She couldn't believe the result. Suddenly she felt more like a woman again. Only her hair let down the ensemble. Despite the lengthy shampooing last night, it still looked lank and dull. She decided to hide it with her scarf.

She put her old clothes in a carrier bag and then took them down to the common-room for disposal. Again, she gave Melos to one of the helpers who was entertaining the children. They were all having a great time and Katya was quite confident in leaving him; it would give her a break.

Later that morning, the refugees were offered the opportunity of counselling and Katya decided she would follow this up and after a conversation with Rachel, who was now back at the hostel, she was introduced to a Doctor Fitzgerald. The doctor took her into a room that had been furnished as a counselling suite with sofas, cushions and a hi-fi system which was playing soothing music.

The doctor introduced herself. "You can call me Jane." The doctor explained the process; there would be no pressure and Katya could say as much or as little as she wanted.

Jane started by asking Katya about her background, her time at University, relationships and her family. Katya sat on the sofa and took her time speaking slowly, not wishing to leave anything out.

After the initial introduction, the doctor explored more deeply. "Tell me, Katya, is there anything specifically causing you anxiety?"

After a long pause, she told the doctor about Ibi's capture and then went into detail about her narrow escape at the house, the trek through the woods and the incident in the woodman's hut.

"How do you feel about that?" asked the doctor, allowing Katya a chance to express her feelings.

"Angry," said Katya. Then she paused, reflected and spoke quietly. "I feel nothing for the soldiers... They were animals but sometimes... I feel..." She thought for the appropriate translation. "We say *'faj'*.. Guilty...? I think… Is that the right word?"

The doctor made no comment on the description.

"Don't worry it is quite normal. With these sorts of traumas, you will feel a range of emotions, but they will pass with time."

After an hour, Katya left the doctor with offers of further sessions. She was not sure if it had helped but it was good to talk to someone about her experience. On her way back to the common-room, she noticed Rachel talking to one of the supervisors. She broke off her discussion and addressed Katya.

"How did it go?" she asked.

"It was ok, thank you," Katya replied.

Then the burning question which all the refugees wanted answering. "Do you know what is going to happen to us?"

Rachel looked at Katya. "We've got several Local Authorities very keen to support us and the media coverage has helped a great deal in getting some momentum to the relief effort." Katya wrestled with the translation but got the meaning.

Rachel took Katya to a map of the north of England on the wall. Children were running around noisily, along the corridors releasing days of pent-up energy. It was mayhem.

"We are here." She pointed to Leeds on the map.

"I thought this place was called something else... Leeds... uh, Bradford, I think... That's what they told us at the airport."

"No, this is Leeds. Bradford is another city, about twenty miles away. The airport serves both communities, which is why it is called Leeds/Bradford."

"Ah I see," said Katya.

Rachel smiled and continued. "We have offers from Sheffield, Hull and Newcastle as well as Leeds of course." She pointed to the cities in turn on the map, but the names meant nothing to Katya.

"We'll be selecting the most appropriate places depending on each families own requirements; we want to keep family groups together. That's most important."

That evening, several of the group were in the common-room watching television. Most couldn't understand what was going on but seemed to derive some pleasure and distraction from it. A documentary about meerkats was showing which had them laughing uncontrollably at their antics. Then the ten o'clock news came on and the group went quiet.

There was a graphic account of the bombing in Yugoslavia, more on the refugee crisis in the camps, and the arrival of more groups in the UK. Then, a piece which made Katya cry out in horror. It was an eye-witness account of someone who had been released from a Serb prison. The commentator was seen talking to a small group of emaciated men sitting on the floor of a tent. Those watching, of course, didn't need the translation; they could understand the refugee's account.

The voice-over went on: "They say they were robbed, imprisoned, starved and beaten unconscious in a Serbian prison in an attempt to force them to confess to knowledge of the Kosovo Liberation Army. They say they were held, dozens to a cell, forced to kneel with their heads down and their arms behind their backs for hours at a time. Prison guards chose one man in each cell to be in charge and threatened that if there were any sound of talking, they would beat these leaders to death."

The camera panned around to an older man. The commentator continued. "One middle-aged man tries on his new shirt, revealing spotty blood-red bruises on his upper arms and back from the beatings he received... Then, several days ago, this group of fifty-one was suddenly released and driven toward the border."

Katya couldn't stand it any longer and, picking up Melos in her arms, raced upstairs to her room, sobbing bitterly. She went to her rucksack and found the photograph of her and Ibi which she had rescued from the cottage. It was dog-eared and torn. She held it to her and once again felt very alone.

Over the next couple of days, Katya started to get used to her new surroundings. She enjoyed walking around in her new clothes, but the real tonic was having her hair done by a local hairdresser who had been brought in especially by the Refugee Council. She had two more sessions with Doctor Jane and Katya described her reactions to the newscast she had seen on TV. Again, the doctor reassured Katya that in time these feelings would gradually lessen but without closure on Ibi it could take some time. She offered to prescribe some drugs to help her sleep if she wanted but Katya declined.

Katya had also made some new friends, particularly a couple called Shefqez Gosalci and his wife Anita. They had a two-month-old baby daughter, Dielleza, and had fled from a village not far from where Katya lived. They exchanged experiences and hopes for the future. The family were keen to return as soon as possible. They both had parents back home and Anita had a brother in the KLA but had had no knowledge of his whereabouts. Katya had described how she had heard of Ibi's capture and feared that he was almost certainly dead, but the Refugee Council were trying to get some news.

That evening the group were called together. They were being assigned their new, more permanent homes. Katya was quite happy to stay in Leeds, which she had not yet seen in detail, but from the coach looked very nice. The names were called, and locations allocated.

When Katya's name was announced, she was surprised to be placed in Newcastle. She had never heard of the city until Rachel had mentioned it earlier and was sad that Shefqez and his family were going somewhere different; she had started to bond with them.

They would be leaving in the morning; the coaches would be arriving at nine o'clock. Another single mother called Edona was also to be relocated to Newcastle. Katya had seen her a few times around the common-room but hadn't really spoken to her. She had a three-year-old daughter called Arjeta. Katya waved to her as her name was called out.

They were probably about the same age but that's where

the similarity ended. Edona was more an ethnic Albanian with dark hair and was shorter than Katya with a fuller figure, quite plump for a refugee. Katya noticed she had been engrossed in her daughter since their arrival at the hostel and wouldn't let her out of her sight. She appeared obsessively protective of her and would not even allow any of the assistants to pick her up or look after her. As a result, Arjeta followed her mother everywhere.

Katya thought this strange; she had welcomed the occasional respite from Melos while she had been at the hostel.

The next morning, Katya felt anxious again at more change; she wondered what her next home would be like. She was in her new clothes and wore her trainers, even if they didn't really match her skirt. She put all her clothes in her rucksack, but she also needed an extra carrier bag to hold the rest of their belongings. Melos was back in his familiar place in his papoose. Katya was sure he was getting heavier. They congregated in the hallway as the coaches pulled in. Rachel and the doctor were among the well-wishers who had come to see them off. The doctor caught Katya's arm.

"I don't know if this is any good for you." She was holding a fold-up baby-buggy. "It belonged to my sister, but her children are far too big for it now. It's been in their garage for a while, but we've cleaned it up and it seems to work ok." She proceeded to open it up like a concertina.

"Oh, that would be wonderful. That is so kind," and Katya hugged her.

They took Melos from his papoose and lowered him into the buggy and strapped him in. He sat there, seemingly content in his new mode of transport.

"It will give my shoulders a rest. Melos is quite heavy now."

Given that only two passengers were going to Newcastle, Leeds City Council had provided an eight-seater mini-bus for the journey and Katya and Edona got onboard with their entourage.

"I'm Frank," said the driver as he helped them stow their

belongings on the spare seats.

"Hello," said Katya. Edona didn't reply.

"Make yourself comfortable, it's gonna take us around a couple of hours I reckon… as long as we don't get stuck in traffic," he added.

Katya translated for Edona who appeared to have only a limited knowledge of English.

The women sat back quietly in their seats, anxious about what the next stage of their adventure would bring. The minibus pulled away down the drive and headed north.

Chapter Five

A shout rang out. "On me head, Slate."

David Slater, daft as a brush but with a sweet left foot, skipped nimbly past the defender and took aim. The ball curled in from the wing and Brian 'Bigsy' Worrell timed his run to perfection. He met it with his head. 'Like a rocket,' he would say later, and left the keeper groping for the ball in mid-air.

2 – 1.

Bigsy peeled away and ran towards the corner flag, arm raised in triumph, acknowledging the adoration of the capacity crowd. For a nanosecond he was Alan Shearer, the man for whom no accolade was sufficient, revered as a God by any self-respecting Geordie. But this was not St James' Park, the temple of worship for Shearer's adoring flock.

A dog barked and Bigsy opened his eyes. He could see his missus, Carole, shivering on the touchline her feet moving up and down to maintain circulation. Standing next to her was Danny Milburn, a forty-something ex-miner, the team's trainer. Rumour had it, started by Danny, that he was a distant cousin of the great 'Wor Jackie' - Jackie Milburn, who had also earned messiah status locally, albeit in another time. It was said, again by Danny, that he once had trials for United, although most believed it was for North Shields and not Newcastle.

The referee blew his whistle and the Heathcote Rovers team trudged off the pitch, covered in layers of thick mud. Bigsy looked back at the churned up ground, not a blade of grass could be seen. He turned to a couple of the team. "I reckon if we was in Africa, we'd have fookin' hippos wallowing in that lot."

There were nods of agreement. "Aye, you're not wrong there, Bigsy," commented one.

The drainage of Council pitches was notoriously bad; there was no money for upkeep and the local recreational ground, or 'rec', as it was known, had six of them. Strange as it may seem, there was a waiting list to be allowed to play on the not-so hallowed turf.

Sunday morning meant football, the South Tyneside Intermediate Sunday League Division Four and the victory felt good.

Bigsy, a natural leader and team captain, was a big lad, hence his name, over six-foot tall and strong. He was quickly joined by James Polglaise, known by all as Polly. At nineteen, he was the youngest member of the team but was showing some promise; he was also Carole's cousin. Bigsy wrapped his arm around his shoulders in a camaraderie kind of way as they sauntered towards the changing rooms.

Danny 'Wazza' Walker, caught up with them; centre-half and almost as wide as he was tall, his nickname derived from his hero and fellow Geordie, Paul Gascoigne. Finally, the last of the Heathcote Tower gang, Colin 'Chirpie' Longton, jogged alongside the small group. His nickname was ironic; he had a reputation of being a bit of a miserable so and so according to everyone. He could play a bit though, another over six-feet tall and a tenacious midfielder. Unfortunately, after a few drinks on a Saturday night, he was frequently still hung-over on Sunday morning and was a regular addition to the referee's yellow cards. Five games suspended so far and one broken leg - not his, an opponent's, and there were still three more matches to play before the end of the season. The mood was upbeat, the banter incessant.

Bigsy, Wazza and Chirpie always hung out together having lived for several years in Heathcote Tower, a twenty-story monstrosity of the late 50's austerity stock. Polly was at Art College and also lived in the tower block but didn't tend to knock around with his three older teammates. Davie Slater was also not in the gang. He lived in one of the council houses on the other side of the estate; the posh end Bigsy liked to call it.

Bigsy, Wazza and Chirpie did have a reputation locally, mostly for flogging dodgy videos and knocked-off cigarettes but nothing serious. They had been interviewed by the local police - 'bizzies' as they called locally, a couple of times but no charges were ever made, lack of evidence and no witnesses, much to the frustration of the constabulary.

The group made their way with the rest of the team inside the communal changing rooms which became full at the end of the Sunday games around midday. Today, all six pitches had been used, so there were over a hundred muddy footballers and the retinue of coaches, trainers and referees all trying to get showered and changed. Actually, that's not quite true, the referees usually drove home in their kit, thus avoiding any unwanted confrontations.

Covered with dirt and grime, the players waited in a line for the showers which were by now starting to run cold. Nevertheless, the conversation in the Heathcote Rovers dressing room was positive and upbeat.

"You played a blinder today Bigsy, lad," said the coach.

"Ta very much Danny... Did you see that goal, man...? Like a fookin' rocket... Goalie never had a chance."

He jumped up and nodded his head as if re-enacting the event, his man-bits bouncing up and down to the amusement of his teammates.

A stream of water hit his shoulders.

"Shite...! That's fookin' freezing!" he yelled.

"Aye, it was sure enough. Shearer would have been proud of that one," said Danny in feigned admiration.

Eventually cleaned up, they made their way to the gravel car park.

"Bigsy, you going to the club for a bevvie?" asked Danny.

"Just check with the missus, like, but, aye, see you there," said Bigsy. "Hey, give us a ciggie, man, I'm gasping."

Danny handed him a cigarette from a twenty pack which had

an 'Export only - not for sale in the UK' label on the top.

Bigsy found the rather battered VW Golf where Carole had parked it on the patch of waste ground that was used as a car park. She was sat inside with the engine running and the heater on full blast trying to get the circulation back into her legs. Carole wound down the window.

"Can you drop us off at the club, pet...? Just going to have a quick bevvie with Danny and the lads."

Bigsy opened the passenger-side door and pulled down the front seat allowing Polly, Chirpie and Wazza to squeeze in the back.

After a short exchange, Carole drove off, her body language showing her displeasure. Bigsy wasn't allowed to drive since he was banned for three years after his third drink-driving charge.

The windows quickly started to steam up and Carole vigorously wiped the windscreen with the back of her gloves, smearing the condensation in greasy streaks.

After a few minutes, they stopped outside the Seaton Working Men's Club.

What a misnomer that was. Out of the present membership of over fifteen-hundred, the club secretary, Stan Hardacre, reckoned there was less than fifty in any sort of full-time work. The steelworks at Consett, shipbuilding on the Tyne, the pits in County Durham had all gone leaving nothing in their place apart from the new Call Centres - pronounced 'cal'. While they had provided a welcome boost to the local economy, they had done little for the estate and tower block populous that spoke in a language that was totally unintelligible to anyone outside the locale; not much use in a 'cal' centre.

The club was showing signs of age now. Although there had been a building catering for workers on this site since the 1920's, the present building was built in 1969. There was a black and white picture in the entrance lobby of Vic Feather, the General Secretary of the TUC at the time, pulling the first pint.

It was a haven for the community with events on most nights;

the Bingo sessions on Sunday, Tuesday, Thursday and Friday, were particularly popular. There were a couple of full-size snooker tables and a TV lounge with a giant screen where the members could watch football on Sky Sports.

Saturday night, there was usually a band or disco and occasionally, when funds allowed, there would be the odd 'celebrity', usually a tribute act. It didn't matter; it was a chance for the locals to let their hair down.

In an effort to boost custom, Stan had tried Karaoke nights but the fact that nobody could actually sing had caused attendances to drop and they were abandoned. They had also put on 'men-only' nights with a comedian who would tell a few 'blue' jokes followed by a couple of strippers but, again, such was the quality of the girls - 'a right bunch of slappers', Bigsy had described them, they had not proved an overwhelming success.

The four lads climbed out of the car, and as the VW was pulling away, Carole wound down the window and shouted to Bigsy. "There's mud on your boots. You make sure you clean 'em off before you take 'em in the house."

"Aye pet, will do," Bigsy shouted back.

The lads made their way to the bar. Danny had already arrived with Slate and a couple of the other team members and was stood talking to Alice, the seventy-year-old barmaid.

"What're you having lads?" asked Danny.

"Champion, Danny lad, it'll be four broons," replied Bigsy. Newcastle Brown, or 'broon', the famous local beer, was the staple diet of the Heathcote Estate.

Danny looked aghast at having to pay for the four of them.

"Hey Slate, lend us a fiver, kidda," said the coach. Slate sheepishly extracted a dog-eared five-pound note from his pocket and handed it to Alice.

The group stood at the bar drinking and completing the autopsy of the game, and it was turned two before Bigsy, Wazza, and Chirpie, with Polly tagging along, made their way back to Heathcote House. They were forced to walk, in the absence of the offer of a lift. Danny was going the other way, he had said.

The complex around the Heathcote Estate probably looked good in the early sixties but had long since lost its lustre. It comprised of two tower blocks, Heathcote House and Wesley House. A pedestrian walkway connected the two. In front of the towers, a service road led to a small precinct where there was an off-license, which looked more like an armoured fortress with metal grills where the windows should be; a general store where you would buy your lottery ticket, run by Mr Ali and his family; and a video store where Bigsy had an interest. The rest of the estate consisted of rows and rows of pebble-dashed council houses. Small twenty-seater buses ran a regular service to the Bus Station in Gateshead.

It was a tight-knit community and two thousand souls lived there seemingly abandoned by the rest of society. It was said that you could enter the estate from the expressway, and it would take you an hour to find your way out again. Some had never made it out at all, having come with mal-intent. They looked after their own on Heathcote.

An underpass took a cycle-track under the Newcastle to the Western Bypass Expressway, onto a small industrial estate on the other side, and then onto the recreation ground where the football was played earlier. The noise of the traffic was constant but, after a while, residents got used to it.

The lads arrived at the tower block about twenty minutes later and took the only lift to their respective flats.

"Do you fancy coming 'round later, Polly lad, there's some snooker on the telly?" asked Bigsy to the younger cousin-in-law as the lift reached the twelfth floor. It was just the two of them now, Chirpie and Wazza having disembarked on previous floors. The metal doors shuddered open.

"No thanks, Bigsy, there's a good wind, I think I'll take the kite out," replied Polly.

"Suit yourself... You're kites mad, bonny lad," said Bigsy.

Polly left and the lift closed to complete its journey to the next stop, the fourteenth floor. There was no thirteenth; it was superstitious.

The two-bedroomed flat that he shared with Carole, number 1405, was small but tidy. She made him stand at the door while she took his kit-bag from him, taking it straight to the washing machine in the kitchen.

"Have ya got any scram, pet, I'm starving here?" asked Bigsy as he settled down in the armchair in front of the TV.

"I'll make us a couple of sarnies in a bit," shouted Carole, as she emptied the contents of Bigsy's kitbag onto the kitchen floor. "Anything on the box tonight, pet?"

Bigsy picked up the News of the World and looked at the TV listings.

"Na, not much, usual garbage."

He soon became engrossed in an article with the headline, *'Cocaine-fuelled three-in-a-bed romp by footballer – exclusive'*.

"Have you seen what these footballers get up to, jammy bastards," exclaimed Bigsy as his wife brought in two huge sandwiches filled with what looked like chicken nuggets. He took the plate, "Champion, thanks pet... Any chance of a brew?" he added and carried on reading the paper.

"What did your last slave die of, eh?" responded Carole, but got up anyway.

Carole was the brains of the Worrell family. She had met Bigsy as a sixteen-year-old while she was still at school and they eventually got married three years ago on her twenty-third birthday. Despite being three years younger, she had a knack of letting Bigsy believe he ruled the roost, but she knew who really wore the trousers.

She had done well for herself, gone to college and was now a fully-qualified beautician. Her job, in one of the larger department stores in the city, meant she had to look after herself and spent much more than Bigsy knew on her creams, makeup and fake tan. Her hair alone cost twenty pounds a week, enough to keep Bigsy in 'ciggies' for the same period. She was attractive and much admired by the cosmetic reps who were always trying it on, but although she would flirt, was never tempted to stray.

Bigsy was a different character altogether. He had been out of work for over two years since the small engineering factory where he had worked as a machinist, following his apprenticeship, closed down. He signed on the dole every Tuesday and picked up his benefits which he pretty much used as spending money. Carole, being the breadwinner, paid all the bills. Bigsy had got used to filling his days knocking around with his buddies or doing the odd turn at the video shop on a cash-in-hand basis. No longer able to drive since his ban he had to rely on others for transport which had somewhat curtailed his freedom.

But there was an opportunity that had recently passed his way which he had kept from Carole.

He had gained a reputation for being reliable and resourceful which had attracted the interest of a local 'face' who controlled the South Tyneside drug trade.

Everton Sheedie was a hard man with a propensity for violence. Although a Geordie through and through, his Rastafarian roots were firmly embedded in the West Indian community of Brixton, London, where he had a lot of relatives and contacts. This had enabled him to build up quite a power-base through his supply chain, which was unrivalled and unchallenged, in the area.

Initially trading a bit of 'ghanga', as cannabis was known locally, he now had a distribution network which stretched from South Shields on the coast, through Gateshead and into the estate areas of Bensham and the Team Valley.

Everton had moved up from providing the locals with a few spliffs for a Saturday night high to more hard drugs including cocaine and heroin, but his latest big money-spinner was Ecstasy, known as 'cowies' or 'tabs', which were in high demand with the clubbers. His cousin would bring them up from London on a Thursday night in a Transit and then his runners would hit the clubs on Friday and Saturday night and clean up.

With the growth in business came personnel problems and

this is where Bigsy came in. His reputation on the Heathcote Estate had come to the attention of Everton when he had dropped off a supply of cannabis to one of his distributors, Bunny Gordon. Bunny lived in one of the council houses that lay in the shadow of the tower blocks. Unfortunately, Bunny had suffered a heart attack and although he survived, just, he was only in his early forties and knew he had to change his lifestyle if he was going to see his fifties. Now it was common knowledge that people didn't normally retire from drug-dealing. You either got picked up by the police and did a long stretch in prison or were 'pensioned off' and turned up in a sack floating down the River Tyne.

Everton however, appreciated Bunny's industry and loyal service; he had made a lot of money on the back of it. The deal was if Bunny could find someone reliable to take over then the 'pension' element would be waived. So Bunny recommended Bigsy.

A meet had taken place the previous Friday in the underpass and Everton had explained the set-up and what Bigsy was expected to do. Although not intimidated by Everton, Bigsy knew his reputation and was suitably cautious before the meet so he'd asked Chirpie to stand at one end of the underpass with a metal pipe hidden down his jeans, and Wazza at the other, as back up. Everton, also a big man, entered the underpass. He was an imposing figure, in his forties with flowing dreadlocks which were kept in place by what looked like a tea-cosy. He was accompanied by two equally hard-looking accomplices. They gingerly approached each other in the dim light of the tunnel, splashing through the puddles that had accumulated from a recent shower.

Everton and Bigsy met in the middle and the large West Indian offered his knuckles for a touch as a sign of respect. Bigsy complied with the gesture which, to be honest, felt a bit strange he would tell his buddies later. Everton explained the way he operated, the drop off points, when to deal, who to deal with and what Bigsy could expect financially for his labours.

Before leaving, Everton gave Bigsy a brief reminder, if any was needed, of the potential penalties for screwing up.

Bigsy was on trial starting Sunday night when he would receive his first delivery, a small supply of coke and a hundred tabs of cowies. He was to meet the courier at nine o'clock in the service area behind the precinct and would be given further instructions by the driver. He was to look out for a white Transit with a 'South Shields Caterers' logo on the side.

"I can do you a good deal on some knocked-off porn if you're interested, like?" was Bigsy's parting shot to Everton. The big man winced as he walked away, wondering if Bunny's recommendation was a wise one.

But Bigsy's problems were far from over. He had not told Carole and needed an alibi to be able to get out on Sunday night which was normally their 'night in'. Bigsy was either off his head on a Saturday or saving himself for the game the following morning, so Sunday night had become a bit of a ritual. Carole would have a long bath with candles and soft music, and Bigsy would slip one of his adult films on the video to create a suitable ambience.

He hadn't worked out a solution yet. He'd arranged to meet Chirpie and Wazza at eight-thirty outside the video store. Wazza, for a fee, had agreed to be the driver as he was the only one with the correct credentials - a valid licence and a car. Chirpie had also lost his for failing to have any insurance, or MOT, or tax... or permission to drive the vehicle he was caught speeding in on the Inner Ring Road. He had told the officer he had just borrowed it which, unfortunately, was disputed by the owner who had reported it stolen. The community service he was given in addition, was a joke, he had said.

Bigsy was still sat in his armchair scanning the Sunday newspaper for more salacious gossip. He came across an article and started up a conversation with Carole in the hope of leading it to the topic of this evening's pass-out. "Says here those Kosovans are coming up here to live. Did you read that, pet?"

"Aye, I think it's terrible what they must've gone through. I've been watching it on the news," replied Carole.

"If you ask me, like, I don't think they should be allowed in. We've got enough problems up here without them dumping a bunch of gyppos on us," parried Bigsy.

"Give over, pet, you've got no heart you haven't. Have you not seen what's been happening to them?" Carole looked at Bigsy frowning disapprovingly.

"I'm just saying that's all," recognising when to back down.

After a respectful pause, Bigsy continued, sheepishly. "I'm going out tonight pet. You don't mind do you?"

"Where to? It's Sunday night," queried Carole, somewhat surprised.

Thinking quickly, Bigsy replied. "A new batch of videos have just come in from Amsterdam, I said I would pick them up from Stan at the club."

"How are you going to get them back to the shop? You can't drive and I'm not going out," said Carole in a huff.

"Wazza said he would take us, like," replied Bigsy.

Just then his mobile phone rang. He listened to the caller. "Wazza, bonny lad, I was just telling our Carole how you're taking us to fetch them videos tonight." Bigsy put his hand over the phone. "It's Wazza," he whispered.

"I gathered that," replied Carole, sarcastically, and stormed out of the room to check the washing turning in the tumble dryer.

Wazza was just checking arrangements and confirming that Bigsy would fill the car with petrol as the warning light had come on. "We're not gonna get very far otherwise," he warned.

"Aye, I'll see to that, bonny lad," Bigsy confirmed. "We'll meet the bloke at the back of the precinct to pick up the gear... He'll tell us what to do, like... Aye... see you downstairs about quarter past." Bigsy rang off.

The coke was to be taken to a local dealer called Trevor Rankin, or 'knob-head Trev' as Bigsy called him. He lived on the estate on Brompton Road, about twenty minutes' walk away from the flats. The ecstasy tablets were to be taken to three clubs in Gateshead, 'Metal Guru', 'Transformers' and 'Lucifer's'. The doormen would be the contact point and Everton had provided them with descriptions and names; a code word was also agreed.

"Thinks it's the fookin' Great Escape," said Bigsy to Wazza when he was explaining the process.

To Bigsy it was just a game; that's how he thought of it. No hint of danger, or any morality issues, just business, fuelled by the need to make money.

At eight-fifteen Bigsy left the flat.

Carole, ignoring his departure, was watching TV and was clearly upset.

"I'm off now, alright, pet...?"

There was no response.

"I've got me key so I'll not disturb you when I come back," he continued, recognising he would be in the spare room.

He shut the door feeling guilty and knowing he would suffer for this; nookie definitely off the agenda for a bit.

He decided to take the stairs; actually, he had no option, the lift had failed again, and he was faced with a thirteen flight slog to the ground floor. He made his way to the precinct to meet up with Wazza and Chirpie outside the video store.

He approached his waiting buddies. "Hey, Chirpie, give us a ciggie, man, I'm gasping," said Bigsy; he wasn't allowed to smoke in the flat.

Chirpie handed him a cigarette and they proceeded to discuss the plan.

At just before nine o'clock, they made their way to the service area at the back of the precinct. It was almost dark and within a couple of minutes, a white van with the logo 'South Tyne Caterers' on the side came around the corner and stopped in a service bay. The driver, Bigsy recognised, was Layton, one of the henchmen they had met in the underpass. He took out two bags and handed them to Bigsy.

"Dis am de coke, dese are de tabs." He spoke with a strong

Jamaican accent. "I'll meet you here tomorrow night at de same time for de money. You know de price Everton wants, what you charge is up to you, but don't get too greedy or de punters won't buy."

"What's the normal going rate?" Bigsy asked the guy, not wishing to look stupid when meeting the customers. The driver winked and shut the door. "Same time tomorrow, wid de money... and don't screw up." He accelerated away, leaving Bigsy's question unanswered. The whole thing took less than a minute.

"What do we do now?" asked Wazza.

Bigsy looked at the bags in his hands.

"Let's make us some money," said Bigsy. They piled into Wazza's car with Chirpy in the back and left for their first contact.

Knob-head Trev's house was only a few minutes away and they agreed they would drop off the cocaine there before heading out of the estate to the nightclubs. "We'll need some petrol soon," said a concerned Wazza as they headed off.

The exchange with Trev was straight forward enough. They knew each other so there was no need for the charade of passwords. Wazza stopped outside his house and Bigsy got out and took the bag with the coke. He rang the doorbell and Trev answered in a string vest and a pair of brown corduroy trousers held up with braces, a pair of slippers on his feet. A cigarette hung from his lips. A woman's voice shouted from inside but Bigsy couldn't make it out. As it happened, Bigsy was expected and Trev was ready with the money so there was no haggling or discussion on price. He gave Bigsy a roll of notes and Bigsy handed over the bag. Nothing was checked - honour among thieves.

"Well that went well enough" said Bigsy as Wazza pulled away.

Bigsy put the money in the pocket of his jeans.

They left the Heathcote and stopped off at the first garage they came to and Wazza was able to fill the car with petrol.

The car was a one-off; a bit too conspicuous for a drug's run, it should be said. It was originally a Ford Escort but there had been several customisations with a widened wheelbase, sports tyres and a 'go-faster' stripe. The sound system was the pièce de résistance. Massive speakers sat on the back shelf which looked like it had been carpeted. The hundred watts it pushed out was enough to make your ears bleed at close quarters, Wazza had said proudly. Bigsy had told Wazza to turn it off to avoid attracting attention.

Wazza filled the car and peered through the driver's window, looking across at Bigsy expectantly.

"You still got me videos in the boot, bonny lad?" asked Bigsy.

"Aye," said Wazza.

Bigsy got out and followed Wazza to the back of the Escort. Wazza opened the boot to reveal a box of forty or so hard-core videos, recently imported from Amsterdam. Bigsy picked out three at random and put them under his coat.

Wazza and Chirpie watched from the car as Bigsy weaved his magic. Sure enough, payment in kind was very acceptable to the lad on the till.

"There's plenty more where they came from, bonny lad," said Bigsy as he left the kiosk. He returned to the car and they drove off.

As it happened, the evening's exercise went smoother than Bigsy had imagined.

Wazza had already worked out a route based on where the drops were to take place. The punters were aware of the new arrangements and paid 'what they paid Bunny,' Bigsy making out he was a close associate of the former supplier. The codes and formalities were all observed and overall, it had been a very satisfactory excursion.

It was deathly quiet as they returned to the precinct; the noise from the Escort's throaty exhaust seemed to reverberate around the towers. As they parked up, Bigsy gave Wazza two twenty-pound notes and Chirpie thirty pounds for their evening's labours, explaining that Wazza had provided the transport.

The tricky bit was yet to come for Bigsy as it was now one-forty in the morning and, while he had tried to phone Carole at around ten, she didn't answer.

He decided to tough it out, and carefully opened the front door. He took his shoes off, which weren't allowed in the living room anyway, and quietly dropped the latch behind him. He tip-toed into the lounge, which was in complete darkness. He walked towards the bedroom, but then suddenly yelped in pain as he stubbed his toe on the corner of the sofa. He quickly stifled the scream.

He made his way past the 'master' bedroom door and into the spare room where a blanket and his pyjamas had been piled on top of the bed in a heap. By now his eyes had acclimatised to the light and he was able to find the switch to the bedside lamp and switched it on. Bigsy got undressed down to his underpants and made his way to the bathroom, trying not to make any noise. He brushed his teeth but did not flush the toilet, then noticed his big toe was bleeding and there were a couple of spots of blood on the carpet. "Shite" he muttered. He took some toilet-paper and put it under the tap and bent down under the sink to dab the marks. He was almost finished and about to make his way back to the spare room when a shape appeared at the door and he jumped up in alarm, cracking the top of his head on the basin. He let out a cry... "Shite." He got to his feet and stood there holding his head.

"And what time d'you call this?"

It was Carole, not best pleased; which was an understatement.

"Eh, Carole, pet, I tried not to wake you." He was still rubbing the top of his head.

"Too bloody late now isn't it. I said, what time d'you call this?" asked Carole again indignantly.

"I can explain, pet, we ran out of petrol, I did try to call you."

"I know you did; I was in the bath."

"Why didn't you call us back?" countered Bigsy.

"What? For more lies...? I phoned Stan at the club and he knew nottin' about collecting any videos. You must think I'm stupid."

"No pet, I can explain, honest."

"Well?"

"We did have to make a delivery… over at Lucifer's and, well you know how it is, the boss invited us in, like, and we stayed for a couple of drinks."

"You've been to a club in Gateshead? Where did ya get the money from?"

"It was free… the boss likes the videos and I slipped him a couple of specials, honest, pet."

It seemed to be reasonably plausible to Carole and, although far from happy with the explanation, she had made her point and needed to get back to sleep for fear of bags under the eyes in the morning. She had to look her best.

"Well, you can stay in there for tonight and don't think you'll be getting any action for the foreseeable, if you catch my drift."

Bigsy slunk into the room and closed the door, the reception having taken some of the gloss off the night's adventure. Before turning in, he wrapped a piece of toilet paper around his damaged toe to avoid getting blood on the sheet. He was in enough trouble as it was.

The next day, Monday morning, Bigsy woke at nine-thirty. There was a lump on the top of his head; his big toe had gone a strange brown colour and it was stinging. The toilet-paper he had used to staunch the bleeding was nowhere to be seen. He checked the sheets but could see no traces of blood; he breathed a sigh of relief.

Carole had gone to work as usual at seven-thirty without waking him up or saying goodbye. He limped to the kitchen, made some toast and brewed a strong tea and sat down to watch the TV. The news still carried the report of the Kosovan refugees' arrival at Leeds/Bradford airport the previous day. They were showing pictures of a four-year-old in a wheelchair and interviewing a family about their initial reaction to arriving in the UK. He took little notice and looked out of the window. It was cloudy but reasonably bright and he could see the hills of Northumberland in the distance. The traffic on the Western bypass was crawling as usual for this time of the morning, winding its way up the hill past the Metro Centre towards the new river crossing.

He picked up his mobile and rang Wazza. "What are you up to?"

"Nottin' much, may go into town later... Need a new pair of jeans," replied Wazza.

"You still alright for tonight...? I could do with you about when the heavy turns up for his money."

"Aye, bonny lad, I'll be there... about nine?"

"Aye, that's champion, man, see you then."

Bigsy went to the spare room to check that the money from last night was safe. He took the cash from the security belt he had worn and counted it out on the bed. He put Everton's stake in a polythene bag and totted up the rest. After paying Chirpie and Wazza their cut last night, Bigsy had cleared one hundred and twenty pounds, not bad for starters. He put his cut in the pocket of his jeans and placed the money for Everton in the drawer in the bedside cabinet; it would be quite safe.

Having put a plaster on his injured toe, he went out and took the lift to the ground floor. The engineers had clearly fixed the elevator issue. He stood in the entrance and lit up a cigarette and noticed a couple of removal vans outside. He moved out of the way as a couple of lads in overalls were negotiating a bed through the front entrance.

"Best of luck with that, bonny lad. You'll never get it in the lift," said Bigsy as they struggled past.

"Cheers for that mate, where's 1410?" said one of the lads.

"That'll be the fourteenth floor," replied Bigsy.

"I was afraid of that," said the deliveryman. "Oh well, here we go," and the two lads started their long journey upwards.

Bigsy was intrigued. There weren't many flats vacant and he thought there was a waiting list. In fact, he and Carole had lived with her parents in Jesmond before they got married and were on the council waiting list for several months before they were offered a flat at Heathcote, which, it had to be said, was not Carole's first choice. She was keen to stay around Jesmond, which was a much nicer area, but, as she admitted at the time, beggars can't be choosers.

He finished his cigarette and took the lift back up to the flat. As the door slowly juddered opened on the fourteenth floor, Bigsy could see the two lads staggering with their cargo from the stairway. They stopped, put the bed down and took a breather.

"You two look knackered," commented Bigsy.

"Where's 1410?" asked the lad nearest him.

"Just round the corner, I'll show you," said Bigsy and led the way. The removal men put the bed down and one of them opened the door.

"So what's this all about?" enquired Bigsy. "We getting new neighbours?"

"Don't know, looks like it. We've just been asked to deliver some furniture here, 1410, and to flat 607, which I suppose will be on the sixth. They've got sparkies, plumbers and decorators on the way, so something's definitely up."

"Fancy a brew lads, after you've dropped the bed, like?" asked Bigsy.

"Aye, that would be champion," they said almost in unison.

Bigsy went back to 1405 and put the kettle on leaving the front door ajar. He ignored the house rules about shoes but made sure there were no marks on the carpet. He always said cream was a daft colour for a floor covering. After a few minutes, there was a knock on the door and the two lads came in and were presented with a mug of tea each.

"Sugar's on the table, lads," said Bigsy.

They helped themselves to three teaspoons of sugar each and made quick work of the drink. Bigsy noticed they were sweating and kept an eye for anything dripping on the carpet. His balls were literally on the line.

Bigsy pressed further on the new occupants but the removal men could give him no more information apart from the fact that the two flats were being kitted out in full - washing machine, microwave, cooker, television, new bed, a cot, sofa, table, chairs, cutlery, crockery, even an iron and ironing board.

"You don't think it's for them gyppos they've been showing on telly, do you?" pondered Bigsy.

"Dunno mate, only know what I've told you," said the man.

For the rest of the day, Bigsy watched the comings and goings around the precinct. He was doing the afternoon shift at the video shop before meeting up, hopefully, with Carole around six o'clock. The removal men were on the go all morning and didn't finish until lunchtime. Luckily the lift kept going and most of the gear went up that way, only the bed and sofa requiring the long haul. Various tradesmen were coming and going, Viking Electrics, Dempsey's Plumbers, RightPrice Carpets and Johnson's decorators. Goodness knows who was co-ordinating it all, seemed a right bugger's muddle.

Bigsy left the video shop at around five o'clock; it had been a fairly quiet afternoon. As usual, "Reservoir Dogs", "The Texas Chainsaw Massacre" and "Driller Killers" were most in demand, especially with young teenage lads who were bunking off school.

He made his way back to the flat and waited for Carole to arrive. He did think about getting something out of the freezer and starting the dinner, but she would definitely be suspicious with that sort of gesture. Plus, apart from the grill, he had yet to master the intricacies of the cooker. No, he would make a brew, put the TV on and sit tight.

Five-past six he heard the key turn in the lock and Carole walked in.

"Oh, hi pet, how was your day?" grovelled Bigsy.

"Why're ya askin'? You're not usually that interested."

"Just asking… Can I get you a brew…? Kettle's just boiled pet."

Bigsy disappeared in the kitchen while Carole went to the

bedroom to change. Ten minutes later she reappeared looking tired but still very smart in tight jeans and a white tee shirt. Bigsy handed her a mug of tea as another news article appeared on the TV on the 'Crisis in Kosovo'. For once Bigsy listened intently until the item was finished and called out to Carole who was in the kitchen preparing a meal.

"You know Carole, pet, some strange things have been occurring today," and he recounted the events he had seen. "I reckon it's them gyppos... the one's off the telly, like. I reckon they're movin' in here, pet. What do you think?"

"I hope they do after what they've been through," said Carole.

"Aye, but there's no work up here and they'll jump the queue for a house. We had to wait months to get this... and we had to buy all our own furniture. You'll remember that alright."

"Most of it was nicked if I recall, Bigsy," said Carole.

"Aye, but that's not the point. Doesn't seem right, that's all I'm saying, we've got enough charity cases in this country without shipping in more."

Bigsy sensed this was not a good time to pick a fight and dropped the subject; he was already confined to the spare room and it was clear Carole had not forgotten last night's little caper.

"I suppose you'll be off clubbing again tonight," said Carole, twisting the knife.

"No, but I do have to pop out at nine for a few minutes... If that's alright, like?"

"Why bother asking me?" said Carole frostily.

"Just being polite, like" he paused, and continued. "Look, pet, I don't want to fight with yas. I've got a bit of business on the go that's all."

He took out a couple of twenty-pound notes from the roll in his pocket and gave it to her.

"Where d'you get this from...? You're always skint."

"Like I said, some business that's all and if it goes as well as last night, there could be a lot more, maybe enough to get us out of this dump."

Bigsy had her attention now and was starting to press the right buttons but she wasn't letting go yet.

"What sort of business...? Not them mucky videos is it? You'll end up getting nicked again and this time you'll get banged up."

"No, no nottin' like that, pet. I've got a contact that can get some cheap gear and I've also got someone who wants to buy it, like, and I make a bit of cash in the middle."

Carole looked at him closely for any signs of lying. She saw none and again gave him the benefit of the doubt. He did after all give her some cash which would come in very handy. She had just seen a new dress in the sale in one of the discount stores which she was anxious to buy but had no spare until payday and would have to put it on her credit card which was already up to its three-thousand-pound limit.

"Why didn't you say last night, I would have understood?"

"Didn't want to worry you, pet."

She beckoned him over to the sofa. "Come here ya daft lump," and Carole planted a big kiss on his head.

"Does that mean I'm out of the spare room?" asked Bigsy with doleful eyes.

"Maybe, but you better be back before ten if you want any real action tonight."

Bigsy smiled knowingly.

"Aye, no problem there, pet."

Chapter Six

Tuesday morning and Bigsy did get his brew in bed at seven-thirty. Last night had gone well on all fronts; although Layton, the courier, was concerned at the activity going on at the flats. The tradesmen were still on site and their various vans were parked in the service bay area. Luckily, another white Transit was not going to attract any attention and the workers were all in the flats. Bigsy gave the driver the cash in a polythene coin bag and Layton stopped and counted it.

"Don't you trust us, bonny lad?"

"Can't be too careful, mon," said Layton, counting the cash until he was satisfied it was all there. "Everton will be in touch."

He was about to pull away when Bigsy put his hands up and furtively moved closer to the open driver's window. Looking around and cupping his hands to his mouth so no potential lip-reader could eavesdrop on the conversation, Bigsy whispered to the driver: "Look, do you think you can perhaps leave out Sunday nights in future, bonny lad, cos it's causing some grief with the missus, like?"

Layton was taken aback. "Everton will call you, just be ready."

Bigsy watched him drive away. He wondered if he had made the right call with his request, but it was done now, and he thought it was worth mentioning.

Fortunately, Bigsy had returned to Carole just before the cut-off time, which might have been literal in this case. She was laid on the sofa sipping from a glass of red wine wearing a dressing gown. She looked at Bigsy and slowly removed it, revealing her best Sunday-night lingerie. Bigsy caught his breath.

The following morning, Bigsy was up early and walked past the growing number of white vans parked behind the precinct, their owners going to and from the towers like soldier ants. He made his way to the bus which would take him to the dole office in Gateshead to sign on and collect his weekly government pay-out. The journey took about three-quarters of an hour by the time they had picked up all the pensioners and other 'job-seekers'.

He saw his case officer who had long given up any hope of placing Bigsy in meaningful employment, signed off the usual form and Bigsy left, putting the eighty pounds in his pocket with the remainder of last night's earnings. He felt good. Most of that would be gone by the weekend, squandered on cigarettes, bevvies and ancillary bits and pieces which came under the general heading of entertainment.

This week might be different; he had a bit more money and thought he might use it to invest in more stock of videos from Stan at the club.

Stan had a nice little racket going on. As well as porn videos, he could also get a seemingly unlimited supply of duty-free cigarettes. He had also recently taken delivery of some nice tracksuits, 'all the way from India', which were very much in vogue in the area and had turned a very good profit. No-one was really sure of his sources, but he did have a brother who worked the ferries from Newcastle to Norway and sometimes Hull to Rotterdam. The club made a good front for distribution and there was no shortage of happy customers and Bigsy was one of the best.

Having completed his weekly pick-up, Bigsy caught the 'Hoppa', the local bus, to Bensham. He stared out of the bus window considering recent events watching the drab scenery go by. It had started raining and the topic of transport came to mind. He was used to cadging lifts when needed and his buddies were generally obliging but he would need to keep Wazza happy. A few notes now and again would be required if he was going retain his services as his regular driver. He would work on it.

As well as picking up his own money, Bigsy was also responsible for collecting his parents' pension from the post office. He had been doing this for some time since his Dad had been confined to his chair in the front room.

Mr. and Mrs. Worrell senior lived on the Bensham estate, which was not far from Heathcote, in a small old people's bungalow. Joe Worrell was an ex-shipbuilder who had worked on the Tyne for the best part of thirty years before they closed the shipyard. He had come down to Newcastle from the Clyde when he was in his early twenties looking for work and stayed. Now at the age of sixty-seven, he was wracked by poor health. He had had a small stroke a couple of years earlier and rarely went out. They had lived in one of the council houses on Heathcote until Bigsy had left home, but then found the house was getting too much for them to manage. They were offered the bungalow on an exchange basis and jumped at the chance.

Joe and Mar Worrell, as she was always known, had had Bigsy late in life, their only child, but viewed him as a blessing and looked after the young lad as best they could. There was never much money; regular strikes and short-term working, particularly in the seventies and eighties had seen to that. Mar struggled to balance the weekly budget but given all the obstacles, not least Joe's drinking and gambling, did an amazing job. The young Bigsy had never gone without food on the table or a clean pair of socks and pants. Bigsy thought the world of his parents and the sadness he had when he looked at the two of them, old before their time, was overwhelming.

Bigsy got off the bus at the end of the road where his parents lived. He reached the pebble-dashed house and knocked on the door. There was a warm glow on Mar Worrall's face when she opened the door to her son.

"Hello pet, come on in; I've made us a brew," said Mar, and gave him a peck on the cheek.

"How're you doing, bonny lass, is the radgie gadgie still stuck in his chair?"

The phrase was a term of endearment from Bigsy, but in the Newcastle dialect, 'radgie gadgie' usually meant a stroppy or difficult person.

He walked into the front room to see his dad glued to some chat show on the TV, oblivious to his son's arrival.

"Hiya Dad, you alright?" It was his standard greeting to his father.

"Oh, hiya bonny lad, didn't see you there," said Joe, somewhat startled.

Mar brought in the tea and some biscuits and Bigsy sat down and gave his mother the pension money. The three of them started chatting and catching up with the news, Bigsy recounting his goal on Sunday morning which, having described it in detail for the umpteenth time, had now taken on such a picture of skill and dexterity that the God Shearer would have been proud.

"Hey, did you see them asylum seekers on the news...? I reckon they're putting some in at Heathcote," said Bigsy.

"Why d'you say that?" asked Joe, and Bigsy described the comings and goings at the flats and the conversation with the removal men.

Joe Worrell had always seen himself as working-class and would always vote for the Labour party candidate whoever that was. Whatever his political leanings however, his views on race, immigration and asylum seekers were uncompromisingly right of Genghis Khan. He thought the National Front was too moderate, and the Ku Klux Klan was closer to what depicted a reasoned society. He pulled a cigarette from another packet marked 'Export only-not for sale in the UK' and handed one to his son. Joe lit up and coughed violently.

"You should give them things up, Dad, before they kill yas," said Bigsy.

Joe ignored the advice and started a lengthy diatribe about the loss of British jobs to foreigners and the expansion of the immigrant population.

"Those fookin' Pakistanis, they're the worst; breed like

fookin' rabbits. Enoch Powell had the right idea but it's too fookin' late now... we're being overrun with them. He was right ya know. I would've voted for him despite him being a Tory," said Joe animatedly.

Bigsy smiled at the passion of the man who had walked out of the shipyard at the drop of a hat or the whistle of a shop-steward in bygone years.

"What are you going to do about it, bonny lad?"

"Nottin' we can do, Dad."

"It's not right, shouldn't be allowed, fookin' asylum seekers," and Joe started coughing again to such an extent that he was losing his breath and going red.

"Hey Dad, you settle down before you do yourself a mischief," said Bigsy fussing over his father.

"Now then Joe, you shouldn't be saying such things. Have you not seen the news? They've been bombed out of their houses, put into camps, everything. How would you like it if it happened to our Brian," as Mar preferred to call Bigsy, "and Carole?"

"You sound like our Carole, Mar, that's what she's sayin'," replied Bigsy.

"Well, she's right... We should be helping them; it's only for a while anyway," countered Mar.

"Aye that's what they say, but I bet they'll end up sticking around and we'll be footing the bill," said Bigsy. He paused, "Ah well, we'll have to wait and see, but they'll be a lot of people not want 'em 'round here, that's for sure."

They continued the discussion for a short while until finally, Mar could see Joe was getting very tired, his attention span having been exhausted, and called the debate to a halt. Bigsy finished his tea and gave his cup to his mother and started to leave.

"Now don't be going doing anything silly, Brian; it'll be all over the papers and we don't want to see any trouble," counselled his mother.

"No, Mar, don't worry I won't," said Bigsy.

He made his farewells, kissing his father on the forehead and giving his mother a big hug and told her not to worry. Joe was once again totally engrossed in his chat show.

It was gone midday before Bigsy returned to Heathcote House. The various tradesmen had nearly all gone. A couple of decorators' vans were left parked behind the precinct. Just then, his mobile phone rang. 'Caller's Number Withheld', it said on the screen.

It was Everton and Bigsy jumped to attention, putting his finger in his right ear to make sure he was not distracted by any extraneous noise. Everton said that he had been pleased with the work on Sunday and the punters had provided him with 'favourable feedback'. His next delivery would be Wednesday night and, as well as the 'cowie' drops at the clubs and knob-head Trev's coke, there would be some more deliveries at two pubs outside Gateshead and one at the Washington Services on the A1. "Just a bit of weed," said Everton.

Timing would be important, and Everton gave Bigsy the times he would have to meet the various punters and the price he expected. He also explained identification and the various code words. Bigsy would have to devise a route to coordinate the trip; it would not be straightforward. Everton made Bigsy repeat the instructions and rang off.

"Shite", Bigsy mumbled to himself recognising things were moving up a gear.

Bigsy called Wazza on his mobile. "Hiya bonny lad, you up for a bevvie?"

"Yeah, ok, see you in ten minutes," replied Wazza.

"And can you pick up Chirpie if he's about? I've got some news."

Bigsy rang off and checked his top-up credit. He waited outside the video store in the precinct and a few minutes later the familiar sound of Wazza's stereo could be heard booming out, the Ford Escort not yet in view. It came around the corner from the direction of the garages and Bigsy could see Chirpie in the passenger seat, head bouncing up and down like a nodding dog. Chirpie got out and Bigsy got in the front seat confining Chirpie to the rear next to the speakers.

"Turn that fookin' noise off for fook's sake, you'll wake the fookin' dead," said Bigsy, as they pulled away. They headed off to the working men's club.

Entering the club, there was a long entrance lobby which led to the main bar and dance area where a doorman would sit and collect entrance money on Saturday nights when there was a 'turn' on. To the left was the snooker room and at the end of the lobby past the snooker room, there was the members' lounge where they could play a game of cribbage or dominoes without being disturbed.

The lobby doubled as an information board with notices of every description; 'what's on this week', 'lunchtime specials', 'darts league fixtures', and so on. There was a section for the football club with some newspaper cuttings of previous headline matches. A fading photograph of The South Tyne Sunday League trophy-winning team 1976, took pride of place with a young-looking Danny Milburn, or so he said; it was difficult to tell, holding the cup in front of his proud teammates. There was even a row of pictures of past celebrities who had performed at the club including an 'Opportunity Knocks' winner from 1978. Nobody had heard of them now.

A notice caught Bigsy's eye. "Hey, hold up... do you see that...? They've got me favourite band on," he exclaimed excitedly, pointing at the advert.

Bigsy was a big fan of Oasis, the Britpop band. His version of 'Wonder Wall' was one of the reasons for the decline of the Karaoke nights. There was a Geordie tribute band who called themselves, 'Why-Aye Sis' who played the local circuit, and Bigsy never missed seeing them when they played at the club.

"When is it?" asked Wazza.

Bigsy checked the date. "Saturday week... I'm well-up for that lads. What d'you think?"

"Aye, I'll be there," said Wazza.

"What about you Chirpie... you coming?"

"I'll see," the big man replied, without a hint of enthusiasm.

"Suit yourself, but we'll have to get the tickets soon in case they sell out," said Bigsy and they walked into the club.

It was busy at lunchtimes, both snooker tables were in use and there was a lot of activity around the two dartboards. The bar area was largely taken up with men downing bottles of Newcastle Brown. The three strode up to the bar across the thread-bare beer-stained carpet. It resembled a scene from an old western movie where the gunslingers arrived in town. Several members looked at them and Bigsy would nod in acknowledgement. He ordered three bottles from Alice and went and found three seats by the window. A thick fog of cigarette smoke hung in the air.

Bigsy, ensuring they were out of earshot from anyone, outlined the next delivery schedule to his pals. He assured Wazza that he would be suitably recompensed for expenses plus a bit of money for his back pocket. Chirpie was his usual laconic self and was up for anything. Bigsy couldn't have wished for a more loyal band of brothers.

Wazza's background was different from Bigsy's. Although now twenty-seven, he still lived with his mother on the sixth floor of Heathcote House. Hazel Walker was in her late forties and regularly helped behind the bar at the club on Saturday nights. She was considered 'fit' by the club's male members and when she wore her special barmaid's outfit attracted a lot of male admirers, though not in Wazza's earshot. At six-foot and eighteen stone he would be a serious match for most takers and would never countenance any salacious comments about his mother. Wazza's father had long since disappeared and he had little recollection of him. According to Hazel, he worked on the North Sea oil rigs, working a fortnight on, a fortnight off. He would commute back and forth from Aberdeen to Newcastle at the end of his shift and one day never came back. He sent Hazel a letter explaining he had moved in with someone else.

Hazel was left with Wazza as a four-year-old. She had to sell their house as maintenance payments were rarely forthcoming, and she had no chance of keeping up the mortgage repayments. The council moved them into Heathcote, and they had lived there ever since, over twenty-three years.

During the day, Hazel worked at a baker's shop in Gateshead town centre where she had been for over twelve years. She doted on her son, regularly supplementing his income with a few quid here and a few quid there. It was Hazel who bought Wazza his pride and joy Escort and paid for all the running costs in return for the occasional lifts to the club. Wazza had been less fortunate on the work front. Like Bigsy, he had gained an apprenticeship as a welder, but once the shipyard had closed, there was no work and he relied on the dole or the occasional back-pocket job for money.

Chirpie Longton lived on the seventh floor of the tower block and was married to Joy, a large lady, at least nineteen stone according to a neighbour, and for that reason rarely ventured out. Bigsy had once said that when she fell out the ugly tree, she hit every branch. They had no children.

Chirpie's features were the product of the university of hard knocks. He was also a big guy, not fat, his regular football had seen to that. But his face looked like it had been hewn from granite due to the regular broken noses, cheekbones and jaws he had suffered from his time playing rugby in his youth. He switched to football following a serious back injury which confined him to a wheelchair for a couple of months. The doctors warned that he could end up paralysed if he continued with the sport, so he made the change. He was generally an insular individual, preferring to keep his own council which had earned him the ironic name 'Chirpie'. He did have a temper however, and Bigsy had seen him take two guys out at one go following a set to and too many broons one Saturday night. He was definitely someone you wanted on your side and Bigsy was pleased he was a mate.

Bigsy went over the arrangements for Wednesday night,

meeting times and routes. The gear would be dropped off as usual by Layton at seven o'clock but this time, given the activity at the flats, they had agreed to meet at the Working Men's Club car park which was fairly quiet at that time of night, and the caterer's van would cause little suspicion. They would meet up at the flats at six-thirty.

Alice bought three plates of sandwiches and chips which they had ordered, Bigsy paid, which was virtually unheard of.

It was around two-thirty by the time Bigsy, and his gang got back to the precinct and Wazza parked his car in his garage which was in a row of lock-ups on the other side of the shops. There was still some activity in the flats, and they noticed three council workers in Hi-Viz vests picking up litter from around the two tower blocks while road-sweepers crept up and down the service road and around the front of the shops.

"Fookin' hell," exclaimed Bigsy. "You don't think the Queen's coming here, do you?" They all laughed but Bigsy was still intrigued.

"Well, I've seen nottin' like this all the while I've been here, man, that's for sure."

They walked together to the entrance lobby of the tower and two more council officers were disinfecting the lifts. A sign was hung across the entrance that read 'out of order - maintenance in progress'.

"You make sure you get all that piss out of the corners, bonny lad," said Bigsy to one of the labourers who looked at Bigsy and gave him the two-fingered salute. Wazza and Chirpie made for the stairs.

At that moment, Polly appeared coming in the opposite direction, almost knocking into the lads; he was holding a kite in his arms.

"Hiya bonny lad, where you off to?" asked Bigsy. "You're not bunking off college are you?"

"Nah, home study... Just testing a kite for my art project," replied Polly.

Bigsy was impressed. He liked young Polly; he was the only one in the family with any real potential. He was the son of Carole's Aunt Alison, who lived on the twelfth floor, and from a young age Jamie Polglaise could draw well and showed real promise in design work, but since he started his course at college, he'd taken it to another level and his talent was beginning to really blossom. He was also an excellent photographer.

Bigsy had bought him a Nikon SLR camera for his eighteenth birthday. Actually, it was provided by Stan from the club at a substantial discount, no questions asked, but some of the results Polly had achieved were quite stunning and he had had some framed and displayed at the college. He was coming to the end of his Higher National Diploma course at Gateshead College and had been conditionally accepted at Northumberland University to study art and media.

Polly's passion, however, was making kites. He became interested in them when he was about fourteen, and some he had made had earned him top grades in his school exams. He constructed them himself, learning about the aerodynamics from his art teacher at secondary school, and decorated them with an amazing grasp of colour and tones, taking his lead from some of the Chinese designs he had read about while he was studying for his Art GCSE. He had joined a local society; he was the youngest member and could be seen regularly flying his latest prototype on the rec. With so much open space, it was an ideal testing ground.

Bigsy watched with pride as his cousin-in-law walked on in the direction of the rec, while he began the all too familiar trudge to the fourteenth floor.

Chapter Seven

The minibus made good progress getting out of Leeds, heading up the A58 and joining the A1 at Wetherby.

Katya looked at the countryside, which was so green and fresh, the fields in different shades interspersed with swathes of yellow from the rapeseed which was now in full bloom. As they headed up the motorway, suddenly a rainbow spread out in front of them following a recent shower, a good omen perhaps.

She watched Edona fussing with little Arjeta who was already bored being cooped up in her seat. Edona gave her a colouring book and crayons that she had been given by the children's nanny at the reception centre. Melos was fast asleep in his buggy, which was secured in the central aisle between the seats. Katya struck up a conversation with her travelling companion, although initially, it was not easy.

She asked where she had come from and how she ended up in England.

The story she heard was a familiar one. Edi, as she wanted to be known, came from a village to the north of Pristina not far from Obilic where she lived with her husband Liri. Liri worked as a labourer on her parent's farm and the small cottage in which they lived came with the job. Although an engineer by vocation, he had been caught up in the expulsion of students at Pristina University where he was studying and, because of the crackdown, he was unable to get a job that matched his qualifications, resorting to farm-work as the only alternative.

Edi described when Liri came looking for work and it was she who persuaded her father to take him on. It was only a small farm with hardly enough money coming in to feed the family. There were a few cows, goats and chickens, a fruit orchard and enough land for a crop of vegetables which enabled them to be virtually self-sufficient but there was little left to sell for cattle-feed and other items.

To make ends meet, Edi's mother, Marianna, worked in a small haberdashery in Pristina which sold material and accessories for clothes. She was also an experienced seamstress and sold some of her own garments in the shop, which helped the family budget. She had taught some of her skills to Edi who was starting to show the potential to be good with fabric and also a talent for design. She had hoped to go to college, but the war had changed everything.

The decision to take on Liri had several consequences; first, it had lessened the burden on Edi's father who was unable to do much heavy lifting due to a painful back injury; secondly, within months Liri had reorganised the farm, becoming far more efficient, and for the first time in years, was actually showing a small profit. Thirdly, Liri and Edi had become lovers and very soon she fell pregnant with Arjeta.

A quick marriage service was arranged, and their daughter was born in February 1996. They moved into their cottage and had become a family with her mother and father close by. It worked well for a while but, with political tensions growing in Kosovo, life was becoming increasingly difficult. The Serbs had imposed a new regime abolishing Kosovo's autonomy and the local government responded by pursuing a policy of peaceful resistance.

That same month, the Kosovan Liberation Army, which until then was seen as no more than a guerrilla outfit, started to become more active and undertook a series of attacks against Serbian targets that included police stations, government offices and Serb civilians in Western Kosovo. The Serbian authorities denounced it as a terrorist organisation and increased the number of security forces in the region. By April that year, more militant Kosovans were actively attacking Serb security personnel, and retaliation by the Serbs precipitated what became known as the

Kosovan War.

Locally, the KLA was getting more and more support. Not surprisingly, Liri was drawn to the cause and soon became an active sympathiser. He had had contact with some of the people involved through his former University friends and had decided to join them. Katya could readily identify with the situation, but unlike her and Ibi, Edi had managed to keep in touch with Liri who had been able to get back to the farm fairly regularly. She described Liri's growing involvement with the KLA. He was seen as having good leadership qualities and he quickly rose through their ranks. Liri had told her about a raid which was of particular importance.

She recounted the story to Katya. In these early days, the KLA were not well-armed and were desperate to get their hands on as many weapons as possible. Liri led an operation to capture ordnance from a former military base just across the border in Albania, a country also in turmoil at this time. The raid was a resounding success and Liri was praised by the KLA command for his prowess in the exercise. Edi spoke with pride but sadness.

Edi carried on her story with more emotion as she recounted the day of March 24, 1998, when Serbian forces surrounded the village of Glodjane. There was a fierce battle. Tragically, Liri was wounded and died later that evening in a field hospital. One of Liri's university friends called at the farm to give her the news and told her that he was a hero of Kosovo and would be remembered for all times. As she recounted the event, Edi began to cry; she had not told anyone, not even the counsellors at the reception centre.

Frank, the driver, could hear the exchanges from the passengers but being in Albanian, he could not understand what was being said.

Edi continued. "After I found out about Liri, I lost all interest in the farm."

She explained that despite the support from her mother and father, she became reclusive and obsessed with looking after her daughter. "I had to protect Arjeta; I couldn't let anything happen to her."

Then a few weeks later a Serb patrol arrived at the farm looking for supplies.

"They were like animals," Edi said in between sobs. "They shot my mother and father, just like that." She clicked her fingers. "In cold blood, as if they were nothing. Then they went through the farm taking anything they could... Then they set it on fire. They killed all the cows... the pigs, even our pet dog."

Edi was crying bitterly now.

"Is everything alright, love?" asked Frank, with a degree of concern.

Katya reassured the driver.

"Not too long now," he replied.

Edi composed herself and carried on with her story.

"I was in the fields with Arjeta; I had taken her for a walk. I heard the gunshots and saw the smoke from their cottage. I rushed back but by the time I reached the farmhouse, it was well ablaze. I knew it was a risk, but the Serbs had gone and the bodies of my mother and father were just lying in the farmyard alongside the corpses of the dead animals... I was in total shock," she sobbed. "But I managed to stumble my way to a neighbouring farm about three miles away carrying Arjeta. I can't remember walking there. It is just nothing."

Luckily, the neighbours had escaped any visits from the Serbs as they were in a more remote location, and took them both in. The farmer and his son went back to Edi's farm that evening and buried her mother and father and collected the few belongings that were salvageable from the burnt-out cottage.

Given Edi's status as the wife of a prominent KLA soldier, she was in grave danger and the farmer quickly made arrangements for Edi to escape to the border. This was not an easy task and involved several different people at some personal risk, all keen to help Edona Bukosi, a widow of Kosovo.

Edi described her escape. She and Arjeta were hidden in

the back of a lorry to Pristina and from there she was taken to Kacanice before crossing the border near Blace in Macedonia. The journey had taken four days. Katya just listened; Melos was fast asleep.

Edi described the conditions in the camp at Blace. Katya was aware of some of the difficulties from her time at Vratnica but had not heard a first-hand account. Edi explained it became so bad the Red Cross was left with no alternative but to disperse some of the refugees, as the food was in short supply and sanitation non-existent. There were concerns about a possible epidemic.

"We were told some people had died. Then one night we were just herded up, put into buses and taken to Stenkovec. We were treated like cattle," she added. "Then, after a few weeks, we were offered the chance of a place on a plane to England. I thought it would keep me and Arjeta safe, anything to get away from the camp... even start a new life; there was nothing in Kosovo to stay for."

They had been on the road for well over an hour when suddenly Katya broke off her conversation with Edi; she had noticed something out of the window - a huge metal statue on a hill.

"What's that?" she asked Frank.

"That's the 'Angel of the North'," replied the driver. "They put it up last year. Supposed to mean something but it's a bit of an eyesore if you ask me. 'Round here they call it the 'Gateshead Flasher'."

The meaning was lost on Katya.

"Oh no, it's beautiful," said Katya, stretching her neck to get a better view.

"Should be there in a few minutes. We're on the Newcastle Western Bypass… only two or three miles now."

They turned off the bypass onto the Team Valley and in the distance, they could see the two tower blocks dominating the skyline.

"That's where we're going," said Frank pointing in their

direction.

Katya had mixed feelings, partly apprehension, partly excitement. She translated to Edi and pointed. Edi just looked bemused.

Melos was awake now and Arjeta was playing with him which suited Katya. He had been asleep for most of the journey and would want some attention. Having someone else to keep him occupied was a bonus.

Katya looked at all the pebble-dashed houses with their front gardens, but it was different from what she had seen in Leeds; this was not a prosperous area. Many of the buildings looked dilapidated, and the gardens were generally unkempt. The rooftop skyline was littered with satellite dishes and TV aerials. They came past the shops in the precinct and into the service area in front of the tower blocks. Katya looked in dismay and horror. There was a huge crowd of people, including journalists and TV crews; it was just like at the airport.

Frank stopped the bus and opened the side door and Katya and Edi were mobbed like pop stars. Two burly policemen made their way to the front of the melee and shepherded the women to a space closed off with police tape. It was surrounded by the press cameramen, all jockeying for the best positions. A smart-looking man in a suit made his way through the throng and approached the two women, Katya trying to keep hold of Melos and Edi hugging Arjeta. Both children were now crying. Frank appeared with the buggy and luggage and placed it next to them.

"Hello and welcome to Heathcote, I am Counsellor Jim Beardsley," the man said. A woman stood next to him stumbled a translation.

"I speak English," said Katya.

"Excellent, excellent," said the counsellor, pulling out a set of door keys from his jacket pocket and with due ceremony handed them to Katya. He attempted to look humble as he scanned the banks of cameras, panning along the row of flashing lights with a fixed smile. He then gave another set to Edi. Some onlookers applauded, others walked away.

More flashlights lit up the blocks of flats. A news-reporter with a strange orange complexion approached them with a microphone; a cameraman followed her. The reporter looked straight into the camera and spoke into her microphone, applying suitable gravitas. "We are here live from the Heathcote Estate where two Kosovan refugees have just arrived from the reception centre in Leeds to start a new life in the North East."

She fired her first question at Katya.

"How does it feel to be safe in Newcastle away from all the fighting in your homeland?" Another woman next to her translated into Serbo-Croat; Katya and Edi spoke Albanian.

"It's alright. I speak English," said Katya. The news reporter looked at her expectedly.

"Very nice, very happy to be here," Katya said.

"What were conditions like when you left?" asked the reporter.

"Not good," replied Katya.

"Have you a message for your loved ones back home?" The reporter thrust her microphone to Edi. Katya translated. Edi replied in Albanian.

"They are all dead," translated Katya.

Taken aback by the answer, the news reporter turned to the camera. "So there you have it, two families relieved and grateful to the people of Newcastle to be safe and away from the killings and starvation back in their native Kosovo. This is Chrissie Franklin returning you to the studio."

She walked away without a backward glance, followed by the cameraman like a faithful puppy.

Just then a large lady of Caribbean origin in an ill-fitting suit approached Katya and Edi.

"Hello, my name is Clara, Clara Davenport... I am the community liaison officer for the local council, and I'm here to help you settle in. I will take you up to your new flats in a moment and answer any questions." She spoke slowly and deliberately;

yet another woman translated, also in Serbo-Croat.

"It's alright. I speak English," said Katya.

"Thank goodness for that, it costs us a fortune in interpreters."

She dismissed the translator and continued talking slowly as if Katya was a child.

She led them away from the crowd, which was now starting to disperse, and towards the entrance of the first tower block.

A journalist shouted out, "How about an exclusive Clara, pet...? It'll be worth your while."

"We'll chat later Harry. Let's get them in first, eh?" replied Clara.

The entourage entered the tower block, a policeman carrying the bags. The children were still crying but now more spasmodically. Arjeta was hiding behind her mother's skirts bemused by all the attention. Melos was in his buggy, confused by what was happening. Clara ushered Katya and Edi in the lift with the children; there was an overpowering smell of disinfectant.

"The luggage will follow on the next lift," said Clara, and pressed the button to floor fourteen.

The lift juddered its way up and opened at the selected floor. Clara got out and led the women to flat 1410 and asked Katya for her keys.

"This one is yours, Katya."

Clara opened the door and they went inside.

Still trying to get the stench of the lift from her head, Katya looked around. It was mind-boggling. There was more than a hint of fresh paint lingering in the air, but everything looked so clean. A brand new sofa was in the middle of the room facing a television, with a dining table and two chairs in the corner. There was warm-air central heating and the room had been completed with a beige-coloured carpet. They went into the kitchen. There was a stainless steel sink and drainer, a washing machine/tumble dryer, fridge and an electric cooker. There was also a microwave oven which Katya did not recognise.

"What is that?" asked Katya.

"A microwave," replied Clara.

Katya nodded. "Oh," she pondered, none the wiser.

They then went to the main bedroom where there was a double bed, a cot and a large wardrobe. The smaller bedroom had a single bed and a tall-boy. Finally, there was the bathroom and although quite small, contained all the necessities including a modern shower. Back to the kitchen and Clara opened the cupboard which had been stocked with tinned food and coffee, and there was a selection of cups, saucers, dishes, and various cutlery. The fridge held some fresh milk, bread and vegetables.

"This is wonderful," said Katya.

"Oh, there is something else," said Clara, and she produced two boxes containing brand new mobile phones from her bag. "These are for you. If you have the numbers you can phone home... Kosovo," she clarified. "They're from the Refugee Council." She handed them both a box. Katya looked in amazement.

"For us?" said Katya.

"Yes... They're encouraging refugees to try and make contact with relatives. It's very confusing at the moment and it may be difficult but we're hoping things will improve soon. The phones have been charged up, I think, and we've topped them up with ten pounds credit... They're 'pay as you go'."

Katya had no idea what she was talking about but smiled, not wanting to appear ignorant. The only available phone back in Kosovo that she knew of was at Afrim's, the farmer who had taken her back to her cottage on the tractor. She had not got his number. But it was a nice thought and who knows?

Clara continued. "You'll get a weekly allowance and other benefits as well as help to find work while you're here, but I'll explain this to you when I call again. You'll want to settle in, I expect," said Clara, looking at the two women who seemed dumbfounded by the whole thing. "A social worker will call tomorrow to talk through any welfare issues and check on the children," she added. Katya translated for Edi.

"Oh, nearly forgot... I have some money for you here to keep you going until we can collect your weekly allowance."

She opened her purse and handed Katya and Edi fifty-pounds each which they looked at with a degree of curiosity. They hadn't worked out the exchange rate yet.

Clara looked at Katya. "I'll take Edi down to her flat on the sixth floor and show her around. I'll see you again tomorrow."

Katya offered to go with them to translate but Edi thought she would manage with her rudimentary English. Clara and Edi left with Arjeta holding her mother's hand, leaving Katya to take in her new surroundings.

After a couple of minutes, there was a knock on the door. Katya opened it and there was a policeman with Katya's belongings, the rucksack and carrier bag.

"These are yours, pet, I think. Sorry for the delay but the lift stopped on the third floor and I've had to walk the rest of the way, like."

Katya had difficulty in picking up the accent but expressed her gratitude. "Thank you."

A cameraman hovered behind him and took pictures. Katya retrieved the bags and shut the door ignoring the calls from the cameraman.

She picked up Melos from his buggy, hugged him and went to the window. The earlier rain had cleared up and it was now a bright day and the sun was warm through the glass. She looked across the Expressway, past the industrial estate and the football fields on the rec towards the Western Bypass. In the distance, she could see the Northumberland hills which dominated the skyline. She noticed someone with a brightly coloured kite on the playing fields and watched for a while as it rode the thermals then dropped back with a tug of the string.

Katya began exploring her new apartment excitedly. Her own house had been homely but without all the modern appliances on offer here. They had a television of course, but all the programmes were in Serbo-Croat, and Yugoslav propaganda dominated the broadcast, so she rarely watched it. There was no washing machine in the cottage; she would normally wash her clothes in the sink and dry them on the outside washing-line in the garden or on a clothes-horse by the fire in the winter. The cooker was different too. She looked at the dials and knobs in total confusion. The microwave oven was something totally new and she decided to leave it alone for the moment.

She found the electric kettle and filled it with water and switched it on, a cup of coffee to celebrate her new home. She took her rucksack and carrier bag into the bedroom and started putting her meagre collection of clothes in the wardrobe. She put Melos into the cot while she was busy, and he seemed to like his new bed and it wasn't long before he was sound asleep. It had been a long and eventful morning.

Back in the kitchen, she took a mug from the cupboard and put in two teaspoons of instant coffee. Topping up with boiling water, she took the mug into the lounge and tried the TV. The lunchtime news featured a report on the war in Kosovo, and as she watched, she was surprised to see the camera focus on the tower blocks.

The anchor woman made the announcement. *"We have exclusive pictures from the Heathcote Estate where two refugee families find new homes in the North East;"* and suddenly there she was, looking dazed and confused, trying to answer the reporter's questions surrounded by dozens of cameras and journalists.

Seeing herself on TV was a shock and she couldn't believe how dowdy and tired she looked, certainly compared with the reporter. It made her sad and she quickly turned off the television.

She finished her coffee and decided once Melos was awake, they would go to find Edi in flat 607. In the meantime, she would start to arrange the flat to her own taste.

Earlier that morning, Bigsy had gone down to the entrance of the flats to have a cigarette and was amazed at all the commotion. Police and cameramen, vans with satellite dishes on their roofs;

Sky TV, BBC, ITV, and CNN, were all there. Bigsy dodged around the corner out of sight just as Wazza appeared from the direction of the precinct carrying a bottle of milk. Bigsy tried to attract his attention in a conspiratorial whisper.

"Psst... Wazza... over here, man."

Wazza spotted Bigsy and went over to join him.

"What the fook's going on?" said Bigsy.

"No idea, man. Ain't seen nottin' like this before," replied Wazza.

"Well, I can do without all this attention, like. We've got a job on tonight," said Bigsy.

"What are you going to do Bigsy, lad? You can't call off the drop, Everton'll eat you alive."

"Aye, I know that, man."

There was a pause while Bigsy pondered the situation.

"I think we'll just keep our heads down for a bit and see what happens," said Bigsy. "Tell you what, meet us at the video shop in an hour and we'll see what's happening then."

At the agreed time, Wazza was waiting, ensuring he was out of the line of sight of any straying cameras. Bigsy made his way from the tower wearing dark glasses and his shirt collar up to conceal his face. Walking quickly away from the crowd, which had now reached worrying proportions, he met up with his buddy. They both surreptitiously peered round the corner of the wall at the back of the video shop to take a closer look at the events that were unfolding before them.

A minibus approached the service road and the crowd pushed forward and Bigsy could see a couple of policemen escorting two women with children from the vehicle. TV lights followed their move.

"I was right... It's them Kosovans... you know, the refugees; they've been on the telly. They'll be moving into 1410 like I said," commented Bigsy in hushed tones.

"Aye, you're not wrong bonny lad... and 607, I bet," added Wazza.

A man in a suit made a few remarks which Bigsy couldn't hear and handed something to each of the women. Some of the audience clapped their hands in appreciation; others walked away.

"There's that tart off the news," remarked Wazza.

"Aye, what's her name?" said Bigsy. He thought for a moment. "I know... Chrissie fookin' Franklin," he added.

"Aye, that's it," replied Wazza.

"You know I've heard she really puts it about a bit, if you know what I'm saying," replied Bigsy. "Mind you, she must be knocking on a bit now; she's been on the telly ever since I can remember."

"What're you going to do Bigsy, lad?"

"Nottin'... I reckon once this lot have gone inside, they'll all be off like rats up a drainpipe."

Sure enough, once the women had gone inside the crowd dispersed. A couple of reporters were giving pieces to camera using the tower block as a backdrop, but they too packed up their gear and within half an hour the whole scene was deserted. A couple of policemen were the last to leave driving away at speed in their patrol car.

"It's a pity they don't turn up that quick when they're really needed," commented Wazza.

"Well, I'm not unhappy to see the back of 'em; now we can get down to some serious business," said Bigsy.

Bigsy and Wazza headed back to the video shop; Bigsy had promised to work a shift. Wazza was going on to pick up his car from the lock-up and fill it with petrol. Bigsy had given him two twenty-pound notes to cover the cost.

"Meet us here at half-past six and bring Chirpie," Bigsy called out to his partner.

"Aye, will do," responded Wazza.

Chapter Eight

That afternoon Katya, with Melos in the buggy, had taken the lift down to the sixth floor to see how Edi was getting on. The smell of disinfectant was nauseating, and Katya tried to hold her breath during the descent. She knocked on the door of flat 607 and waited. After a couple of minutes, she knocked again. Katya could hear someone trying to turn the latch. Slowly the door opened, and Edi peered around it.

"Hello, we've just come to see if you are ok."

Edi stood to one side to allow Katya and the buggy to pass. As soon as they were inside, Edi started to cry. In deep sobs, she told Katya that she was really homesick and didn't know how anything worked and thought she would starve to death.

Arjeta was pleased to see Melos and ran to the buggy. Katya watched as she made a fuss of him. Katya hugged Edi and tried to reassure her. "Yes, I know it will seem very strange, but it is only for a short time. Remember, we are safe here in this nice apartment and soon we can return home to Kosovo."

Edi started to calm down and Kata took her into the kitchen and showed her how the kettle worked. Edi's family had always used a range on the farm and boiled water on the open fire in a saucepan. They laughed when Katya said she had no idea what the microwave was for, and would need some help with the washing machine, but was sure they would soon master it.

Edi explained that she was also worried about her lack of English and Katya had promised to give her some lessons. She would speak to the lady in the morning and made a mental note of things she would need to cover.

Once she was happy that Edi was more settled, they returned to the kitchen and started to work the cooker. After a bit of trial and error, Katya had found that it was fairly straightforward, once they had got used to the various switches and dials. She made Edi and Arjeta some toast using the grill and then made them both a coffee.

After another twenty minutes, Katya could see that Edi was more relaxed and she could leave. Arjeta made a pouting face wanting Melos to stay. Katya did her best to placate the girl by promising to return the following day after the visit from the social worker.

With Melos having been cooped up all day, Katya decided to take him for a walk in his buggy and get some fresh air. She could do with some exercise and clear her head from the smell of paint and all the commotion of the morning. It would also give her a chance to explore the new surroundings.

Outside the tower, children were playing. Schools had obviously closed; earlier than at home, she noted. They paid no attention to Katya as she made her way to the underpass which went under the busy dual carriageway. She wanted to take a closer look at the kite which she could see flying in the distance. She had worked out a route from her window which would take them to the recreation ground.

It was dark and noisy as she pushed the buggy along the short tunnel. All the lights had been vandalised and the bulbs missing. Some kids were messing about on their bikes at the exit and stared at her as she walked past. For a moment, Katya felt threat but continued walking.

It took less than ten minutes from the tower block. After leaving the underpass, she walked the back of the industrial park and straight onto the field. It was muddy in places from the earlier showers and Katya was still wearing her trainers, but there was a cinder track leading around the playing fields to another entrance on the other side of the park.

It was heavy going pushing the buggy along the uneven path. She could see the kite-flyer in the middle of the field, and she stopped at a couple of benches thoughtfully provided by the local council. They were splattered with bird droppings, but Katya found a clean spot on one of them and sat down. She watched as the person with the kite worked the string like a master puppeteer coaxing every last swoop and rise. Melos looked on and appeared to take notice of the object in the sky and followed it with fascination.

Katya started to relax for the first time since she arrived and felt the sun warm on her face.

She looked at Melos in his buggy. "I think we are going to like it here."

The kite was now on the ground and its owner winding the string around a bobbin. Carrying it in his arms, he walked towards Katya. She suddenly caught her breath. She looked at the silhouette, the slim features and longish curly hair; it could have been Ibi in his youth. She had seen photos of him at senior school before he went to the University and the resemblance was uncanny. As he got closer, however, she could see that facially there was no similarity, but just for a moment…

"Hiya," said Polly.

Assuming this was a greeting, she replied, "Hello."

"You like kites then, pet?"

"Oh yes, they are wonderful, and you fly them very well," said Katya warmly. Strangely she felt like she knew him even though it was the first time they had met.

"Not seen you around here," said Polly in a strong local accent.

"Sorry, I don't understand… Can you speak more slowly; it is quite difficult for me?"

"Sorry pet, I have not seen you 'round here," he repeated deliberately.

"Thank you. No, we arrive today. We come from Kosovo."

"Ah, I see, so you've moved into Heathcote, like. I saw all the crowd this morning,"

"Yes," said Katya and she got up and walked alongside Polly as he made his way back along the cinder path.

"What's the bairn's name?" asked Polly. "Sorry, the young lad, what's his name?"

"His name is Melos and mine is Katya."

"Mine's Jamie, but everyone calls me Polly."

"How do you do... Polly?" said Katya as a question.

"Are you going back to the flats?"

"Yes, I will need to feed Melos soon."

"Ok, I'll walk with you; I live in Heathcote...I'm on floor twelve."

"I am on number fourteen," said Katya.

As they walked along, sharing a conversation, Katya had to keep checking some of the phraseology which she had not seen in any textbook. Polly explained to Katya how he had got involved with kites and about his work at Art College, and Katya told him where she came from and about her job as an English teacher.

In no time they were back at the flats and sharing a lift. Polly got out at floor twelve and said his goodbyes, promising to look out for her. Katya rode to the next floor and opened her door, pushing the buggy inside. She decided to have a coffee and get Melos something to eat. She checked through the stock in the kitchen cupboard. There were several jars of baby food. She had stopped breastfeeding when they had reached the reception centre; it was too much of an effort. One thing she needed, though, was more disposable nappies. Clara had explained about the shops and the general store in the precinct that was open until eleven o'clock at night. Katya decided she would explore further after she had eaten her evening meal.

Bigsy had got back to his flat about half-past four. Earlier, he had noticed what looked like Polly and a woman with a buggy walking from the rec. He made a brew and watched TV until Carole came home from work. She walked in just after six o'clock.

"Hiya pet, you should've seen the goings-on here today.

It's been manic," said Bigsy and he explained the arrival of the refugees and the media scrum that ensued. "They just had it on the news. That tart Chrissie Franklyn was here and everything. It was amazing."

"Do you know where they are?' asked Carole.

"Aye, one's along the corridor in 1410; you know the flat they've been doing up... Other's on the sixth, next to Wazza."

"I'll keep my eye out for 'em. It must be very strange being in a new country an' all," said Carole.

"How's your day been, pet, alright?" enquired Bigsy.

"Aye, not bad, got the day off tomorrow, thought we could go to the Metro Centre. I want to get a new outfit."

"Aye, that'll be fine. I've got a delivery to make tonight, pet, not late mind, but with a bit of luck I should be able to make a contribution towards your gear."

"What time'll you be back?"

"Shouldn't be late... About eleven, if we don't break down," said Bigsy, casting a knowing look towards Carole.

"Aye, ok, I might wait up for yas if there's a good film on the telly."

Bigsy put on his tracksuit top and headed down the stairs. Wazza and Chirpie had just arrived and were parking up. Bigsy got in the front and Chirpie was back in his usual place among the speakers. The hi-fi was turned off.

Katya had fed Melos and eaten her first meal in her new flat - scrambled eggs and toast with a mug of coffee. After she had cleared up, she made her way to the lift; she needed to get Melos's nappies,. The smell of disinfectant still lingered. She made her way across the service road and around the corner to the precinct. She noticed the graffiti scrawled on the wall, like some urban tapestry. It reminded her of Pristina except that was propaganda. This was a bit strange. 'Freddie loves Suzie' in a love heart, people's initials in artistic swirls, apparently someone called Rikki Rankin was a 'wanka', whatever that was.

She reached the general store and a few customers were milling about looking along the racks of produce for ready meals, buying cigarettes or some beers for the evening. Katya stared at the selection of food, dairy produce, fruit, cold meats, cosmetics and toiletries and, what she was looking for, a baby section. She chose a pack of disposable nappies which appeared to be the right size, the same brand as she was given in Leeds, and carried on looking at the array and choice of goods. Then she thought back to her time in the camp in Macedonia and sighed. In the toiletries section, she chose some bubble bath and soap, shampoo and lipstick.

She reached the till and watched as Mr Ali totalled her shopping.

"That will be ten pounds, forty-five pence, please."

He recognised her from the television news which they had been watching for most of the day to catch a glimpse of themselves; he had been interviewed earlier by the local BBC. The interviewer asked him what he thought of the refugees coming to live nearby and what the publicity would do for the community. He had no complaints; his takings soared during the morning to such an extent he had had to send his son, Jamal, to the Cash and Carry for more supplies.

Katya opened her bag and looked in bewilderment at the money which Clara had given her.

"Don't worry, pet," said Mr Ali in an accent that was part Newcastle, part Pakistani. "I will help you. It must be very strange for you today. How are you settling in?"

"Very well," said Katya. "Everyone has been so kind."

Mr Ali looked in some surprise; he had not always enjoyed that welcome. His window had been 'egged' or broken many times and he was forced to use steel shutters when he closed at night, a requirement of the insurance company. He had also been subjected to disgusting racist graffiti which had caused him a great deal of sorrow and worry.

He quickly explained to Katya the value of the money in her

purse, ignoring the ten Deutschmark note which was folded in the bottom. There was a small queue starting to form behind her. He took the fifty-pound note that Clara had given her and counted out the change slowly into her hand.

"Thank you, and I hope you are very happy here," said Mr Ali, putting the small items in a carrier bag and handing it to Katya. She placed the bag on the buggy handle and carried the carton of nappies under her arm. The three people behind her at the counter stared at her inquisitively as though looking at some exhibit in a zoo.

She made her way back to the tower block and, as she approached the lift, she could see someone waiting. She was about Katya's age and looked very glamorous in tight-fitting jeans and a sloppy white tee-shirt with a logo across the front which Katya could not make out. Rather incongruously, she was carrying an empty waste bin. The lift arrived and the woman held the door open while Katya negotiated the buggy and nappies into the lift. She pressed the button for floor fourteen.

"You must be the girl from the telly, from Kosovo," said the woman.

"Yes," replied Katya.

"I think we might be neighbours. We live on fourteen... My name is Carole."

"Hello, my name is Katya."

"That's a bonny name, pet, and is this your bairn?" The same phrase from this afternoon Katya recognised.

"Yes, his name is Melos." The boy looked at the inquisitor and started to smile.

Carole made some unintelligible baby noises to the boy. "Goodgie, goodgie, goo," it sounded like. Katya noticed Carole's clothes and makeup and how glamorous she looked.

The lift reached floor fourteen and they extricated themselves from the confined space.

"Listen pet, I'm just making a brew if you fancy one."

"Thank you, that is very kind. That would be nice," replied

Katya, not really understanding what she had agreed to, but not wanting to push away any hospitality.

Carole opened her door of her flat and Katya followed her inside, pushing the buggy. Katya surveyed the room. It was the about the same size as her flat, maybe a bit bigger, with a large sofa facing an enormous television with a satellite receiver, video player and hi-fi system. There was a coffee table between the sofa and the TV, and in the corner against the wall was a dining table. Katya picked up Melos and sat down on the sofa with the boy on her lap.

"What'll you have Katya, pet? I've got tea, coffee or I can open a bottle of vino if you like."

"Coffee will be fine thank you," replied Katya, trying to make sense of the word 'vino'.

"No, I don't suppose you drink wine, do you?"

"I do, but not for a long time," said Katya, recognising the connection.

Carole disappeared into the kitchen and soon a percolator was starting to make bubbling noises.

"You speak English well, pet," Carole shouted from the kitchen.

Katya shouted back. "Thank you, I was a teacher back home... I studied English at the University in Pristina, but it is very different here, I think. It is not the same as I learned it."

"Aye, that's the Geordies for you," said Carole as she returned to the lounge carrying a tray with two mugs and a plate of digestive biscuits. Katya returned Melos to his buggy and he seemed quite content watching proceedings.

"Would the bairn want a drink or anything?"

"No thank you, I will give him some milk when I get in before I put him to bed."

Carole was a natural people person, gregarious and comfortable with conversation; she had to do it every day with clients.

"So how come you ended up here?" asked Carole taking a

sip of coffee and Katya gave her a short recount of her journey from the time she was forced to flee her cottage to the journey through the woods to the refugee camp in Macedonia. She left out the attack.

Carole was captivated by the story and couldn't begin to comprehend the suffering Katya had endured. She could see the pain in Katya's eyes as she told her story.

"Well, while you're here pet, I'll make sure you're not troubled with anything or anyone. So if you need anything, anything at all, you just have to ask."

"You are very kind," said Katya, and having finished her coffee made her excuses. "I think we had better go now before Melos starts to get hungry."

She got up and Carole gave her a hug.

"There is just one thing," asked Katya. "What is a..." She paused to remember the name. "A micro... something?"

"What one of these?" said Carole leading Katya into the kitchen. She pointed at the appliance in the corner.

"Yes, what is it? I have one."

"A microwave?" Carole laughed and explained the concept of instant cooking. "I will pop across tomorrow pet and show you how it works."

Katya said her goodbyes and headed back to her flat with Melos and her bags.

After putting Melos to bed Katya had some time to herself. She put on the TV and flicked through the channels on the remote. Nothing much appealed so she decided to run a bath. The water was hot from the tap, a luxury she could only dream of a couple of weeks earlier. She poured in some foam bath and watched the bubbles rise.

She got into the bath and lay there, contemplating her day. So much had happened, the journey from Leeds, and Edi's story, the reception at the flats and the media furore, the new apartment and the briefing by Clara. Then she thought of her walk to the park and her meeting with Polly. She couldn't get over how he had initially reminded her of Ibi, but there was a boyish charm and enthusiasm about Polly that Ibi definitely did not have. Ibi had always been the cynical one; he wanted to change the world, conditioned, of course, by events back home. The thoughts of home started to get to her, and she started to cry, not with sadness this time, not as a grieving widow, but just an outflow of emotion and, perhaps, relief.

Wazza, with Bigsy and Chirpie on board, headed the Escort out of the estate and off to the working men's club ready to meet Layton. They got there just after quarter-to-seven and as they waited for the courier, Bigsy recalled the commotion from that morning.

"I hope we don't get any more of 'em," said Bigsy. "My nerves canna stand the strain."

Wazza and Chirpie laughed.

Layton arrived in the courier van at exactly seven o'clock. Bigsy went to the driver's side and was handed three bags. Layton instructed in his Geordie/West Indian accent.

"De big one is de weed; dare's tree bags inside for de two pubs and de service station drops. De small one is wid de tabs for de clubs and the odder is wid de coke. Don't be late and don't screw up. We meet here again, same time tomorrow wid de money. Ya got dat?"

Bigsy nodded, "Aye, bonny lad, I got it alright, tomorrow, seven, here."

Layton pulled away, watched by the three lads.

"Right," said Bigsy. "Let's get to work," and Wazza opened the boot of the Escort and Bigsy stowed the merchandise.

"Where to?" said Wazza as he started up the car.

"Trev's" said Bigsy as he put on his seat belt.

Ten minutes later, they had arrived at knob-head Trev's and Bigsy's knock on his door. Trev was swaying from side to side and slurring his words incoherently, totally out of it, when he answered. Nevertheless, he paid up without any problem, just pleased to get his hands on his next hit.

Then it was off to Gateshead and the clubs to drop off the 'cowies'. They were eagerly expected by the doormen and at Lucifer's they were given the opportunity of a free entrance.

"Better not," said Bigsy. "But thanks for the offer, like... more deliveries to make."

The next call was 'The Grapes', an old pub just outside Gateshead and not far from the fly-over where the old A1 crosses the road to Sunderland. They arrived in the car park, a good ten minutes before their allotted time.

"Chirpie, you come with me and bring the package. Wazza you stay in the car and keep your eyes peeled for any bizzies."

Chirpie put one of the bags of weed under his jacket.

"You got a ciggie, Chirpie, man? I'm gaspin'," said Bigsy as they approached the entrance. Chirpie handed him a cigarette. Bigsy had got a name and description of the contact and Bigsy related this to Chirpie.

"You keep your eye out for him, Chirpie, bonny lad."

They went inside.

"What a dump," said Bigsy quietly. "Did ya smell them bogs as you passed? They were reet hacky."

"Aye, you're not wrong there," said Chirpie.

There were only two people in the bar, dragging on cigarettes and watching a TV in the corner that was suspended from the ceiling by what looked like string.

"What can I get you?" asked the man behind the bar.

"Nah, you're alright, man, we're waiting for Donny Pembleton," said Bigsy.

Out of respect, Bigsy handed the barman a five-pound note which was gratefully received.

"Aye young Donny is usually in about now. Take a seat and I'll give him a call."

The barman picked up his mobile phone and pressed buttons. Someone answered and the barman made conversation but Bigsy couldn't hear all the words, but he did catch the phrase "two chancers," which did nothing to endear him to the barman.

"He's on his way. He is expecting you," and, a few minutes later, a short, stocky man with a strange military-style haircut and tattoos up both arms came through the door and walked over to Bigsy and Chirpie. They exchanged pleasantries and the appropriate code word, then went out of the bar and towards the toilet.

"Aw no, man, we can't go in there; it's minging," said Bigsy.

"We ain't hanging about, man," said Donny.

So the two went inside, leaving Chirpie on guard, and Bigsy immediately noticed the graffiti which decorated the walls. A large example stood out. 'It's no use standing on the seat, the crabs in here can jump three feet.' A different class of poet, thought Bigsy.

They exchanged goods. Bigsy checked the cash and Donny smelt the weed and seemed satisfied with the quality, although how he could tell above the stench from the toilet Bigsy could not comprehend.

"See you next time," said Bigsy and they left. Donny went back to the bar.

"Well, that went right enough," said Bigsy as he got in the car.

"Where to now?" asked Wazza.

"'The Roundhead' in Low Fell", said Bigsy.

"I know it," said Wazza. "Couple of miles up here and left at the lights."

"Aye, that's it, up the hill on the right," agreed Bigsy.

They arrived on time and made their drop with another unsavoury character called Sid Merrick. Nick-named 'The Monster', he was a real head case and definitely someone to avoid unless absolutely necessary. With Everton's people however, there was a bit of reflected respect for Bigsy and Chirpie and the deal went down without a hitch.

Bigsy checked the money was safe in his money belt and Wazza headed the Escort out towards the service station on the A1 about five miles away. They chatted excitedly; their nervousness having abated following their successful exchanges.

They were waiting for a guy from out of town. Everton had told Bigsy this was the first time that he had done business with him and had been instructed to be very careful and take no chances. "Make sure ya gets de money," Everton had instructed.

They were early for the meet as they approached the services, but suddenly Bigsy let out a gasp and felt his stomach churn.

"Shite, I don't know if it's fookin' north or southbound... Look there's one on each side," Bigsy exclaimed.

"I'll pull in here and you can call Everton and check," said Wazza, trying to be helpful.

"I can't do that, he'll think I'm a right wazzock," exclaimed Bigsy who was starting to go white.

"Well, what else can you do, bonnie lad?" enquired Wazza.

"I don't know, I'm buggered," said Bigsy. "Everton'll have my balls on toast."

There was a long pause as Wazza negotiated the car to a stop in the car park.

"Hang on a minute... You see that footbridge?" said Bigsy, animatedly, pointing to the pedestrian walkway which crossed the motorway.

"Aye," said Wazza.

"Well, that's going to save me a good kicking," said Bigsy, breathing a sigh of relief. "We'll park here and you and Chirpie head over to that side and I'll wait here. Then you can call me if he comes your way and I'll call you if he comes this way."

Bigsy made Wazza repeat the description of the guy and his car. "It's a black BMW 3 series." He gave the registration of the car and the code word 'extreme'. "His name's Hughie Bonner."

Chirpie and Wazza headed over the footbridge, the traffic pounding away underneath them.

Time seemed to drag but then after about twenty minutes, Wazza called, which made Bigsy jump nervously.

"I think your man's here." He repeated the registration of the black BMW, a match.

Bigsy hared across the walkway with the bag of hash as fast as he could and joined up with his buddies in front of the Service Station entrance. The sweat was dripping from his brow, the underarms of his tracksuit top glistening. They waited for the man to park up and get out of his car.

As he approached them, Bigsy walked towards him, head down, and gave the arranged greeting. "Have you got a light, man?"

He presented the man with an open packet of cigarettes.

"It's a bit extreme here," said the man emphasising the code word and accepting a cigarette from the packet.

"Mr Bonner?" replied Bigsy, as the man flicked a cigarette lighter and offered it to Bigsy. The flame momentarily illuminated Bigsy's face,

"Yeah," said the man.

While Wazza and Chirpie stood guard, Bigsy and the man went behind the lorry park and completed the deal. Bigsy handed the man the bag of cannabis and Bonner handed over the cash. Bigsy checked the money then pocketed it in the purse on his belt. The man headed back to his car.

As they walked back across the bridge, they were recounting the meet.

"Aye, it was like something out of that film Casablanca," said Bigsy. Wazza and Chirpie fell about laughing.

"Seemed a canny bloke," said Wazza.

"Aye, not from round here though," replied Bigsy. "Sounded more like a Scouser."

"What's a Scouser after weed over here for? I'd've thought there was enough over there to fill the Tyne Tunnel," said Chirpie.

"Aye, that's a fact. Fook knows… We got paid, that's all that counts," replied Bigsy.

They reached the car in the south-bound car park and assumed their positions. "Hey, let's have some music on," said Wazza. The mood was upbeat, and he switched on the sound system. The noise rocked the car.

"Turn that fookin' racket off!" shouted Bigsy and Wazza complied realising his error.

They headed out of the service station in silence and took the next exit slip road, turning right under the motorway and back on the northbound side towards home.

They continued steadily along the A1 and were congratulating themselves with a job well done when, seemingly from nowhere, the back window lit up like daylight. Wazza blinked as the reflection from the rear view mirror temporarily blinded him. A blue flashing light replaced the dazzle and filled the back of the car.

"Shite, it's the bizzies!" shouted Wazza in a panic.

"Don't worry, everyone stay calm. You've not been speeding. I've been keeping an eye out," said Bigsy.

He quickly crammed the money belt into the void behind the dashboard, hoping that he hadn't shorted out any wires.

"What about the videos in the boot, man?" said Chirpie, who always had an uncanny knack of bringing clarity to a situation.

"Shite!" said Bigsy, "I forgot about them. Just keep your head down, that's all we can do."

They were on the Western Bypass near Team Valley only two or three miles from the estate.

Wazza eased the Escort onto the hard shoulder and waited. A policeman in a Hi-Viz jacket walked to the driver's window. Wazza lowered it slowly.

"Can you get out of the car, sir." It was an order, not a question..

Wazza got out and shut the door. The policeman shone a torch around the inside of the car and Bigsy turned his head away from the beam of light. Chirpie was cowering lower in the rear seat trying to hide behind the speakers. Bigsy would never admit it but he thought he was going to be sick.

Bigsy was straining his ears, trying to find out what was going on. He noticed Wazza was being escorted to the white

BMW parked behind them.

"That's a serious piece of kit they've got there. It'll do one-fifty no bother." said Bigsy to Chirpie, trying to lighten the tension.

After about twenty minutes, Wazza returned to the car and almost collapsed into the driver's seat.

"What was all that about?" said Bigsy.

"Rear fookin' number-plate light not working... They wanted all me documents and wanted to know where'd we been tonight and everything. Even had to do a fookin' breathalyser. Managed to blag it though; let us off with a caution, like. I was fookin' shiting myself I don't mind telling you."

"What did you tell em?" asked Bigsy.

"Said we'd been down to me Nan's in Chester-Le-Street to see her as she's was sick, like," said Wazza.

"I'll say she's sick, she's been dead for six years, you big divvy," said Bigsy.

"It's all I could think of at the time," said Wazza, the relief almost palpable.

Wazza eased his way back onto the motorway followed by the BMW which then shot passed them with the blue lights flashing.

"Looks like they've got another shout," said Bigsy. "Come on let's get the fook out of here; I've had enough excitement for one night."

A few minutes later, Wazza pulled into the service area in front of the flats and Bigsy retrieved his money belt. Fortunately, the electrics had not been disturbed. He gave Wazza two twenties and a ten to fix his light and gave Chirpie his thirty pounds. He seemed happy enough, if Chirpie was ever happy. It was difficult to tell.

Bigsy and Chirpie made their way to the lifts, while Wazza headed back to the lock-up to park his pride and joy still cursing his luck for being stopped.

It was ten-thirty when Bigsy opened the door to the flat; Carole was sat on the sofa watching a film on TV.

"Hiya pet. How d'you get on?" asked Carole.

"Champion, pet", and he reached into his money belt and pulled out three twenty-pound notes and gave them to her. "Thought you may be able to use this tomorrow if you need some new gear."

"Ta pet, that's champion. You sit down and I'll pour yas a glass of wine."

She poured Bigsy a large red and disappeared into the bedroom. Ten minutes later, she reappeared in a dressing gown. She removed it, revealing her latest purchase.

Bigsy nearly choked.

Chapter Nine

Thursday morning, flat 1405, Carole was sat at the table in her housecoat eating toast and drinking lemon tea, her make-up already immaculate, her hair in coloured plastic rollers, ready for combing out.

She was used to getting up early and, despite having the day off, she would always make an effort. Sitting opposite was Bigsy, looking like the morning after the night before, in need of a caffeine fix and a shave. He was sat at the table in his boxer shorts scouring The Sun newspaper, his bourgeoning stomach starting to creep over his waistband. Carole was telling Bigsy about her meeting with Katya.

"She's a canny lass, no mistake, and the bairn, he's a real bonny lad, dead cute."

Bigsy looked up from his paper. "I could still do without 'em here mind... The place'll be crawling with social workers and all that crowd you see."

After breakfast, with Carole in the bathroom, Bigsy made his way back to the bedroom and retrieved the money belt from the back of the wardrobe and began counting out the cash in preparation for the meet with Layton. After expenses, he was a hundred and eighty pounds up, including Carole's clothes money. He put Everton's cut to one side in a supermarket plastic carrier bag, rolled it up and placed it back in the wardrobe behind his shoes. He slipped his spending money into the pocket of his jacket and smiled with satisfaction.

In flat 1410, Katya had washed her hair and was sitting in her blouse and skirt, drinking coffee and trying to feed Melos who appeared engrossed in a cartoon on the television. She heard a buzzing noise coming from the table and realised it was her mobile phone. It had been on there since Clara had given it to her and Katya had not studied it in any detail. She thought she would wait for someone to show her how to use it. Totally bemused, she looked at the front of the handset and logic told her to press the button with the green telephone. She put the phone to her ear. "… H… h… hello."

"Hiya Katya, girl, it's Clara."

Katya had to concentrate really hard to understand her.

"Just to let you know the social worker won't be calling today. She's gone down with the lurgy."

Katya was lost. Clara then went on about absenteeism in the social services, which was apparently to do with the pressure of the job.

"I'll get someone 'round tomorrow first thing. There's also someone from the Refugee Council who wants to meet you too, so we'll come over about ten o'clock if that's ok."

"Yes, yes, that will be fine," said Katya, having managed to piece together the message. She was almost overwhelmed by all the sudden attention. It was as though everyone wanted a piece of her.

"How are you settling in?" Clara asked. "Everything ok?"

"Fine, good, thank you," replied Katya.

"What about Edi how is she? I haven't been able to contact her."

"I will call in to see her later and make sure she is ok," said Katya.

Suitably reassured, Clara said her goodbyes.

"That will give us some time to ourselves," Katya said to Melos, somewhat relieved.

She got up to go towards the bathroom and noticed something by the front door, an envelope. She picked it up and felt there was something squashy inside; it felt like jelly. She opened the envelope slowly. The smell knocked her back and she dropped the envelope on the floor.

"Eurgh, eurgh," she caught her breath, ran to the sofa and

picked up Melos from his buggy. She grabbed her keys and ran out through the door, along the passageway and knocked frantically on the door of 1405.

Carole opened the door and was confronted by Katya who was visibly shaking and breathing heavily. "Katya...? Whatever's wrong pet?" said Carole and Katya told her about the envelope.

"It is dog's, I think," said Katya, not really sure of the correct translation.

"You come in, pet, and sit down. Don't you worry yourself; I'll soon sort it for ya."

Bigsy walked in, wearing a tracksuit top and jogging bottoms. "What's all the rumpus about?"

"This is Katya, the one from Kosovo I was talking to you about. Someone's put some dog shite through her letterbox."

Bigsy looked at Katya and could see her shaking and straight away felt sympathy for her. "I'm Bigsy, Carole's hubby, and I'll sort this out for you, don't you fret. You won't be having this trouble again I can guarantee you of that." Bigsy's voice was firm and reassuring.

Carole took Melos from Katya who was starting to calm down.

"You sit there; I'll make you a brew," said Carole, rocking the young lad up and down in her arms. She looked at Bigsy. "What you going to do, pet?"

"I've a good idea who's done this. I saw some kids hanging around over by the lifts when I came in last night, that fookin' Rikki Rankin and some of his mates. They're out of control that lot, I tell you. I won't be long, pet."

Bigsy slipped on a pair of trainers grabbed his keys and went out the door, leaving Carole comforting Katya.

Bigsy headed for the precinct, and sure enough, Rikki Rankin, the son of knob-head Trev, was riding around in front of the shops doing wheelies with two of his friends. At fourteen-years-of-age, school had long since lost its appeal and Rikki was already the subject of an Anti-Social Behaviour Order, a new initiative that had been recently introduced by the government to reduce youth crime.

"What a joke that is. They'll all want one round here," said Bigsy, when it was announced. He had been proved right; it was soon seen as a badge of honour among the youths of Heathcote who had long since given up on the framework of society.

Rikki, it had to be said, had not had the best start in life. His Dad was a 'crack-head' and his step-mother, Pauline, who was, at twenty-five, twelve years younger than Trev, was already on a bottle of vodka a day.

Rikki's real mother had abandoned her husband and son years earlier when she had got fed up with the drunken beatings that Trev unleashed on her on a regular basis and was now living with a Call Centre agent in Cramlington. She had severed all contact with her previous life and had a new family of her own. Trev had spectacularly failed as a father and Rikki had virtually brought up himself.

Bigsy thought quickly. "Rikki, bonny lad, got a minute?"

Rikki approached Bigsy a little apprehensively.

"I got some new videos you might be interested in, straight from the U.S. of A. I've got them in the back office if you want to see them, like."

Rikki looked suspiciously at Bigsy.

"Aye, ok I'll take a peek," said Rikki, getting off his bike and leaving it on the pavement.

Bigsy took Rikki around the back of the shops and unlocked a side gate. He led Rikki through and closed it behind him. Without warning, Bigsy swung his fist around into Rikki's stomach, the air escaping the lad's lungs with a rush and doubling him up. Rikki crouched on the floor and another punch hit him on the side of his head that made his ears ring.

"What d'you fookin' do that for?" Rikki groaned, holding his head and gasping for breath.

Bigsy grabbed Rikki's tee shirt under his throat and lifted him off the floor, cutting off his circulation.

"Now this is how it's going to work, bonny lad. I know it was you messing around pushing dog shite through people's letterboxes."

"I was only having a laugh Bigsy, honest," coughed Rikki, who was now going quite red.

"Well I don't think it's very funny; so, listen carefully, bonny lad, cos this is what you're going to do. You're going to be my guardian angel. You and your buddies are going to keep an eye out for us and if I hear of any problems, any problems," he repeated, "with the Kossies," - Bigsy's new name for the Kosovans, "you'll be eating dog shite for a week. Do I make myself clear...? I'm holding you personally responsible. And if you can't handle it or if you see anything I should know about, you tell me, and I'll sort it. Is that understood?" Bigsy was very assertive and there was no mistaking his message.

Rikki was in danger of losing consciousness and Bigsy loosened his grip.

"Aye Bigsy, anything you say," groaned Rikki.

"Now fook off and take your mates with you."

Bigsy opened the gate and pushed Rikki out still holding his head and trying to catch his breath.

Bigsy made his way back to the flat where Katya was still talking to Carole, drinking a coffee. Carole was holding Melos and jigging him up and down, making him laugh out loud.

"How did it go, pet?" asked Carole as Bigsy came into the flat.

"It was Rikki Rankin alright, and I've had a quiet word, like."

He looked at Katya, who now appeared a lot calmer. "Don't you worry, pet, he won't be causing you any more bother."

"You are so kind. Thank you so much," said Katya.

"Look, I've got an idea, pet," said Bigsy to Carole. "Why don't you take Katya to the Metro Centre and get her kitted out, like. I've got some business 'round here to take care of, so I don't mind."

Bigsy took out his wallet from his jacket pocket and pulled

out a couple of fifty-pound notes and gave them to Carole, relieved that he had avoided the trek around the shops holding Carole's carrier bags. "I can't think of anything worse," he had once told Wazza.

"What d'you reckon, Katya, pet, are you ready for some retail therapy?" asked Carole.

"What is Meh'ro Cen-na?" asked Katya, repeating the words phonetically as she had heard them.

"Paradise," replied Carole, and she and Bigsy roared with laughter.

"It sounds good," said Katya.

"Oh it is," said Carole.

Carole followed Katya back to 1410 with a plastic carrier bag and took the envelope and dropped it inside and wrapped it up tight.

"Don't worry, pet, I'll sort this out for you. What time can you be ready?"

"I need to go to see Edi, check if she is ok, so about an hour, if that's alright?"

"No, that'll be fine, I've got a bit of tidying up to do an' all," said Carole and went back to her flat.

Katya put Melos in his buggy and went down to the sixth floor and knocked on Edi's door. She answered it in what appeared to be her nightgown. Arjeta was drawing pictures on the table in the corner. The television was on with the sound turned down, the light was on and the curtains drawn.

Katya went inside and spoke to Edi in Albanian.

"How are you today?"

"I'm ok," said Edi but Katya was not convinced.

Katya went to the window and pulled the curtains open. Sunlight brightened the room. She looked out and saw that there was little in the way of a view, just the side of the other tower block. It was not as appealing as Katya's vista. Not surprising, then, that Edi had kept the curtains closed.

Arjeta looked up and made a joyous shriek. "Melos! Melos!" She rushed to the buggy and started making a fuss of the lad. "Edi, have you eaten anything?"

"A little… But I don't feel very hungry."

Katya went into the kitchen and checked the supplies. They were similar to what she had had when she arrived but noticed, apart from the bread and a bit of milk, nothing seemed to have been touched.

"Let's see what we have," said Katya, concerned at Edi's situation. She produced some eggs, butter and milk and started to make an omelette. After a few minutes, Katya made Edi and Arjeta sit down at the table and they started eating.

Katya looked at Edi. "You must make an effort, Edi, for Arjeta's sake."

Edi looked down. "Yes, I know you are right, but it is so hard... If it wasn't for Arjeta, I don't know what I would do."

She looked so forlorn as she picked at her breakfast. The trauma of recent weeks was beginning to surface. Katya could identify with the emotion.

Edi eventually finished and Katya collected the two plates. Arjeta got down from the table and immediately went to Melos.

"I also came to tell you that the social worker is not visiting today but they will be here tomorrow. They are bringing someone from the Refugee Council; they may have some more news. They will be here at ten o'clock. You must be ready for them."

Edi thanked Katya. "Yes, I will be ready."

Before leaving, Katya showed Edi again how to work the cooker and what the tins of food contained.

"Everything is so different," said Edi. "I have lived all my life on a farm. I have only been to Pristina a few times. I hated it… all the cars; everywhere rush, rush. Here, it is so noisy… All the time the traffic, broom, broom." She held her hands to her ears.

"It's ok, yes, I understand, but it's only for a short while. I have seen the news and they say that peace is coming."

"But what do I have to go back to?" Edi looked down, so

forlorn.

It was a rhetorical question that Katya couldn't answer. Unfortunately, returning to Kosovo scared Edi almost as much.

Then Katya remembered her date with Carole. "Look, I need to go, Edi, I have things to do, but I'll come back later, and we can go for a walk… to the shops, perhaps, get some more things. While I'm gone, get yourself cleaned up and look after Arjeta."

Edi gave a thin smile and nodded; the pep talk was what she needed.

Katya left the flat and ascended the lift back to 1410 with Melos in the buggy.

Back in her own flat, Katya got her purse and put it in her old rucksack. She then put on some lipstick for the first time in over a year. She dispensed with her scarf which had always worn when she was out for as long as she could remember; it was time for a change. She combed her hair, which lay in natural blonde waves falling just short of her shoulders; if only her clothes looked better.

She wheeled the buggy out of the flat and across the corridor to 1405. Carole was waiting for them and grabbed a jacket. She shouted something to Bigsy then walked with Katya to the lift.

"We'll take my car. It'll be quicker than the Hoppa," said Carole.

Katya smiled, not letting on she had no idea what a 'Hoppa' was.

"Thank you."

They walked to the garages, which were only a few minutes away from the tower entrance. Carole opened one of the lock-ups and got in the elderly Volkswagen and reversed out. They put the buggy and rucksack in the boot.

"You'll need to sit in the back, Katya, pet. We don't have a car seat for the bairn, and it might be a problem if we get stopped by the bizzies," said Carole and pulled down the passenger seat. Katya wrestled with the words but just about understood.

Katya got in and Carole passed Melos to her. As soon as they were comfortable, Carole drove off towards the Western Bypass, giving Katya a travelogue as they went.

"That's the Consett Road," she pointed, and explained about the steel works.

It only took a few minutes and they were on the Bypass making their way in a line of traffic towards the Metro Centre. After about five minutes, they came off the motorway and drove along the approach road to the enormous car park. Carole found a parking spot in the red zone.

"That's so we can find it again," said Carole, smiling and pointing at the sign with a red circle. "They've got different colours for different areas, so we don't get lost."

Katya found it hard to take in. They had passed several hotels, office blocks and a huge supermarket. Then there were the cars, thousands of them. Katya's eyes were wide open. Carole opened the boot and took out the buggy.

"What d'you think?" asked Carole as she unfolded it.

"I don't know what to say. I have never seen anything like it. Not even in Pristina; we have nothing like this."

"Aye, it was one of the biggest shopping malls in Europe when it was built."

They headed to the entrance and walked in. The sheer size, the noise, the lights, the colours, were just mind-boggling. Katya was totally transfixed. There was even a fun-fare in the entrance with waltzers, a helter-skelter and other rides. She noticed the people; they seemed much larger somehow.

"Aye, that'll be all the beer and burgers," said Carole.

Katya saw that many were wearing black and white striped football shirts with the words "Newcastle Brown" on the front.

"That'll be the Toon Army," said Carole, leaving Katya thinking they were some sort of private militia.

"This is, amazing," she exclaimed, not really doing the description justice to her actual feelings. Her eyes were wide trying to take in everything.

"Come on, Katya, pet, let's spend Bigsy's money," said

Carole and they headed into a women's clothes shop which had loud dance music coming from it.

"Have you got any breeks?" asked Carole, almost shouting to be heard.

"I don't know... what are they?" asked Katya.

"Sorry pet, trousers, jeans that sort of thing."

"I only have what I am wearing, and a spare shirt and skirt," she replied.

"We'll have to do something about that."

There was a bargain rail where the end-of-line stock had been placed at reduced prices.

"Hey, these are alright," said Carole, and they sorted through and found a pair of jeans that looked as if they would fit Katya.

"You've got a cracking figure, Katya, you just need to make the most of it," and they walked to a changing room, Melos seemingly mesmerised by all around him. She tried on the jeans and Katya loved the way they hugged her hips and bottom.

"Wow, they look champion pet; how much are they?"

"Fifteen pounds," replied Katya, reading the label and she went to get her purse from her trusty rucksack which was hanging from the back of the buggy.

"You put that away; this is my treat, or should I say Bigsy's," Carol said, and laughed. "Have you not got a handbag?"

"Only the rucksack."

"Next stop, handbag city!" cried Carole with a smile.

Carole knew the layout by heart and soon found her favourite leather store.

"This is it..." said Carole as they stood outside a shop selling leather coats, bags and luggage. "They've got some great stuff in here… and they're quite reasonable."

After a good look around, Katya chose a leather sling-bag which went around her shoulder and hung at her waist; it would be more practical with Melos to contend with. Again, it was in the sale and a very reasonable price.

"What about undies?"

"Only what I'm wearing," replied Katya.

Carole grabbed her hand and, like a couple of schoolgirls, headed for the first lingerie and night-attire shop they came to. She went into the changing room with Katya to supervise the fitting.

"You'll be in agony if you get the wrong size, pet," said Carole as she watched Katya try on some bras.

"Wow, Katya, pet, you've certainly got an amazing figure... great boobs."

Katya made the translation. "They have grown since I had Melos. I hope they stay this shape once my milk has gone."

They continued to shop for a couple of hours and Carole made sure Katya was kitted out with everything a good Geordie lass would need. Loaded with carrier bags, they stopped for lunch at a burger bar where Katya had her first beef burger. Melos was in a high chair and had a milkshake.

Finally, they called into a huge baby store which had everything a mother and child would ever need. Toys, clothes, buggies, prams, feeding equipment, Katya was amazed at the choice. She wanted to spoil Melos but settled on a recliner which would mean she could sit him down without having to constantly watch him in case he fell on the floor. She also bought him a new romper suit to replace the one she had been given in Leeds. Katya insisted on paying for these with her own money from what she had been given by Clara.

"That was incredible," observed Katya, who was now running out of superlatives.

"Aye it's not bad, but I think we take it all for granted you know," and Carole realised that she was right and maybe she, too, had learned something today.

It was around two o'clock when they made their way back to the car and headed home. That was a word that Katya couldn't use yet, but it was getting closer, and it had only been a day; all due to the people, particularly Carole.

They went back to 1405 and Carole made a brew. Bigsy was

out.

"Probably on the rec playing football; they usually train on a Thursday," Carole said, as she brought in two coffees. "Come on, let's see what you've got."

Melos was fast asleep in his buggy, worn out by all the excitement, as Katya opened the various carriers and laid the clothes out on the sofa. A pair of jeans, a pair of brown casual trousers, two pairs of shoes, a handbag, underwear, some makeup, with the promise of a lesson from Carole on how to apply it properly, three different tops, and two tee shirts; all paid for by Carole and Bigsy. Katya felt as excited as a kid on Christmas day.

"I don't know what to say," said Katya.

"D'you know, pet, I'll tell ya something, I've enjoyed myself more than if I was shopping for me... and I really mean that."

"But what will Bigsy say?"

"He'll not bother; I can always get 'round our Bigsy."

"Thank you, and thank Bigsy for me also," and Carole escorted Katya back to 1410 helping her with some of the bags.

Later, Katya spent an hour with all the clothes trying them on and checking in the mirror. She tried different combinations and couldn't believe the transformation; she looked a different woman. After putting the shopping away into the wardrobe, she changed into her new jeans, a tee-shirt, and finally a pair of brown casual flat shoes. She left the flat with Melos in the buggy to go to see Edi.

Edi opened the door and looked at Katya in amazement.

"Katya...? Is that you? You look so different."

Katya described her visit to the 'Meh'ro Cen-na' and explained the concept of retail heaven.

"We will go there when we have enough money and get you some new clothes," said Katya.

Edi looked at her second-hand skirt and top which she had got at the reception centre in Leeds and her face saddened. Her shoes were just about wearable, having survived the refugee camp, but were scraped and worn, the soles starting to show signs of holes. Her coat was stained from all manner of things; there had been no opportunity, or money, to get it cleaned. Arjeta looked at Katya and said how beautiful she looked. Katya thanked her.

"Come on Edi, get dressed. We will go the shops in the precinct; it will do you good to get out. You need some fresh air."

Edi looked disinterested but Katya was not to be moved. She went to collect her coat. "And don't wear the scarf; you have nice hair," she shouted to her.

The four of them made their way to the General Store. Like Katya the previous day, Edi could not get over the range of goods on offer. Edi said she wanted to make some pastry to make a pie in the Burek style which she regularly cooked back on the farm. So they looked for flour, milk, more eggs and margarine. She also bought some leeks, spring onions, cabbage, mushrooms and some spices that she had recognised by their smell. Katya also needed some more milk and some disinfectant for the bathroom. They queued up at the till and Mr Ali recognised Katya straightaway.

"You look different today, very pretty," said Mr Ali, and Katya thanked him. He helped them both with the money, Katya translating for Edi.

"Don't worry, you will soon get used to it," assured the proprietor as they left the shop.

Outside, three lads had turned up and were riding their bikes rather aimlessly around the precinct. Seeing the two women, they scarpered at full-speed away from the shops and towards the garages. Katya took little notice.

They went back to Edi's flat and took the bags into the kitchen.

"I am going to cook us a pie like back home," Edi said as she put all the ingredients on the worktop. Arjeta looked on with interest.

"What sort of pie?" asked Katya looking at all the ingredients.

"A burek with vegetables, like my grandmother taught me back on the farm," replied Edi.

The two of them looked at the cooker trying to work out the temperatures. Katya had used a stove before but that was primitive compared to this one. Edi had never cooked on one having always used a range. Between them, they managed to figure it out and the oven soon reached the appropriate temperature. Edi got all her ingredients together, ready to make her traditional Albanian dish.

"Would you like to stay for tea. I would like the company, " said Edi.

"Yes, that would be nice, thank you," said Katya.

So Katya sat down with Arjeta who was entertaining Melos.

"Is it ok to turn on the TV? The news is on about now and we can catch up with what's going on," shouted Katya to Edi who was in the kitchen.

"Of course, " Edi shouted back.

Katya turned on the TV and the news had already started. Then, the almost daily report from Kosovo was featured. The programme showed the bombing of Belgrade which was still continuing.

Edi, hearing Kosovo mentioned, left her cooking and joined Katya in the lounge. She watched the pictures but was unable to understand the commentary.

Katya translated. The news wasn't good. The Serb leader, Slobodan Milošević, despite the military action against him, was still not bowing to the pressure of the wider global community to give up his hold on Kosovo. The bombings didn't seem to be having any effect. There were disturbing pictures from the refugee camps and suddenly the war and suffering became all too real again.

Edi started to cry. "We will never go home," she sobbed and rushed back to the kitchen.

Katya turned the TV off and went to help Edi; she gradually calmed down.

The cooking and preparation took almost two hours, but the result was delicious. Afterwards, Katya felt full and as they sat around the table, Edi was more talkative; her demeanour boosted by the activity.

Despite his injured toe, Bigsy managed to finish his football training and wandered back to the flat. Carole had made a casserole and the aroma was wafting from the kitchen.

"Something smells good," he called out as he took off his shoes and socks at the front door and started to examine his feet.

"Have you had a good day, pet?" he asked, bending down and poking his bruised toe with his finger. It was starting to shed the nail. He winced as he disturbed the scab.

Carole took his kit-bag from him and kissed him on the cheek. "Aye, I've had a great time... What's wrong?" she asked, looking at his bare feet.

"Nottin'," said Bigsy. "Just a bruise."

Carole soon lost interest in Bigsy's injured toe and started to recount the day.

"Sounds a bit pricey, pet," he observed as Carole started listing the clothes she and Katya had bought.

"Ah, give over Bigsy, after what she's been though, it was magic to see her looking at all the clothes. It was like watching a bairn opening their Christmas presents. Anyway, I might have a little surprise for you a bit later, like." She winked at him mischievously.

"Aye...? Well, I've got to see a bloke at the club at seven, but I shouldn't be late back."

Bigsy finished his tea and went out around six-thirty to meet Wazza and Chirpie. They walked to the garages to pick up the car and discussed the next football match on Sunday, away to Sacristan Old Boys. "Very old some of them," said Bigsy. "I feel three points coming on." They were very upbeat since Sunday's victory.

They arrived at the club and waited for Layton who pulled into the car park in the caterer's van spot on seven o'clock.

"You can't say he's not punctual?" Bigsy said to Wazza,

Bigsy went over to the van and handed him the money in the plastic bag. Layton laid it on the passenger seat and began counting it laboriously.

"It's all there, man," said Bigsy, who was watching him closely.

"Always check it. It's what I do," said Layton and, satisfied it was all accounted for, he wound down the window. "May have a big one for you for tomorrow… Friday's always a busy night. Everton will call you."

Layton wound the window back up and reversed the van and left the car park in a cloud of cinders and gravel.

"Flash git," said Bigsy under his breath.

"Who fancies a bevvie then, my shout?" said Bigsy and the three of them wandered into the club.

Bigsy ordered three broons. He looked around the bar and there was one or two faces whom he acknowledged, and then Davie Slater walked through the door and came up to them.

"Hiya lads, good practice today."

"What you having Slate, bonny lad?" asked Bigsy.

"A broon, Bigsy, ta," Slate replied.

The lad had a reputation, not totally justified, as a bit of a comedian and never wasted the opportunity of an audience.

"Hey, here's a good one for you." Without waiting for a response, Slate continued his joke. "If they have referees in football and umpires in cricket, what do they have in bowls?"

Wazza, Chirpie and Bigsy looked at each other.

"I have no idea," said Bigsy.

"Goldfish!" said Slate, who roared uncontrollably with laughter.

"You daft bugger," said Bigsy.

"I don't get it," said Chirpie.

"You're as mad as a box of frogs," said Wazza. "And your jokes are no better."

They enjoyed an hour or so discussing 'men things', football, particularly Newcastle United, girls and cars.

"Have you seen anything of them Kossies, Bigsy lad?" asked Wazza using Bigsy's name for the Kosovans.

"Aye, that Katya's a bonny lass, not seen the other though," and he went on to explain the envelope incident and what he would do to Rikki Rankin if there was any repetition.

"You've changed your tune a bit," observed Wazza.

"Aye well, they're alright when you get to know 'em, like," said Bigsy.

He took another swig of his broon and put the empty bottle on the table. "Back in a sec, lads."

He got up and headed for the gents.

On his way back to his seat his phone went; it was Everton. Bigsy listened closely with his finger once more stuck in his right ear to hear properly. After about five minutes, he joined his buddies.

"We need to get going lads, work to discuss."

They got up from their seats and said their goodbyes to Slate, who finished his drink and went off to try his comedy routine on some other unsuspecting club member. The lads headed for the car park at the back.

Sitting in the car, Bigsy outlined the next job. "Good news, lads, Everton's pleased with us and we've got a big drop tomorrow. If we want it, like" Bigsy said. "What d'you think, are you up for it?"

"Aye, alright with me," said Wazza.

"Count me in," said Chirpie.

Bigsy explained that there was a big demand for cowies on Friday night in the clubs and there would be some extra drops.

"It could be a late one… There's a couple more pubs an' all," Bigsy added.

"What about the Washington Services?" asked Wazza.

"Nah, I think that was a one off," said Bigsy.

"Same meet with the courier?" asked Chirpie.

"Aye, here at seven-thirty," said Bigsy.

Business concluded, Wazza started up the Escort and they

made their way back to the flats.

It was about nine-thirty when Bigsy let himself in and Carole was on the sofa in her dressing gown with a glass of red.

Bigsy sat down and she poured him a glass.

"Alright pet?" asked Carole.

"Aye," said Bigsy. "Got another job on tomorrow night," he added as he took a sip of wine. "Should be good earner."

"You must be getting rid of a lot of trainers."

"Aye, and other stuff, like," replied Bigsy.

Carole got up and took off her dressing gown revealing her latest purchase; a black camisole and matching knickers.

Bigsy wanted to say something but the words wouldn't come out.

Chapter Ten

It was just before ten o'clock when the expected visitors arrived at flat 1410. Katya was ready. The incident with the envelope yesterday had been forgotten and she didn't feel any threat, confident that Bigsy had dealt with the situation. "Just kids messing about," he had said.

Katya heard the knock and opened the door to find an entourage before her. Clara was there with two other women and a man in a grey suit and red tie. They exchanged pleasantries and Katya motioned for them to come in. There was that uneasy moment, like 'musical chairs', when no-one knew exactly where to sit. The sofa was clearly too small for four people, so the man sat on a chair. Melos was in his new baby-recliner.

Clara made the introductions. "This is Michelle Dexter, who is the case officer for Heathcote Tower and will be looking after any welfare problems you might have." They exchanged greetings. "This is Jenny Wheatley from the Refugee Council and she has further information about contacting loved ones back home."

"Hello," said Katya.

"And finally, this is Mr Potter, who is Head of the Children's Department for the local council and, as you might have gathered, has a particular interest in Melos's welfare."

Introductions over, Katya offered to make them a coffee and went into the kitchen followed by Clara. "I'll give you a hand, girl."

The other guests got up and went to the window to admire the scenery. The day was clear, giving a vast panorama across the Expressway and onto the distant hills.

"An incredible view you have," said Jenny, as Katya and

Clara came in from the kitchen and handed around the mugs.

"Yes I am very lucky," said Katya remembering Edi's outlook.

"Have you any sugar?" asked Mr Potter.

"I am sorry, no," said Katya, "I never use it."

"That's ok. I can drink it without," replied the man.

Jenny spoke: "I better go first as I expect you're anxious to learn what's happening."

"Yes, thank you," said Katya and she took a drink of coffee.

"Well, I don't know if you've seen any of the news programmes since you've been here," continued Jenny.

"I saw it on television yesterday," replied Katya.

"Well, Milošević is digging his heels in." Katya hadn't understood. "Sorry, he's not budging," A blank look from Katya which Jenny again detected. "He's resisting any attempts to get him to make peace," Jenny clarified. "NATO's continuing to bomb Belgrade but there's still a lot of fighting going on in Kosovo. It's definitely too dangerous to return at the moment."

Katya nodded; her face etched in sadness. She looked down into her mug. Jenny continued and embellished what Katya had been told in Leeds.

"The UK has agreed to let in around four and a half thousand refugees and they're still arriving. Some are making their own way and claiming asylum; others are being flown from the camps similar to the process that you went through… As you know, you'll be able to stay here for a year if necessary and claim asylum if you wish or go home when you want. All your travel costs will be paid and there's a small resettlement grant."

Jenny paused and took a drink of coffee.

"We're encouraging refugees to make contact with loved ones if it's possible… You've got your phones, I think,"

Katya nodded. "Yes."

"Good… Well, we're in regular contact with the authorities in Pristina but it's still difficult, as you can imagine. Most of the phone lines have been cut but we've had some successes in tracing relatives, mainly by letter."

"What about relatives?" asked Jenny

"My husband was captured by the Serbs; he is dead, I think."

"I'm so sorry," said Jenny. The others looked down not wishing to make eye-contact with Katya.

"What's his name?" inquired Jenny.

"Ibi... Ibrahim." Jenny wrote down the name on her pad.

"I'll make enquiries and see if I can find out anything. We're getting some details of prisoners of war. Maybe I can get some information on him."

"Thank you," replied Katya.

"Is there anyone else we can try and contact?

"My mother lives in Lapusnic," said Katya. "But I have not heard from her since I left last month."

"Do you have her name and address?" asked Jenny. Katya provided it and Jenny made another note.

"That is very kind," said Katya.

Jenny looked at Mr Potter, indicating she had finished her piece.

"Hello Katya, my name is Potter," he announced formally. "I'm head of the Children's Services in South Tyneside and, as you might have gathered, I have responsibility for children's welfare in the area. We will want to keep an eye on Melos to make sure he hasn't suffered any ill effects from all the upheaval."

He bent down and held Melos's little hand in his fingers.

"He looks in good shape." The boy was smiling. The man looked up at Katya.

"I've been speaking to some of my colleagues in other areas. It seems many of the refugee children have been traumatised by the events in Kosovo. They've had to arrange special counselling for them... There've been some tragic cases. We've even had examples of some of the older children seeing their parents being shot or beaten up. It really is quite terrible."

Katya looked down in sadness.

"Is there anything you need from me?" asked Mr Potter. "Anything for Melos? I can arrange for a supply of disposable nappies or baby food. There's a lot of stuff being donated by some of the multi-nationals to help the aid effort."

"That would be very kind," said Katya.

"I'll have some delivered on Monday. How old is he?"

"Seven months," replied Katya.

Mr Potter made a note. "You and Edi are the only refugees we have in Tyneside. Most are in London and the South East but there are some in Leeds, Hull and Sheffield."

That had answered a question Katya had wanted to ask.

Michelle then explained her role as a social worker, and that she would call on them at regular intervals to check they were ok.

Clara wanted to draw the meeting to a close as they wanted to see Edi.

"And then I want to take you on a bus ride into Gateshead to show you where you need to go to collect your benefits. I've got some vouchers for you as well from one of the supermarket chains for clothes, or food if you like."

Katya again expressed her gratitude and collected the mugs and took them to the kitchen; she noticed that Mr Potter hadn't drunk his. The visitors gathered up their things and Katya agreed to accompany them down to the sixth floor to translate for Edi.

On the way down Clara turned to Katya. "You were a teacher, weren't you, back home?"

"Yes, that is true. A... how you say? First school."

"Primary school," Clara corrected.

"Yes, er... the primary school, in the village where we lived."

"That might be useful. I may be able to find a job for you. We're quite short of primary school teachers in this area." Clara made a mental note.

They arrived at Edi's flat; it was almost eleven o'clock. Katya knocked on the door and Edi answered. The flat was tidy, and Edi had made an effort to look her best, but her clothes gave away her situation. The smell of last night's cooking still lingered heavily. The introductions were made, and Katya translated all the information for Edi. Mr Potter paid particular attention to Arjeta and her drawings. After about half an hour, Michelle, Jenny and Mr Potter left, leaving Clara behind.

"Right," said Clara. "How about a bit of shopping?"

Katya translated for Edi. "Clara is taking us on a bus so we can get our money."

"But I want to stay here. I don't want to go," Edi exclaimed.

After some persuasion, she put on her old coat and followed Katya and Clara to the elevator. Katya was pushing Melos in the buggy and Clara was holding Arjeta's hand.

As they waited for the lift to arrive, Katya had noticed Arjeta with Clara. "You are very lucky," said Katya. "Arjeta doesn't usually let anyone get close to her except Edi."

Clara made another mental note.

As they left the tower block, Clara led Katya and Edi to the bus stop just around the corner in front of the shops. Three boys on bicycles rode past them as they walked across the service area. The women waited for about five minutes and then a small bus arrived with the word 'Hoppa' on the side in large letters. Katya made the connection.

The group got on the bus and Clara spoke to the driver before joining them in the seats.

"You won't have to pay if you use the bus," Clara said as she sat down. "I'll arrange a pass for you both." Katya translated.

The journey to Gateshead town centre took about forty-five minutes after they had picked up a few pensioners and a couple of errant teenagers who had bunked off school. Edi found it difficult to come to terms with the noise and traffic, the smell of diesel fumes and the general hubbub. She looked out of the window in trepidation. The bus pulled into the terminus and they got off.

Clara took them first to the council buildings and the Job Centre and showed them the forms they would need to fill in. Edi looked at the melee around her and just stared blankly, a mix of confusion and fear.

Clara introduced them to one of the officers called Ruby who would have the responsibility for dealing with their claims. Katya and Edi were told to ask for her each time they called, and she would make sure they received their benefits.

Clara reached into her handbag and pulled out several coupons. She counted them out to Katya.

"These are the vouchers I mentioned earlier. I will take you to the store where you can get some clothes and things for the flat. There is one hundred pounds each."

Katya was flabbergasted and roughly converted it to Deutschmarks for Edi.

"Thank you," said Edi, the first time Katya had heard her speak any English in public.

Clara took them along a covered way which was lined with shops. Edi was almost in shock. Arjeta just stared. *"Shiko nënë!"* she kept saying, *"Shiko nënë!"* "Look mummy, look mummy."

They came to the large supermarket which had provided the vouchers and went inside.

"It's quieter today; on Saturdays you can't move," said Clara. Katya translated for Edi and she smiled. She was beginning to feel more relaxed.

They found the clothes section and Clara explained sizes to them. Katya had mentioned her trip to the 'Meh'ro Cen-na' earlier, explaining her new jeans and top. Clara laughed when she heard the pronunciation.

"We'll make a Geordie out of you yet." Katya smiled but had not really understood the humour.

After almost two hours, the party emerged from the store loaded with bags of clothes and supplies. They had bought wisely. Katya was able to buy a new jacket, a hairdryer and some more things for Melos who was now fast asleep in his buggy. Edi bought some new clothes and shoes for herself and a new dress and shoes for Arjeta. They had nothing left of their vouchers at the end of the trip.

The shopping had proved great therapy for Edi who was now

much more animated and talked excitedly to Arjeta.

Clara had to return to her office in town but saw them back to the bus station. She told Katya the number of the bus to look for and the stand where it departed. After a few minutes, the Hoppa came and Clara got on and spoke to the driver.

"He will tell you where to get off," said Clara, indicating to the driver.

"Thanks you... for everything," said Katya.

"That's ok; it's what I'm here for... I'll call again next week but phone me if you have any problems."

Clara gave Katya and Edi her business card. "My number is on there; you can contact me any time."

She turned and left them to make their journey back to the flats.

The bus dropped them off at the shops in the precinct where they had got on, and they made their way back to the tower block loaded with carrier bags. It was now mid-afternoon, and Katya caught a glimpse of a kite high in the sky in the distance. She would go for a walk later.

Edi and Arjeta left at the sixth floor and Katya and the buggy rode to the fourteenth. She had noticed the change in Edi and hoped that the journey had been a turning point for her and Arjeta.

As she was trying to get the buggy and bags out of the lift, Carole was just about to go into her flat and turned around to help Katya.

"Hiya, Katya, pet, what's all this, more shopping?" she teased. "Here, let me give you a hand."

"Thank you," said Katya and as she off-loaded some of her bags to Carol, she explained their journey to Gateshead.

"That sounds great, Katya, pet," said Carol and followed Katya towards her flat. "Hey, here's a thought, how do you fancy coming for tea tonight? Bigsy's going out and won't be back till late."

Katya thought for a second or two. "I have a better idea, why don't you come round to me? I will cook you a Kosovan meal. It is the least I can do to say thank you for everything you have done for Melos and me."

"Aye, ok pet, it's a deal. That'll be great. What time?"

"About eight o'clock, if that's ok? Melos will be asleep by then."

"Aye, ok, I'll be there."

Carole left, and Katya put her things in the bedroom then made herself a coffee. She looked out of the window and saw the kite still flying. "Polly!" she exclaimed under her breath. She finished her drink and went back to the bedroom and changed her tee shirt for a brand new pale blue blouse. She put Melos back in his buggy then headed to the lifts.

"Come on Melos, we're going to see the kites."

She made the journey to the rec and sat down on the same bench she had used on the first day. Polly was concentrating on his kite flying and didn't notice them for a while.

It was another mild day and Katya felt sleepy following her shopping expedition and shut her eyes for a moment. Then she heard what was now a familiar greeting.

"Hiya, Katya, pet, how're you doing?"

It was Polly. She was deep in thought and his appearance had made her jump.

"Oh... oh, hello Polly... How are you?"

"Sorry pet, didn't mean to startle you, like."

"That's alright; I was just enjoying the sunshine."

"Well, I should make the most of it if I was you, pet. We don't get much up here."

Katya laughed. Polly made her laugh; it was his enthusiasm and his positivity… and his smile.

"Have you finished for today?"

"Aye, the winds dropped, not get any lift now," explained Polly. "Are you going back to the flat?" Katya again wrestled with the strong local accent.

"Yes, I suppose we should, Melos will want his tea."

Polly looked at Melos in his buggy and pulled some funny faces. "He's a bonny lad alright."

Katya got up from the bench and started walking alongside Polly. She told him about her visit to the 'Meh'ro Cen-na' with Carole. Polly was in hysterics at her pronunciation. She then described the earlier trip to Gateshead with Edi and Clara. Polly listened to Katya's travels with interest then he explained his latest project for college. He was putting together a collage of old decaying buildings and would be going down to the old docks the following morning to take his photographs.

"You can come with us if you like."

"Really…? Yes, I would love to. What time are you going?" replied Katya, without giving it a moment's thought.

"About nine o'clock. The Mags are at home tomorrow and the place'll be crawling by twelve."

Katya had lost the translation completely but was happy with the time.

"Yes, good, but I will have to bring Melos, if that's ok."

"No, that'll be champion, that."

They got to the lifts and Polly helped her in with the buggy. Neither of them talked in the confined space but it wasn't an awkward silence. At the twelfth floor, Polly got out.

"I'll see you tomorrow downstairs by the front entrance at nine then."

He smiled again. She felt a shiver, but it wasn't the cold.

"Yes, ok, I will see you then."

As the lift doors closed, she giggled to herself like a schoolgirl. She told herself not to be silly.

When she got to the flat, she put Melos in his recliner and switched on the TV. He seemed quite content watching the children's channel while Katya checked in the kitchen and made a list of ingredients she would need for her meal.

In Kosovo, filo pastry is a speciality and Katya had been taught how to make it at a young age by her mother. It had been a while, but it would be good to try again to make sure she had not lost her touch. She would make a pie with a casserole of some beef steak, onions, mushrooms and potatoes. She checked her purse and thought she would have enough money. She would need to make the remainder last until she could collect her benefits the following Tuesday.

She put Melos back in the buggy and headed back down to the shops. She collected all the ingredients she would need, and Mr Ali helped again with payment. He introduced her to his son, Jamal, who was filling shelves behind the counter. It was busy, being Friday teatime.

Back at the flat, she fed Melos and left him in the recliner while she prepared the dinner. She knew she would need a good couple of hours to cook the dish and she started to make the pastry. Once the mixture was ready she rolled it out. Without a proper rolling pin she had to make do with a milk bottle. The result looked fine and having cooked the meat and vegetables she put them in a casserole dish and covered it with the pastry then put it in the oven. She hoped she had set the dials to the right temperature.

As the dinner was cooking, she put Melos to bed and read him a story. Once he was asleep, she went back to her wardrobe and chose a pair of slacks and another top; she was ready for her guest.

At just turned eight o'clock, Carole knocked on the door and presented Katya with a bottle of wine and two glasses. "I've bought us a drop of vino and these. Wasn't sure if you had any or not."

She handed the glasses to Katya. "Thank you, that's very kind."

The smell from the kitchen caught Carole's attention, "Katya, pet, that smells amazing."

"It will be ready in a few minutes. I hope you enjoy it. It is a while since I have been able to cook properly."

"I'm sure I will," replied Carole.

Carole had on a smart pair of jeans with a pattern up the side of each leg, a pair of loafers and a skimpy white tee shirt that looked a bit small for her and revealed most of her cleavage.

"Make yourself at home," said Katya.

She took the bottle of wine and the two glasses and went to the kitchen, Carole followed.

"Mmmm, that does smell good." She looked at pie through the glass door of the cooker.

Katya examined the wine bottle to see how to open it. Carole took it from her and unscrewed the top. "Oh, that is good," said Katya. "I don't have, what you say...? A thing to open," said Katya. Carole poured two large measures.

"Ah, a corkscrew you mean... I never bother, our Bigsy can open 'em with his teeth," said Carole and they both laughed.

"When did you last have a glass of vino then, pet?" asked Carole as she took her first sip.

Katya thought for a moment. "When Ibi and I got married I think, a long time ago."

"I didn't know if you drank at all being Muslims, like," said Carole as the pair walked back into the lounge.

"I am not a Muslim," Katya explained. "My grandfather came from Sweden. That is why I have blonde hair. We were brought up as Christian. In Kosovo, it is mostly Muslims, but we have quite a mix of faiths. In Pristina, we have churches and mosques together."

They carried on chatting, Katya talking about the trip to Gateshead and the events of the day. She told Carole how much she had enjoyed watching the kites and how nice Polly was.

"Aye, he's a canny lad our Polly. The only one of the family who's got any talent... or brains for that matter," said Carole.

"You and Polly are... er... family?"

"Oh yes," Carole replied and gave Katya a potted history. She listened with interest but didn't mention she was meeting him the next morning.

After a few minutes, Katya served the meal and they sat around the table. Carole poured out more wine in slightly bigger measures.

"No, I can't drink all that, I will be, how do you say...? Pissed," said Katya, looking at the three quarters filled glass. Carole roared with laughter.

"Aye, don't you worry pet; we'll get pissed together, eh?" and Carole took a large gulp.

"This is champion," said Carole after taking a few mouthfuls. "How do you make pastry like this? It melts in your mouth," and Katya explained her mother's tutorage and the importance of getting the right ingredients.

"You'll have to give me the recipe," said Carole, although the chances of her actually cooking pastry were non-existent.

After the meal, they both cleared the plates away and sat down on the sofa. Carole shared out the remainder of the bottle. They started talking about families and Katya started to feel the effects of the drink and was a bit woozy.

"So how long will you be staying here, pet? Do you know?"

"I don't know... They say we can stay for a year, maybe more if we want. We can ask for... er, asylum, I think. But I will say this, what is there to go back for? Everything it is destroyed now... and there are so many bad memories."

Katya examined her wine glass, looking at the contents like some connoisseur. It was almost empty. She seemed to be overwhelmed by sadness, locked in a moroseness fuelled by the alcohol.

She looked at Carole. "I will tell you something." Then, overcome with emotion, Katya described in detail the incident in the woodshed and the rape by the soldiers and her subsequent escape.

"Ee, you never... what...? You killed 'em...?! What, both of 'em...?" exclaimed Carole. "Fookin' hell!"

She was extremely sober now having listened intently to the story. "I can see why you're in no hurry to go back, pet, I really can."

Katya burst into tears. "I haven't been able to talk about it to anyone," she sobbed, "except the doctors."

"Don't worry, pet, I'll not breathe a word. I think you were very brave, and you mustn't blame yourself. I'd have cut their balls off."

Katya continued sobbing for a while and Carole held her. Later, having calmed down, Katya went into the kitchen and made some coffee. Carole joined her.

"I'll say this, pet, you've certainly seen life," said Carole, as Katya poured boiling water into two mugs containing a measure of coffee in each.

"Yes, that is true," replied Katya, and they returned to the lounge.

They continued to talk until around eleven when Carole got up to go. She kissed Katya on the cheek and said goodnight.

"Will you be alright, pet?" asked Carole.

"Yes, I will be fine," said Katya. "Thank you for coming 'round and bringing the wine; it was very kind."

"No bother, pet... Thanks for dinner; it was champion. See you soon."

Earlier that evening, Bigsy waited for Wazza and Chirpie by the shops ready for the latest drop. Right on time, he heard the boom of the dance music coming around the corner. The Escort pulled to a halt and Chirpie got out and went into his usual place in the back holding his ears.

"Turn that fookin' racket off. You'll have every bizzie in Tyneside down on us," said Bigsy. Wazza complied.

Bigsy went over the evening's drops, timings and code words and they arrived at the club around seven-fifteen. Layton, as usual, arrived at half-past seven on the dot. "I don't know how he does that you know," said Bigsy.

The car park behind the Working Men's Club was quiet at this time and the caterers' van pulled up alongside the Escort. Unusually, Layton got out, went around the back of the van and opened the rear doors. There were two large duffle bags.

"Dis one has de coke and tabs... an' dis one de weed," said Layton in his strange dialect. "You know where you've got to go and how much it all costs. Any questions?"

Bigsy shook his head "Nah... Everton gave us all the details, like. I'll meet you here same time tomorrow, ok?"

"Aye, and don't screw up," was Layton's parting reminder.

Bigsy and Wazza put the bags into the boot of the Escort next to the videos. Chirpie looked on from the back.

"I take it you've got the number plate fixed this morning Wazza, bonny lad, cos if we get stopped with this little lot they're going to throw away the key," said Bigsy.

"Aye, took it round to Tyre-Fit first thing. Good as new," said Wazza.

"I'm pleased to hear it... and don't go speeding," said Bigsy.

"What in this? It won't do above sixty," said Wazza.

"Aye, but we're in a thirty so don't you forget," retorted Bigsy, and they set off to the first drop.

The drops were the same as Wednesday night, except the service station was replaced by another club not far from the Metro Centre. There was also another pub just off the Team Valley. The night club Ecstasy supplies were nearly three times the mid-week drops, ready for the weekend, the busiest time, and Bigsy realised that there was some serious money going down this time. While outwardly pleased at another good earner, inside he was seriously panicking about the responsibility and the potential hazard of being caught. He was in it up to his neck now, no mistake and what Carole would say if she found out didn't bear thinking about. He tried to put it out of his mind.

The first drop was at knob-head Trev's place and Bigsy made the call. Trev opened the door and seemed more coherent than the other days.

"I'm glad you called round Bigsy, I understand the lad's been giving you a bit of grief, like. Well, I sorted it. He won't be going out for a while and his bike's down the Money Maker Store waiting for a buyer."

This concerned Bigsy as he knew Trev had a tendency to be a bit free with his fists and he had already dealt with the situation.

"You're alright Trev, it's all been sorted. No need to take it further, like. Thanks anyway."

"Fair enough... Have you got something for us, Bigsy?" said Trev.

"Aye, you got the money?"

And with that, the deal was done, but Bigsy was feeling a bit guilty of his treatment of Rikki. Maybe he could have given him a verbal warning. Still, what's done is done, and he got back in the car.

The rest of the drops went off without a hitch and Wazza did keep below the speed limits. "If we go any slower we'll catch ourselves coming back," Chirpie commented at one point, and they all laughed. He never said much but when he did it was always worth a listen, Bigsy said.

It was nearly twelve-thirty before they got back to the precinct. Bigsy had done a quick calculation and reckoned that his cut from the evening's work was at least five hundred pounds after paying Everton his whack. He was keeping the money in one of the duffle-bags; the other empty one was left in the boot next to the box of videos. He pulled out some notes and gave Wazza one hundred pounds and Chirpie fifty; they seemed pleased with their evening's work.

"All in it together now," said Bigsy, as he gave them their slice.

He watched Wazza and Chirpie as the Escort disappear towards the garages, then headed inside to the lift. As the elevator slowly rattled its way up the fourteen floors, he thought that Carole would be pleased with another sub; it would ensure his continued entry into her good books. He stifled a yawn. He also hoped she would be asleep when he got in. He was utterly knackered and didn't think he could raise an eyelid never mind anything else.

Chapter Eleven

Saturday morning, seven-thirty, Flat 1410, and Katya was already up and showered. She was in the lounge drying her hair with the new dryer she had bought in Gateshead. The TV was on showing cartoons and Melos was in his recliner watching avidly.

She went into the bedroom and looked at her clothes hanging in the wardrobe. It was not a lot compared with Carole, but far more than she had had in the camp, and probably more than she had had in the cottage; she and Ibi had always made do. She chose to wear her jeans and, remembering Carole's outfit from the previous evening, put on a white tee shirt which made the most of her new figure.

After another coffee and some toast, she put Melos in the buggy and her purse in her new sling bag, its first proper outing. She had dispensed with the old rucksack but had not thrown it away; she had put it at the back of the wardrobe as a memento. She slipped her jacket around her shoulders and made for the lift. She pressed the button for the ground floor. The lift arrived and when the doors opened the pungent smell of urine assailed her.

It was just on nine o'clock as she pushed the buggy out of the lift and spotted Polly pacing up and down outside the lobby. He turned around and saw her; he smiled nervously. He was dressed casually and looked like a student with his unkempt hair and baggy tee-shirt, tracksuit bottoms and trainers. He had a Nikon camera-bag around his shoulder. He did not usually take it out. The last thing he wanted to do was to advertise the fact he was carrying an expensive camera, but he thought it might impress Katya.

"Hiya, Katya, pet, you look good."

"Thank you," said Katya.

He looked at Melos, who was wide awake and looking at Polly. "And how are you, bonny lad?" he asked, dropping the Geordie twang for a moment in the hope he might understand.

"Oh, he's fine," said Katya.

They walked to the bus stop and Polly was explaining their journey. "We need to take the Hoppa into Gateshead and then we'll get another bus and head over the river and along to Scotswood; should get some good pictures there."

The places Polly mentioned meant nothing to Katya, but she was happy to go along with the plan.

After a few minutes, the Hoppa turned up and Polly showed his student pass. The driver recognised Katya from the previous day and waved her and the buggy on without charge.

Polly was intrigued. "How d'you do that?"

Katya explained the free travel arrangements that had been agreed for her and Edi.

They changed buses at Gateshead Interchange and got on a double-decker that would take them over the Tyne Bridge, through the City Centre and out on the west road along the north bank of the Tyne.

Katya was intrigued with these vehicles which she had seen in Leeds and from her window at the flat, but this was her first journey in one and she was determined to go upstairs even if it meant carrying the buggy, or more correctly, Polly carrying the buggy. She was amazed at the scenery, especially when they crossed the Tyne Bridge and she looked down the river. Polly proudly gave her a running commentary.

"I didn't realise how big this city is."

They passed St James' Park, the football ground, which was already bustling with activity.

"It'll be manic here on the way back," said Polly. "The Mags are playing Everton this afternoon."

"What is Mags?" asked Katya, and Polly explained the nick-name for the local football club, what it meant to the local community, and how he was on the waiting list for a season ticket. He changed the subject when he could see Katya was losing interest.

They arrived at a stop about a mile out of the city centre and Polly helped Katya with the buggy down the stairs and off the bus. It was still mild, though cloudier than the previous day, but there was no hint of rain. Katya looked around and could see the dilapidated buildings, broken down gates and general dereliction. It was only missing the bullet holes and she could have been back in Kosovo.

They approached an old factory, the gates had long since been boarded up but with a bit of persuasion, Polly was able to push the wire mesh fence far enough from its post to create a space that they could climb through.

"Is this ok?" asked Katya. "We don't want to be in any trouble."

"It's fine, pet," said Polly. "We'll not be doing any harm. Just taking a few pictures if anyone asks."

Polly helped Katya through the gap with the buggy and pushed the fence back in its original position. There were bricks and all manner of debris on the ground and Polly and Katya carried the buggy until they reached what looked like an old service area which was relatively clear. Melos seemed unconcerned at the transportation. They went through an archway.

Katya surveyed her surroundings. It was an old factory with rusting metal and broken machinery, discarded remnants of a bygone age. Clumps of weeds were growing out of the brickwork, doors with faded paintwork with letters stencilled indicating their previous use - wages office, works manager, canteen. Behind the factory, she could see a deserted dock where supplies of raw materials would have been unloaded from boats and barges on the brown/grey waters of the Tyne which flowed silently past. She looked on the floor and in the corner she could see old syringes and discarded condoms; others had been there before.

Polly took off his bag and got out his camera. He loaded a

roll of film.

"Are you ok here, pet, while I take a few shots?"

"Yes, I'll be fine."

"Be careful, you'd better not touch anything in case it comes down on your head," Polly added with a smile. He always seemed to be smiling Katya noticed.

Melos was now asleep in the buggy and Katya watched Polly as he went about his work. She saw the way he framed his subject, discarding some views but snapping away at others. After about ten minutes, he came back to his bag and loaded another film, putting the spent one into a container.

"I'm using black and white for this project. It'll add to the atmosphere," he explained.

After another twenty minutes, he returned and, as he approached Katya, he aimed his camera and shouted "smile", then clicked the shutter. Katya quickly turned her head away in embarrassment.

Polly quickly put his hand up in apology. "Sorry, pet, didn't mean to upset you."

He walked closer. "It's alright I won't take any more, I promise, but you looked so canny stood there, like."

Katya assumed it was a compliment. "It's ok.... I just wasn't ready...I am not used to having my photograph taken. It was a surprise that is all."

She let go of the buggy for a moment and moved into an open doorway a few yards away. "What about here?"

She lifted her arms up against the frames and looked straight at Polly.

"Aye, that's champion." He clicked off three shots.

"Turn sideways," he instructed, and she obliged. He took another couple of shots.

She noticed that her nipples were erect and clearly visible through her tee-shirt. A shock of excitement shot through her body.

"Thanks for that," said Polly. "You'd make a cracking model, you know. You're really beautiful."

Katya was blushing. "Thank you."

They returned to the camera bag and buggy where Melos was starting to wake up and grizzle. Polly unloaded the film and put it in another container and dropped into his bag.

"That's it I'm afraid, no more films left."

Katya felt strangely disappointed; she was enjoying the attention.

"Come on, we can get the bus and stop for a bite to eat in Gateshead and you can see to the bairn."

They struggled through the fence and back onto the pavement, then crossed the road and waited at a bus stop.

"Did you get the pictures you were looking for?" asked Katya.

"Aye, and a few more besides." He grinned.

After about ten minutes, a bus came and took them back across the Tyne Bridge towards the Interchange at Gateshead. As they passed the football ground, there were now thousands of people milling around, most wearing the black and white shirts she had seen at the Metro Centre.

"So that's the Toon Army?" Katya said and laughed.

"Aye, the Toon Army... I say this, you're a quick learner, Katya, lass."

It was almost midday when they got off the bus in Gateshead. As they walked away from the double-decker, Polly turned to Katya who was manoeuvring the buggy through the crowded walkway. "Have you been introduced to stotty cake yet?"

Katya looked at him trying to understand. "I don't know. What is... er... stotty cake?"

"I'll show you, follow me."

"I'll need to find somewhere to change Melos and give him some food," said Katya.

"Aye, no bother," said Polly.

Polly led them into a large bakers shop. There was a long queue of people waiting to be served. At the rear there was a cafe and, having taken over buggy pushing duties, Polly made his way through the crowded tables and managed to find a seat. Katya following him. Melos was taking in all the people around him. Katya was looking at the array of bread and cakes in wonderment.

She turned to Polly as they made themselves comfortable at the table. "I've not seen anything like this."

Her mind again briefly wandered back to the refugee camp in Macedonia.

"There's a baby changing place through there." Polly pointed to a sign on a door indicating a baby's bottle. "You sort out the bairn and I'll get us some food."

Katya took Melos into the baby room. Polly placed the buggy against the table then turned to a family on the adjoining seat. "Can you look after that for us?" They acknowledged, and he joined the queue at the counter. He still had his camera bag around his shoulders; no way was he leaving that out of sight.

He eventually got served and ordered two salad stotty cakes and a coffee that Katya had asked for, and a glass of coke which he took back to the table on a tray. One of the staff got a baby's highchair and put it against their table. Polly waited for Katya to return. After a few minutes, Katya came out of the baby room and made her way past several tables and dropped Melos into the highchair and strapped him in. She then squeezed onto the seat next to Polly.

"This looks nice," said Katya, looking at the flat-bread encasing a generous portion of salad.

"Welcome to your first stotty cake, bonny lass."

"That looks very good. How much does it cost? I will give you the money."

"No you won't, pet; this is on me," said Polly and they both started eating.

"This is lovely… Thank you so much."

"My pleasure," said Polly.

After finishing their meal, Katya fed Melos from a jar of baby food which a waitress had heated up in a microwave, and then they left the cafe to get the Hoppa back to the flats.

As they made their way back to the lifts, Katya turned to Polly. "Thank you for today, I have really enjoyed myself."

"Aye, me too," said Polly.

They reached the twelfth floor and Polly held the lift doors open for a moment preventing them from closing.

"I'll be developing the photos on Monday at college… I can pop 'round Monday night if you'd like to see them. I'll bring my portfolio as well; see some of my other photos."

"Yes, that would be good. I would really like that," said Katya, and she leaned over and kissed Polly on the cheek. "Make it after eight o'clock Melos will be asleep by then."

After getting back to the flat, she changed into a pair of trousers and decided to do some washing. Clara had shown her how to use the machine, but this would be the first time she'd tackled it alone. She had bought some washing powder the previous day and measured it out and put it into the chute on the top of the machine. She opened the glass front, put in her jeans and her original skirts from the Leeds reception centre. She would hand wash a couple of tops and underwear; she didn't want the colours to run. She then selected the temperature and pressed the 'on' button. After a few seconds, it shuddered into life and she could hear the sound of water gushing through. Success!

It was mid-afternoon and she had decided to go to see Edi and see how she was coping. She took Melos in the buggy and made her way to her flat on the sixth floor. When Edi answered the door, she looked pale and drawn.

"Are you ok, Edi? You don't look very well."

Edi held the door while Katya negotiated the buggy into the flat.

"No, I do not feel good; I have not slept, and my stomach is upset," said Edi.

"What about Arjeta?" asked Katya.

"She's ok, just really bored," replied Edi.

The curtains were again still closed, and the light was on in the lounge. Katya pulled the curtains back. Arjeta rushed in from the bedroom where she had been sleeping.

"Melos, Katya," she shouted excitedly, with a big smile on her face, and went straight to the buggy to play with the young boy.

"Have you eaten anything?" asked Katya

Edi looked down forlornly, which Katya took as a 'no'. She explained she had given Arjeta a bar of chocolate and yoghurt that she had bought from the store the previous day.

"I don't think the food here is good for me," said Edi. "It makes me sick. When I am on the farm, always we have fresh vegetables, milk, eggs and meat," she explained. "And I can't use the oven. It is too difficult. All those knobs and things... I don't know what they mean."

She showed Katya a nasty blister on her forearm. "I did this too. It is very painful."

"How did you do that? asked Katya.

"On there," she replied, pointing to the hotplate.

"Ok, you rest on the couch; I will make you and Arjeta another omelette."

Katya went to the kitchen and poured a glass of bottled water and took it to Edi.

"Here, drink this."

Later, Edi ate the omelette and, feeling better for some food, started to perk up a bit. They were sat at the small dining table in the lounge, Arjeta was playing with Melos.

Edi looked at Katya. "How do you manage with the flashbacks?"

"What do you mean?" asked Katya.

Edi described the nightmares which didn't seem to stop even when she was awake. She kept seeing her parent's bodies and could even smell the burning buildings.

"Yes, it is hard," said Katya. "I do think about things that happened and have nightmares sometimes too, but I am trying to be strong and shut them out."

Edi then began to elaborate further and spoke of her time in the refugee camp.

"There are things that I have not told you."

Edi looked down at the table.

"We were so short of food... I thought that Arjeta would starve."

"Go on," said Katya. "You can tell me if it will help."

"One of the Albanian soldiers who was protecting us in the compound had access to the Red Cross supplies and he told me he could get anything I needed if..." Edi hesitated for a moment. "If I gave him 'services' in return."

"What sort of services?" Katya asked.

"The soldier said that if I had sex with him, he would bring me extra food and drink."

Edi started to cry.

"So you were forced to have sex with the soldier for food?" Katya summarised.

"Not forced exactly, no," said Edi. "I could have said no, other women did, but I had to think of Arjeta, so I gave in."

"How many times?"

"Many times," said Edi. "And not just with one, for three weeks, I had six different soldiers."

"And what did you get in return?"

Edi explained that she and Arjeta had been given chocolate, fresh fruit, bread, cake and milk as well as the HDR rations that were given to them by the NATO people. No wonder she had looked well-fed compared to the rest of the refugees on the plane.

"Have you seen a doctor?" she asked. "You must get checked out for infections."

Edi said that the men had all worn condoms as they were afraid of catching AIDS, but she had seen the doctor in Leeds and was told she was ok.

Katya was not a trained psychiatrist but had learned enough from her teaching degree that Edi needed specialist support.

"Would you like me to get in touch with Clara, see if there is any help?"

"I don't want to cause any trouble; they might send us back to Kosovo, or they might take Arjeta away from me... I couldn't risk that. I would sooner kill myself... and Arjeta."

This disturbed Katya even more, although she was sure she didn't mean it. They talked for another hour and gradually Edi began to snap out of her depression, but Katya repeated she would phone Clara and try to get someone to see her as soon as possible.

When Katya left Edi she seemed a lot brighter and more positive. Katya had invited them both for a meal that evening as she didn't want to leave her friend alone for any length of time at the moment. As soon as she got back to her flat, she found her mobile phone in the kitchen drawer and punched in Clara's number. She looked at the handset for a moment, but nothing happened. She pressed the button with the green telephone as she had done previously. There was a series of beeping noises and then what Katya assumed to be a ringing tone. After about thirty seconds, a voice came on. "You have reached the voice mail of Clara Davenport, please leave a message after the tone and I will get back to you as soon as possible."

Katya spoke slowly, slightly unnerved by the formality of leaving a message. "Hello... this is Katya... Gjikolli....I am worried about Edi... I think she is not well... she really needs to see someone can you, er, arrange something... please?"

She switched off her phone and looked at it with suspicion hoping her message had got through.

Earlier that day, the residents of flat 1405 had slept in and it was past ten o'clock before Bigsy had made his way to the kitchen to make a brew. Carole was already up and sat at the table in the lounge eating toast in her dressing gown, hair and makeup immaculate as ever.

"What time did you get in this morning, pet?"

"Not sure, but it was late, about half-twelve, I think."

"Was it successful... your business, like?"

"Very," said Bigsy, still not fully awake.

She didn't press further and went into the bedroom to change. When she returned, she announced that she was popping down to the shops to get some more milk and bread. "Won't be long pet."

When Bigsy heard the door shut, he went to the spare room and found the duffle-bag which he had hidden under the bed. He started to count out the takings. Everton had done very well for himself.

As he had done previously, he put Everton's cut to one side and wrapped it in a carrier and put it back in the duffle-bag. He counted the rest, four hundred and twenty pounds, and that was after he had paid Wazza and Chirpie their money. He had to find another place to hide it; he couldn't leave it in his jacket pocket, he might get mugged. Now, how ironic would that be?

He found a new pair of shoes in a box at the back of the wardrobe which he had yet to wear. "They're for best," Carole had instructed when they had bought them a few weeks earlier. He took the shoes out and placed the money inside. He still had over one hundred pounds in his jacket. He took fifty pounds from his stash and put it in his trouser pocket and replaced the shoebox at the back of the wardrobe.

When Carole returned, Bigsy had washed and shaved and was beginning to feel like a human being again.

Carole made them both a coffee and sat down on the sofa. She could not keep it to herself any longer.

"You'll never guess what Katya told me last night, pet?" and she told Bigsy about Katya's escape and the incident in the woodman's hut.

"You what...?!" Bigsy nearly spilt his coffee. "She topped two soldiers?"

"Aye, knifed one and shot the other... That's what she says, and I believe her."

"Well, she's certainly gone up in my estimation, pet. That's one brave lass there," responded Bigsy ruefully. "You just don't know what goes on, do you. I mean, you see it on the telly, like, but when it's on your front doorstep, it's hard to take in."

"You keep it to yourself, mind. I told Katya I wouldn't tell anyone, but she would have expected me to tell you."

Bigsy pondered while he finished his coffee.

"Are you going to the match this afternoon, pet?" asked Carole, changing the subject.

"Is the Pope Catholic?" replied Bigsy with a grin and put his hands in his trouser pocket and pulled out a note.

"Here you are, pet, a little something to treat yourself, from last night."

He gave her the fifty pounds. Any more and she might get suspicious.

"Ah, pet, that's champion, might pop into town later... See if our Katya wants to come," said Carole, who then gave Bigsy a lingering kiss. "I hope you're not saving yourself tonight, pet, because I've got some extra time planned myself, like," and, grinning, rubbed his groin. Bigsy groaned.

"No," he stuttered, "I'm meeting Wazza and Chirpie at one o'clock to go to the match. Should be back about six. I've got to see my supplier at seven but that won't take long."

He reluctantly broke off and went into the bedroom to change into his match attire, his number nine replica shirt with the immortal name 'Shearer' emblazoned on the back and tracksuit bottoms.

The traffic going to the game was horrendous and from experience it was easier and quicker to catch the bus; it had been a regular pilgrimage every fortnight.

Bigsy would have liked to go to away matches but never had the money. A round trip to, say, Arsenal, Manchester or Liverpool cost a fortune, although it was a lot cheaper to get to Leicester or Coventry, but the opponents weren't much cop and the games were often grim, so they never bothered.

Today it was Everton, a tough game as they were doing well. Although the Mags' league form was not brilliant they were doing well in the cup. Two weeks previously they had beaten Tottenham two-nil after extra time to reach the Cup Final at Wembley. Alan Shearer had scored both goals. So cup-fever was definitely in the air.

Getting a cup-final ticket was impossible, there were rumours that grown men were willing to sell their daughters to get their hands on one. A ticket was recently advertised in the Newcastle Evening Chronicle for five hundred pounds. Bigsy and the boys had contented themselves that they would watch the game on the big screen at the club with a few broons. In any case, they were playing Manchester United and the chances of a win were fairly remote, although on their day they could beat anyone, Wazza had remarked to a general consensus.

The three of them had bought season tickets before the league started so there was no financial outlay today apart from the obligatory meat pie. It was reckoned that over half of the season ticket holders at Newcastle were out of work and it was a mystery how they could lay their hands on enough money to buy one. Rumour had it that there was a government grant available, but that was just malicious and probably started by their arch-rivals, Sunderland. Bigsy had saved up for his from the proceeds of the porn-video sales which, although not terribly lucrative compared with their present venture, proved sufficient to subsidise his precious ticket.

Bigsy, Wazza and Chirpie got to the ground around two-thirty and picked up their pies from the catering shop behind the main stand. The game kicked off and, within three minutes, Campbell had put the visitors ahead which had quietened the Toon Army.

"Fookin' a mile offside!" shouted Chirpie, fully animated now. Wazza had said that Chirpie was a different person when he was either drunk or at St James' Park. By half-time, Campbell had scored again and doom and gloom had descended on the Geordie faithful.

The second half started, and the Mags were playing a lot better. "Our Ruud's stuck a boot up their arses," said Wazza, referring to the manager, the Dutchman, Ruud Gullit. Shearer converted a penalty in the 82nd minute giving the adoring crowd a forlorn hope, but they hadn't played at all well. The game was sealed when Gemmel struck a third for Everton in the 88th minute. Game over.

Rather gloomily, Bigsy, Wazza and Chirpie made their way out of the stands and towards the exits with thirty-seven thousand others, bemoaning missed chances and poor referee decisions. Suddenly, Bigsy stopped in his tracks and was almost knocked to the ground with the force of the following throng. Wazza and Chirpie also stopped and Bigsy pulled them to the side behind a parked car to avoid being carried along by the sheer weight of the crowd.

"Did you see who that was?" said Bigsy.

With over a thousand people surrounding them, it was a bit of a daft question.

"Where?" said Wazza and the three of them peered through the car windows at the door to the mobile Police station which was always parked there on match days.

"Shite...! It's the guy from the services," said Chirpie.

"Aye, Hughie, fookin', Bonner," said Bigsy, as they watched him chatting to a uniformed officer before going inside. "Even got the same jacket on... He must be a fookin' bizzie."

"I've got to call this in," said Bigsy and, once they were out of the mainstream of supporters, Bigsy ducked behind a wall and called Everton.

It should be pointed out that Everton Sheedie had been christened after the legendary West Indian cricketer, Everton Weekes, and not the Liverpool-based football team that had just inflicted misery on Mags' fans.

The phone was answered on the third ring.

"Everton, bonny lad, it's Bigsy. I know you said not to call you except in an emergency, like, but you'll want to know about this," and he went on to explain what he had seen.

"Nah, don't think he saw us, there were fookin' thousands

coming out the ground," answered Bigsy.

"Tanks for dat information, mon," said Everton. "You did de right ting in calling. I was saying to Layton I made de right choice putting you on de payroll. You have conducted yourself well in doing de business. I have some good feedback from de customers. I appreciate dat."

Bigsy was trying to make sense of the strange dialect but felt there was a compliment in there somewhere.

"Ta Everton, bonny lad, thanks very much," said Bigsy and he rang off.

Bigsy joined up with Wazza and Chirpie and made their way to the metro station.

"What are we going to do, Bigsy?" asked Wazza. "D'you think they're onto us?"

"I don't know, bonny lad, I left it with Everton, says he'll sort it," replied Bigsy.

The three got off at the Gateshead Interchange and Bigsy told Wazza and Chirpie to go on home, he would see them later for the exchange with Layton; he had some business he needed to do.

Bigsy made his way to the Money Maker Store and went inside.

Money Maker was part of a national chain of what was really a quasi-pawn-broking enterprise. You could take in anything of value and they would pay cash for it, although at a fraction of its true worth. They would then sell it on. Wazza reckoned that half the stuff had been nicked but that was by the by; there were never any questions asked and no-one seemed bothered. They would also cash Giro and other cheques which normal banks wouldn't touch, again heavily discounted. Bigsy was looking for something in particular and spotted it in the corner. An assistant approached him.

"How much for the mountain bike?" asked Bigsy.

"That's just come in, very good quality, only a few months old," said the spotty youth.

"Cut the shite. I asked how much, not a fookin' history lesson," said Bigsy, trying to lay down a marker. He had no love of this store that made a lot of money on the back of other's misfortunes.

"Eighty pounds," said the lad.

"Piss off," said Bigsy, "I'll give you fifty in cash," and he pulled a wad of notes from his jacket pocket.

"I'll have to ask the manager," replied the assistant.

"Aye, you do that, bonny lad," said Bigsy.

The assistant went away and came back again a few minutes later. "I've spoken to him and he said he can't let it go for anything less than sixty pounds."

"Aye go on then, you thieving bastards," said Bigsy, annoyed not at the lad but the principle.

He peeled off three twenty-pound notes from his wad and gave it the assistant. "And I'll need a receipt," shouted Bigsy, as the lad went to ring it up on the till.

Bigsy hadn't ridden a bicycle in probably fifteen years but, as they say, it never leaves you. After a wobbly start, Bigsy got up a bit of speed and headed for the flats about three miles away. It was a bit hairy to start with; there was still plenty of football traffic, mostly Everton supporters making their way to the A1. They took great delight in trying to cut up anyone in a Newcastle shirt which, of course, Bigsy was still proudly wearing. Although reasonably fit from his football training, he was beginning to feel it when he coasted down towards the flats, thankfully unscathed.

About half a mile away he stopped outside a familiar dropping off point - knob-head Trev's. He parked the bike and knocked on the door. Bigsy heard shouting and a dog barking. The door opened, it was Trev holding the collar of a particularly vicious looking canine straining to get at Bigsy and barking ferociously. Bigsy stepped back from the doorstep. Trev was remarkably coherent.

"Bigsy...? What d'you want...? You're not due a drop tonight, are you?" asked Trev, somewhat surprised and hanging on to the dog with all his strength.

"It's your lad I've come to see, is he in?" asked Bigsy with one eye on the dog.

"What's he done now...? I'll fookin' kill him if he's been up to no good." said Trev.

"No, nottin' like that," said Bigsy.

"Rikki!" shouted Trev loud enough for the neighbours' curtains to start twitching. He opened an adjoining door and threw the dog inside and shut it in. Bigsy could hear the dog clawing at the door trying to get out and barking even louder.

"Sorry about that Bigsy, lad... Just got him, like, not yet properly house-trained," said Trev, presumably talking about the dog.

Rikki sheepishly went to the door and nearly ran back when he saw who it was, but his father caught him by the wrist. The lad had a black eye and cuts to his lip which Bigsy knew was not down to him.

"It's ok, Rikki lad, you're not in any bother, I've got summat for you," and led the boy to the pavement and proudly showed him the bike.

"For me?" asked Rikki almost speechless.

"Aye, but the deal still stands, you understand. You'll need a bike if you're going to be me eyes and ears, right?"

"Ta Bigsy, that's great," and he picked the bike up and would have cuddled it if he could.

"One more thing, d'you play football?"

"Aye, when I get the chance, like," replied the lad.

"Well, get yourself some kit and be down the rec at five o'clock on Thursday night for a coaching session. You up for it?"

"Aye, you bet, I won't let you down, honest," said Rikki excitedly, and wheeled his bike into the house. A woman's voice was raised. The dog continued to bark. A neighbour shouted something which Bigsy couldn't make out.

Bigsy turned to the man. "Now look Trev, I'm gonna do you a favour and take that lad of yours under me wing, like. I'll see he doesn't get into any trouble and if he's any good he can join the youth football team, give him something to aim for. Oh, and another thing, lay off the fists, ay, if he's gonna be in my team I want him in good shape."

Trev felt a bit guilty and looked at Bigsy. "Aye, you're right Bigsy, it's the coke, sometimes it does things to your head. I'll see he's alright."

"You better had Trev because you don't want to be falling out with me, if you catch my drift," said Bigsy.

The door slammed shut and Bigsy walked off to the flats. He got in to find Carole watching TV.

"I saw the result... bad game?"

"Aye, we was shite," replied Bigsy.

"Well, never you mind pet, I've ordered you a curry from the Bombay Temple. It'll be here in a few minutes."

Bigsy enjoyed a good curry and it was handy that the local takeaway at the other end of the estate had a very popular delivery service, particularly on a Saturday night.

Bigsy went to get changed; he was hot and sticky from his cycle ride.

A few minutes later, the doorbell rang, and it was the curry. Carole paid the delivery boy and took the carrier bag with the cartons into the kitchen to dish it out.

"I've got you a Chicken Balti, Peshwari naan, boiled rice and chips. Oh, and there's a couple of papadams. That ok?"

"Aye, pet, champion, I'm starving," replied Bigsy making his way to the table. "What you having, pet?"

"I'm just having a couple of them onion bhaji things and a salad... Got to look after my figure," said Carole.

After sampling the east's finest cuisine, well east of Consett anyway, Bigsy went to the bedroom to get his duffle-bag.

"I'll see you about nine o'clock, pet, I won't be late."

Carole was engrossed in the TV. "Aye, ok pet," she replied, and he left the flat to meet his buddies.

Within a couple of minutes, Wazza' Escort appeared with

Chirpie in the back in his usual place. He hadn't bothered sitting in the front from the garages. The music was turned off. They made their way to the club for the meet with Layton who pulled into the car park at exactly the allotted time, seven-thirty.

"I still don't know how he does it," said Bigsy.

He parked next to the Escort and wound down the window of the transit. Bigsy handed him the duffle bag and, as was now customary, Layton emptied the money onto the passenger seat and began to count.

"Good take last night," said Bigsy.

"'Bout average for a Friday," replied Layton.

Satisfied it was all there, Layton gave Bigsy an envelope. "From Everton," he said and started reversing away. "Expect a call," was the last Bigsy heard. He watched as the van pulled out of the car park.

Bigsy looked at the envelope in his hand and tore it open. Then he nearly passed out. Inside there were three front-row seats for the Cup Final. He read it again and again, "Saturday 22nd May 1999. The Football Association Challenge Cup Final - Manchester United versus Newcastle United seat number J65. Price £120."

"What's up, Bigsy?" said Wazza, seeing his buddy in a state of shock.

"Ah need a drink, lads," and he showed the contents to Wazza and Chirpie.

"Fookin' hell," said Wazza.

"Fookin' hell," repeated Chirpie.

"You're not wrong there,' said Bigsy

They went inside and Bigsy ordered three broons. Bigsy paid, then gave Wazza and Chirpie their tickets out of sight from any prying eyes. They would get torn limb from limb if they were spotted with Cup Final tickets.

"Don't you lose those, lads, whatever you do," said Bigsy.

"We'll have to sort out some transport, like," said Wazza.

"No bother, there'll be loads of coaches going down," replied

Bigsy.

Chirpie was deep in thought and his Newcastle Brown.

It would have been a long night, but for Carole's expectations, so around eight forty-five Bigsy set off back to the flats leaving the lads watching this week's turn, a Daniel O 'Donnell tribute act who was getting a bit of stick from the punters. "D'you know any Black Sabbath, bonny lad?" was one cry, prompting howls of laughter from the meagre audience.

"Don't fancy his chances tonight," thought Bigsy as he walked back.

It had just turned nine when he got back to the flat. The walk had done him good and his curry was pretty well digested.

Carole greeted him in her dressing gown. "You get yourself in the shower, pet, and I'll be waiting for you."

She opened her dressing gown. Bigsy took in the sight in front of him and suddenly felt the curry repeating on him.

Chapter Twelve

Hughie Bonner could have been an actor; as events were to unfold, he should have been.

The life of an undercover policeman takes a special sort of person, one who can blend in with whatever low-life his duty of the day requires. It's not just a case of looking the part, that bit is easy. It's getting into the psyche, being accepted as one of them, whoever 'them' happens to be. Then, having built up relationships as the cover develops, bringing them crashing down. A great way of acquiring enemies.

Hughie, having got to know one or two villains in the line of duty, understood their motivation, their ways and methods; he spoke their language. He'd actually quite liked one or two characters he had crossed over the years. He discovered life was much simpler on the streets. Incongruously there was a lot more honesty; you screwed up, grassed, double-crossed - you died, simple. No bleeding-heart lawyer, no jury, no psychological profile that said you came from a broken home or were abused as a child, as if that somehow justified almost any possible atrocity. There were no mitigating circumstances; you broke the law of the street, you paid.

But he was unequivocal, if Hughie had his way, all the pimps and dealers, all the traffickers and extortionists, all the fraudsters and rapists, all the extremists and bombers would be rounded up, put on a huge ship, tugged out into the North Sea and nuked.

Hughie had been in the police force since leaving University twelve years earlier and had been attached to the Merseyside division for most of that time. He joined their COE, covert operations unit, in 1994 and had some spectacular successes. He was well-regarded by his superiors and had been earmarked as someone with potential.

As a result of his most recent mission, he had been instrumental in bringing down a large drug cartel involving members of the local Chinese community, major players in the area who, between them, controlled a sizeable chunk of Liverpool's thriving heroin traffic. The gang, it was discovered, were also providing slave-labour to the cockle-picking trade-in Morecambe Bay.

It had taken several months to infiltrate the organisation, posing as a dealer recently released from prison. Hughie had spent weeks frequenting known hang-outs until he became part of the wallpaper, part of the fabric of the scene, so his presence became familiar and caused no alarm. From there he gradually worked his way in.

When the arrests were made, such was the impact, the price of heroin on the street went up fourfold if you could get any at all. Hughie wasn't Hughie Bonner then, he had a different pseudonym; he was Jason Caldwell, and he was a very wanted man. Rumours of the contract started at five-thousand pounds but, whatever, it was time for Jason Caldwell to bow out. Recognising the danger, arrangements were made for Detective Sergeant Craig Mackenzie to move away from the North West and he accepted a transfer to Newcastle.

The Mackenzie family had lived on the Wirral for several years and were close to the grandparents, so moving his wife and young family had been a strain. Jean Mackenzie was a Personnel Manager for a local building society with her own career and circle of friends. The two boys were just five and seven and were doing well at school. The relocation, unsurprisingly, caused marital problems which they eventually resolved. Jean managed to get a transfer with her employers to Newcastle which made the move easier, that, and a generous allowance from Merseyside police in acknowledgement of Mackenzie's work in Liverpool. The family found a suitable house in Morpeth, a town with a similar socio-economic status as the Wirral, just half an hour from Newcastle city centre and only twenty minutes to the Metro

Centre. It is a much sought-after place to live.

After a few weeks familiarising himself with the area, D.S Mackenzie was given his first assignment. His background in Liverpool had made him an ideal choice to work on a new initiative to clamp down on drug trafficking in the area – Operation Snowball.

For this project, he chose the name Hughie Bonner, a name he made up while doing a crossword.

Tyneside's drug cartels were in two distinct areas, north of the river – Newcastle city; and south of the River - Gateshead and South Shields. The River Tyne made a natural demarcation line and the rival gangs tended to keep to their own patch. However, the Newcastle side with its numerous clubs, had a much larger potential custom and was generally wealthier. There was, understandably, a great deal of protectionism surrounding the catchment areas but there were signs of some local discontent with the status quo, with the South Tyneside gang trying to make inroads into the north, a position which the north side would rigorously defend. It was a potentially explosive situation.

As far as the police were concerned, the couriers tended to be small fry and, while their arrest had some merit, it was unlikely to lead to any major reduction in drug crime as the gang leaders would just employ new carriers. Operation Snowball's main objective was to identify and apprehend the main protagonists.

Hughie Bonner started his attempt to infiltrate into the gangs by frequenting the clubs in Newcastle and South Tyneside.

The first part of his plan involved introducing himself to the DJ's. He'd acquired a very good collection of rare dance records, through a source in London, which were much in demand at the clubs. He would visit a venue and take with him a selection which he would then sell. Gradually, over a few weeks, he was supplying several DJ's. His cover was secure; he'd become part of the scene. Hughie hoped that this, in time, would lead to the drug suppliers.

During his undercover work, he'd had a tip-off that Scalleys Night Club was a regular haunt where drugs were freely available.

Scalleys was a popular haunt in the Newcastle area, regularly announcing 'house-full' signs, particularly at weekends. From the outside, it resembled a warehouse of some kind, a common sight along the north-side waterfront. Inside, the dance-floor would probably hold two or three hundred people and was separated from the bar area by a metal balustrade surround. There was a seating area which allowed space for those who wanted to socialise rather than dance. The seats were worn, some bearing the scars of having been deliberately cut with a knife.

During his investigations, Hughie had learned that Ecstasy tablets were being supplied at the club, but it took three weeks of patient observation before Hughie managed to spot the exchanges. He noticed that one of the doormen, in particular, seemed to be in great demand, regularly slipping off to the toilet area or disappearing around the back where there was a service area, conceivably to meet possible clients. Hughie followed him discretely on a couple of occasions and twigged.

The 'swap' was done in a split second so that only a trained eye could see the sleight of hand that secured the switch. Usually, it would take the form of an accidental bump into each other whereby the punter would hand over a rolled-up note, either a ten pound or twenty-pound note, depending on the quantity. The money having moved from punter to doorman, the same move would take place a few minutes later when the drugs would pass the other way, ingenious and very successful. There was a variation where the exchange was done on the pretext of asking for a light for a cigarette; the result was the same.

Having worked out the methodology, it was time to move things along. Two days later, he was in Scalley's and paying particular to the doorman whom he was now convinced was one of the 'players'. About nine-thirty, he noticed the large

West Indian walk through the bar area and approach one of the scantily-dressed clubbers. This time he could see the transaction quite clearly.

After the exchange had been completed, Hughie made his play for the girl. She was at the bar.

"Hi, can I get you a drink?'

She eyed him up and down, assessing the potential. Hughie was a good-looking guy and it looked promising.

"Yeah... ok... rum and black." He ordered her drink and took a lager for himself.

"You on your own?"

"With me friend Tracy, but she's copped off," she replied.

"Fancy a dance?'

"Yeah... why not."

She got up from her stool. "I'm Kerry by the way."

"Hughie."

After a few turns on the dance floor, they returned to a table and their drinks. It was quieter in the corner away from the speakers and some semblance of conversation was possible.

"So what do you do?" asked Kerry.

"Work, you mean?" replied Hughie.

"Yeah," said the girl taking another sip of her drink.

"I'm a roadie."

"What with bands and stuff.".

"Yeah," said Hughie. "Just been setting up at the local arena... I look after the lighting... Worked with all the big bands."

"Really...? Like who?"

"Just finished a U.S. tour with Dire Straits but loads... Used to work with Queen before Freddie passed on."

"Wow, that must've been brilliant."

"Yeah, it was," said Hughie.

She was smitten and moved closer to her new acquaintance. Her hands started to wander freely up his leg towards his thigh.

"I know a place we can go," she whispered, anxious to consummate their brief encounter.

"Yeah, I would love to but I'm meeting Joey Eden at twelve... Next week perhaps... I can give you my number," said Hughie.

"What <u>the</u> Joey Eden?" she exclaimed.

Joey Eden was a guitarist with one of the major Newcastle bands and the revelation clearly impressed the lovelorn Kerry.

They swapped mobile phone numbers and over the next few days, various text messages were exchanged; it was clear Kerry was more than interested in her new acquaintance. They made arrangements to meet again at Scalleys the following Saturday.

Nine-thirty, they were sat in one of the alcoves, closer than Hughie would have liked. The club was packed. Kerry was keen to hear more stories of Hughie's exploits on the road. When he felt the time was right, he made his play.

"Look, I don't know if you can help me."

"Yeah, ok, pet, why not?"

Hughie looked around to make sure no-one was in earshot.

"Do you know where I can get some good shit...? Weed... or h?" he added. "I'm new 'round here and my regular supplier's gone back Stateside with his band."

"Yeah, I can get you fixed up, no problem," she replied as quick as a flash. "But it'll cost you, mind."

"Sure, ok, will this cover it?" He produced a twenty-pound note and put it on the table.

"Yeah, that should do, but I was thinking of other ways you could pay me." She looked left and right, then pulled down the top of her dress to reveal her breasts.

"What do you think?"

"Wow, yeah, fantastic, but let's just do the business first, eh?" replied Hughie.

"Hmm. ok, stay here," said the girl, looking disappointed.

Hughie watched as she headed towards the exit. He had an idea where she was going.

Ten minutes went by, twenty; Hughie was beginning to think he'd been stood up. But then he could see her walking across the dance-floor accompanied by the doorman.

The girl had given Lionel some background to the request and said she could vouch for Hughie. Lionel was taking no chances and made additional enquiries through the DJ who also confirmed Hughie's credentials. The pair approached the alcove where Hughie was seated. The West Indian introduced himself.

"Hi, I'm Lionel, I understand you're looking to do some business."

The doorman joined Hughie at the table.

"Leave us, we're discussing business," said Lionel to the girl and she headed off to the bar to spend Hughie's money.

"Do you want a drink?" offered Hughie.

"I'm cool," said the man. "What is it you're wanting? I can arrange the commodities, but I'll need a few days to process the order."

"A bit of weed, just enough for a few spliffs," said Hughie.

"Yeah, ok," said Lionel "I can do that. Call in on Wednesday and I'll have it for you."

They agreed on the amount and the price and shook hands.

Hughie didn't re-join the girl again that night. He spotted her on the dance-floor with another guy with tongues down each other's throats. He gave a sigh of relief; he wasn't looking forward to giving her the push.

Wednesday night, as arranged, Hughie took delivery of a small quantity of Jamaican hash. The deal was done in the car park. He was in.

During this phase of the operation, he was reporting back to his boss, D.I. Pete Grove, at regular intervals by meeting in appropriate pubs where he would provide an update. He was meticulous about security; his personal safety was paramount. A lot of work had gone into his cover being tight.

He met Grove the day after the deal at Scalleys and handed over the Cannabis; this was protocol and would protect Hughie from any prosecution. They discussed strategy for the next phase which they hoped would lead to identifying the main players.

They conceived a plan.

The following Saturday as he entered Scalleys, Hughie approached Lionel again. He was in his customary position on the door. Seeing no-one was waiting behind him, he shook hands with the West Indian and leaned close.

"Lionel, my man, I have some business for you, if you're interested?" Hughie spoke just loud enough to be heard over the music emanating from inside the club.

"Yeah, cool, man, I'll catch you later."

"I'll be at the bar," said Hughie.

Lionel eventually joined Hughie an hour later to hear his proposition.

"What can I do for you, man?" said Lionel as he sat down on an adjacent stool with an orange juice.

Hughie whispered his story.

"I've had a call from one of my band connections wanting a larger supply of weed. He's going on a European Tour in a couple of weeks and wants enough to see them through the gigs."

Hughie was hoping to get to the next level in the organisation which was rumoured to be another West Indian called Everton but had no further details. Hughie outlined his needs which he knew were larger than could be safely exchanged at the club.

"I think I can arrange that for you" said Lionel. "But not here, too dangerous... Someone will call you to make the arrangements... Give me a number."

Hughie gave Lionel his mobile number and the man returned to his door duties.

A couple of days later, Hughie was sat at home watching the news which was dominated by the war in Kosovo and the refugee crisis. He noticed the local news report showing a couple of the Kosovan refugees being resettled into the flats on Heathcote.

He turned to his wife. "That's like taking vestal virgins and putting them into Sodom and Gomorrah."

Just then, his phone rang; it was Lionel from the club.

"That Hughie...? Lionel... Expect a call tonight regarding the proposition we discussed," and he hung up without further formality.

A couple of hours later, Hughie did receive a call from someone with a strong West Indian accent.

"Is dat Mr Bonner?"

"Yes," replied Hughie.

"I understand you want to take delivery of a certain consignment," said the voice.

"Yes, who am I speaking to?" said Hughie.

"You don't need to know dat. Are you wanting to buy or not?"

"Of course," and Hughie explained what he wanted and why.

"Right den diss is what we will do," said the West Indian.

The voice told Hughie he would arrange the exchange and gave him details of how it would work and the price. He told Hughie about the password he would need to provide, and they agreed on a word, 'extreme'. Hughie told the voice that he would be driving a black BMW and gave him the number and said he would be travelling up from Peterlee. The man suggested the Motorway services on the A1 at Washington as a convenient drop point and Hughie agreed, but it would need to be the northbound side as he would be travelling in that direction.

"Dat's cool... Someone will approach you in de car park and ask for a light... and den you say de password... You got dat?" said the voice.

"Yeah... got that,' said Hughie.

While not entirely satisfactory, it was a start and it was likely he would meet at least one more member of the gang. This could lead to further introductions he hoped.

The night of the switch went well enough. He pulled into the services, parked up, and as he walked towards the main entrance, a heavy set man in a cheap black tracksuit came up to him and asked him for a light. The man appeared to be sweating profusely for some reason. He gave the appropriate code and they went around the back of the services and did the swap. Hughie was making a mental note of the man and his two colleagues who also looked serious players judging by their demeanour. Better still, he would wait at the end of the slipway from the services and see if he could spot their car, a quick check on the license database and they may have a significant lead.

As he pulled away, he noticed them cross the footbridge over the motorway. Very clever, very clever indeed, clearly seasoned pros, parking on the southbound carriageway knowing that there was little chance of the car being recognised going in the opposite direction.

So, Hughie pulled away, none the wiser as to the identity of his suppliers, but there was no rush. He would definitely recognise the main courier again.

The following Saturday, he decided to go to St James's Park, not because he was a great fan of the Mags, he had spent too long on Merseyside for those allegiances to be jeopardised, but he thought it might be a good place to mix with the locals and maybe get some more intelligence. He would also keep his eyes open. He may even spot the man who had done the deal at the services; a remote chance, but who knows.

Hughie decided to wear a replica 'Shearer No 9' shirt, with his jacket over the top. He didn't think he would stand out.

Towards the end of the game, one of his colleagues called him on his mobile and asked him if he wanted to check out the CCTV footage in case it may show up someone. So it was at this point he made his way to the on-site police station. A decision that would ultimately cost him his life.

Later that evening, just after nine o'clock, Hughie was at home watching TV when he received a call.

"Hello dere, Mr Bonner? I trust you was happy with de consignment?" said the familiar voice.

Hughie went into the kitchen. "Yes, it was good... My friends were very happy."

"Dat is good. I like a satisfied customer... De reason for de call. I have taken a delivery of a large supply of de finest leaf and tought you may be interested in a bit of business. I can do a good price, a one-off deal but you will need to move quickly... widdin de hour. I will make de drop myself. Give us a chance to get to know each odder."

Hughie thought fast. "How much?" The man gave him a price.

"Ok, yeah, I can do that."

Hughie kept an amount of cash for emergencies such as this.

He didn't like it, but this could be an important break, so he agreed; particularly when the voice said he would be turning up himself, another piece in the jigsaw.

The West Indian gave Hughie details of where the meet would take place, an old abandoned factory down the Scotswood Road. The voice gave him the details and time, ten o'clock; it would be pretty dark by then. "Don't want to broadcast it," said the voice.

Normally he would have phoned in and logged this meeting, but it would take him a good twenty minutes to get there from Morpeth and with most of the team still wrapping up at St James's Park, he had decided to do the paperwork in the morning; he hoped to have more to report.

It was just before ten as he parked his black BMW about one hundred yards from the factory. He locked up and walked back until he found the gap in the fence he had been told to look for. As instructed, he walked through the archway and waited. He was beginning to feel a little uneasy, but he had been in worse places. He looked around at the dilapidated building and wondered what they used to make there. That was his last thought.

He wouldn't feel anything. A baseball bat across the back of the head and it was the end of D.S. Hughie Bonner. He was probably dead before he hit the ground, such was the force, but with the river only fifty yards off and well out of the way of any prying eyes, they could make sure. Everton and Layton dragged the body to the edge of the abandoned dock and dropped it into the Tyne. The fast currents would retain it for a few days before spewing it up on a beach somewhere down the estuary.

Chapter Thirteen

Sunday morning, Katya was sitting at her table looking out of the window. She could see the rec was busy with footballers doing their thing; all six pitches were in use. From the distance of the flats, and the height, the players looked like they were in a table soccer game with Katya being able to move the players with her fingers.

Melos was in his recliner watching the television, healthy and happier than she could remember, giggling at her pulling funny faces, even smiling at cartoon characters. Katya also thought he was starting to understand English words. She had made a conscious decision to speak to him more in her second language now, believing, long-term, it would be to his advantage.

She reflected on how her life had changed during the last couple of months. She had gone from a fairly shy village schoolteacher to a confident and self-contained woman and it was the events of the intervening weeks that had moulded her. Her survival instincts had given her an inner strength that she had never had before. The subconscious mechanisms of her brain that controlled her thought processes had managed to block out the worst of her ordeals and replaced them with a new and positive outlook. It was her way of coping.

With time on her hands, she had spent many hours in contemplation, but it was time to look forward. She was determined she would make the most of life, having almost had hers taken away. She believed she had been given a second chance by whatever God was looking after her and was determined to make the most of every opportunity and experience that came her way. She had to let go of the past for her own peace of mind and for Melos. It was her epiphany and she made a pact with herself to do that; trust your own instincts.

In 1405 Bigsy was up early. Carole was dead to the world as he dressed and collected his football gear. He had scrutinised his injured big toe the previous evening and was pleased to see there were no lasting effects, the bruising virtually disappeared and the nail healing; a bit of plaster and he had declared himself fit to play.

He quietly left the flat so as not to disturb his sleeping wife and joined Polly, Wazza and Chirpie in front of the flats for their trip to Sacriston. Wazza had sensibly left the Escort at the club the previous evening and the walk to collect it had cleared their heads of the copious broons that had been consumed. It would take them about three-quarters of an hour from there. They shared lifts so that they took as few cars as possible and Polly had taken the spare seat in Wazza's car. Slate had accepted a lift from Danny Milburn with another couple of the team. The remaining team members were making their own way to the ground.

Wazza's car was full of conversation about the previous day's game at St James' Park and Polly took particular interest as he was rarely able to get to matches. No mention was made about the Cup Final tickets. Bigsy had not even mentioned them to Carole. He had otherwise been occupied last night and he wasn't going to disturb her this morning.

The match went the way Bigsy had predicted with a four-nil win, Bigsy getting a hat-trick and Slate hitting the fourth with a left-foot shot from outside the box. After the game, Danny was really upbeat. "You were on fire today, Bigsy lad, what d'you have for breakfast?" Bigsy smiled to himself.

Later that same morning, Katya took Melos down to see Edi.

When she opened the door, Edi was dressed and wearing one of the new tops and a skirt she had bought in Gateshead. The curtains were open, letting in a stream of weak sunshine.

Although about the same age, Edi had a different body shape from Katya, and coming from Romany stock, her hair was very dark and tied back from her face that gave her a stern look. Katya had never seen her wearing jeans or trousers and couldn't imagine Edi in them. It had taken some persuasion for her to dispense with her scarf.

She looked much better than the previous day and she told Katya that she'd had some cereals and toast for breakfast. She was determined to look after herself for her daughter's sake.

Arjeta was watching the television and Katya suggested the four of them go for a walk. It was a dry day, if fairly cool for the time of year. Katya took them to the rec where the football matches were being played and they took the path that went right around the pitches to a small kiddie's playground in the corner.

Edi and Katya took it in turns to push Arjeta on the swings. There was also a roundabout and the three of them had great fun in riding it as Melos watched on from his buggy. It had been a tonic for all of them. They called at the shops on the way back and bought some more food and provisions. Edi was still struggling with the money but, again, Mr. Ali was only too pleased to help them. More disturbing though, Katya noticed that Edi had only a few coins left in her purse.

"Where is the rest of your money?" asked Katya.

Edi looked at Katya sheepishly. "It is all gone… I wanted to give Arjeta some nice things. I spent it in the supermarket."

Katya hadn't kept track of what Edi was buying at the time.

"Here, you better have this," said Katya and, despite leaving herself a little short, she gave Edi a ten-pound note.

"But I will need you to pay me back next week when we collect our money."

"Yes, thank you," said Edi. "Of course."

Katya stayed with Edi for most of the afternoon and practised some English with her. She discovered that Edi had a reasonable understanding of the language and it was mainly a question of confidence that was holding her back. With a bit of practice, she would soon be able to communicate which would make a huge difference for her. They turned on the TV and found a film on one of the channels and Katya let the dialogue run for a while and then asked Edi to translate. Katya explained that it was how she had learned.

It was late afternoon when she eventually returned to her flat to make Melos's tea. She looked across to the recreation ground; all the footballers were gone but she could see Polly was out with his kite. She wanted to go and see him; she had really enjoyed his company but decided she would wait for his visit the following night. Instead, she wrote another letter to her mother to give to Clara to pass on to the Refugee Council.

Later that evening she was watching the television news when she heard a buzzing noise coming from the kitchen and realised that it was her mobile phone. She still hadn't got used to having a phone that wasn't plugged into the wall. It was Clara returning Katya's call. She pressed the green telephone button and listened.

"Katya, girl... it's Clara. I got your message and I'll be coming around at ten o'clock tomorrow morning to see you and Edi... I've managed to contact a doctor and I'll bring her with me... How is she?"

"Hello Clara," she replied. "Thank you... yes, Edi, she seemed better today but I think she should still see someone. I am worried about her," Katya explained, and after a brief catch-up, Clara rang off.

Bigsy returned from the match just after two and Carole was ironing in front of the portable TV in the kitchen watching the omnibus edition of a soap opera. Bigsy was full of the joys of spring and replayed his three goals in minute detail. Carole listened in mock interest with one eye on the TV.

"By the way pet, you'll never guess... Wazza, me and Chirpie have got tickets for the cup final. How good is that?" said Bigsy, trying to play it down. The more he was likely to enjoy the event, the more it would cost him in recompense.

Now he had her attention.

"How d'you get them? They're as rare as hen's teeth 'round here."

Bigsy told her that his supplier had been so pleased with the work he had been doing that this was his way of saying thank you; which was almost right.

"And what am I supposed to do while you and your musketeers are swanning around Wembley then?" said Carole, not really entering into the spirit of Bigsy's good fortune.

"Ah, don't you worry pet, I'll see you've got plenty of readies for some serious clothes shopping," said Bigsy.

"Aye, it'll need to be some serious money an' all," replied Carole, trying to look affronted, but starting to consider this was not a bad deal. She had no wish to travel down to Wembley with a bunch of drunken idiots to watch a football match, even if it was Newcastle United, and the promise of extra spending money was the icing on the cake.

They enjoyed a lazy afternoon, Carole continuing ironing and Bigsy falling asleep in front of the four o'clock football match.

That evening Carole suggested that they shared a bath and Bigsy eagerly agreed but was starting to wonder how he would keep up with his wife's newfound libido.

Monday morning, Carole brought Bigsy his usual brew at seven-thirty. She normally worked a five-day-week; she did not work Sundays and had one in four Saturday's off. When she worked Saturday, she would take a day off in the week. The department was fairly flexible and with a small team, it wasn't difficult to agree a rota.

Bigsy was going to meet up with Wazza at lunchtime and then work a shift at the video shop until Carole got home. He hadn't heard from Everton since the call on Saturday and was wondering if anything was up. He mentioned this to Wazza later but said he would leave it for a day or two; he didn't want to do anything to upset Everton.

At flat 1410 Katya had quite a day ahead. She was expecting Clara at ten o'clock with the doctor to speak to Edi.

At about half-past nine, there was a knock on the door. They are early, thought Katya.

She was on the floor playing with Melos who looked quite at home in his recliner. She left him watching the TV and answered the door. She was confronted with a large box and Katya could see a head trying to peer over the top.

"Katya, Ju, ji, colly?" said the man.

"Gjikolli," corrected Katya with the appropriate pronunciation.

"Parcel for yas.. Can you sign for us, pet?"

Katya let the man in, and he put the package on the floor. She signed his clipboard, thanked him and he left. After he had gone, she got a knife from the kitchen drawer and opened the package. It was three large packets of disposable nappies and probably twenty or thirty jars of baby food in two long cardboard containers. There was a note, "Compliments of the Baby Store". Katya was amazed at the generosity.

At just turned ten o'clock, there was another knock on the door and this time it was Clara and Michelle Dexter, the social worker, and another lady who was introduced as Doctor Stephanie Peterson, a psychiatrist attached to Newcastle University, who specialised in post-traumatic stress disorder.

Introductions over, Katya went to make the coffee with Clara while Michelle and the doctor kept Melos amused.

Clara asked about Edi. "You sounded very concerned on the phone yesterday."

"I was," replied Katya. "She was not well at all on Saturday but yesterday, she seemed better."

"What about her daughter?" asked Clara.

"She seems fine, a bit quiet, but ok," replied Katya.

"We'll need you to come with us to translate. Doctor Peterson would like to make an initial assessment," said Clara.

"Of course, it will be no trouble," said Katya.

Katya and Clara carried in the coffees. The doctor and Michelle were looking at the view from the window.

"Goodness you are so high up," remarked Doctor Peterson. "It's like you're on top of the world."

"I've got used to it now," replied Katya.

They finished their coffees and Katya handed Clara the letter which she had written to her mother. "Can you give this to the lady from the Refugee Council?" asked Katya. "It is for my mother. I have printed her address on the front. I hope she can contact me. I have put my address and telephone number in the letter."

"Of course, I'm seeing Jenny this afternoon. She wants to know how this morning's meeting goes."

They cleared away the mugs and Katya put Melos in his buggy, and they all crammed in the lift to the sixth floor. Katya noticed that the doctor appeared to be trying to hold her breath.

Edi answered the door in her new top and skirt and looked reasonably refreshed. Arjeta was sitting at the table with a colouring book.

Introductions were made and Katya translated. They declined more coffee but sat down on the sofa and Doctor Peterson took out a notepad. She started her questions with Katya translating.

"Hello Edi, my name is Doctor Peterson and I specialise in the effects of trauma."

Katya translated, but it was difficult to know if Edi really understood.

"Can you tell me how you are feeling at this moment, mentally I mean? Are you having nightmares? Do you have feelings that you want to harm yourself or Arjeta?"

Edi was quiet and didn't respond. The doctor tried another tack.

"Ok, don't worry. What about any physical issues - pains, headaches, tummy problems, rashes, are you eating properly?"

Edi explained the queasiness that she had felt over the weekend, which she put down to getting used to the food. She hadn't felt very hungry and she was not sleeping well. She was, however, suffering headaches, nightmares and flashbacks.

The interview continued for over two hours and Michelle and Clara also asked some questions and made notes. But it was not like an interrogation. The three of them had been very sensitive and talked slowly and almost comforting. Edi did understand a lot of what they were saying and answered in English when she could; otherwise, Katya translated as accurately as possible recognising the different nuances in the respective languages.

As Doctor Peterson concluded, she spoke to Katya, Michelle and Clara; Edi had gone quiet.

"It's my opinion that Edi is showing typical signs of PTSD... sorry, post-traumatic stress disorder," she clarified. "I can give her some pills which will help her sleep." Katya translated for Edi. She looked at Katya blankly.

"Can I have a word in private?" said the doctor to Katya and they went into the kitchen out of Edi's earshot. Michelle was making notes on a writing pad while Clara was trying to entertain Arjeta. Edi looked on, feeling totally lost.

"I am concerned about Arjeta. Do you think Edi is capable of looking after her at the moment?" asked Doctor Peterson.

"Oh yes, certainly, Arjeta is the only thing keeping Edi going," said Katya, which did little to reassure the doctor. Katya noticed the doctor's expression and was beginning to realise there was a possibility that Arjeta could be taken away from Edi. She was desperate to head-off any suggestions in that direction.

"I want to say…" Katya paused to get the words correct. "Edi has been through a great deal and just needs a little time to get used to it," Katya said. "I will make sure she is ok."

The doctor thought for a moment. "Hmm, ok, thanks… but I do need you to keep an eye on her. I'll call again on Wednesday." She gave Katya her card with her mobile number. "Ring me any time if you are worried in any way."

They went back into the lounge. Michelle was just packing her things into a briefcase and Clara was still playing with Arjeta.

The three visitors left, and Katya talked to Edi, summarising what was going to happen and giving her reassurance that they weren't going to take Arjeta away from her.

Katya suggested they go for some fresh air, so Edi got their coats and, with Melos safely tucked into in his buggy, they headed to the shops. They walked further into the estate away from the precinct and talked. Katya noticed the front gardens and how some had been tended with care and attention while others looked overgrown and neglected. They walked past one house and could hear people shouting and a dog barking ferociously. They eventually came to another row of shops among which was a newsagent's, an amusement arcade, a launderette, an Indian Takeaway, The Bombay Temple, and a sandwich shop. Katya bought them both a sandwich for lunch.

Katya was keen to keep Edi as occupied as possible and continued to talk to her in English, translating where necessary. "What is that called?" - a shop. "What is that called?" - a bus, and so on. She made Edi ask for the sandwiches, rehearsing before they went in. They walked back to the flats and Katya stayed with Edi until late afternoon when she made her way back to 1410 to prepare for her visitor. The time with Edi had been well spent as, not only had she seemed more at ease, it also turned out to be good for Arjeta who was occupied with Melos for most of the time.

Meanwhile, Bigsy and Wazza had spent the afternoon in the video shop replenishing stock. They had called around to the club earlier to meet up with Stan Hardacre who had received another consignment of under-the-counter videos. They agreed on a price and loaded them up in the back of Wazza's car. Bigsy had an arrangement with certain customers that were on the 'friends' list and would allow them to rent one for a night at five pounds a time. There was a back room at the shop where they could browse undisturbed.

Wazza parked the Escort at the back entrance to the store and carried the box of videos in. They left a float of about ten in the boot of the car to exchange for petrol.

The system worked well. The adult videos were by far the most popular choice and the regular clientele, mostly, but not exclusively, men, were very happy to pay the going rate for the real thing. Bigsy shared the proceeds with the shop owner, with two pounds going to the proprietor. Over the last couple of years, they had done quite a lucrative trade, enough to pay for Bigsy's season ticket anyway.

About five o'clock, Bigsy's mobile rang; it was Everton. Bigsy had had no contact with him since the call on Saturday and, while not too concerned, given the situation, being kept in the dark had been a little worrying.

Bigsy was still in the video store and had to strain his ears to hear Everton. There was a TV in the corner of the store playing noisy trailers of new releases on a loop to attract customers. Everton spoke in his usual West Indian drawl which did nothing to aid Bigsy's comprehension.

"De probalem of de police officer has been sorted but just to be certain tings are cool, we have moved de operation to a new place."

Bigsy didn't know the original whereabouts in any case.

Everton explained there would be a new phone number, a Pay-as-you-go mobile, which he gave to Bigsy to memorise. Layton had changed the transport and would now be using a five-year-old Mercedes van. He provided a description.

Everton continued. "Dere will be no drops for de next few days to let tings cool down… Sorry for de inconvenience, mon, but if everyting is ok, de next drop will be Friday. Dere will be more customers dis time so it will make up for de loss of business."

Bigsy caught the drift.

"Cheers Everton, bonny lad, and for the Cup Final tickets, like, much appreciated."

"No probalem mon... Ah hope dat ya enjoy de game. Ah will

cal you again, Wednesday."

Everton dropped the call.

Katya fed Melos and then checked her purse, emptying the contents out on the kitchen worktop. She examined each coin and found she had around three pounds in loose change and a five-pound note in her purse plus the ten Deutschemark note which at the moment was valueless. She would speak to Clara to see if it could be exchanged; at present rates, it should be worth at least five pounds.

She decided to go to Mr Ali's in the precinct for some supplies for the evening and bought a bottle of Chilean red wine, which was on special offer, a large packet of crisps, a bottle of milk and a bottle of Newcastle Brown for Polly. She had recognised the bottle from the football shirts. Luckily she still had a couple of pounds left for emergencies.

She put Melos to bed around seven o'clock and went to her wardrobe. It had been a long time since she had dressed for a man and she felt a little nervous. She was probably reading more into the situation than was warranted, and in any case, she had no real expectations or plans for tonight; she would just take it as it came, but she wanted to make an effort. She then realised that she was missing something in her makeup bag - perfume. She hadn't worn perfume for a long time but felt it would help her confidence knowing that she smelt nice.

Checking Melos was asleep, she went along the corridor to 1405 and knocked on the door. Carole answered in her casual gear.

"Hiya Katya, pet... Everything ok?"

"Yes, thank you... Have you some er... perfume I could have?"

"Of course, pet, come in... What's this, you got a fancy man already?"

Katya made an excuse that she would be going into Gateshead in the morning and wanted to feel fresh. Carole wasn't convinced as Katya's eyes betrayed her but decided not to press further.

"Come in," said Carole. "No problem, I get loads of free samples from the reps. I've got a box full you can look through. Just choose anything you want... Hang on I'll get it for you.".

Katya waited by the door. Bigsy was sat on the sofa watching the TV.

"Hiya, bonny lass, how're doing, pet?" said Bigsy.

"Hi Bigsy, I'm fine, thank you," replied Katya.

"Would you like a brew or something a bit stronger, pet?" shouted Carole from the bedroom.

"No, thank you, I need to get back, Melos is on his own."

Carole reappeared with a small grey valise and gave it to Katya. "There you go, you sort through that lot, pet, and you can let me have the case back tomorrow. Take as much as you need, I'll probably end up flogging 'em at a car-boot sale if you don't have 'em."

Katya didn't make the translation but thanked Carole and rushed back to the flat, not wanting to leave the boy on his own for long.

She checked on her son; he was sound asleep, then went to the bathroom with the case to examine the contents. She was amazed. She had never seen such a selection of perfumes, bath oils, and various make-up items, all in small presentation boxes labelled 'sample only, not for resale'. She recognised some of the labels and chose a 'Chanel' which she knew was nice, and also expensive.

She showered and put on her jeans which had been airing following the earlier washing. From her limited wardrobe, she chose the white peasant-style top, which buttoned up the front, and the new underwear that she had bought at the Metro Centre; a pair of flat shoes completed the look. A dab of Chanel behind her ears and on her wrists did the rest. She dried her hair and checked in the mirror; she had not looked nor felt this good in a long, long time. She undid three buttons revealing her cleavage and sat on the sofa waiting for Polly feeling like a teenager.

At just turned eight o'clock, there was a knock on the door. It made her jump. She still felt nervous but didn't know why.

Polly was dressed more or less as Saturday with a tee shirt and tracksuit bottoms and a pair of trainers, looking every bit a student. It was how Katya remembered the lads dressing at University in Pristina; it must be universal. He had a large portfolio folder and another, what looked like a photo album. He had also brought his Nikon camera bag.

Katya greeted him with a kiss.

"Hello Polly, come in."

Polly, too, seemed nervous as he entered the flat.

"Please, sit down I will get some drinks."

Polly made his way to the sofa and sat down with his portfolios and camera on his lap. He looked around the flat anxiously.

"I wasn't sure what you liked to drink or even if you did, so I got you one of these," shouted Katya from the kitchen. She returned and presented him with the Newcastle Brown.

"Aye, that's champion that is," said Polly. "Have you got a bottle opener?"

Katya felt embarrassed. "No, sorry, I haven't."

"No bother... Can I use your kitchen a minute?"

"Of course," said Katya and followed him.

He placed the rim of the bottle top on the edge of the work surface and hit it hard with the side of his hand like a karate chop, and the top dropped off onto the floor.

"You have done that before," said Katya laughing.

"Aye, once or twice," said Polly.

Katya poured herself a glass of red wine and went back to the lounge. Polly didn't do glasses and drank from the bottle, student-style.

They chatted for a while about kites and whether Polly had made any more and about the previous day's football match at Sacristan, which Katya did more out of politeness than interest. After a few minutes, she pointed at the portfolio. "Are those the photos from Saturday...? I can't wait to see them."

Polly unzipped the side of the folder and opened it up. The photos were A5 size and arranged in neat rows with captions underneath. The ones Polly had taken at the factory were stunning. In black and white, the pictures had captured the feeling of dereliction and decay familiar in World War II photographs. There was a great use of light and shade. Shafts of sunlight glinting through the windows gave them an almost ghostly effect. Katya looked at them in amazement.

"Oh Polly, they are so beautiful. What does your tutor think?"

"I only finished developing them this afternoon; he hasn't seen them yet," he replied. "You might want to see these as well," and he opened his photo album which was crammed with probably a hundred photos. He took another slug of his beer.

On the first page was the one that showed Katya with the buggy. She was looking towards the camera and her face was smiling, the focus was good, and it captured her in an off-guard moment.

"That was just before you turned away," said Polly.

"I was a bit, how you say... surprised," said Katya, "I am not used to being photographed."

"Well, you would never have guessed it."

He turned the page to reveal Katya framed in the doorway looking at the camera, her arms raised against the wall on either side.

"I can't believe that is me. I look so... different."

She turned the page to another equally stunning shot. "Wow... they are amazing," she added, using one of Carole's phrases.

Katya was feeling quite emotional, or it could have been the wine; she was already halfway down her glass.

Polly asked to use the toilet.

"Of course; it is just through there."

She pointed to the corridor and continued to look through the photo album. There were some of what seemed like a college fashion show, and a local band, all in black and white. Then, as she turned the pages, she suddenly came to one which took her aback.

It was a figure study, a young woman, sitting on a chaise-longue, looking at the camera; she was naked. She had a good figure, almost voluptuous, with dark cropped hair. There was a tattoo on her shoulder, and she had a pierced belly button. She had shaved most of her bikini line with just a strip of hair visible. Katya could hardly keep her eyes off the picture; she didn't know why. Curiosity, certainly, but for some reason, felt a twinge of jealousy.

She jumped like a guilty schoolgirl as Polly came back in the room.

"I like this one… Is she your girlfriend?" said Katya, showing Polly the nude study.

"Oh, I'm sorry, pet, I forgot they were in there. No, she was just a model they hired at college."

"Are there more?"

"Aye, about twelve I think," and Katya looked through the set of photos examining them closely.

"They are lovely photos, and she is very pretty."

"Aye, they're ok, but she's definitely not as pretty as you," said Polly.

"You think so? I don't know... It is difficult for me to say. I have never thought that way."

There was a moment's silence; she was starting to feel warm. She noticed that Polly had finished his brown.

"Would you like a glass of wine? I have no more beer, I am sorry."

"Aye, that would be champion."

Katya finished her glass and went to the kitchen and returned with two glasses; she gave one to him.

"You really think I am beautiful, Polly?" she asked, putting her drink down on the table.

"I think you're the most beautiful girl I have ever seen," said Polly staring at Katya as she stood leaning against the table.

"Would you like to take my picture?" she asked, looking

straight into his eyes.

Polly put his drink down on the floor next to the sofa and reached for his camera bag. He picked out his camera.

"Aye, that would be champion, pet. I've put a new film in tonight."

"Where is best?"

"Over by the window, the light is better there," said Polly, and at fourteen floors up they would not be overlooked.

She looked at Polly and he started to frame the shot. Katya undid the next two buttons on her blouse; her bra totally exposed. She felt suddenly wanton and desirable. Two clicks, two flashes.

"Shall I take this off?"

Polly nodded and she took off her top. She'd had no training, but, without any hint of self-consciousness, she found herself posing provocatively for the camera.

"That's champion," was all Polly could say.

She undid the button to her jeans and pulled down the zip and gently eased them off watching Polly's face for his reaction. His face was reddening.

Katya stood there in her underwear continuing her seductive posturing for Polly. She had no idea where it was coming from, just following her instincts. She felt alive. Three more flashes. Then, she slowly removed her bra. Her breasts firm, her nipples fully erect, she put her hands over them, teasing Polly, and then dropped her arms to her side. Polly gulped, trying to maintain his composure.

Four more flashes as she posed in different positions, guided by her photographer.

"Over on the sofa."

Katya obeyed and lay down; he took several more pictures.

"Would you like to see the rest?"

Polly couldn't speak as she slowly pulled down her panties.

Polly's nerves were going to get the better of him; camera shake was starting to become a real issue. He paused, trying to slow things down. He wanted to take beautiful photos, but he also wanted her, and it was starting to become obvious.

Katya could see Polly was aroused and she loved it. The power, the thought of how she could make him feel; she controlled him now. He took the remaining shots of Katya with her on the sofa, lying on her back, on her stomach; she had nothing to hide from him now. The camera stopped clicking, the film exhausted. "That's all I'm afraid."

Polly sat down next to her on the sofa. She took his arm and pulled him onto her, and their lips met. They kissed passionately; Katya had never known such intensity. Polly's hands moved to her breasts and he gently started fondling them. She tilted her head back, moaning softly as Polly broke from the kiss and started sucking her nipples like a baby.

She tugged at his tracksuit bottoms and pulled them down. His boxers came with them and his erection was now in front of her. She held it in her hand, rubbing, caressing... loving every second.

"Just a sec, pet," said Polly and he went to his jacket and pulled out a condom and slipped it on. She wasn't sure if he was presumptuous or sensible but right now she didn't care. She just wanted him.

She lay on the sofa and gasped as she felt his hardness enter her.

It was over far too quickly and, as sexual Olympics go, would not have won a gold medal. She hadn't climaxed but as she lay there holding Polly in her arms, she felt at peace and a deep contentment.

Later, they made love again later. It was slower, more satisfying, and this time she did come.

Katya would have liked him to stay but she had to think of Melos, so it was almost midnight when they said their goodbyes. Polly promised to call again soon to show her the photographs.

After he had gone she ran a shower and thought about the evening; it gave her a warm glow. Then she had a thought; how could the same act create such differing emotions? Just a few weeks ago she had killed a man for doing what Polly had done to her. What had happened to her? Where did this liberation come from, because liberation is what it was? Was it some form of dissociating response, a reaction to the traumas of her escape from Kosovo? Maybe... all she knew was that it felt so right. She hadn't experienced anything like it before, not with anyone, not even Ibi who had been her only lover until now. She had trusted her instincts.

Her mind suddenly thought of her husband and sadness crept over her - not guilt, she hadn't done anything wrong, but of missed opportunities.

Chapter Fourteen

Katya had slept but restlessly, going over the events of the previous evening. She knew very little about Polly apart from the brief meetings they had had, but she felt comfortable with him. There was the age difference, however, and that bothered her. Although it was only five years, she was a lot worldlier than Polly. She recognised she would have to guide the relationship along slowly if it was going to develop further than just a physical thing or, worse still, be a one night stand.

Today was to be their first unaccompanied trip to Gateshead to draw their benefits and Katya called for Edi just after the morning rush hour. She and Arjeta were ready and with Melos in his buggy, they left for the bus stop. When they got there, Bigsy was also waiting for his own journey to the benefits office and Katya said hello and introduced him to Edi.

"Hiya, pet how are you doing? How's the bonny lad?" he asked, looking at Melos.

"Very good, thank you," Katya replied.

The bus came and he sat opposite to them and they made small talk during the journey, Katya involving Edi at every opportunity. Bigsy asked Edi how long she had known Katya, where she lived in Kosovo, were they following events on the news – if not he could fill them in; when did they think they would be going home, and so on. Then he had a thought.

"What're you doing Saturday night?" he asked. "Only there's a good band on at the club, 'Why-Aye Sis'. They're brilliant. You'll be very welcome, and it'll be a great night?"

He could tell the girls looked uncertain and he tried to reassure them.

"Our Carole's going, like, and some of our mates. It'll be a good chance to meet some more people."

Katya translated for Edi, although she had worked out the meaning herself.

Edi responded to Katya in Albanian. Bigsy looked bemused.

"No, we are not doing anything. We would love to come. That is very kind," said Katya.

Edi smiled but spoke to Katya in Albanian to express concern about Arjeta. Katya outline Edi's worries to Bigsy.

"Nah, don't you fret, pet. It'll be no bother. Saturday night's family night, there'll be plenty of kiddies about."

Katya checked the translation and relayed it to Edi. Reassured, she nodded and smiled.

They reached Gateshead and joined the queue at the benefits office and said goodbye to Bigsy, who was off to the Post Office to draw out his parents' pensions. When they reached their turn, it was Ruby who was waiting to serve them and that made things a lot easier. They completed the paperwork and their allowances were paid, eighty pounds and some change. Katya put her money in her purse, and her purse in her bag, grateful that she was now able to buy some food and maybe something for the wardrobe. Edi was keen to go to the supermarket they had visited with Clara and so they walked along the covered shopping area.

Just before they reached the store entrance, Katya noticed there was a small bureau-de-change kiosk with one till and a cashier. She went to the window and, rummaging in her purse found, the now very dog-eared ten deutschemark note. She presented it to the cashier and after a moment or two, he gave Katya a five-pound note and some more loose change. She watched the cashier put the note in his till and thought about the journey that it had made. He would have no idea.

They spent some time loading up their trolleys with supplies. Edi was looking for more of the traditional basics that she was familiar with back on the farm, vegetables, fruit, chicken, even rabbit which she had cooked many times. Her father was good with a shotgun, she explained. Katya was looking to be more adventurous and wanted to try some of the ready-meals and sauces on offer. She looked at the rows and rows of food – Italian, Mexican, Chinese, Indian, Thai. The variety was incredible compared with the meagre offerings in the local store in Lapugovac, especially since the blockade; they were lucky to get even the basics. Momentarily, Katya's thoughts went back to the refugee camp and she wondered how her former inmates were fairing.

Katya watched Edi and was concerned that she was also loading up chocolate bars, snacks and other treats, presumably for Arjeta. She then went to the clothes section and bought a couple of outfits suitable for a three-year-old girl.

"Be careful Edi, that money will have to last until next week; you won't be getting any more."

Edi looked a bit sheepish. "It will be ok; I just want to give Arjeta something special to make up for the hardship. Don't worry I will manage."

Katya could see Edi was becoming more confident now and appeared less uncomfortable in her new surroundings. She had got used to the noise and bustle and was starting to use her English much more.

They made their way back to the flats and Katya stayed with Edi for a while before returning to her 1410 to put the shopping away and feed Melos. She looked out of the window, hoping to see the kite flying, but Polly would be at college now. She hoped she would see him later.

Just after lunch, the phone rang. Katya was hoping it was Polly; he now had her number, but it was Clara.

"Hiya Katya, girl, I've been making a few enquiries... Would you be interested in a part-time teaching assistant role at the local pre-school centre? It's not far from you? Twenty hours a week... pay's not bad, five pounds twenty an hour."

Katya was taken aback, momentarily.

She took in the offer and agreed immediately. "Yes, of course. That would be wonderful."

It would mean she could be productive again; she missed interacting with children and being able to make a difference. She also thought it might open up opportunities to get back into a full-time teaching role, with slightly older children, which was what Katya ideally wanted.

"You'll need to have an interview, but they want you to start next Monday. What do you think?" said Clara.

Katya couldn't contain her excitement. "Yes, yes, that will be fine, thank you. What will they want me to do?"

Clara explained the role would not be babysitting but trying to engage young children by play and education giving them a good grounding before they started proper school.

"You'll have a mentor, one of the other teachers, who'll sit with you for a short time to show you what they do and help you settle in. It sounds ideal... Now that I know you're interested; I'll give the centre manager a call to meet you for an interview... her name's Mel Henderson."

"Thank you, that is very kind," said Katya.

Clara rang off and Katya sat for a moment taking it all in. She was really excited but a bit daunted at the same time She was dying to tell someone, but Carole was at work.

A few minutes later there was another buzzing noise from her phone; it was different from the normal ring. She had received her first text message. She pressed the green button and the message was revealed. '*Photos r gr8, c u l8er Polly xx*'.

It was like a secret code and she had no idea what it meant; nor did she know how to text back. She also noticed there was a tiny picture of a flashing battery in the top right-hand corner of the screen which she deduced must indicate the battery was running out. She looked for the box which came with the phone which was in the kitchen drawer and looked inside. Clara had said there was a battery charger inside but hadn't opened the box. She found the device and plugged one end into the slot in the bottom of the phone and plugged the other end into the wall socket and flicked the switch down. A notice flashed up saying *'battery charging'* and Katya felt pleased with this discovery. She started to read through the instruction book that was also in the box, but was baffled by the language; she would ask Polly.

Bigsy had spent the morning with his parents having collected their pensions and was concerned that his father's health was deteriorating. He noticed he was coughing far more frequently and, for his age, seemed frail. Mar said he had not left his chair in front of the television all week except for food, sleep and the call of nature.

While Mar was making a brew, Bigsy tried to cheer him up. "You'll never guess what, Da... I'm going to Wembley to see the Mags... You'll be able to see us on the telly," he joked.

His father just looked at Bigsy. "That's nice," he managed to respond.

"What's this about the cup final?" said Mar as she brought in the tea and a plate of Digestive biscuits. Bigsy explained his good fortune.

He looked at his father. "He doesn't look too good."

"No, I called the doctor yesterday, but he just fobbed us off with some more cough medicine. To be honest, I don't think they've got a clue what's wrong with him... I told him, why don't you do some proper tests, like, but he didn't want to know."

"Why did you not say, Mar...? You should have rung me, I'd have sorted him out," said Bigsy.

"Didn't want to trouble you, Brian. You've got enough to see to without worrying about us an' all," said Mar.

After his tea and a brief catch up, Bigsy left to get back to the flats. He shouted to his father but there was no response; he'd drifted off to sleep, then he kissed his mother on the cheek.

"I'll pop 'round again later in the week, but make sure you call me if he doesn't get any better."

"Aye, pet, will do," said Mar as Bigsy left the bungalow.

Carole returned home at her usual time looking drained.

"You look knackered, pet, you ok?" greeted Bigsy as she came through the door.

"I'm ok pet, but nookie will be off the agenda for a bit, if you catch me drift."

"No problem pet, you put your feet up and I'll get us a brew." Bigsy feigned disappointment; it would give him a chance to recover. "Would you like us to make the tea?" he offered, which was pretty well unheard of.

"It's ok pet… I'll just have a jacket potato and some salad. There's a shepherd's pie in the fridge you can have. It won't take long in the microwave."

Bigsy went into the kitchen and returned with two mugs of tea.

"Did you see Mar and your Dad today?" asked Carole. as she took a sip of the reviving drink.

"Aye, Dad's getting worse I think. Been stuck in his chair all week," said Bigsy, with a look of concern.

"Has Mar called the doctor?"

"Aye, but they're not interested. Fobbed 'em off with some more cough medicine. I told Mar to ring the doc again if he gets worse. Said I'll go 'round there; soon sort them medics out… I reckon, if they lived in Morpeth it would be different, you mark my words."

"Aye, you're not wrong there," said Carole.

"I saw Katya and the other Kossie on the bus this morning. I invited them to the club on Saturday. Thought they can sit with us… You don't mind do you, pet?"

"Of course not, no, that'll be champion, that," replied Carole. "I'll be glad of the company."

Bigsy was usually bonding with his buddies and doing business with copious broons whenever they visited the club, frequently leaving Carole on her own.

Earlier that evening, Katya received another call from Clara to say she had arranged for her to meet Mel Henderson at the school the following morning at ten o'clock. She gave Katya the directions, it was only a twenty-minute walk or so. Katya was excited at the prospects of being with children again.

After a light meal of vegetable soup and some bread she put Melos to bed around seven o'clock and took a shower. She didn't know whether Polly would call but reading his text message again, thought he might. She chose a tee shirt and a pair of slacks but decided to dispense with a bra; she was feeling adventurous.

There was still a glass of wine left from the previous night which she poured out and sipped. She had bought another bottle while at the supermarket which she would open if necessary.

She switched on the TV but couldn't concentrate. Eight o'clock came, eight-thirty, nine o'clock. She stared out of the window; it was raining, and her mood began to match the weather. Then, at about nine-fifteen, there was a knock on the door. Katya's heart raced. She opened it and there was Polly, carrying a photo album. Katya smiled and invited him in.

"I wasn't sure if you would come today or not."

"Did you not get my text?"

"Yes," replied Katya, "but I couldn't understand it."

Polly made a gesture that involved hitting his forehead with the palm of his hand, which indicated, 'what an idiot'.

"I'm sorry pet, I didn't think. I was trying to get here sooner, like, but I had an assignment to finish for tomorrow and I've run out of credit on my phone, so I couldn't call you."

"That's ok. I'll forgive you," she teased.

She offered him a drink. "Only wine I'm afraid," and she opened the other bottle.

She gave Polly a glass and he looked at her. "You look amazin', pet."

"Thank you," said Katya and she sat down next to him on the sofa and folded her legs underneath her, facing Polly. She took a sip of wine. Polly was wearing his obligatory tee shirt and tracksuit bottoms, although both were different from the previous night.

"So, you have the pictures?" asked Katya, unable to contain her excitement.

Polly handed her the photo album. "Aye, I've got a new book for these," he explained. He watched her as she opened the cover.

Katya gasped.

She searched for the right words but not really coming close. "Wow, Polly, these are... wonderful."

She started turning the pages slowly, one at a time examining each picture in turn. Polly had captured something in her, which she had difficulty in recognising; it looked like a different person. For a start, it was so out of character; she would never do this. When it came to sex, she had always been slightly self-conscious and reserved. Even with Ibi, although she was content, she was always a little inhibited; she preferred the lights out. But this was something totally different; passionate, erotic even, an emotion she had never experienced before.

As she turned the pages, she could feel herself getting more and more aroused. She looked at Polly. His face was flushed. They started kissing, deep and urgent, tongues working overtime. He started to feel her breasts through her tee-shirt, and she moaned in pleasure. She stroked him through his tracksuit and could feel him hard and firm and they were soon naked on the floor. After the rush of the previous night, this was more measured, Polly taking his time, trying new positions to fulfil his partner. Katya was in ecstasy.

When they were both exhausted, Katya went to the kitchen and made them both a coffee. She returned carrying two mugs and sat close to Polly on the sofa. He put his arm around her.

There was so much she wanted to say, but, instead, there was reflective silence as they sipped their drinks. She had no intention of getting into any deep analysis; just treasure the moment.

Katya eventually initiated the conversation.

"Will you be flying your kite again soon?"

"Aye, pet, tomorrow probably, if there's a wind."

"Oh, that is good, I will like to join you. It is good for Melos to have the fresh air and he enjoys watching the kite."

"Aye," replied Polly.

"Clara called me today," continued Katya.

"Clara?" queried Polly.

"Yes, she is from the, er... council; she is looking after me and Edi. She told me there is a teacher's job at the school and I am going to meet them for a... er... how you say...? Er, interview... tomorrow," said Katy, and explained what she would be doing.

"Wow, that's champion, pet. I'm pleased for yas. I hope you get it." He kissed her on the forehead affectionately.

She continued recounting her day.

"Bigsy was on the bus this morning. He's invited Edi and me to the go with him and Carole on Saturday night."

"What the 'Why-Aye Sis' gig?"

"I think so. I can't remember."

"That's great. I'll be there as well. I know the drummer; he goes to the same college as me. They've asked me to take some photos of the band for publicity, like. I'll be able to see you there."

"That will be good," said Katya.

It was gone eleven before Polly left; he had college in the morning. Katya escorted him to the door, and they kissed.

"I'll call you tomorrow, pet, after I've topped up the credit on my phone."

The next day, Katya was experiencing a mixture of excitement and anxiety as she took Melos in the buggy to the appointment with Ms Henderson at the Pre-school centre.

As she passed the bus stop on the other side of the road, she noticed Edi and Arjeta getting onto the Hoppa. She called out but Edi hadn't heard, or, if she had, she had ignored Katya. She was surprised and a little concerned about this as Edi had said nothing about going into town and was unsure how she would cope on her own. It would be pointless trying to ring her, she hadn't even switched the phone on to Katya's knowledge. She would call round later to find out what was going on.

Katya arrived at the Pre-school centre just before her allotted time at ten o'clock. It was in a large, fairly run-down building, not far from the shops at the bottom of the estate. She went to the reception office just inside the main entrance door where a heavy-set woman wearing a smock was typing something on a computer keyboard. Katya introduced herself.

"I'm Sonia," said the receptionist. "You must be calling about the new assistant's position. I will get Mel for you... take a seat," and she disappeared through another door where Katya could hear children singing.

Katya sat down on one of the seats in front of the desk. A few minutes later, another lady came through the same door and introduced herself. "Hi, I'm Melanie Henderson, everybody calls me Mel. I'm the manager of the Seaton Pre-school centre." She shook Katya's hand.

She would be in her mid-thirties, medium build, brown hair cropped very short, with a small diamond stud in the side of her nose. Katya introduced herself.

"Nice to meet you... come through," said the manager.

Mel led her through what appeared to be a small sports hall - there was a badminton court painted on the wooden floor with climbing bars on the two side perimeter walls. Children's drawings were pinned to cork-boards on the back wall. About twenty or thirty children were sat with a teacher talking to them. They went into another room which led off from the main hall and into a small office. There looked to be a kitchen opposite. It brought back memories of the NATO centre at Pec.

Katya noticed that Mel did not have a local accent and it was easier for her to understand. She parked the buggy and sat down. Mel went to make some coffee and came back with two mugs.

"Would your son like anything?"

"No, he's fine."

"He's a lovely looking lad," said Mel taking a sip of coffee.

Katya started to relax; this was not going to be the interrogation she had feared.

They talked for almost two hours, Mel asking a lot of questions about Katya's training and the work she had done in Kosovo, how she felt about working with the children. The manager took notes. She outlined the work of the Centre, the curriculum they were expected to cover, hours she would work and the administration that would be required. She would need Katya's passport and several forms filling.

"What about Melos?" asked Katya, after Mel had finished detailing the administration.

"It's fine, you can bring him. Several of the staff have their kids with them."

Mel concluded the interview.

"Any more questions?" asked Mel.

Katya shook her head. "No."

Mel looked at her. "Ok." She paused and pushed her notes to one side. "Well, Katya, Clara's spoken highly of you and I have to say I've been impressed with your experience and background during the interview, so, I'll be very happy to take you on."

Katya was overjoyed. "Thank you."

"There's a probationary period of one month. Then your position will be confirmed," said Mel. "Come on, I'll show you around and introduce you to one or two people."

Mel got up and Katya followed her back to the main teaching area with Melos asleep in the buggy. She was introduced to other members of the team. Katya was trying to take in everything and remember the names.

After another half an hour, Katya left the building and walked back to the flats with a feeling of excitement about her new job. She couldn't wait to start.

Back in Gateshead, Edi had managed to get to the bus station without any problems; the bus driver had recognised her and let her on without paying. She made her way to the supermarket just along the mall from the Interchange and went straight to the children's section with Arjeta in tow.

She looked at the racks of clothes and toys and Arjeta was having a great time playing with the dolls and cartoon figures. Edi had taken a carrier bag with her from her trip the previous day and as she saw something that Arjeta liked she dropped it into the bag. After a half an hour, the bag was full of stuff. Finally, she hung the old carrier bag on the back of the trolley, took a couple of dresses from a shelf and dropped them into her trolley and went to the checkout.

Once there, the cashier scanned the two dresses and told her the price, sixteen pounds forty-nine. Edi took out a twenty-pound note from her purse and gave it to the cashier who gave her change. The dresses were placed in a new carrier bag. Edi wheeled the trolley to the front entrance and took the old bag off the back and bundled the two carriers under her arms and walked out of the store.

Then all hell broke loose.

Bells and sirens echoed around the mall and people were rushing everywhere. Two tough-looking security guards descended on Edi and held her by her arms. She screamed in Albanian at them. Arjeta was in shock, unable to take in what was happening. The guards bundled Edi back into the store through a side door and into an office which had a desk and two chairs. Behind the desk was a bank of security camera monitors and a man in the same security firm uniform was sat on another chair staring intently at them. Iron railings protecting the windows which were of frosted glass. They closed the heavy metal door behind them; it was like a prison cell.

Edi was petrified and was still screaming abuse in Albanian when a woman, formally dressed in a creased business suit, walked in through another door behind them. The guards still had hold of Edi who was struggling and cursing them. Arjeta by this time was crying uncontrollably. The woman asked Edi to open the large carrier and the lady took out all the items and placed them on the table. They still had their security tags on them.

"Where is your receipt for these?"

"Nuk po kuptoj!" she kept shouting. "I don't understand."

One of the security guards took her purse and opened it looking for identification. Edi screamed at them and was getting hysterical. In her purse they found Clara's business card and seeing she was a community liaison officer rang the contact number. It was answered straight away.

"Clara Davenport, Community liaison office," was the reply, and the woman spoke.

"My name is Yvonne Stacy, head of security at Pricewise Departmental Store in Gateshead. We have a... Edona Bukosi," she spelt out the names; "in custody here at the store. She was caught shoplifting. We cannot interview her; she doesn't seem to understand English and she's hysterical."

Clara explained who Edi was and the woman's demeanour changed. She asked the guards to let her go and for Edi to sit down. She asked one of the men to get a cup of tea and some orange juice for Arjeta who was by now convulsing with fear. She then gave the phone to Edi who listened to Clara and gradually she calmed down. Edi passed the phone back to the woman and she continued her discussion with Clara. The call finished and she spoke slowly to Edi. "You ... wait... there... Clara... is... coming... here."

"Clara... here...? That is good," said Edi, still shaking and sobbing.

It was almost half an hour before Clara arrived. She had tried to reach Katya to help with translation, but her phone was switched off.

There was a look of relief on Edi's face when Clara entered the room, she kept saying, "I'm sorry, so sorry," and started to weep pitifully. This started Arjeta crying again, seeing her mother upset. Clara had some real damage limitation to do. The Kosovan refugees were high-profile and if this was to get into the papers, it could jeopardise a lot of hard work.

"How much are we talking about?" asked Clara.

"Over eighty pounds worth of items," said the Head of Security, gravely.

"Can you give me an exact figure?" asked Clara.

"Exactly...? Eighty-four pounds seventeen pence," replied the woman.

Clara continued. "You have no idea what these people have been through. Edi has already been diagnosed with post-traumatic stress disorder and was making good progress; goodness knows what this episode will do to her."

"That's not really my problem," said the woman. "She has been caught shoplifting... red-handed."

"Yes I know, and I am sorry for that, but your company has just donated a lot of money towards the aid effort for the refugees and Edi received some free goods from here last week. She's probably got confused."

Clara paused, took out her chequebook from her bag and started writing. "I am going to pay for the items... Here's my cheque, and I want you to let her off with a caution, no police and no journalists. Do we have a deal?"

"Well, it's not standard procedure or company policy," said the woman.

"I can always talk to Sir Lucas if you prefer. He has been extremely supportive," Clara said, referring to Sir Lucas Menzies, the company chairman who recently chaired a meeting with the Refugee Council which Clara had attended.

"No... No... I am sure we can come to some... arrangement," said the lady, and Clara picked up the two carrier bags and put all the items from the desk into them. She explained to Edi they were going home.

"No polici?" asked Edi.

"No Edi... no polici," said Clara.

Edi looked at Clara, tears flowing down her cheeks. "*Faleminderit*, thank you."

She turned to Yvonne, picking up the lady's hand and holding it to her face pitifully. "*Faleminderit*, thank you, thank you."

Yvonne, showing little emotion, unlocked the metal door and escorted Clara, Edi and Arjeta out onto the street through a side entrance.

"Follow me," Clara said to Edi. "I am in the multi-story," which of course she didn't understand but she did as she was told.

Clara took Edi back to the flats in her car and parked in the service area. They made their way to Edi's flat and Clara said she would see if Katya was at home. It was gone twelve o'clock by this time.

Having left Edi, Clara took the lift and knocked on Katya's door. Katya had just returned from her interview at the school. Before she could say anything, Clara spoke to her. "Can you come down to Edi's? There's been a bit of a problem."

"Of course... what has happened?"

Katya grabbed her jacket, put Melos in his buggy and followed Clara down to the sixth floor. Clara outlined the incident as they took the lift.

When they arrived at Edi's, she opened the door and hugged Katya sobbing bitterly. Arjeta pushed the buggy into the corner and started playing with Melos. Clara went into the kitchen and made herself a mug of coffee and then sat down to find out why Edi was trying to steal the goods from the store. Katya translated.

Edi was staring blankly ahead, not making eye-contact. She replied in Albanian, Katya translated for Clara.

"I do not know..." She looked down; her hands wringing together, under, over; fingers nervously entwining then unentwining, tears starting to fall down her cheeks. "I just wanted some new clothes and things for Arjeta. She has suffered so much."

"I understand," said Clara "But it could have been very serious. You could have gone to court or even been sent home." Katya translated.

This horrified Edi and she looked at Clara in despair. "I am so sorry," she replied in English. "I am so sorry."

Clara explained that she had paid for the goods to stop it going further but would need Edi to pay it back every week from her benefit allowance. Edi began to cry again.

"Yes, er… I will pay, of course… Thank you, thank you."

"Ok… It's alright." Clara unfolded her arms and leaned forward slightly continuing in a more conciliatory manner. "I have also contacted Doctor Peterson and asked her to come and talk to you again. She is going to call 'round in the morning."

Katya translated.

Edi looked at the pair, her face etched in despair. "*Faleminderit*, thank you."

Clara and Katya stayed for a while until they were satisfied that Edi was calm, but as they left, Clara asked Katya to keep a close eye on her.

Later that afternoon Katya was watching from the window and spotted Polly flying a kite on the rec. She wanted to see him after the trauma with Edi and made her way with Melos in his buggy to watch.

As soon as she got to the playing field where he was working his kite, he beckoned her over and asked her to take hold of the string. He showed her how, by pulling it would make the kite rise and letting it out would cause it to drop. But there was an art to it, knowing when to pull and when to let it out, depending on the strength of the wind.

The first time Katya went solo, the kite just crashed to the ground but fortunately, it wasn't damaged. Polly laughed and showed her again. Melos looked out from his buggy and appeared to be smiling as he watched the two of them.

Then something caught Polly's attention; something dark running at speed towards them. It got closer and he could see it was a dog, which was not unusual on the rec; but this one was different. He was not on a lead for a start, contrary to the many notices surrounding the park, and it looked savage. It was snarling rather than barking and was running very fast close to the ground as if to make it more aerodynamic.

Katya gasped in horror as she, too, noticed. It was making straight for the buggy.

They were only four or five yards away from the boy, but it seemed much further. Without thinking, Polly hurled himself at the dog, which was now only feet away. The dog grabbed Polly's left arm between its teeth and held on. Polly was wrestling with it, hitting it with his other fist trying to get it to let go. The dog continued to snarl, foam and saliva dripping from his mouth, shaking Polly's arm like a toy doll.

Just then, a teenager appeared, out of breath, and carrying a dog lead.

"Sabre, down, down Sabre, let go," he shouted, and he whipped the leather lead with some force down on the dog's back.

It gave a yelp. His voice must have carried some sort of authority, or it might have been the threat of another beating, the dog let go of Polly's arm.

Katya grabbed Melos from the buggy and cradled him, turning away from the dog, protecting her son. The lad grabbed hold of the dog's collar and in one movement slipped the lead through the metal ring attached to it.

"Are you ok...? He just slipped his lead, like," said the youth.

Polly recognised Rikki Rankin. The dog was still snarling, straining at the leash almost standing on two feet to get at Polly who was now sat on the ground holding his left arm. There were several ugly puncture wounds and he was bleeding profusely. It was taking all the lad's strength to keep the dog from attacking again.

"Call an ambulance," cried Polly and the youth reached for his pocket and pulled out the latest Nokia.

Rikki, tugging on the dog's lead with one hand, gave the ambulance service details of what had happened and where they were. There was a small access road to the rec which was used by the council for grass cutting and maintenance, which led to the main road; that would be their entrance. Polly pulled out a handkerchief from his pocket and Katya dabbed the bleeding as best she could.

It took around ten minutes for the ambulance to arrive and the two paramedics quickly checked his arm and stemmed the bleeding.

"We need to get you in," said one of the medics and they put Polly onto a stretcher. He was going into shock and looked as white as a sheet.

"I'm coming with you," said Katya and the paramedics lifted the stretcher into the ambulance and, as one got in the front to drive, the other lifted Melos and the buggy on board, closely followed by Katya. Rikki shouted, "I'll look after your kite for yas," and having tied the savage dog securely to a tree, wound the string onto the bobbin and put the kite under his arm.

Rikki was joined by two other lads.

"What're gonna do? Your Da'll go crazy," said one.

"I don't know..." said Rikki. "But this fookin' dog's for the knackers' yard."

Chapter Fifteen

The ambulance raced through the rush hour traffic, blue lights flashing and sirens blaring. Melos started to cry frightened by the noise and Katya picked him up to comfort him, but her thoughts were really with Polly. He was in some pain but seemed ok and the paramedics were happy he was in no danger. She held his hand for most of the journey; she had a lot to thank him for. She was in no doubt that, but for Polly's intervention, Melos could have been very badly hurt or worse.

It took only about ten minutes before they arrived at the main Accident and Emergency hospital in Gateshead. The ambulance crew wheeled Polly on the stretcher and Katya followed, pushing Melos in the buggy. They went into an emergency room and a nurse stopped Katya. "You better wait in the waiting area."

"But I want to be with him," said Katya. "He saved my baby's life."

The nurse let her through, and she watched as a doctor examined Polly's arm. The bleeding had subsided but there were a couple of nasty gashes and some puncture wounds. However, it did not look as bad as it had on the field. Polly was also beginning to get his colour back.

"It seems fairly superficial," the doctor said looking at the arm. "I don't think there is any major damage. You were lucky though you could have severed an artery. It was some dog that did this."

"A Pitbull," said Polly.

"I thought they were illegal," said the doctor.

"So did I," said Polly.

"I will get these larger tears stitched; the smaller ones we'll just tack up and bandage, and you will need a tetanus jab. You may have some battle scars to show for it depending on how the wounds heal," said the medic.

Katya was so relieved and held his good hand. "You were so brave. I thought you were going to die."

He had fully regained his senses and was smiling. Katya kissed him on his forehead.

By the time he was released, it was gone seven o'clock. His arm was in a sling and bandaged from his fingers to his elbow. There were some smaller scratches above that. He got his mobile out of his pocket with his good hand and dialled with his thumb. "I must phone me Mam, she'll be fretting."

His mother answered, "Jamie, where are you, pet...? I've been worried sick, our Bigsy came down to say you've been taken to the hospital, something about Rikki Rankin's dog."

Polly explained what had happened but played down the extent of his injuries. "I'm just leaving the hospital."

"How are you getting home, pet?" asked his mother.

"I'm waiting for a bus, Mam," replied Polly.

"You'll do no such thing, pet. Get yourself in a taxi, I'll settle up when you get back."

"Thanks Mam," said Polly and rang off.

Several taxis were hanging around the hospital and Polly hailed one. They put the buggy in the boot. Melos was fast asleep in Katya's arms. During the journey, Polly talked about his mother whom he hadn't discussed with Katya in any detail.

He explained that her name was Alison and she was the sister of Carole's mother, June. She was in her forties and had been married to Polly's father for ten years before, like so many others in the block, the family split. At that time they lived in Cramlington but moved to Heathcote Estate when they divorced. Polly was about nine-years-old at the time. Alison worked as an assistant in the accounts department for Newcastle City Council.

They arrived at the flats and Alison was in the lobby, smoking a cigarette waiting for them. She paid the driver and made a big fuss of her son. Katya had taken the buggy from the boot; Melos was now awake. Polly introduced Katya to his mother.

"Pleased to meet you," said Katya. She looked at Polly. "He was so brave, he saved Melos."

"Bigsy told us a bit about it, bought your kite back... Said Rikki Rankin bought it 'round. Let's get you inside pet, I've got a bit of tea for you," said Alison and they all got into the lift.

The lift stopped at twelve and Polly and his mother got out. Alison went to open the door to the flat, leaving Polly behind. With his mother out of earshot, Katya called out, "I'll call you tomorrow... Love you."

Polly waived his bandaged arm, "Better already Katya, pet," and winked at her.

The doors closed and Katya felt strange but in a good way. She quickly snapped out of it; she had a child who needed feeding.

Back on the playing field, moments after the ambulance left, a police van turned up and headed over to where Rikki and his mates were. The friends quickly rode off leaving Rikki to face the music. The dog was still tied to the tree, barking manically, as Rikki was trying to wrestle with the kite in the squally wind.

An officer got out wearing complete body armour and carrying a pole with a loop at the end like a lasso. He approached Rikki. "Is that your dog, son?"

"No, it's my Da's," said Rikki. "I was just walking it, like."

"Ok, well I'm going to have to take it to the pound. There's been a report that it's attacked a member of the public."

"Aye, they've just taken him away to the hospital."

"Can you control it?" asked the policeman.

"Aye," said Rikki.

"I want you to steady the dog while I get this noose on him, ok?"

It was still tied to the tree by its lead but barking threateningly. It snarled as the pair approached, white foam dripped from the corners of its mouth.

"I've got his lead on," said Rikki.

"Not taking any chances," said the policeman and he slipped the noose around the dog's head and pulled it tight.

"Now untie the lead, lad," said the policeman.

The dog was going mad trying to escape its captive and it was taking every ounce of the officer's strength to hold it.

"Jeez he's strong.... It looks like a Pitbull."

"It is," said Rikki.

"Sorry lad, but they're illegal in this country. It's against the law to have one of these."

"Aye...? Well, you'll have to talk to me Da about that," countered Rikki.

The officer opened the back of the van with his free arm and, showing a great deal of strength, lifted the animal into the back and shut the door. The barking was almost demonic by now.

He turned to Rikki and asked him his name and address and made a note. "I'll be round to see your Dad later," and he got into the van and drove away. Seeing the police leave, Rikki's mates reappeared.

"What're you gonna do?" said one of the lads again to Rikki.

"I'm gonna see a man about a dog," said Rikki.

Bigsy was about to finish his shift at the video shop when Rikki Rankin came in with his two cohorts carrying what looked like one of Polly's kites.

"Hiya Rikki, bonny lad, how're you doing?" asked Bigsy.

"I need your help, Bigsy," said Rikki and he explained the events at the park and that the police would be around later to talk to his Dad.

Bigsy of course, had a vested interest in this information as knob-head Trev was one of his clients and he certainly didn't want any unnecessary attention, certainly not from the police.

"Well, I think we better have a word with your Da, don't you?" and they walked down Brompton Road back to Rikki's house still carrying Polly's kite. Trev was in the kitchen buttering some toast when they went in.

"Hiya Bigsy, bonny lad. What do you want? We seem to be seeing a lot of yas lately," said Trev.

"There's been a bit of trouble with the dog, like," Rikki said anxiously.

Bigsy took over and outlined the story as Rikki had told him.

"The problem is Trev, we don't want to be drawing any unnecessary attention to us, like, if you catch me drift."

"Aye, I can see your point, bonny lad. What d'you want us to do, like?" asked Trev.

"Well we can't have the bizzies 'round here, can we? So I suggest you give them a call, like, and you go and hand yerself in."

Trev could see the logic and they concocted a story about how Trev was just minding it for a friend who had gone to Spain and he had no idea it was a Pitbull in the hope that they would let him off with a caution.

"But you'll have to go down the nick. We don't want 'em round here," said Bigsy and he waited while Trev made the call.

The local police station seemed happy, even pleased that Trev had offered to go to them. There was no rush for volunteers to visit Heathcote.

As Bigsy left with Polly's kite in his arms, Trev was putting his coat on to go for the bus. "And you leave the boy alone, this is down to you Trev, lad," was his parting farewell from Bigsy.

Thank goodness he was not off his face, thought Bigsy; now that would have been a problem.

Back in the flats, Bigsy stopped off at the twelfth floor to speak to Alison Polglaise and return Polly's kite. He told her that Polly had been taken to hospital after wrestling with a dog on the rec but didn't have any more information. He then went back to his flat where Carole was in the kitchen preparing dinner.

"Had a good day, pet?"

"Don't ask," said Bigsy.

The next day Bigsy had nothing special on, so he decided to

call around to his parents to see how his Dad was. His mother thought he seemed a bit better but Bigsy was not so sure. He was reasonably communicative, but he still didn't want to move out of the seat even when Bigsy offered to take him to the club for a drink. A couple of years ago he would have 'bitten your arm off', he told Wazza later.

At lunchtime, he was in the club discussing things with his buddy when his mobile rang; it was Everton.

"Give us a minute," said Bigsy and he grabbed a pen and paper from the bar and went outside. He was keen to hear what was going on.

"Aye, go on," said Bigsy when he had composed himself.

"Tings are cool again, mon," said Everton and he explained that Friday's drop was on. It was going to be a big one so Bigsy would need to be very careful with security. It would be a long night.

Everton gave Bigsy the details which he wrote down.

As well as the usual venues there were going to be two new night clubs, "Rockies'" and "Mr Flint's" in South Shields for the Ecstasy tabs, which was a bit of a trek but Bigsy knew where they were, plus there were a couple more pubs, 'for de ghanga', said Everton.

There was also a new club just over the Tyne Bridge called Scalleys, on the Waterfront, a popular haunt of clubbers. Bigsy thought this was strange as they had always kept south of the river but didn't question it. They had decided to give knob-head Trev a miss this week, given the police attention he was getting.

There would be extra amounts of merchandise due to the missing drops earlier in the week. Everton would be taking delivery from his supplier later that evening and would label and put everything together so that he would know what went where. They would need plenty of space in the boot. Bigsy made notes; drop off points, contacts and code words. "Don't forget, my mon has new wheels," Everton said. They were to meet Layton at seven-thirty at the club. Everton was confident that their operation had not been compromised.

Katya had difficulty sleeping; she was worried about Polly and realised how close she was to losing Melos. She had made a fuss of the lad and played with him until he fell asleep, which was well past his normal bed-time. In the morning she called Polly from her mobile. "How are you? I have been so worried," said Katya.

"I'm ok," said Polly. "Arm's been hurting a bit but I've taken a couple of painkillers... I'm not going to college though. I called in and told 'em what had happened. They were ok about it. I'll be fine in a couple of days."

"Thank God," said Katya.

"The bizzies came round last night... Had to make a statement."

Katya didn't understand but didn't question it; she was just relieved that Polly sounded back to his old self.

"I can come and see you later if you like," said Katya.

"Aye, that would be champion, pet."

"I need to call in on Edi, but I will see you after."

"Aye, ok, no bother, I'll be here," said Polly.

Katya and Melos called at Edi's around nine-thirty and Katya could see she had regressed. She had not bothered to make herself up, and her hair was lank and unkempt like it was when they first arrived. Again, the light and TV were on with the curtains drawn. Arjeta was sat at the table drawing, but seeing Katya, rushed to Melos to play with him.

Katya was firm with Edi.

"Look, Edi, it is no use feeling sorry for yourself. You must make an effort, or Arjeta could also start to suffer and you know what that would mean." The words shocked Edi and she started to cry.

Katya left her for a moment and made them both a coffee, then helped Edi sort herself out.

By the time Clara arrived, Edi was looking and feeling a lot better. Dr Peterson was with her and they had a long discussion about the events the previous afternoon. The doctor was trying to get to the root cause, the motivation for the shoplifting. Edi tried to explain as best she could and the doctor told her that it was not unusual for people with PTSD to act out of character, but she would continue to need support. She wanted to make sure that Edi was taking the anti-depressants which would take a few days to start working.

During the discussions, Katya mentioned to Clara that she would be starting at the Pre-school centre on Monday and wondered if it would be a good idea to take Arjeta as well as Melos to give Edi a break.

"Yes, that's an excellent idea," said Doctor Peterson. "It will also help Arjeta having contact with other children."

The idea was put to Edi who, not unexpectedly, was very reluctant, worried that Arjeta was being taken away from her. Eventually, after reassurance from Katya, she agreed.

Feeling more assured that Edi was beginning to make a slow recovery and there would be no repetition of the incident, Clara and the doctor left with the promise of a further visit the following week.

After they had gone, Katya made Edi and Arjeta some eggs and toast. She continued to counsel Edi as they ate their breakfast.

"Edi, you must try harder, we have Saturday evening to look forward to. We will meet new people there. It will be a nice time"

Edi looked aghast.

"But what if they find out about me stealing clothes?"

"They won't find out," reassured Katya.

What they didn't know was, half the estate had previous convictions in that regard; she would have nothing to worry about.

Katya was anxious to see Polly and eventually, she left Edi and made her way up to Polly's flat. He answered, wearing his usual tracksuit and tee shirt and Katya kissed him warmly.

"How are you Polly? I have been so worried."

Polly held up his arm which was now out of the sling. "Feeling a lot better, thanks. I'll be able to juggle again in no time. Fancy a brew?"

"Yes, please," Katya replied and sat down on a chair while he made a coffee.

She looked around at the family photos on the bookshelves. The room definitely had a woman's touch.

"My Mam likes to have photos around," said Polly, as he walked in with the drinks, noticing that Katya was looking at the pictures.

"I was just looking at the photographs of when you were a boy... So nice."

"I don't know about that, pet," replied Polly.

"Did you mean what you said when you were in the lift last night pet?" asked Polly as he handed Katya a mug.

"Yes," replied Katya, knowing exactly to what Polly was referring. "I have only known you for a short time, but you have made me live again. There were times in Kosovo when I thought I would die. Things happened that I cannot talk about... but now... now I feel I can look forward and you have given me that."

"Sometime, when you feel up to it pet, you can tell me about your life back home," said Polly.

"I already feel this is my home now," said Katya.

"I feel the same way," said Polly looking into her eyes, and they kissed again, this time more passionately. Melos right on cue started to grizzle and they broke off and laughed.

"You can come 'round tonight if you want, about nine after Melos is in bed." She paused. "You can stay with me the night... if your mother doesn't mind."

Polly kissed her again. "Aye, I would like that, pet. I'll take another day off college, they'll be ok... and don't worry about my Mam, I'm a big boy now."

Katya felt a warm glow.

That evening, after dinner, Bigsy was recovering from football training. He had kept his word and given Rikki Rankin some coaching and was sat reading the evening paper with a cup of tea. Carole was watching TV.

"Have you heard how our Polly is today, pet?" she asked.

"Aye, I rang Alison this morning and she said he was on the mend."

Suddenly as he scanned the pages, he noticed a picture, a sight that made his heart almost stop.

"Fookin' hell...! Shite no...! Oh my god...!"

He read again; "Jeez no!"

"Are you ok, pet?" asked Carole. "You look like you've seen a ghost."

"Aye, pet... I've just got to see Wazza... Won't be long," and he got up from his seat and dialled Wazza's number. "Get down the stairs now. I'll meet you in the lobby. Can't talk. I'll tell you when I see you."

"Where're you going with the paper, pet?" asked Carole.

"Just some business... Nottin' to worry about."

He grabbed his jacket from behind the door and left with Carole wondering what the urgency was.

Bigsy got to the lobby in the lift just as Wazza was coming down the stairs.

"What's up Bigsy lad? Is it about the drop tomorrow?"

Not answering Wazza's question, Bigsy opened up the paper and showed him the headlines:

"Missing Policeman's body found on South Shields beach."

Under the dimmed lights of the tower block lobby, they both read the article:

'Police confirmed that the body of a man found on the beach at South Shields last night was that of a missing police officer, Craig Mackenzie (34). Detective Sergeant Mackenzie had been reported missing while on duty since Saturday night. Police would give no further details. D.S. Mackenzie was married with two young children and came from Morpeth. This afternoon

the Chief Constable paid tribute to the officer saying he had served the force and community with distinction and would be sadly missed by his colleagues. His thoughts went out to his wife Jean and the two boys. The police would not confirm how D.S. Mackenzie died but said they were treating his death as suspicious.'

"So?" said Wazza.

"Look at the picture, man!" said Bigsy.

"Fookin' hell!" said Wazza.

"Aye, you're not wrong there," said Bigsy.

"Hughie Bonner!" said Wazza, recognising the man on the grainy marriage photograph that some hack had retrieved from the grieving widow.

"What you going to do, Bigsy, lad?"

"I have no idea, man, but whoever did this is going to have his balls stomped on big time if they get caught, that's for sure," said Bigsy.

Katya awoke Friday morning with Polly beside her. He was still sleeping, and she wanted to hold him. It was the first time she had slept with anyone for a long time and she realised how much she had missed the closeness and security of someone next to her. She thought of their love-making the previous night and felt a warm glow.

She could hear Melos wanting his breakfast so, slipping on a pair of pants and a tee shirt; she went to his cot and picked him up. She didn't know how anyone could sleep through a baby crying, but then Polly was a student. She put Melos in his recliner, turned on the television and went to the kitchen to make two cups of coffee. As the kettle was boiling, she watched the news from Kosovo on the TV and there was no change in the situation. Peace still seemed a distant dream.

She took in a cup to Polly and stood there for a moment watching him, and then smiled as he started to stir.

"What time is it?" asked Polly with a groan.

"Half-past seven," replied Katya.

"Aw no," he groaned. "That's the middle of the night for a student when he's off college." Then he winced in pain as he moved his arm.

"How is your arm?" asked Katya, seeing Polly's discomfort.

"Sore, but getting there," said Polly, moving his arm up and down to stimulate the circulation.

"What are you doing today?" she asked.

He winced again as he gingerly sat up to drink his coffee.

"I've got some course work to finish off. I wasn't able to do much yesterday."

"Yes, you must study hard," said Katya and smiled.

"I need to call in on Edi and spend some time with her. She is not well I think. The doctor said she is... er, having problems caused by what she went through in Kosovo. I said I would watch her and make sure she is ok."

"Are you coming back to bed, pet?" said Polly as he finished his drink.

"I need to feed Melos, I am sorry. I'll make us some breakfast in a minute."

"Aye, ok," said Polly. "I'll get up in a sec."

Back on the sixth floor, Edi was sitting down, eating some cereal and watching the TV. She too had been watching the news and, although she couldn't understand all the dialogue, she was able to glean some comprehension and it didn't look good.

She looked in her purse, realising she would need some more milk this morning but was horrified when she worked out how much she had left. It was less than ten pounds and it would be nearly five days before she could get any more money. She couldn't keep borrowing off Katya, it would not be fair; she had to think of another way to get some cash for her and Arjeta. One solution came to mind.

She got washed and dressed and told Arjeta she was just going to the shops she would not be long. Arjeta shouted and screamed, she wanted to go too, but Edi firmly told her to stay and finish her picture, she would only be a few minutes. Picking up her purse, she shut the door, she could hear Arjeta screaming, "Mami, mami".

She went to Mr Ali's shop and got a bottle of milk from the dairy section. She was also looking for something else. She had a plan which had worked in the camp. She went through all the aisles but couldn't see what she wanted so she went to the counter to pay. Then looking at the cigarettes and medicines behind the counter she spotted what she was searching for.

Mr Ali was his usual jovial self and asked how Edi was, and her daughter, and how she was settling in. She found she could understand most of what he was saying and was able to answer, "I am well thank you, Arjeta is fine." She placed the milk on the counter and Mr Ali put it in a bag.

"That will be sixty-four pence. Was there anything else?" and she looked at the medicines and other goods behind the counter and pointed.

"This?" asked Mr Ali, pointing at some headache pills.

"No," replied Edi and he pointed to a heartburn cure.

"No", and Edi was leaning over almost within touching distance of what she wanted. Then Mr Ali twigged.

"These?" he asked, somewhat shocked and took down a pack of three condoms.

"Yes... please," Edi confirmed.

Mr Ali looked somewhat quizzical and, unwittingly, with some disapproval. He quickly put them in her bag; luckily, the counter was empty, and he took the money.

Edi hurried back upstairs. One hurdle out of the way, now the question was how she was going to find customers.

At the camp it was a lot different, the men had approached her, but somehow she was going to have to find suitable clients herself, and at this moment she didn't know where to start. Edi also knew if she was going to earn any money, she was going to have to change a few things. She looked in the mirror and realised that the way she looked would not attract anyone; there was work to do.

While she was considering her idea, she started to feel a lot better; her depression seemed to lift. She had an objective, a goal which would help her and Arjeta and give them the lifestyle they deserved. She went to the bathroom and started to look at her limited supply of make-up. She would ask Katya who seemed to have plenty. She had a plan.

When Katya arrived later that morning, she was surprised to see Edi in a more positive frame of mind; after yesterday, Katya was expecting something different. Arjeta seemed happy playing with a doll which was part of the result of the previous day's escapade at the supermarket. Edi asked Katya if she could borrow some make-up for the visit to the club tomorrow evening.

"Of course, I will bring some down tomorrow morning."

Bigsy had been on the phone early to Wazza. Given the Hughie Bonner situation he was trying to think of some sort of contingency plan but without knowing what was going on, they had nothing to work with, so Bigsy decided that they should just carry on as normal. They would meet at the club as planned.

That evening Bigsy had been more nervous than usual but tried not to show it to Carole. She had finished her period and was thinking of outfits to wear for the gig at the club the following night.

"It'll be good for you to let your hair down; you've been a bit peaky these last couple of days... And you've been off your food a bit, pet, an' all, which is not like you. You hardly touched your mash tonight."

She got off the sofa and went to Bigsy who was staring out the window. "And don't think of saving yourself tomorrow night either, I've got plans for you." She leaned up and kissed his cheek. "And no getting lagged up either. I think it's about time you had one of my special massages."

She winked at Bigsy.

Now, this did start to register; Carole's special massage was a particular treat. Bigsy wondered what the occasion was as it tended to happen only when a) Carole was drunk, b) when she had had a particularly good day shopping or c) it was Bigsy's birthday, and that wasn't until September.

Bigsy turned from the window and his brooding. "I'm sorry, pet, got a lot on my mind just now. I'll be fine for tomorrow," said Bigsy and checked his watch.

He grabbed his jacket. "Sorry pet, got to go. I'll be late in, another delivery to make tonight. Don't worry about waiting up," and he blew her a kiss and headed for the precinct.

Wazza and Chirpie were waiting in the service area as Bigsy exited the lobby. The music was again turned off. He got in and as they drove away, he decided to share his concerns about the Hugh Bonner situation with his buddies; he had not seen Chirpie since the newspaper story.

As practical and to the point as ever, Chirpie expressed his views. "As I see it we've done nothing wrong. We didn't kill the guy and they can't prove anything that connects us to those that did."

"The problem with that argument, bonnie lad, is that we have a pretty good idea who was behind it and it was probably due to our tip-off, which probably makes us an accessory to murder, like," commented Bigsy dolefully.

"They can't prove a thing. We don't know whether it was Everton who topped that bizzie, and they can't prove that you grassed him up so we might as well move on," argued Chirpie.

"He's got a point, Bigsy, lad," said Wazza.

"Aye, I guess so." Bigsy looked down. "But to see his picture in the paper. He had a missus and a couple of bairns. It got to me a bit, that's all."

"Bigsy, bonny lad, you can't be going soft now, it's too late for that. You've got to tough it out man, you'll go mental otherwise," said Chirpie, with an insightful appreciation of the situation. Bigsy acknowledged the comments but soon drifted back to his retrospection.

They arrived at the club a little after seven and sat in the car out of sight. Although the car park was virtually empty, the main road was still busy with the remnants of the rush-hour traffic. Fortunately, being at the back of the club, meant that they were out of sight from the main road. Layton, as had now become a standing joke, entered the car park at seven-thirty exactly. "You could set your watch by him," said Bigsy.

It was the new van as Everton had described, and they got out of the Escort and went to meet their supplier. Layton got out and opened the rear doors. "Hope you've got plenty of room in dat crate, mon," pointing at the Escort.

He took out three duffle bags and went to the car. Wazza opened the boot and Bigsy's latest box of videos was still in there. "I told you to take them out," said Bigsy.

"I forgot," said Wazza.

"We'll have to put them on the back seat next to Chirpie, and pray we don't get stopped," said Bigsy, and in a scene reminiscent of an Ealing comedy, they began shifting a box of pornographic videos onto the back seat of the ancient Escort and replacing them with three bags of class A drugs.

"Well, if we get stopped tonight, lads, they'll throw away the fookin' key," said Chirpie, accurately describing their predicament.

Layton went through the drops again with Bigsy. This time they both had pieces of paper with the details written down; it was getting quite complicated. He paid particular attention to the Waterfront drop. "You'll have to be careful dare, mon, it's off de normal patch. But it's cool," said Layton.

Satisfied it was all in order, Layton headed out of the car park with the pay-off arranged for the following night at the same time. Bigsy had forgotten there was a band on, and, at that time on a Saturday night, the car park would be busy. They would need to be vigilant.

"Seemed more respectful tonight," Bigsy observed as they

got into the Escort.

Bigsy was still anxious and twice had to answer the call of nature in what he termed were 'minging netties'- unsanitary toilets, but the deals went without a hitch.

As they crossed the Tyne Bridge for their last drop, the Waterfront delivery, Wazza turned to Bigsy.

"Are you sure this is right, Bigsy, lad?"

Bigsy checked his itinerary.

"Aye, that's what it says… Scalleys on the Waterfront."

"Yeah, I know it," replied Wazza. "It's north of the river, that's all."

"Well, I guess we'll soon find out, bonny lad," replied Bigsy.

Wazza negotiated the Escort around the backs streets adjacent to the river and pulled up in front of the club. The whole area was buzzing; the pubs seemed to be bursting and many people were drinking outside on the street.

It was gone midnight, but there was still a long queue waiting to get into Scalleys. They sat in the car watching until the line had been cleared and Bigsy got out of the car and approached the doorman. He checked his notes again. 'A brother called Lionel,' it said.

Wazza and Chirpie were in the car keeping an eye on Bigsy in discussion with the West Indian; ready in case they were needed. Then after a couple of minutes, Bigsy walked back to join them.

"Aye, he's expecting us, all right… We need to go 'round the back; he'll meet us there."

There was a service road that went along the side of the club to a delivery area at the rear. They sat in the car for a couple of minutes and then the back door opened; the doorman beckoned them.

Bigsy got out and went to the boot and took out the remaining bag, labelled with a 'S'. It felt heavy. Bigsy knew its contents were particularly valuable by the amount of money being paid. It contained several hundred tabs of 'cowies' and a bag of heroin.

The exchange was made and Bigsy checked the cash. Lionel

had presented the notes in bank-sealed envelopes which made counting easier. The longer it took, the more vulnerable they were.

Satisfied it was all there, Bigsy shook hands with West Indian.

"Nice doing business with you, man," said Lionel as he went back into the club.

As they returned south over the Tyne Bridge, there was a genuine feeling of relief; the Escort was quiet. Bigsy broke the silence.

"I don't know about you two but I'm fookin' knackered."

"Aye, you're not wrong there, Bigsy, lad," replied Wazza. Chirpie seemed to be asleep in the back.

Twenty minutes later, they were in the precinct outside the tower blocks. Bigsy, again, had kept all the money in one duffle bag as it would be easier to count and, as he got out, he gave Wazza two fifty-pound notes and Chirpie two twenties and a ten. They said their goodbyes and Bigsy looked back and saw Chirpie putting the box of videos back in the boot of the car and climbing in the front.

He took the lift to the fourteenth floor and quietly let himself into the flat. He crept through the lounge, avoiding the sofa leg, and put the duffle bag in the spare room; he would sort it out tomorrow. He pushed the bedroom door open and saw Carole was snoring gently.

"Thank goodness for that," he whispered under his breath.

Chapter Sixteen

Saturday morning, and on the sixth floor, Edi was planning her wardrobe for the night to come. She had carried her small sewing kit in her bag all the way from Kosovo, consisting of a pair of scissors, a tape measure, a number of silks, needles and different coloured cotton.

She tipped the contents onto the bed and rummaged around until she found what she was looking for. The colour of the cotton more or less matched the skirt and she set to work creating her ensemble. She measured the right length and cut a good six inches off the bottom. Then she folded over the hem to create a smooth edge and started stitching. She tried it on and was pleased with the result, her first mini-skirt.

Katya joined her about eleven o'clock and Edi showed her the outfit. "What do you think?" She spoke in Albanian.

"That's incredible," said Katya. "You look so different."

Katya had brought Carole's sample briefcase with her and helped Edi choose some make-up.

"I will call back later and help you put it on."

Polly hadn't stayed over the previous night. It was a mutual decision; he had some college work and was finishing a new kite and wanted to be on the rec early to try it out. After the incident with the Pitbull, Katya was anxious about going back to the sports ground and watched from her window. She had of course spoken to Polly; his arm seemed to be healing well and he was not experiencing any pain. He arranged to see Katya at the club after he had completed his assignment as the official photographer for 'Wye Aye Sis'. She looked forward to it.

Back on fourteen, Bigsy had counted the money from last night's job. He had almost twenty-thousand pounds in the duffle-bag. He got his calculator and worked out his twenty-per cent cut, around four-thousand pounds, he noted. He was thinking about how he could explain his new-found wealth to Carole as he put his share in the shoebox in the bedroom. There would be questions asked that was for sure; he would think of something.

Carole was working and he had the flat to himself, a chance to slob-out. He phoned Wazza and everything was set for the meet with Layton.

By six o'clock that evening, the estate was a hive of activity. It seemed everyone was going to the club. Bigsy had checked the football results and was a bit disappointed that the Mags could only manage a one-all draw with Sheffield Wednesday, but at least his hero was again on the score sheet with a forty-fourth-minute penalty. Bigsy had ordered a takeaway for quarter-past six so Carole wouldn't have to cook when she came home. Just after six o'clock, there was a rattle of keys as she let herself in and hearing her arrival, Bigsy got up and made her a brew.

"How was your day, pet?" he shouted from the kitchen.

"Aye, not bad," she replied and disappeared in the direction of the bathroom.

The news was on the TV and things were still not improving in Kosovo. It looked like ground forces would be sent in. Bigsy had taken a special interest in the war since meeting Katya.

Carole grabbed a quick shower and by the time she was drying her hair, the chicken jalfrezi, boiled rice and naan with extra chips was waiting on the table, together with her onion bhajis and salad.

Katya, meanwhile, had spent an afternoon of pampering herself while Melos was asleep. She luxuriated in a long bubble bath, then spent some time trying out some of the samples in Carole's case. Afterwards, she felt vibrant and refreshed and so alive. Was this really the same woman who had narrowly escaped with her life from Kosovo only a few weeks earlier? She found it difficult to comprehend the course of events that had completely changed her world.

Katya had already chosen her outfit, her jeans and the white peasant-top which had worked so well for her when Polly had first visited.

Edi, meanwhile, was trying to create her own look; she was now on a mission. Her top was tight and emphasised her figure to good effect. Her skirt looked much too short, but she had good legs, if a little on the plump side, and, having had some coaching from Katya, was applying her makeup. Arjeta watched her mother with fascination. She had never seen her looking like this. "Like a princess," she observed.

Further down the road on the estate, knob-head Trev was also getting ready. Like Bigsy, he enjoyed the music of Oasis, and was looking forward to the evening.

His young wife, Pauline, was tarting herself up in the bedroom, the customary glass of vodka next to her.

"You go steady with that stuff, my girl, you don't want to be off your head before you get there," said Trev.

Her look, totally inappropriate for the Working Men's Club, but quite acceptable at the Waterfront hostelries, consisted of high clumpy heels, black fishnet hold-ups and a skirt that was so short you could see the tops of her hosiery without any difficulty. Her top, if you could call it that, was cropped below her red bra which was clearly visible. The ensemble was complemented with some garish makeup and red lipstick.

"You look like a fookin' prossie," commented Trev when she made her way down the stairs into the living room.

"Piss off," was her riposte. Things were not sweet in the Rankin household.

Trev was still angry. His run-in with the police regarding the dog was playing on his mind, that and the fact that the dog had cost him nearly a thousand pounds and was now dead in some pound somewhere with no chance of a refund.

The desk-clerk at the Police Station had taken all the details and he had been interviewed by an officer who informed him he would be facing a charge under the 1991 Dangerous Dogs Act. It was likely he would face a hefty fine, which of course he wouldn't be able to pay, so it would mean some boring community service, unless he could find a benefactor to pick up the tab. He would have to appear before Gateshead Magistrates at a future date.

It also meant that his supplies had not been delivered, so he had not earned any cash that week and had only his regular benefit cheque to live on. He was also in need of a fix himself; anything to get him away from this 'shite-hole' of an estate.

Rikki was watching the TV. He had been grounded since the incident on the rec, although with his father and step-mother out for the evening, he would be able to get up to all kinds of mischief. His two buddies would call later when the coast was clear.

In 1405, Carole was adding some final touches to her make-up in the lounge when Bigsy came in from the bedroom carrying Everton's duffle bag around his shoulders.

"Where're you going with that manky old thing, pet?" asked Carole. "Hey... be careful... you're dropping dust all over my carpet."

"Just a bit of business, pet," replied Bigsy, quickly making his way to the front door before any further questions were asked. Carole put on her coat and followed Bigsy out of the flat.

In the corridor, Katya was just manoeuvring Melos out of her flat in his buggy towards the lift.

"Hiya Katya pet," said Carole, walking towards them. "You look fantastic."

"Thank you," said Katya.

Bigsy extended his greetings and they walked together to the lift and Bigsy pressed the button. Carole was making strange noises to Melos.

"Is Edi still coming?" asked Carole as the lift opened.

"Yes," said Katya. "I will call for her." Bigsy pressed for the sixth floor.

"We'll wait downstairs for you," said Bigsy as Katya got out to collect Edi.

The lift closed and Katya went to Edi's flat and knocked on her door.

Edi was waiting and answered straight away; she was wearing her new outfit.

"Wow," said Katya. "You look so different."

"*Si një princeshë*," said Arjeta.

"Yes," said Katya. "She is a princess."

Edi smiled, but it was a tense smile. Katya talked to her as they headed back to the lifts trying to get her to relax.

When they reached the ground floor, Bigsy and Carole were waiting for them outside the block. A couple of minutes later, a taxi pulled up.

"This is for us," said Bigsy. There weren't many who would be travelling to the club from Heathcote in a taxi.

As they were about to get in, Wazza and Chirpie appeared from the flats.

"Carole, pet, the cab's a bit crowded, like. You take the girls, I'll go with Wazza and Chirpie and meet you there," said Bigsy.

There was no dissension and he watched the taxi pull away before joining his buddies to collect the Escort from the lock-up. Wazza reversed out and Bigsy put the duffle-bag in the boot.

When they arrived at the club, the car park was almost full. Wazza parked in a corner away from the main block which he thought might be more inconspicuous. Bigsy howled with laughter. "Inconspicuous... this…? It stands out like a fookin' pimple on a laddy's nose." Chirpie roared with laughter.

The three made their way to the main entrance where the girls were waiting and Bigsy paid for everyone to go in. The band had set up on the stage and tables were placed around the sides of the dance floor. Bigsy had reserved two tables at the back of the room. Katya and Edi felt very self-conscious as they followed Carole to the seats, but they soon made themselves comfortable. The men went to the bar.

It was busy and there was a couple of temporary staff on duty to help Alice, including Wazza's mum, Hazel. This was usual for a Saturday night when there was a band playing. Bigsy got to the bar and gave Alice two fifty-pound notes.

"Put that behind the bar for my mates will you and have one yourself, pet."

"Ta, Bigsy, pet," said Alice.

The lads returned with the drinks, Katya having a glass of rather watery looking red wine and Edi having lemonade; she didn't touch alcohol, she explained. Arjeta was looking around at all the people and thought they were staring at her; she grabbed her mother for protection. After some initial curiosity, that gradually subsided, and the onlookers soon went back to their respective conversations.

Just before seven-thirty, Bigsy, Wazza and Chirpie made their apologies and went back to the car park to wait for Layton. Bigsy scrounged a cigarette from Wazza and they sat in the car and waited.

"He's late tonight," said Bigsy at seven thirty-one, and they chuckled.

But he didn't come; seven forty-five, eight o'clock.

At eight-fifteen, Bigsy said that he would have to go back in or face the wrath of Carole. Wazza and Chirpie agreed to wait for a little while longer.

"He's going to come inside looking for us anyway, I would think," said Chirpie.

"Aye, well, give it twenty minutes, bonny lad, and if he doesn't show, you come back inside, and I'll leave a message on the door for them to tell us when he comes."

There was a frosty greeting from Carole as Bigsy walked towards the table.

"Where've you been all this time? We're dying of thirst here."

"Sorry, pet, just a bit of business."

"You alright? You look like you lost a pound and found a penny?" observed Carole.

"Aye, everything's fine... Same again for everyone?" said Bigsy and went to the bar to get the drinks.

Polly, with his camera bag around his shoulders looking very professional, and his Mum, Alison, came in shortly afterwards and went and joined the table where they were all sitting. Bigsy went to the bar and bought them drinks and Katya moved up to ensure Polly could sit next to her. Polly made a fuss of Melos who was smiling at him in his buggy. The body language was obvious, especially to Alison who, as his mother, could tell there were shared secrets.

Davie Slater who had been sitting with Danny Milburn, came over to say hello.

"Hi Bigsy, Carole, Polly, Alison." He nodded to Katya and Edi. "Hey, here's a good one for you," and Bigsy groaned, expecting another of Slate's jokes; he was not to be disappointed.

"A ghost walks into a bar, right, and says to the barman, 'a double whiskey please', and the barman says, 'sorry we don't sell spirits'."

Davie roared with laughter. Bigsy groaned, Carole and Alison politely chuckled and Katya and Edi just looked at each other in confusion. There was no equivalent translation into Albanian.

Another followed: "A man goes to the doctors and says, 'doctor, can you give us something for the wind?...'" There was a pause for the punch line. "So he gave him a kite."

Davie almost curled up in hysterics. After a few minutes of further excruciating banter, Davie went back to join Danny.

Bigsy's mind was elsewhere, however, and had not joined in with the merriment which hadn't gone unnoticed by Carole.

"You sure you're ok, pet?"

"Aye, won't be a sec just going to the gents," and he got up and went outside to see if Layton had turned up. Wazza and

Chirpie were outside the entrance; there was still no sign.

"I don't think ya man's going to show, Bigsy lad. What're you going to do?" said Wazza.

"I don't know, I really don't know," said Bigsy.

"Why not call Everton?" said Chirpie.

"Aye, that's an idea," said Bigsy and he made a call to the number Everton had given him.

Bigsy held his mobile to his ear. There was a discordant sound. 'Number unobtainable', it said on the screen.

"Nottin' more you can do," said Wazza.

"Aye," said Bigsy and he put his phone back in his pocket.

Having given up on Layton, Bigsy went back inside with Wazza and Chirpie in tow and walked back to the table. Everyone moved up to accommodate the new arrivals. Carole made the introductions.

The band came on at nine o'clock to great approval. Bigsy stood up and whistled using his thumb and forefinger, his problems momentarily having disappeared.

Polly had left Katya and had gone down to the front with his camera trying to concentrate on his work. The group started up with 'Champaign Supernova', one of Bigsy's favourites. The band were good and with your eyes closed, you could almost believe it was the real thing. They were real enough for this crowd anyway; it would be the nearest they would ever get to their heroes. The lead singer had his microphone stand fully extended with the microphone bent down at forty-five degrees singing up into it with his hands folded behind his back, just like Liam Gallagher. The guitarist had an Epiphone guitar emblazoned with a Union Jack just like Noel. Nobody would notice, or care, it was a copy made in Korea. Polly took more pictures.

The band finished their first set with 'She's Electric', which went down a storm and they left the stage to rapturous applause.

During the break, Stan Hardacre, as he was inclined to do, took over the microphone and made numerous announcements –

future events, prize draw and so on. He asked for mothers to keep their kids off the dance floor. Several children, seeing the vast empty space, were running around creating mayhem and making a lot of noise. Others were pushing model cars to see how far they could go. "Health and safety, you know," he explained.

Then he called for quiet and he waited for the noise to subside. He blew into the microphone to get everybody's attention.

"Order," he shouted again. "I have a special announcement to make."

It went very quiet, just the low hum of voices and the gentle clink of glasses at the bar.

"Now, some of you may have been watching the news on the telly about them two refugees." His voice echoed around the room in grave tones; attention was total. "I am delighted to say we have 'em with us here tonight."

Everyone looked around the room and suddenly all eyes were focused on Katya and Edi. Stan continued, sounding presidential.

"We are honoured to welcome these two brave ladies here this evening, who against all the odds, have escaped from their home in a war-torn country and are safely in our fold; 'Katya Ju... ju... colly and Edona Bukosi.'" He read from a scrap of paper in his hand. The crowd applauded.

Bigsy had, of course, told Stan of Katya's experience and that she had killed her two assailants and the story had spread like wildfire around the estate. Katya, without knowing it, had become a local hero and celebrity.

Then Alice and Hazel came out from the kitchen carrying two large cardboard boxes.

"Would you like to come up here to the stage for a minute," said Stan addressing the women.

Rather self-consciously, Katya almost dragging Edi, went up to the front. Stan presented them with the two boxes of food, donated by the members of the club. Katya and Edi accepted their gifts graciously; the crowd clapped, whistled and cheered their approval again. Polly took a photograph.

Stan gave Katya the microphone which she viewed with some suspicion. It went quiet again and she spoke nervously. "Thank you, thank you… you are very kind."

She handed the microphone back to Stan. The crowd continued to cheer as the pair went back to their seats carrying their 'hampers'. Carole, Alison and Polly were cheering as they approached the table. Arjeta was holding the buggy looking very bemused by the whole thing.

Bigsy meanwhile had been trying again to get Everton on the new phone number but was still getting an unobtainable tone. There was nothing he could do. The money, for now, would have to stay in the back of Wazza's car before deciding what he should do with it.

On the Rankin table, things had gone from bad to worse. Pauline was now completely inebriated and becoming abusive to anyone within earshot. She was stood up trying to sing to the records playing in the background.

"Sit down and behave yourself," said Trev pulling her into her seat. "You're going to get a fookin' good hiding when you get in."

"Piss off, you fookin' bully; I've had enough of you. I'm going into town to see me mates and go to a club." She got out her mobile made a couple of calls and ordered a taxi. "And don't bother waiting up," was her parting shot to Trev.

A few minutes later, the band kicked off again with a rousing rendition of 'Roll with It' and everybody got up on the dance floor. Katya hadn't been to a dance since her college days and had forgotten what it was like to lose yourself in music. Polly grabbed her hand and Carole nodded. "Go on, Katya, pet, I'll look after the bairn."

Melos seemed quite content in his buggy.

Edi was sat with Arjeta on her lap watching and listening but appearing to be enjoying herself. After a few numbers, Edi was persuaded to join them. Somewhat nervously, she got up and joined the group, not really knowing what to do. She had never been to a dance before in her life. After a while, she was beginning to enjoy it and without realising was actually attracting some attention. One person who was taking a keen interest was Trev Rankin who was sat drooling at her legs. Eventually, he got up and approached the dancing group.

Now, Trev had a bit of a reputation when it came to dancing, not that he had done much recently. This was due to his nasty habit of thrusting his pelvis in between the unsuspecting dance partner's thighs and pulling her towards him with his hands pressing firmly against her buttocks.

Unfortunately, this had led to several incidents, including him being laid out by one particular woman from Byker who put him in hospital. He had however had some successes, not least with the erstwhile Pauline, who by now would probably be throwing up in an alleyway outside some nightclub in town. There would be few dancing partners, however, in the club.

Trev cut in and fronted the unsuspecting Edi. Within a couple of minutes, he made his move and Edi felt something hard nudging her pubic bone and it wasn't a mobile phone. Her first reaction was to pull away but then suddenly thought this might be her chance.

She leaned closer until she was close to his ear and said in her broken English, "do you want sex?"

Trev couldn't believe what he was hearing, he loosened his grip.

"Come again, pet."

Edi repeated it loud enough for him to hear against the noise of the music.

"Are you asking for a shagging, pet?" said Trev.

Edi had no real idea what he was saying. "Sex…? Yes," she clarified. "Ten pounds."

Trev was totally taken aback and looked into her face.

"You're telling me I can shag you for ten pounds?" said Trev into her ear.

"Yes," said Edi.

"When?" asked Trev.

Edi looked around and everyone seemed caught up in their own worlds.

Katya had only one thing in mind the way she was staring into Polly's eyes while she danced.

"You have..." she was recalling the word she had been practising for this very opportunity... "Er... protection?" asked Edi.

Trev was having difficulty handling this.

"Aye, I've got Johnnies, always prepared, me, like a good boy scout."

Edi didn't understand.

She looked around again. Arjeta seemed to be really enjoying herself playing with Melos and watching the band. This was a whole new experience for her.

"Now.... Outside."

Trev let go and Edi went back to the table and asked Carole to look after Arjeta while she went to the Ladies.

Trev met Edi in the corridor by the toilets and led her outside to the car park. There was a dark area away from any lights close to Wazza's car. "Here will do," said Trev.

"You have... money?" asked Edi and Trev pulled out a grubby ten-pound note from his pocket and gave it to her. Edi pulled down her pants, hitched up her skirt and lent against a fence and Trev was soon in full flow. It only lasted a few seconds before Trev let out a groan and collapsed backwards, his legs wobbling, nearly falling over.

"You're certainly a surprise one you are," said Trev, zipping himself up and discarding the used condom over the fence.

Edi quickly put on her pants and made her way through the car park towards the club entrance. That wasn't too difficult, she thought.

Trev caught up with her. "Hey, wait up... Are you up for it again, like, for ten pounds, pet? Not now, next week."

Edi turned; she understood the gist. "Again…? Yes... ten pounds."

"Aye, ok, champion… What's your number?"

He meant phone number. Edi didn't understand. "I live... Heathcote."

"Aye ok, pet, which flat?" Edi told him the address.

"Ok, I'll call 'round on Monday morning about eleven. Will that be ok?"

"Yes, ok," replied Edi.

Edi turned and went back into the club, Trev headed for the gents.

Back on the dance floor, everything was going well, and no-one seemed any the wiser to Edi's departure; she had been away for less than ten minutes.

Arjeta put her arms up to her mother and shouted "*kërce, nënë kërce!*" - "dance, mummy; dance," and Edi picked up her daughter and went back to the dance floor. Trev was back at his table with a bottle of broon and contemplating his good fortune.

The last number had to be "Don't Look Back in Anger", and the whole crowd was sharing the chorus, "*So Sally can wait…*"

Katya was unsure of the words but tried to join in. She was holding Polly close and Alison was in no doubt that something was going on; even Carole had taken more than a passing interest. "Your Polly seems a bit struck with our Katya."

The night ended, the band said their farewells and gradually the crowd started to drift away.

The taxi Bigsy had ordered was waiting outside the front entrance of the club. Polly was carrying Katya's hamper while she pushed the buggy. Melos was fast asleep. Wazza was carrying Edi's box. The taxi driver opened the boot and they were able to stow the hampers. Katya lifted Melos out of the buggy without waking him and Polly folded it up and put it on top of the boxes. The driver closed the boot.

"We can't all get in," observed Carole.

"That's ok, I'll go with Wazza," said Bigsy. "There'll be enough room for Polly and Alison."

Bigsy gave the driver a ten-pound note. "Keep the change, bonny lad."

The passengers managed to squash in with Arjeta sitting on Edi's lap. Bigsy watched the taxi drive off then joined Wazza and Chirpie in the car park. They started discussing what they should do with Everton's money.

"Well, we can't leave it in the car," said Wazza. "It could get nicked."

"Aye, then our balls would really be in the mangle," said Bigsy.

They decided that Bigsy would keep the money in the flat for the time being in the hope that Everton would contact him.

They made their way back to the flats. Remarkably, Wazza had managed to stay sober, Bigsy had insisted on it; he couldn't afford to lose his driver. They dropped Bigsy off at the flats; Chirpie said he would keep Wazza company back to the lock-up.

Bigsy headed for the lift with the duffle bag over his shoulders and pressed the button. He waited and waited... nothing. It had broken down again. He cursed, then trudged his way up the thirteen floors to the flat trying to think of a place to hide the bag. Carole was forever curious and would want to know what was in it. Twenty thousand pounds, it didn't bear thinking about; there would be much explaining to do, that's for sure.

For now it would have to be under the bed in the spare bedroom. Carole had indicated that they would be otherwise engaged when they got home to be bothered about it tonight.

When he got in, he took his shoes off and quickly made straight for the bathroom, dropping the bag under the spare bed en-route. Carole, luckily, was in the kitchen opening a bottle of wine. He flushed the toilet and breathed a sigh of relief. One hurdle crossed.

When she came out of the kitchen, Bigsy was back sat on the sofa in the lounge and she handed him a glass of red wine. "That was a champion night, Bigsy, pet... Thanks for paying for us. I shan't be long," and she disappeared into the bedroom.

Bigsy's mind was elsewhere but in a few minutes, she returned in a dressing gown.

"Now how about that special massage I promised, pet?" said Carole.

Polly stayed with Katya that night. Alison, as all protective mothers would do, had told him to mind what he was doing but inside she was pleased for him. To her knowledge, he had not had a serious relationship and she was certainly happy with Katya as a potential partner; she had liked her from the first time they had met.

The following morning it was football again, so Polly was up early. His arm felt much better and the pain had completely gone. Katya made them both some toast and coffee; she would come and watch later.

"We're playing Fenham Rangers today pet. It'll be a tough game they're top of the league."

He kissed her and left to get his kit.

Bigsy had also got up early and, very quietly so as not to disturb Carole, went into the spare room and retrieved his bag. He checked again; Carole was still fast asleep. He went into the kitchen and got a screwdriver from the 'man-drawer' where he kept his bits and pieces, then went back to the spare bedroom. He removed the screws from the central heating vent in the wall opposite the window. Moving quickly, he took off the grill-cover and stuffed the bag in the space behind before replacing it.

It was a tight fit, but it would be out of sight at least for now. Fortunately, the central heating was not likely to be required for a couple of months yet, even on Heathcote. He then went to make a brew, still deep in thought about what was going to happen about Everton's money.

There were more than usual watching the game; this would

be the last home fixture of the season. Stan and a few others from the club had turned up to give some support and were standing next to the coach, Danny. Fenham had also bought a few supporters with them. Carole was there in a new light-weight jacket which, although very smart, was a bit overdressed for a touchline appearance on the rec, but then you have to keep up appearances, she had said.

Katya had taken Melos down in his buggy; the lift now repaired. She decided not to call in on Edi but would see her later. She had not seen Polly play football before and soon got caught up with the excitement of the match.

The game was as tough as they had expected and, despite the various exploits of the previous night, Seaton acquitted themselves well, Bigsy equalising ten minutes from time with a penalty, one-all was the score.

The players trudged off to the changing rooms and the watching fans dispersed. There was the usual throng around the entrance to the changing rooms with the players waiting to use the showers; a queue of cars formed trying to leave the rec,

Katya declined the offer of going back to the club; she wanted to check on Edi. Polly had arranged to go for a drink with the rest of the team but had promised to call around later.

Katya was walking beside Carole back to the flats pushing the buggy. Carole had something on her mind. "I think our Polly's got a thing for you."

Katya turned and looked at Carole. "Yes, I am very fond of him, too."

Monday morning would be another defining moment for the two refugees.

Katya was up early. Polly had not stayed; he had college. She was getting ready for her first day at the Pre-school centre. She was naturally a little nervous but felt a twinge of excitement at the same time. The hours were ideal. Every week-day - ten until two o'clock, although there was some flexibility and a chance of extra hours if required.

She got Melos ready and went down to the sixth floor to pick up Arjeta at nine-thirty as arranged with Edi the previous day. Katya was expecting some resistance from Edi and wasn't sure whether she would let her go. She was surprised, therefore, when she answered the door wearing makeup and her hair washed and combed. Arjeta was stood at the door ready with her coat on. Katya also noticed that Edi was dressed in her skirt from Saturday night. Katya teased Edi and asked her if she was going dancing again. Edi just smiled. After a bit of cajoling Katya managed to persuade Arjeta to come saying she needed someone to look after Melos while she worked.

Arriving at the centre, Katya was greeted by Sonia who led them to the staff room, which also happened to be the kitchen. Mel was already in front of the children and waved and mouthed, "won't be a minute."

Sonia took over from her and Mel joined Katya and the two children. Straightaway Mel made a fuss of them. Arjeta was understandably shy at first but quickly seemed to relax and wasn't as tearful as Katya had feared.

"Will she be ok?" said Katya. "Only she doesn't speak any English."

"She'll be fine," said Mel. "We have several children from immigrant families. We engage them through pictures and drawings. They also like singing... She'll soon pick up a few words."

Mel made them both a coffee and gave Katya some background to the children they were responsible for. Over half were the offspring of single mothers who were working. The rest were where both parents were either employed or couldn't be bothered looking after them. Several children had learning difficulties and others had psychological issues but generally, while at the centre at least, they were reasonably well behaved.

After about half an hour's briefing, Mel led Katya back to the main hall where the children were at little tables drawing. They were asked to stop, and Katya was introduced to the group.

"That's the Kossie who killed all them soldiers," whispered one five-year-old to his mate. Respect had already been earned.

Her first task was to supervise a drawing session and she went around the room praising the children's efforts. After lunch, the children were relaxing, and Katya had offered to read them a story. They were sat on the floor, very attentive, hanging on her every word as she read the story of the 'Three Little Pigs'.

A blond lad who was about four years of age and sitting at the front was particularly enthralled, his eyes wide in wonderment as the plot unfolded. Katya used all her dramatic skills to make the episode as scary as possible and as she spoke the words, "he huffed and he puffed and he blew the house down," the blond lad looked up at her and said... "the bastard!"

Mel, who had witnessed the episode, had to go to the kitchen to recover in fits of laughter. Sonia too was almost hysterical; they had never heard that response before. Katya was the complete professional and ignored the comment. Later, Mel praised Katya for her work and thought she would fit in very well.

"How you kept a straight face when you read the 'Three Little Pigs', I'll never know."

Another lady called Kelly turned up at two o'clock to take over and was introduced to Katya, "This is my partner, Kelly Meredith," said Mel and explained she did the afternoon shift.

Earlier that morning, around eleven o'clock, there was someone stood outside Edi's flat. He appeared to be looking around to check no-one was watching. Coast clear, he knocked on the door. It was Trev.

"Hiya, pet, can I come in?"

From what she had gleaned from the conversation on Saturday, she thought he would call which was why she had put on the same outfit.

Edi moved to one side to allow Trev to pass.

He looked at her. "You look champion, pet."

"I don't understand."

He sat on the sofa and she sat on one of the dining chairs.

"Did you mean what you said on Saturday, pet?" said Trev slowly.

"Yes… Ten pounds."

Trev took out a ten pound note and put it on the table.

"Come." Edi led him to the bedroom.

Again it was a fairly brief affair and Edi spent the whole time staring at the ceiling. After it was over, they went back into the living room and Trev sat down.

"Are… you… looking… for… more… business?" He spoke slowly and deliberately to make sure she understood. Edi squinted her eyes in concentration, trying to make out the words and their meaning.

"Yes, er… I want… er money… for Arjeta," Edi said.

"I have one or two friends who would be interested, like," said Trev. "Nice blokes, no radgies."

Edi was lost.

Trev tried again. "Would that be ok?"

"Yes," said Edi. "Ten pounds."

"Good," said Trev. "Here's what we will do."

He spoke very slowly in mono-syllables as if she were retarded in some way.

"Have... you... a TELEPHONE?" He raised his voice in the hope that it would help the comprehension and made a mime with his hands of a handset by extending his thumb and little finger. She understood and went to the kitchen and returned with the box that Clara had given her.

Trev explained to her what to do and plugged it into the wall socket. He checked the phone settings and found the number which he wrote down on a piece of paper.

"I… will… phone… you… when I have someone and tell you when they can come," she nodded and appeared to understand. Trev made her repeat it.

"I will make sure that they pay. You won't have any bother

with the readies."

Edi had lost it again but nodded. He provided more hand signals as if Edi was deaf.

Trev went over the process again and explained what to do about the phone which she seemed to understand. She repeated it again. After another twenty minutes further coaching she let him out.

Trev couldn't believe his luck, a decent prostitute in Gateshead would cost at least twenty pounds and maybe more at a weekend, so he had found another cash-cow to feed his habit and maybe even pay his impending fine. He would charge clients twenty pounds and keep ten for himself. It would be like printing money. There was no shortage of bored men on this estate, particularly during the day when most of the women were working.

Bigsy was reading the evening paper when Carole got in from work. "Have you had a good day, pet?" he asked almost routinely.

"Aye, pet, not bad," said Carole in the same tone.

"Would you like a brew?" asked Bigsy.

"No ta, pet, better get on with the dinner; it's defrosting all over my bag," said Carole.

Another headline gripped Bigsy's attention and he froze as he read it; then he read it again:

'Police look for killers in gangland murders,' it said.

'Police are looking for two men in connection with the shooting early Saturday morning of three men in what is believed to be a gangland turf-war killing. The two dead men were named as Everton Sheedie (43) from Jesmond and an associate, Layton Gibbons (26) of Wallsend. A third man, believed to be Mr Gibbon's brother, was said to be critical in hospital with gunshot wounds. Mr Sheedie was known to the police and had previous convictions for drug offences. Although not confirmed, it is believed that the killings were drugs-related. It is understood that the three men had visited Mr Gee's nightclub in the City

late on Friday night and were gunned down in an alleyway leading from a side entrance. Yesterday, extensive forensic work was being carried out at the scene and police have appealed for witnesses and for anyone who was at the club on Friday night or Saturday morning to contact the incident room. Police are examining CCTV footage of the area but, as yet, no further information was available'.

"No wonder you were late, bonny lad," muttered Bigsy to himself, and got on his mobile to Wazza.

"You need to see the paper, bonny lad, page sixteen, you can't miss it. I'll meet you downstairs in an hour, and can you get Chirpie?" said Bigsy.

Chapter Seventeen

May was to be a turning point for the war in Kosovo.

The daily news continued to bring disturbing reports of atrocities on both sides of the conflict. There had been continued air raids on Belgrade and increasing pressure on the Serbian leader, Slobodan Milošević, to agree to a peace deal.

At the start of the month, a NATO aircraft attacked an Albanian refugee convoy, believing it was a Yugoslav military convoy, killing around fifty people. NATO admitted its mistake five days later, but the Serbs accused NATO of deliberately attacking the refugees. A few days after that, NATO bombs hit the Chinese Embassy in Belgrade, killing three Chinese journalists which, of course, had impacted negatively on relations with China. NATO claimed they were firing at Yugoslav positions. The United States and NATO later apologised for the bombing, saying that it occurred because of an outdated map provided by the CIA.

These military blunders did nothing to give confidence to the wider watching world that there was any cohesive strategy in bringing the war to a swift conclusion.

Agim Çeku had taken over as commander of the Kosovan Liberation Army which was now being actively supported by NATO. He would later become Kosovo's first Prime Minister. Katya had heard of him but did not know whether he would make a difference or not. She despaired when she watched the developments in her homeland.

On the refugee question, TV reports were showing that an estimated one million Kosovans had been displaced in what was being dubbed by the media as 'ethnic cleansing', and given temporary asylum in numerous countries including Canada, Australia and the US, as well as several European countries. The numbers entering the UK were still being quoted as around four thousand five hundred, although exact numbers were proving difficult to confirm due to the many who were making their way to the UK by means other than the official airlifts.

Back on the estate, Katya continued in her new teaching assistant post and was not only enjoying it but having a positive effect on the children. Mel had complimented her on several occasions on the way that she was able to stimulate even the normally most difficult children. Even Arjeta was blossoming. She had gained more self-confidence and was starting to understand and speak English and therefore interact with the other children. She also seemed to be putting on weight.

When Katya called for her each morning, she was already waiting with her coat on eager to go. Katya had noticed how smart she now looked compared with some of the children. She was wearing new shoes and clothes and often brought a new colouring book or doll with her. Katya had asked Edi about this, but she had told Katya that she had saved up some money from her weekly benefits and just wanted to spoil her daughter. Katya had no reason to question this.

Edi also had seemed less stressed recently, which Katya had put down to the effects of the anti-depressants. Her English was coming on well and she appeared to be looking after herself, regularly answering the door, wearing makeup and fresh clothes, if a little revealing, Katya had thought.

Katya's relationship with Polly was also progressing well and he was very much part of her life now. She encouraged him in his college work, and he had made her a special kite that he had decorated with the Albanian flag which he had taught her to fly. He had stayed over at the weekends and on those days when he had a study day and this arrangement suited both of them; it kept the relationship alive and fresh.

His photographs from the derelict factory had earned him a top grade in his course work and were exhibited in a prominent position in the entrance lobby of the college. Some further commissions had come his way from a Tyne-side advertising agency and another from a local record company who had seen the pictures he had taken of the group at the club. This would provide him with some extra money.

Domestically, they got on extremely well. Katya enjoyed Polly's sense of humour, when she could understand it. Polly had taught her to use the microwave, which had come in very useful when preparing meals, and other gadgets, and she could now text on her mobile phone. Katya had tried some of the local cuisine and enjoyed curry and Thai stir fry, admittedly from a supermarket jar. As Polly had said, she was almost a Geordie.

Katya had also seen quite a lot of Carole in the past few weeks. On the nights when she was free, Katya would pop around for a glass of wine. Bigsy was usually out with Wazza and Chirpie at the Working Men's club or doing business and Carole was always pleased to see her. They had returned to the Metro Centre a couple of times and on the first occasion, Katya was quizzed by Carole on her relationship with Polly. Eventually, Katya had confided in her that they were in fact lovers, as Carole had suspected, but they were taking things slowly as it was early days.

Katya was not sure of the reaction she would get, but Carole was delighted and suggested they went to a wine bar to celebrate. Carole again indulged Katya in clothes and makeup, "now you're almost part of the family, like," she explained. Bigsy again came up trumps as the benefactor with a major helping of cash.

Katya's own financial position, while not flush, was manageable. Clara had sorted out her benefits which meant she would not be paying any tax on her earnings at the Pre-school club. This gave her roughly an extra twenty pounds a week. She shopped wisely, without extravagance, and was content with herself. She was a long way from home not just physically but psychologically.

In her darkest moments, she still thought of her journey from her homeland, the incident, the refugee camp, and her friend Hava Goranovic who helped her in those first few days as she fled the pogrom. She wondered what had become of her and her family. Katya had managed to develop her own coping strategies by compartmentalising the events and traumas. In overcoming these adversities, she had become a more determined and self-assured woman and the support from her new friends, and importantly Polly, had given her much needed emotional stability.

On the sixth floor, things couldn't be more different. Edi, although outwardly seemingly stronger and able to fool Clara and the other social workers who had visited her - and to some degree, Katya, was far from stable. She had become obsessed with ensuring that her daughter had the best of everything. There were always chocolate treats in the fridge, ice cream, crisps, cakes, or anything else Arjeta had decided she wanted. She regularly spent the afternoons in town with Arjeta in the 'Baby Store'. She kept away from 'Pricewise'. She was banned from there in any case after her previous excursion.

There was a price to pay to enable her to feed her shopping habit. In the first week, after her discussion with Trev, he had supplied her with four new clients, two of whom had rebooked straight away for further sessions. Opening hours were obviously restricted to when Arjeta, and Katya, were at school, and when there were no expected visits from the numerous support agencies that wanted to see her.

Trev would phone around nine-thirty to see if the coast was clear and confirm that Edi would be open for business. He would then arrange the client visit and carefully explain who was coming and at what time. Each time he reminded her to recharge the phone in case she lost custom. The money was always paid upfront. On a couple of occasions, there was only a few minutes from one client leaving and another arriving, giving Edi just enough time to clean herself up. She was also becoming more adept at her trade. One or two clients were nervous and needed extra help, others were so excited they hadn't made it to the full act itself; there were no refunds. The quicker it was over with the better as far as Edi was concerned; it was just business.

The first week she had earned eighty pounds, the second, one hundred pounds, and one hundred and fifty in the third. There was an allowance of half an hour for each session which Trev had insisted on, to ensure 'maximum turn-around opportunity'.

Edi, of course, had not understood.

The arrangement had worked very well and gave her the money she needed to be able spoil Arjeta, which was her sole aim. Trev, too, had little complaint. At this rate, he would not only have enough cash for his fine but would be able to give up dealing drugs. He had even been able to enjoy more private sessions with her; there was precious little forthcoming at home.

Edi had shown little emotion about what she was doing; she saw it as a matter of survival, expediency, as she had done at the camp. She felt nothing. It was simply a means to an end; that was all.

May 22, 1999, was an important day for the local population - Cup Final day. The Mags were at Wembley and the whole of Geordie-land was in celebration. It was five-thirty in the morning when Wazza and Chirpie met Bigsy in the entrance lobby of the flats and took the taxi they had ordered to the bus station where the coaches going to the match were departing. There were thousands of people milling about around the bus terminus and dozens of coaches. "Busier than a Saturday morning," observed Chirpie almost excitedly.

"Says in the paper they're expecting almost forty-thousand people'll be going down to Wembley," said Wazza.

"I think most of them are here," said Bigsy.

They carried their luggage - a six-pack of Newcastle Brown each, and some sandwiches that Carole had made up for them, onto their designated coach and by six o'clock they were off on the three-hundred-mile trip which would take them at least six, probably seven hours, given the traffic to Wembley on cup final day.

The worries and anxieties of a few weeks ago seemed to have lessened over this past week as the excitement of the forthcoming match grew.

Chirpie, as usual, was always quick to put a pragmatic and philosophical view on things. "What else can we do?" he counselled wisely. Bigsy was becoming more like his old self again. Carole had noticed a difference and put it down to her special massages that appeared to be almost on tap. In fact, Bigsy was looking forward to a bit of a break from conjugal duties; for one night at least.

They had agreed that Everton's money would stay in Bigsy's central heating vent until either someone called to claim it, or sufficient time had passed when it was deemed safe to share it out. The timescale had not yet been decided, but the switching-on of the central heating would have a bearing on it as there was no way any warm air was getting to the spare bedroom with the duffle bag blocking the flow. An investigation by Carole was bound to ensue. The other possibility – of them getting caught, was never contemplated, not publicly anyway, but each had their own concerns and had to deal mentally with that threat as best they could.

Carole, meanwhile, was having a lie-in. She had sensibly taken the day off. There was no way she was going to earn any serious commission today. The shops would be deserted while every bar in town would be heaving. The city looked spectacular with black and white bunting everywhere. On the estates there were pre-match street parties planned. Street-sellers with flags were out in force and Bigsy had bemoaned the fact that he had missed out on a major business opportunity involving fake replica shirts which were flying off the shelves in the market. A 'Shearer No 9' was selling for ten pounds and being shipped in from some sweatshop in Mumbai for one-pound fifty. "Do the maths," Bigsy had said to Wazza. The real thing from the Fan-

Store at St James was nearer forty pounds.

Katya had an unexpected visitor later that morning. It was Clara with Jenny Wheatley from the Refugee Council. Katya had put Melos in a lobster pot which Mel had given her. This was a useful addition to her baby items, like a plastic cage where you could put babies and they could move around inside without coming to any harm. Melos, ever curious, was starting to crawl really well now and she couldn't leave him out of her sight for a second.

Katya invited them both in and went to make coffee. Clara and Jenny went to the window and looked out across the rec.

"You don't see that very often do you?" said Jenny. "Someone flying kites."

Polly was trying out his latest creation before submitting it to college as part of his project.

Katya brought in the coffees and the three sat down.

"The reason why we're here," said Clara. "Is this," and she handed a fairly scruffy envelope addressed to Katya.

Katya looked at the writing and recognised the hand immediately.

"It's... it's from my mother." Katya found difficulty in getting the words out.

"Yes," said Jenny. "It was delivered to my office yesterday. As you know, we've been trying to make contact with as many relatives as possible. Unfortunately, so many have left, we've not had a great amount of success, so I was very pleased when this came through and I wanted to get it to you as soon as I could. We know how important it is to get information on loved ones."

Katya's hands were shaking as she opened the letter. She translated for Clara and Jenny; she didn't mind sharing her news.

'My Darling Katya, my heart was ...' Katya thought for the right word... *'Overjoyed... when I received your letter. I read it so many times I thought my eyes would wear out. I prayed for you every moment that you and my sweet thing...'* She looked at Clara. "That's Melos", Katya explained... *'would be safe... No one here*

tells us what is happening. There is no television or radio. I am well. I left my house after you went away that morning and went to stay with Afrim and his family ... ' He's the farmer who took me on the tractor the first morning," Katya clarified ... *'The Serbs did not bother us and now they are gone. The KLA are controlling this area now and I feel more safe.'*

Katya was beginning to cry now, tears dropping on the scrap of paper she was trying to read from. She composed herself a little and continued: *'I have now returned home for two weeks and have food from Afrim who brings me vegetables and eggs from the farm. I have been lucky. My house was not set on fire like so many others in the village. I hope you and my sweet thing are well in England and it will not be long before you can return. I pray every day for peace and your safe return. Your loving mami.'*

Katya was sobbing bitterly, partly relief, partly sorrow, but mostly because she realised how much she missed her mother. She wanted to hold her and be held, made safe as her mother had always done when she was a child.

Clara put her arm around her.

"I can take another letter for you now we know we can contact your mother. I'll call around in the week if you like," said Jenny.

"Yes, that would be kind if you could. I will write back today," said Katya, gradually composing herself once more.

After they had left, Katya re-read the letter and decided not to join Polly on the rec for the moment. She wanted to clear her head and take stock.

Thoughts of Kosovo came flooding back. She went to the kitchen and made herself another drink and then to the window and stared at the scenery, deep in contemplation. Then she had a thought; there was something she needed to do. She went into the bedroom and retrieved her old rucksack which was still at the back of the wardrobe. She put it on the bed and started to rummage around in the bottom. Her hand touched the dog-eared photograph and slowly she removed the picture. She turned it over and looked at the image of her and Ibi and felt... nothing. The bond was broken; it was just a photograph of someone she once knew.

Back on the coach, Bigsy and co were in full swing. They were making good time and, providing they didn't have to keep stopping for comfort breaks brought on by the non-stop consumption of broons, they would arrive at Wembley in good time.

Eventually, at one forty-five the coach pulled into the huge parking lot at Wembley stadium and the fans, most of whom were fairly inebriated, got off and made their way to the ground. Bigsy, Wazza and Chirpie had premium seats and found their way to the appropriate entrance area.

The sheer scale of Wembley and the crowd was something none of them had experienced before. St James's Park was one of the largest grounds in the Premier Division and plans were in place to increase it to over fifty-thousand when the finances were available, but Wembley, with all its history and tradition, was at another level. It truly was 'awesome'; the only word Bigsy could think of.

"There's gonna be at least ninety-thousand in here today, man," said Chirpie who seemed almost overcome with the emotion of it all. "Just think of all them famous footballers that have trod these steps down the years."

"Steady on Chirpie, bonny lad, you'll have us in tears if you carry on like that," said Bigsy.

They made their way to the seats that had been provided for them by their former employer and they were really impressed. Almost at pitch level and at the halfway line directly opposite where, in less than three hours, their god, Alan Shearer, would, hopefully, hold the cup to the adoring fans. Bigsy suggested that they said a short prayer for 'absent friends' but as none of them was remotely religious and couldn't think of anything to say, they decided to just enjoy themselves. "It's what Everton would have wanted," said Chirpie philosophically.

The marching band of the Grenadier Guards put on their usual immaculate display and then the crowd all stood to sing 'Abide with me', tears streamed down Bigsy's face with Wazza and Chirpie also having difficulty in holding back their emotions. The teams came out led by Shearer for the Mags and the much-derided Roy Keane for Manchester United, followed by the two managers in their smart suits, Alex Ferguson and Ruud Gullit.

The game kicked off at three o'clock after the teams were presented to the royal dignitary. United dominated the game. Keane was injured early on and was replaced by Sheringham in the ninth minute, and by the eleventh minute, the striker had put United one-nil up. United remained in control for most of the match and a Scholes' goal, set up by Sheringham, put the game beyond Newcastle after fifty-two minutes.

You would think that losing a Wembley Cup Final would be devastating and, to a degree it was, but the experience of it would live forever with those who were there. By five o'clock Bigsy, Wazza and Chirpie were making their way back to the coach and in the Newcastle section of the crowd, there was a subdued silence.

"I thought we were a bit unlucky," said Chirpie.

"Nah, they're a class act no doubt about it, you have to give it to them," said Bigsy graciously.

Back on Heathcote, the whole estate was watching the game. The Working Men's Club was full to the rafters. Such was the demand, Stan had sold tickets to watch the match on the big screen, never missing an opportunity to make money. It had been a nice little earner too, he commented later. Polly had decided to meet up with Davie Slater at the club. Katya realised that it was a man's domain and had politely declined the offer to join them. She wanted to catch up on some housework she had said, but really she needed to be on her own. She was still in a reflective mood following her mother's letter. She had not yet told Polly about it but would do so when the time was right.

Carole had a tidying-up day and relaxed in her own company. Just before kick-off, she switched on the TV. She wanted to see if she could spot Bigsy but with such an enormous crowd, it was a forlorn hope. She was sad when the final whistle went because she knew that Bigsy would be upset.

At about six o'clock she had a phone call. She thought it would be Bigsy on his mobile wanting to share the sorrow of the result, but it wasn't. She listened to the voice on the other end and sat down on the settee.

"When...? Just after the match you say...? Where have they taken him...? Are you ok...? D'you want us to pop round?" There was a long pause. "I don't know what to say I'm so sorry, pet, I really am… of course; I'll let Bigsy know as soon as he comes home."

Without thinking, she went into the kitchen and grabbed a bottle of red and a couple of glasses and headed out of the flat. She walked down the corridor and knocked on Katya's door.

Katya answered and was surprised to see Carole standing there.

"Are you busy, pet?" said Carole.

"No, I have just finished feeding Melos, and Polly is at the, er… club."

"Thank goodness… I could do with a bit of company right now."

"Of course… Come in," said Katya.

Carole walked in and put the two glasses down on the table. Then unscrewed the bottle top and poured out a large measure of wine in each glass.

"Whatever is the matter Carole...? Is Bigsy ok?" quizzed Katya.

"Aye pet, it's his Da, he died tonight... Just after the match, like," Carole replied still in shock.

"Oh, I am so sorry, does Bigsy know?" asked Katya.

"No, he's on the coach and won't be in till late. I can't phone him on the mobile, it wouldn't be right."

Carole sat down on the sofa and explained the phone call she had received. Mar Worrell had gone to make a cup of tea about five o'clock, after the match had finished and when she returned to him, he was just sat there, in his chair just staring blankly at the screen. She couldn't wake him, and she called an ambulance. The paramedic confirmed he was dead, and they took him to the morgue. Mar was ok and she had a neighbour sitting with her.

They talked for a while and Carole told Katya about Joe and his life and she shed the odd tear. Carole did not tend to show that kind of emotion outwardly. She was a strong character and thought that to break down in public was a sign of weakness, but this was different, and she trusted Katya. She had known Joe for many years and had got to like him immensely. There were so many of his qualities that Bigsy had inherited.

About an hour later, Polly arrived and could see that Carole was upset – her usual immaculate makeup was smeared. "Whatever's wrong Carole, pet?"

She explained what had happened. Polly had offered to contact Bigsy or go around to see Mar Worrell, but Carole asked him not to. She would deal with it when Bigsy came home.

"You'll let your Mam know," said Carole, and she got up to leave. She wanted to get back to her flat in case she had any more calls. Katya let her out, offering to pop around if she needed anything. "Ta pet, I'll just put the telly on and get to the bottom of this bottle. I'll be ok."

Bigsy returned home around two-thirty and was surprisingly sober. There was not much appetite for drinking on the way back and most people, Bigsy included, had just slept. "It was like being at a fookin' funeral," commented Chirpie as they were getting off the coach in Gateshead; rather portentously as it happened. They had to wait twenty-five minutes for a taxi as all the coaches had arrived at about the same time as the clubs in town were starting to turn out and there were long queues at the ranks.

Bigsy was surprised to see Carole was still up but any thoughts of special massages soon disappeared when he saw the streaked makeup and smudged mascara.

"What on earth's up, pet?"

"You better sit down, pet." She kissed him on the cheek and Carole told Bigsy of his father's demise.

"After the match you say?"

"Aye," she replied.

"Well, at least he got to see the Mags at Wembley... Just a pity they couldn't have won the game," and he held Carole and started to cry.

The following morning Bigsy and Carole got up early and went around to console his mother. It was an emotional gathering and neighbours were regularly popping in and out to see Mar Worrell and pay their respects; news travels fast on Heathcote. The undertaker called around and arrangements were made to have the funeral the following Friday. Wazza and Chirpie both visited, which Bigsy really appreciated. "You know who your friends are at times like these," he told Carole later.

They went to the club at lunchtime and it was again full with everyone dissecting yesterday's match with 'if only' and 'maybe if', but the result would stand, history was set, and they would have to move on. When Bigsy arrived, he was swamped with well-wishers offering condolences on the death of his father. Several people, when paying their respects had also commented, "at least he got to see the game," hoping that this was some consolation and would help in some way. Bigsy had come to see Stan Hardacre to arrange the post-funeral do. Stan had promised to put on a decent spread, at 'cost', if Bigsy could give him a note of numbers.

The day of the funeral was very pleasant, warm for early summer. The rec was looking colourful from the flats with its array of yellow dandelions and the goalmouths, which had become quagmires during the winter months, had even started to show a tinge of green.

It seemed like the whole estate had turned out for Joe Worrell. Katya was with Polly and Alison who had both taken days off. Bigsy had arranged a taxi to take them to the crematorium. Kelly had agreed to cover at the pre-school club and look after Melos; Katya didn't feel he would keep quiet long enough during the ceremony. Katya had explained to Edi about the funeral, and that she wouldn't be going to the school. Edi said she would look after Arjeta. She would have a day off from her work.

The cortege started at the couple's bungalow on Bensham and made its way to Heathcote where many of the residents wanted to pay their respects. It travelled slowly through the estate. Bigsy, Carole and Mar Worrell followed the coffin at a sedate pace. Onlookers showing great dignity bowed their heads as they passed by. Carole was immaculate as ever in a new dark outfit which looked suitably funereal.

The service passed off well, warm eulogies were said by the vicar and a couple of former shipyard workers who had kept in close touch with Joe. They talked of his inner strength and his character, and above all his fairness, which was a credit to the Worrell family. Many tears were shed at that point.

After the service around thirty of the closest friends and relatives went back to the club for the do and Stan had done a great job. There was a large picture of Joe Worrell on the wall draped in black and some tasteful flowers on each table. As a mark of respect, Stan had closed the club for the afternoon so the mourners could have some privacy; except for the snooker room, which tended to be a good source of revenue at lunchtimes.

It was late afternoon by the time the party had broken up and Bigsy and Carole made their way back to the flats. Katya was dropped off at the Pre-school club to pick up Melos and Polly said he would walk with her back to the flats.

As they got out of their taxi at the service area in front of the flats, Bigsy couldn't help noticing a new black five-series BMW with smoked glass windows parked outside the gates to the rear of the shops. The engine started and it moved at walking pace towards the small group which had congregated on the pavement outside the flats, busy saying their goodbyes. Bigsy looked around as the car glided towards them. The driver's window slowly lowered.

"Bigsy Worrell?" asked the man.

"Who's asking?" said Bigsy.

"Ah'm Errol Sheedie, Everton's brother." He spoke with his late brother's West Indian accent. "Ah believe we may have some unfinished business."

Wazza and Chirpie had heard the conversation and had moved beside their buddy.

"Aye," said Bigsy, recognising the same features and intimidating look as his brother. "I believe we might, but I've just buried me Da; can it not wait for a couple of hours, like?"

"Ok, Bigsy, ah hear dat you's a mon of honour. Everton always spoke well of you. Here's what we will do, ah'll meet you at seven o'clock but not here, too many eyes. Where do you suggest?"

"There's the Working Men's Club on Seaton Road. The car park at the back will be quiet then. It's where we used to meet Layton." He gave the man directions.

"Dat's cool, mon," said Errol. "See you at seven and my condolences on your loss by de way."

"Ta," said Bigsy but the window was up and the car moving away before he could get his acknowledgement out.

"You don't see many of them round here," said Wazza, referring to the BMW.

"Not with all their wheels on anyway," said Chirpie.

After they got back to the flat, Bigsy got his screwdriver and made an excuse to Carole that he noticed the air-vent in the spare room was loose. Carole was in the main bedroom changing and didn't take any notice. Bigsy again moved quickly and removed the old duffle-bag from behind the grill and screwed it back up again. The bag was covered in dust.

As Carole came out of the bedroom, she was confronted with Bigsy carrying the mangy bag.

"Don't you bring that scabby thing into my lounge again, it's filthy. Look, it's dropping dirt all over my carpet... Take it outside."

"I will, pet, don't you fret. I just need to pop out tonight for a couple hours, a bit of business," replied Bigsy.

"But you've just buried your Da... What's so important you've got to go out...? Is it about that car you was talking to?"

"Just a bit of business to finish that's all... Nottin' to worry about," replied Bigsy and Carole let it drop.

Bigsy was waiting outside the tower block pacing up and down, anxiously dragging on a cigarette when Wazza and Chirpie called around at six forty-five. They headed off to the club with the duffle-bag safely stashed in the boot. The 'Beemer' pulled into the car park at seven o'clock precisely.

"What's it about these Rastas? They're always on time," observed Chirpie.

Errol got out. He was a large man, at least six foot three with short curly hair and designer sunglasses; he reminded Bigsy of Morgan Freeman, who was one of his favourite actors. He wore a gold chain around his neck, black shirt, pale green slacks, loafers and enough gold around his wrists to cover the national debt of small African country. The obligatory diamond-studded Rolex completed the look; this was some serious dude. And he was not alone; two equally hard-looking characters got out of the back seat and stood menacingly at the rear of the car. Bigsy, not to be phased went up to Errol and, as Everton had done on their first meet, offered his knuckles for a touch. Errol gave a huge grin and did the greeting.

"I was sorry to hear of Everton's passing Errol, bonny lad," said Bigsy.

His casualness and lack of fear slightly unnerved Errol; he was used to being treated with reverence. At the same time, it also endeared him to Bigsy.

"We had a cracking time down at Wembley. It was a shame Everton couldn't have made it, like, but he was remembered. We said a few words for him during 'Abide with Me'," said Bigsy.

Errol smiled again. "Dat's nice to hear Bigsy, mon," said Errol. "Shall we get down to de business. You have something dat belongs to me."

"Aye," said Bigsy, "Get the bag from the boot, Wazza, lad," and Wazza retrieved the duffle-bag and Bigsy gave it to Errol.

"I kept it safe, like. I said to the lads, someone'll be wanting it, you see. It's all there, man," said Bigsy as Errol looked inside.

"I'm sure it is," said Errol and gave the bag to one of his henchman who put it in the boot of the BMW.

"Everton was right when he said he had found a diamond when he found you. Are you and de lads interested in carrying on working for me?"

Bigsy thought for a moment and eyed up the big West Indian.

"Look, no disrespect, like, but it seems people end up dead working around the Sheedie family so if it's all the same to you, like, I think I'll pass on the offer; if you don't mind, bonny lad."

Errol looked perplexed and seemed to be considering the response.

"I'll say dis, Bigsy, mon, you're one cool dude... respect is due. Ah just come for de money and Ah'm out of dis shit hole and back to civilisation in Brixton. You'll be getting no bother from me and ah'll see dat no-one else has cause either, but if you change your mind here's my number and if you get any trouble, any trouble at all, you give me a call, ok?"

He gave Bigsy a business card. 'Errol T Sheedie Ltd., Security Agents', it said.

They touched knuckles again and Errol let out a huge roar of laughter. "Come on lads, back to de smoke. You take care, Bigsy, mon." He turned and got into the back of the BMW.

The driver fired up the car and it sounded like something from a Formula 1 racetrack. It accelerated out of the car park, the spinning rear wheels stirring up gravel and dust which flew in all directions.

"Well lads, it looks like it's back to the videos, and I'm not unhappy about that either. I've had enough excitement to last a lifetime," said Bigsy and they piled into Wazza's car and went back to the flats.

Chapter Eighteen

Thursday June 3, 1999 came the news that all the refugees had been waiting to hear. The headlines on the TV early morning breakfast programme said:

"Milošević surrenders."

Katya turned up the volume on the TV and listened intently to the commentary:

'Full details are still coming in, but the latest news from Belgrade is that Slobodan Milošević has agreed to cease all hostilities by the Serbian forces and has accepted a NATO-led peacekeeping force (KFOR) into Kosovo. According to a NATO spokesman, the peace-keeping will be undertaken under a special directive from a UN Security Council Resolution. Initially, KFOR's mandate is to help provide a secure environment and ensure public safety and order so that the Kosovan refugees can return home. The possibility of real peace at last. We will bring you further information as we get it.'

Since moving to the flats, Katya had always watched the TV first thing in the morning while feeding Melos to get what news she could about the war. Recent reports were beginning to show that the NATO bombing campaign was beginning to have some effect, but after so many false dawns and dashed hopes, this had come almost out of the blue.

Strangely, she had mixed emotions. The letter she had received from her mother had rekindled her thoughts of 'home' but over recent weeks, she had settled into the new community and felt very much a part of it. Her friendship with Carole, her relationship with Polly, her job at the Pre-school club, and the support she had received from Clara and the other agencies had moved her to consider staying in the UK permanently. She had nothing to go back for apart from her mother, whom she loved dearly, but she wasn't getting any younger and Katya had Melos and his future to consider.

Clara had told Katya she was in no doubt she would be accepted on a permanent residence status. "We need good teachers," she had said, and Katya was a good teacher.

What she didn't know, of course, was whether this new peace deal would mean that the original offer of asylum by the UK Government would be rescinded and there would be immediate repatriation of refugees back to Kosovo, so many questions.

She rang Clara to see if she could fix a meeting with her and Jenny Wheatley to discuss what was happening and Clara said she would arrange it.

On the sixth floor, Edi too had seen the reports and, although she could not understand all of it, she had a pretty good idea what was happening.

She was getting Arjeta ready for her collection by Katya at nine-thirty. Although she had not heard from Trev since Tuesday morning, which, given recent activity, she thought strange, she was dressed in her working gear. She was sure he would call this morning.

Edi was overjoyed of course. She could go home and get away from all this and back to a life that she knew, where she would feel comfortable and safe. It used to be so simple on the farm with her husband and daughter and her parents close by. She yearned to be back to her life as she remembered it.

It would also mean she wouldn't have to sell herself anymore to all those men she despised so much.

She had been giving a lot of thought to what she would do if and when peace came, and she could return to Kosovo. She hated herself for what she had become but, of course, it had been necessary to give Arjeta what she deserved. That was all that mattered.

Although she had no relatives to go back to in Kosovo, she did have good neighbours who had sheltered her. They had told her they would always be there for her. As a widow of a 'hero of Kosovo', she would always be looked after in the new order of things... wouldn't she?

She would talk to Katya about it.

When Katya arrived, Edi gushed excitedly in Albanian about the news. She asked Katya when she thought they would be able to go home and what Katya was going to do. She knew about her relationship with Polly. Katya explained about the possibility of a meeting with the Refugee Council representative and would keep Edi informed.

Elsewhere on the estate events were slowly unfolding that would take any decisions out of Edi's hands.

Pauline Rankin was a piss-head. She was also a manipulating and evil piss-head. Life for her had been hard. She had had an abortion at fourteen and expelled from school not long after for being a 'severe disruptive influence'. That was hardly an imposition; she was rarely there in any case.

She was regularly getting into fights and the assault on one of her teachers was the last straw. Her mother had also lived on the estate but died of a heroin overdose when Pauline was twelve, after which she was put into care. She didn't have a father, not one that was there for her anyway. She frequently ran away from her foster parents and would always end up back on the estate, usually dossing down on a friend's floor.

She learned the art of threat as an influencing tool very early in life. She was a bully and a compulsive liar, in fact, someone that you did not want to make an enemy of – or have as a friend, for that matter. She had also discovered the power that the promise of her body could do to men. She could have anything she wanted. She managed shoplifting gangs like some waif-like Fagan and could always get her hands on the drug of choice, although alcohol, the cheaper alternative, would dominate her late teens and early twenties. Overall the life of Pauline Rankin was, to say the least, colourful if tragic.

Her life had changed, but not necessarily for the better, when she met Trev at a club in Gateshead when she was just eighteen, nearly seven years ago, and succumbed to his easy charm. Trev was twelve years older than Pauline with a chequered past. He was a single father, although the term 'father' was loose in this case; he had had little influence over the development of a, then, seven-year-old Rikki. Trev would regularly leave him on his own and go into town on the pull. And pull he did. Pauline saw him as a way out; he had a council house on Heathcote, and in his own way was attractive enough. He could also get drugs.

They got married, which surprised a lot of people that knew the couple. They were rowing even before the nuptials and Pauline could often be seen in Mr Ali's wearing a scarf or more makeup than was usual to cover the bruises. But she could give as well as receive and had already caused Trev to be hospitalised. In one particularly vicious incident, she drew a knife on him that put a three-inch gash in his arm.

So it was against this background that Pauline heard of Trev's pimping side-line.

Two days earlier, Trev had gone to the club for a game of snooker but instead of staying late and getting drunk as usual, he decided a couple of frames accompanied by a broon or two would suffice and he would head home. He had made an appointment with Edi for the following day and didn't want to cause any impediment to his performance.

He got home to find Pauline in a state of undress with some spotty lad on the living room floor.

"What the fook's going on here?!" said Trev as he entered the room.

Pauline quickly covered herself up but, before the lad could move, Trev had grabbed him by the throat and went mental, giving the lad the hiding of his life. Trev dragged the barely conscious lad to his feet before throwing him out the front door sending him crashing onto the concrete.

He then went after Pauline, who ran into the kitchen and pulled a knife from the drawer. The boy she had been with, happened to be fifteen-year-old Stevie Leonard, one of son Rikki's closest mates. Rikki had been down the video store with Bigsy helping out shelf-stacking to earn some money and was on his way home when he found his buddy lying in the alleyway next to his house, moaning and in need of urgent medical attention. Rikki phoned the ambulance and, while waiting for it to arrive, he held his buddy's head trying to keep him comfortable. There was blood pouring from a deep gash to his forehead, both eyes were black, there were bruises to his cheeks; his nose appeared to be broken and one of his front teeth was loose. He was in a bad way.

"Who did this to you, Stevie?" said Rikki.

"It was your da," he replied in a rasping whimper.

"Why's he done this to you?"

He struggled to speak. "Your Pauline phoned us and said she was having a party for your birthday, a surprise, like. She wanted me to come round and talk about it." He winced in pain, the blood from his head now dripping onto the concrete floor of the alleyway.

He continued, talking slowly in a wheezy voice, "When I got here, Pauline asks if I wanted a drink an' she gave me a glass of water. Then I started feeling really strange, like. My legs were all wobbly and stuff... I must have passed out... The next thing I know she's sitting on top of me in just her knickers... sucking my willie."

He paused, almost losing consciousness, but managed to continue. "Then your Da walks in, and sets into me... It wasn't my fault, Rikki... honest," and Stevie went quiet.

"Hold on, Stevie mate, hold on," said Rikki, cradling his buddy's head.

The paramedics arrived and quickly got him into an ambulance and as soon as Stevie was away, Rikki went into the house and found his father shouting and swearing at Pauline who was now at least dressed, if a little dishevelled. She was holding a knife in her hand in what was ostensibly a stand-off, threatening she would run Trev through if he laid his hands on her.

Rikki screamed at his father. "Why did you fookin' do that to Stevie for...? It was her fault," pointing at Pauline.

Pauline hurled more abuse at Trev. "You're a fookin' coke-head; I need a real man who's up to the job, you useless piece of shite."

"Well, I haven't had any complaints lately," Trev shouted back defiantly.

"What's that supposed to mean?" said Pauline.

Suddenly Rikki shouted. "He's doing the Kossie prossie."

It went quiet. "Now you shut your face," said Trev looking at Rikki, clenching his fist threateningly.

"No... you go on Rikki, lad, you tell us what you mean," said Pauline, eyes wide with anger, fury and mostly hate and with the knife still pointing in Trev's direction.

Rikki spilled the beans.

"I've seen him go in there loads of times," said Rikki, fired up by the anger he felt at the abuse his friend had taken at the hands of his so-called parents.

"Go where?" asked Pauline, who was leaning forward with the knife in her hand ready to defend herself if Trev made a move towards her.

"I'm warning you," said Trev, unable to get to Rikki past Pauline and the knife.

"To her flat in the block," replied Rikki. "The Kossie's... the one on the game."

"What were you doing there, Rikki?" asked Pauline, becoming interested in the story.

"Shut your fookin' face, lad, before you get a good slapping." Trev was beginning to look anxious now.

"You leave him alone, you fookin' gobshite," shouted Pauline, her rage showing no abating.

Rikki continued. "I was looking out for the Kossies for Bigsy, making sure they didn't get bothered or nothing."

"What's that got to do with anything?" said Trev.

"I saw the Kossie in Mr Ali's buying rubbers. Everyone knows she's been at it. I was watching from the stairs," said Rikki.

"And you've seen your Da go in?" said Pauline, her demeanour changing.

"Aye, loads of blokes were going in," replied Rikki.

The atmosphere was tense. Trev was now on the defensive with this major revelation and Pauline, despite her earlier indiscretions, had taken the moral high ground.

"I want to know who else has been round there dipping their wicks," said Pauline. "Or else the whole estate will know what you've been up to and you can't imagine the bother that'll cause."

Trev knew she wasn't bluffing, and the fall out was too grim to contemplate. He tossed a few names; "Pete Draper".

"What? Gemma's hubby?" Gemma was a cleaner at the local hospital and worked long hours to support her family. She was also one of Pauline's closest weekend clubbing mates.

"Aye," said Trev sheepishly. He continued, "Stevie Compton."

"He's living with our Linda," another of Pauline's pals.

And the list went on.

It was not a coincidence that the girls, who were attached to the men involved, were friends of Pauline. Trev's social circle was fairly limited, and, obviously, the men Trev had originally contacted as potential clients were known to them both. Then the client list grew by recommendation.

Pauline, a lot calmer now, was taking control.

"OK, the matter's closed," and she returned the knife to the kitchen table but keeping it within arm's reach. "I'm gonna sort everything out."

She stared at Trev. "And you, you fookin' gob-shite, will give up your agency work and you can apologise to young Stevie when he gets out of hospital, and if I want to recompense him for his pain and suffering in the best way I know how, then you'll just have to put up with it."

Trev hung his head, knowing the game was up.

She looked at the lad. "Thanks Rikki, you've done the right thing telling us. You're a good boy, deep down. I want you to make sure you go to school for the rest of the week, and you'll hear no more about it. If your father lays a finger on you, you let me know."

The threat of exposure hung in the air. Trev was beaten and slunk off out of the house, back to the club to get drunk.

So on Thursday third of June, the day Kosovans could celebrate their freedom, at nine forty-five in the morning, Edi received a knock on the door. Katya and Arjeta were well on their way to school. Edi thought it would be Trev, although she thought he would have phoned; he always had. On the other hand, she had received a lot of visitors from the various support agencies that were helping her through her psychological problems, or so they thought. So there was no reason to fear answering the door; a decision she would regret.

As she opened the door, Pauline and four of her friends barged in and bundled Edi to the ground. Gemma and Linda sat on her while Pauline got a roll of masking tape and wrapped it 'round her head and mouth. Edi was almost paralysed first with shock, but now fear.

"We'll teach you to come over here and shag our blokes while we're trying to earn a crust," said Pauline.

Edi was gagging; her eyes wide with fright. Pauline took out a knife she had hidden in her belt and put it to Edi's throat.

"Now we're going for a little walk and if you make a peep of noise, I'll slit your throat like a pig. Understand?" Edi made no attempt to acknowledge, she was frightened rigid.

"I said do you understand?"

Edi nodded without any comprehension of what was happening, her eyes reflecting the terror she felt inside. She was shaking uncontrollably. Pauline told one of the girls to check the landing and grab a lift. They heard the 'ping' sound a few moments later.

Ensuring the coast was clear, they picked Edi off the floor and the five of them dragged her outside the flat and shut the door. They then bundled Edi into the lift and hit the 'up' button, floor twenty. Thirty seconds later, the lift reached the destination and the door opened.

"I hope you like heights, Kossie," said Pauline sarcastically.

Opposite the lift was the maintenance stairway which led to the roof from the twentieth floor. Gemma and Linda pulled opened the heavy metal access door. They pushed Edi through and closed it behind them. It would normally be locked but there was a routine inspection due that morning the caretaker would say later. Pauline and the four others bundled Edi up the short flight of stairs in total darkness.

They opened the door at the end of the stairway and emerged into the bright light on the top of the building. Edi was desperately struggling against her captors. Three seagulls vacated their perches squawking their disapproval at the disturbance.

The roof area was covered in asphalt and had various aerials, satellite dishes and a maintenance hut where hoists were kept for window cleaning. There was also the housing for the lift which was regularly in use to sort out failures and routine maintenance.

The wind howled across the top of the building, making it difficult to stand. Mini dust-devils danced between the hut and the lift housing raising discarded cigarette ends and other small debris before disgorging them elsewhere. The five women wrestled Edi back on the ground and Pauline removed the masking tape and placed her hand over Edi's mouth so that she could hardly breathe.

"We don't want no evidence do we?" said Pauline.

Edi started to go limp and Pauline released her grip.

"Ah no lady, you're going to experience this trip," and without further ado the girls lifted Edi up and walked quickly to the edge of the building and threw her over.

As Edi hurtled towards the ground, Pauline noticed a kite

flying over on the rec. How appropriate she thought, the Kossie is flying with kites.

Mr Ali was taking some rubbish to the dustbins at the back of his shop when something in his peripheral vision caught his attention. He focused and looked again, aghast, as he saw an object falling from Heathcote Tower. He thought at first it was a wheelie bin. Kids had been known to throw them off the top for a laugh, though not since they had the new security doors fitted. But then it became all too clear as he saw the arms flailing in the air as if clutching, searching for some imaginary hand-hold to slow the descent and save them from oblivion.

There was no discernible noise as she hit the concrete walkway that surrounded the building. Not a crash or clunk or any sharp sound, just a dull thud. No movement, like a discarded rag doll, turfed out of a child's pram.

Mr Ali rushed to the scene. Others walked over quickly to where the remains of Edona Bukosi lay. There would be nothing they could do.

The ambulance and police arrived in around ten minutes, alerted by the storekeeper. Mr Ali stood guard, keeping prying eyes away, trying to provide some vestige of dignity for the Kosovan who came to the community looking for a safe-haven. The perpetrators slipped away without being seen, satisfied that their honour had been served.

The police set up a cordon around the scene with blue tape and started asking for witnesses. News crews also turned up as word got out that one of the Kosovans that only a few weeks ago was being welcomed by the people of the estate and the media had jumped from the roof.

Clara Davenport turned up around eleven o'clock and police activity was well underway. Men were setting up satellite dishes at the front of the building, just like at the reception only a few short weeks ago. Edi's body was shielded under a black plastic sheet. Clara made her way to the tape and talked to one of the officers.

"I'm Clara Davenport, Community Liaison Officer. I've just had a message from one of your officers that one of the refugees has been found dead. Do you know who?"

Mr Ali was still at the scene in a state of shock and was being interviewed by another officer. He heard the question and intervened. "It's Edi... poor Edi. It is so sad; why would she want to kill herself? She had a lovely daughter and seemed so happy here, and just when they say there is peace at last... It just doesn't make sense."

"Oh, no!" exclaimed Clara put her hand over her mouth in shock.

She quickly composed herself and asked the officer if she could see the body. She could confirm her identity. One of the officers lifted the tape and let her through.

"Are you sure you want to do this? It's not pretty."

Clara almost passed out when she saw Edi's broken body, but when she saw the outfit, the same she was wearing a couple of days ago when they had visited her, there was no doubt. She nodded to the policeman.

"Has anyone contacted Katya?" Clara asked.

"Katya...? Who is Katya?" asked the officer.

"Katya Gjikolli, the other refugee," replied Clara. "They were friends."

"No, I don't think so. I'll ask the boss."

Another officer, not in uniform, approached Clara. "My colleague tells me there is a daughter, how old is she?" asked the detective.

"About three, I think; she'll be at the Pre-school club with Katya," said Clara. "I should go and get her."

"Yes, if you wouldn't mind, please. I'll need to have a chat with her," said the officer and Clara got in her car and headed off to the Pre-school club.

Clara parked outside the centre and went in. Sonia was on reception.

"I need to speak to Katya... It's urgent."

She could hear Katya's voice talking to the children. Sonia led Clara through into the main hall and Clara beckoned Katya. Katya waved back and after a couple of minutes joined them.

"Is there somewhere where we can go in private?" Clara asked.

Mel, who had come to see what was happening, led them to the staff room; Sonia took over the group.

"What is wrong?" said Katya as they sat down.

"I'm afraid I have some very bad news Katya," Clara said. There was a pause and she looked down. "There is no easy way to say this... Edi is dead."

Katya was stunned and didn't say anything for a moment.

"Dead, no she can't be I only saw her this morning... How?"

"She was found at the bottom of the Tower block. They're saying she might have… jumped."

"No... no, that cannot be... She would not kill herself, never," said Katya animatedly. "She has Arjeta to take care of... and it is against her religion."

"Yes, I know... It does seem strange, and the police did say that it's only one possibility they're looking at, but if Mel can spare you, I think we should go back to the flats. The police want to talk to you."

Katya looked at Arjeta who was playing with a couple of other children. "How am I going to tell her? She will be totally lost, Edi almost... how you say...?" Katya searched her mind for the right word. "Smothered her with love."

Mel quietly moved away then shortly returned with Melos and Arjeta. Katya took her son in her arms and gently took hold of Arjeta's hand.

"We have to go now, say bye-bye to Mel and Sonia," Katya said, trying to hold back her tears, and then she took them to join Clara in her car. She put Melos's buggy in the boot.

As they got back to the flats, the media circus was in full swing.

"Oh no, not again, it was like this when we arrived," said Katya.

"I will park up by the shops and we can walk the rest of the way," said Clara, but there were no spaces and Clara ended up driving onto the grass verge next to the path that led to the rec.

Katya noticed the lads on the bikes again and Mr Ali was outside his shop viewing the commotion. Jamal was on the till which was now busy with journalists and sound crews, reporters and cameramen looking for lunch-time sustenance. Mr Ali saw Katya and went to her.

"I am so sorry... Edi was such a nice lady."

"Thank you, Mr Ali," said Katya.

With her head bowed, and with Arjeta holding her hand, Katya made her way to the lifts. Clara followed with Melos in the buggy. The police officer in the suit headed them off before they could get to the entrance lobby and some journalists recognising Katya started to circle, firing questions at her.

"Why do you think she jumped?" asked one.

"Didn't she like it here?" asked another.

The officer intervened and told Clara and Katya to go up to the flat; he would join them in a couple of minutes. Clara told him the number.

They got into Katya's flat and Arjeta wanted to know why they hadn't gone to see 'mami'. Katya didn't know what to say and just said that she needed her to look after Melos and left the room.

Clara made them both a coffee. And a few minutes later the police officer arrived with a policewoman.

"This is W.P.C. Maggie Dobbs," he introduced his colleague. "And I'm D. I. Geoff Fielding. I need to ask you a few questions... If that's ok?"

Fielding wanted a complete background on Edi. Clara kept the children occupied and out of earshot.

"How did she seem this morning when you picked up her daughter?"

"Fine," Katya replied, fighting to maintain her composure. "She was excited about the news of the war, she was happy. She thought she could go home soon. I still can't believe she would do anything to hurt herself, it doesn't make any sense... and she had Arjeta to look after."

He continued his questioning. "Have you had any racial abuse since you arrived?"

Katya told them about the dog mess. "Just children," she told them, but nothing since. "Everyone has been so kind."

"Do you know if anything was bothering Edi, you know, money worries, relationship problems, things like that?"

"No, I don't think so. She spent most of her money on Arjeta, clothes, candy, toys and things," replied Katya.

"What about her state of mind? Did she have problems with her mental health?" continued the officer.

Katya told him that she had had difficulties in adjusting and told him about Edi's parents and the traumas she had to endure escaping from Kosovo.

Katya continued. "When she arrived, she was not in a good way, but she had seen the doctor here and the pills seemed to be helping... She seemed happier now."

After about an hour of questions they left. Fielding told Katya they would return again soon; they were just starting the investigation. Finally, he asked if Katya would be prepared to do the formal identification at some stage. Katya agreed.

"Thank you for your help," said the officer as they left the flat.

In the lift, Fielding turned to his colleague.

"What do you think, Maggie?"

"Not sure, guv, but it doesn't add up. Why would she kill herself now just when the war has ended...? And she had her daughter she doted over, according to her friend... I'm not convinced it's suicide."

"Me neither." He made a call. "Get a forensic team up on the roof and we need to look at the flat. Get it marked up as a possible crime scene; I don't want anyone in there treading on the daisies."

A short time later, Polly arrived, having been on the rec most of the morning with his kite. He hugged Katya. "I've just heard about Edi; I can't believe she would top herself."

Katya understood. "She didn't Polly, I am sure... She had too much to live for."

"What was she doing on the roof anyway? How did she get up there? The doors're always locked," said Polly.

"I don't know... It doesn't make any sense... I hope the police will find out," said Katya.

"I'll give our Bigsy a ring and let him know. He may have some ideas," said Polly and got on his mobile.

Katya looked at Arjeta and then Clara. "How am I going to tell her, Clara?"

"Hmm, I don't know... I can get some professional help in to support you. I've already rung Jenny Wheatley and Doctor Peterson and they're coming over later this afternoon." she paused. "I'll say this, if this is a suicide, there's going to be a lot of questions asked."

Polly held Katya; she still hadn't cried yet; she could not take it in.

As Clara was leaving, so Bigsy came to the door. Katya kissed him on the cheek and went to make some coffee.

"I can't believe it, pet. I am so sorry for yas, I really am," said Bigsy. He told Katya that he would be making his own enquiries and if he found out anyone had killed her, there would be trouble.

Chapter Nineteen

The ripple effect of Edi's death had disturbed a great deal of muddy water.

The police had made extensive enquiries and had come to the conclusion that Edi's death was suspicious. There were too many unanswered questions. Why would she kill herself on the very day that peace had been declared? How did she know that the door to the roof would be open; if, in fact, she knew there was a door to the roof?

Was it a coincidence that the caretaker had opened the door earlier that morning for a routine maintenance visit that no one else seemed to know anything about?

The officers had questioned him hard on this point, but he refused or was unable, to give any further information. He explained he had received a phone call that morning from someone from a maintenance company asking for access and he hadn't thought to check it.

The police had established that Edi was devoted to her daughter, everyone had said so; it was also against her religion to kill herself. Although not a practising Muslim, she had been brought up with their broader ideals. Her mental state appeared more stable of late and her psychiatrist had said she had not shown any indications of self-harm. Then there was the flat. Why did she have a box of condoms in her bedside cabinet? Why the revealing clothing which seemed out of character for a Kosovan farm girl? Where did she get the money for all the children's clothes and stuff that were in the wardrobe?

The indication was beginning to suggest that she was acting as a prostitute; it would seem the only logical conclusion. But that opened up other questions; who were her clients? How did she get them? Did she have a supplier?

There were scuff marks on the floor of the flat which could have been a sign of a struggle. There were also several footprints on the gravel on top of the roof, but a recent rainstorm had washed away any chance of firm evidence.

The incident was widely reported in the newspapers and were taking the suicide line, which prompted articles on the effects of post-traumatic stress disorder and the mental health issues of refugees.

The media frenzy continued for a couple of days, even Chrissie Franklin made another appearance.

"It must be serious for that tart to be on the case," said Bigsy to Carole, when they were watching the six-thirty local news.

The local community was in shock and there were genuine outpourings of sorrow. Katya had been given compassionate leave and Mel and her partner Kelly had visited the flat a couple of times to give her some support. She had been interviewed several times by the police and had the harrowing task of formally identifying Edi's body. Clara had accompanied her.

Katya had agreed to look after Arjeta. Clara said it would be in Arjeta's best interests, and she was giving her as much attention as possible. Arjeta continued to ask for her 'mami'. "When is she coming back?" and "Why can't I see her?"

Polly had been a tower of strength. The incident had also hit him badly. He had shown considerable maturity in the way he had supported Katya, and she relied on him now in so many ways. He even took turns in babysitting Arjeta and had made her a small kite.

Once the flat had been processed by the police, Edi's belongings had been given to Katya as guardian of Edi's daughter. Katya was surprised at the number of clothes and baby things Edi had amassed in such a short period, Katya had to put it in the spare bedroom, there was no space in the wardrobe for it. She looked at the pile. Edi could never have paid for all of it through her benefits; it just wasn't possible. There appeared to be hundreds of pounds of stuff, but where she was getting her money from was a mystery.

In the social services department of the local council, panic was setting in. Everyone was covering their backs. The Head of the children's division, Mr Potter, was holding one meeting after another, he'd blanked his diary for the foreseeable future and was only taking phone calls relating to this incident. There was going to be a full enquiry. The press were calling for heads and he wanted to make sure it wasn't his.

Clara, Michelle Dexter and even Doctor Peterson had been interviewed. The Refugee Council had been involved. Mr. Potter had also been interviewed on TV by that Rottweiler of local news reporting, Chrissie Franklyn. He had assured the public that 'no stone would be left unturned', 'lessons would be learned', etc., etc., and the public could be confident in the 'professionalism, dedication and expertise' of their local social services department.

Edi's funeral was a devastatingly sad affair. All expenses had been taken care of by the local council with a contribution from a central fund. Katya, as chief mourner, sat in the car with Clara. Mel had taken Melos and Arjeta to the Pre-school; Arjeta still hadn't understood that her 'mami' would not return.

As with Bigsy's father, the cortege had passed slowly through the estate to the crematorium, and the road was flanked by well-wishers who, as previously, reverently bowed their heads as it went by. News reporters covered the story.

There had been a lot of speculation and rumour around the estate about what had happened, but for now, the appropriate respect was being paid. Bigsy had again come up trumps with a do back at the club. Katya wasn't sure but Bigsy said Edi was 'one of their own' and it was the right thing to do.

At the club, Stan had laid on a small spread and made the

lounge available for mourners but in the event only a few took advantage of this generous offer.

"I don't know what I'm gonna do with all these sarnies left over," said Stan to Bigsy when they eventually left.

Polly, Alison, Bigsy and Carole arranged go back to Katya's flat for a while to give her some support. Clara also said she would come.

While the rest of the group made their way to the lifts, Carole called in to the mini-market to get some coffee, milk and a packet of biscuits; Katya had run short.

As she came out of the store, she noticed Rikki Rankin and his two friends riding aimlessly around the precinct. They scampered off when he recognised her. Carole thought it a bit odd.

When she returned to the flat with the supplies, Carole handed them to Katya who went to the kitchen to make the drinks. "I'll give you a hand," said Clara, relinquishing the babysitting duties to Allison.

Bigsy was sat on one of the chairs talking to Polly.

Carole looked at Bigsy. "You'll never guess who I've just seen, pet...? Young Rikki Rankin and his two mates riding 'round the precinct."

"They're always 'round there," said Bigsy.

"Aye, but when they saw us like, they scarpered smartish, as if they were guilty or something," replied Carole.

Bigsy thought about this.

There was a knock on the door, and it was Mel who had returned with the two children; Katya made a fuss of them. Carole was on coffee-making duties and Mel stopped for a while and chatted.

"If there's anything I can do, please let me know," said Mel as she left. Alison also made her excuses; she needed to get back.

It was quieter. Katya was seated on the settee with Polly and Carole, Bigsy on one of the chairs. Clara was in the spare bedroom playing with the children. Katya looked drawn and tired with the events of the last few days and was in deep contemplation, pondering what had happened.

She was sipping her coffee, then looked up.

"There is something else; something the policeman told me. He asked if I knew why Edi had a box of... how you say?" she paused for the translation. "Er... condoms...? I told him I did not know."

She took another sip of coffee. Carole, Bigsy and Polly were listening intently.

"Edi, er... told me something which I have not told the police. She told me... when she was in the camp in Macedonia she had..." another pause, Katya looked down. "She told me that she had... How do you say? Given herself to the soldiers to get extra food for Arjeta…"

Katya looked at Carole, then Polly. "I don't know, maybe she was doing that again. That could be where she was getting the money from for all the clothes and things for Arjeta... I don't know... I thought I would have been able to tell if she was in trouble. We did talk a lot." She paused again. "She was wearing more makeup and different clothes, but I thought that was because of the dance at the club. She seemed to have had a good time. She had changed since that night."

Katya was becoming upset and Carole her hand to comfort her.

"Do you think I should say this to the police?" asked Katya.

"Nah, I think you should say nottin'…" said Bigsy. "Mind you, the bizzies did stop and ask me if I'd noticed any strange men going into the flats recently. I told them most of the men 'round here were strange, like, but I bet that's what they're thinking."

He thought for a moment, then looked at Carole. "I've got to pop out for a bit, pet; I want to make some enquiries of my own and I think I know where to start."

He made his excuses to Katya and left the flat.

Back on the ground floor, Bigsy walked across the front of the flats towards the precinct. The police marquee which had hidden the spot where Edi had landed was now being taken down by two police officers. A Council cleaning team were stood outside their lorry smoking cigarettes, waiting to clean the site.

Bigsy reached the video store and made a call on his mobile.

"Rikki lad, it's Bigsy. Now, don't you go worrying, you're not in any trouble, promise, but I need to have a quick word, like. Can you meet us at the video shop as soon as? I'll be waiting for you," and he rang off.

Bigsy was in the shop and about ten minutes later a rather nervous looking Rikki walked in. "Come through into the back, bonny lad. Don't fret you're not in any bother."

They went into the back and Bigsy switched the kettle on. The area doubled as a kitchen; there was a sink and drainer with some coffee-stained mugs standing on it. A small fridge was in the corner next to the special video selection display.

Bigsy took one of the mugs from the drainer, rinsed it under the tap and poured himself a cup of coffee. He took a bottle of milk from the fridge and topped up the boiling liquid, deliberately taking his time. Rikki sat nervously on an old chair in the corner biting his fingers surrounded by shelves of adult videos.

"D'you want a brew, bonny lad?" Rikki shook his head.

"Suit yerself," said Bigsy.

Bigsy was getting himself into the right frame of mind. He wanted Rikki to understand that he wanted information but did not want to frighten him into not disclosing anything. Advanced psychology would be required. He started his piece.

"You've been a big help to me since we had that misunderstanding about the dog shite," said Bigsy. "I've really appreciated you being my eyes and ears, like… regarding the Kossies. There's been no bother and that's down to you, Rikki lad, but things have changed a bit lately… you know what I'm saying?"

"Aye, Bigsy, I do. I've been frantic with worry about it."

"Well, I reckon you know what's going on and I need you to enlighten us, like, cos I'm having difficulty here?" Bigsy took a slug of coffee.

Rikki began to cry, but after a bit of coaxing Rikki started to tell Bigsy the story.

"Aye, well, I've been keeping an eye on the Kossies like you asked us to, Bigsy, and I noticed there were loads of men going into the Kossie's flat... You know the one that died... including me Da."

"Your Da an' all, you say?" queried Bigsy

"Aye, then we had a big bust-up at the house after me Da beat up our Stevie and I told Pauline about it." Rikki started to cry again. "I didn't want to get anyone in any bother I was just so angry about what he had done to Stevie."

"That's alright, Rikki lad, and what happened next?" encouraged Bigsy.

"Well, nottin' really. Pauline said not to say anything, and she would sort it," replied Rikki.

"What did your Da say?"

"Nottin'. Pauline told him she would tell everyone he was screwing the Kossie if he said anything and he's been stoned most've the time since then."

"I wish you had told me before, Rikki, lad. I could have sorted all this out and maybe the Kossie would still be alive," said Bigsy, which did nothing to help Rikki's state of mind.

"What's going to happen, Bigsy? The cops have been 'round asking questions and everything. I'm scared, I mean really scared, man. I've been thinking about running off but I've nowhere to go."

"Now, don't you worry, Rikki, bonny lad, your uncle Bigsy's going to sort this out once and for all so keep your head down and don't bunk off school again, ok?"

"Aye, ta Bigsy," said Rikki. He smiled at the thought of Bigsy being his 'uncle' and he left the shop and headed home.

Bigsy had an idea; he had work to do.

He took out his wallet and pulled out a business card, 'Errol T Sheedie Ltd., Security Agents'.

He punched the numbers into his mobile. The call was answered on the third ring. "Yeah," came a gruff voice.

"Errol, bonny lad, its Bigsy Worrell. I need a favour to ask," said Bigsy.

Errol seemed pleased to hear from him. "Bigsy, my mon, what's happenin'?"

Bigsy's favour was large and he knew he might be asked to repay it sometime in the future.

He went over exactly what he needed and gave Errol a little background into the 'why'.

"Dat's criminal mon," said Errol when Bigsy described Edi's unfortunate demise. "Ah tink ah can help here. Would ya like me to send a couple of me lads up. Dey have experience of handling dis kind of ting, ah'll cover der expenses?"

"No, thanks anyway Errol, bonny lad." Errol loved it when Bigsy called him that; it creased him up. "It's something I've got to finish. I owe it to Edi, like."

Bigsy continued, "I'll send the money today recorded delivery and I'll put the address inside. When can I expect the package? Two days... that's champion," and he rang off.

Bigsy headed back to their flat and to the shoe box in his wardrobe. Carole was still at Katya's. He took what he needed and went back to 1410.

"You've been a while, pet," said Carole. "Any problems?"

"Nah... Just a bit of business to take care of," replied Bigsy. "Just going for a wander up to the post office in Seaton, I need to post a letter and I could do with the exercise."

Two days later, Friday, and Carole had gone to work so wasn't around to see what Bigsy was doing. A jiffy-bag arrived at flat 1405; there was no return address on the envelope.

Bigsy took out the plastic bag from inside the container

wearing a pair of thin rubber washing-up gloves and opened it carefully. Then he emptied out the white powder onto a saucer and divided it into two equal portions which he placed in two smaller plastic bags and sealed them. He put the saucer in the sink and poured bleach on it, removing any trace of the substance. He re-sealed the jiffy-bag with the original bag back inside and wrapped it in an old newspaper. It would be in the communal waste bin shortly and, with delivery due today, by lunchtime, it would be rotting on a distant landfill site.

He picked up his mobile phone and made the call.

"Trev, bonny lad, Bigsy. I thought you should know, I've just taken delivery of some of your finest Columbian, if you catch my drift. We're back in business again. My contact has given us some freebees by way of recompense for the interruption in supply, like, and as a good customer, I thought you and your missus could do with some. Rikki tells me things have been a bit fraught in the Rankin household lately."

Trev was a little suspicious at this generous offer; it was not like Bigsy, but then he wasn't about to turn down the chance of a good hit when the opportunity arose. It had been a while; he was making do with vodka.

"That's very decent of you Bigsy, lad; I would be very happy to take it off your hands," he drawled.

Bigsy told Trev to meet him at the underpass in half an hour.

Trev turned up, unshaven, looking distinctly rough and definitely worse for wear, swaying from side to side as he approached Bigsy in the underpass.

"Bigsy, bonny lad," he managed to say, his words slurring almost incoherently.

"Trev," Bigsy acknowledged, and they met in the darkness in the middle.

Lorries trundled overhead on their way to the A1; it was difficult to hear anything, but Bigsy wasn't after a conversation. Coast clear, Bigsy produced the two sealed packets from the pocket of his jeans and handed them over to Trev. He didn't notice that Bigsy was still wearing gloves.

"And don't you go taking it all yourself... Give some to the missus, eh? You never know, you might be on a promise."

"Aye, you could be right, bonny lad," said Trev.

They went their own ways and, once in the flat, Bigsy took off his jeans and put them in the washing machine with copious amounts of washing powder. Carole had no idea that Bigsy knew how to operate it; that was his little secret.

Saturday morning around ten o'clock, D. I. Fielding and W.P.C. Dobbs returned to Katya's flat to give her an update. They sat on the settee, declining the offer of a hot drink. Katya sat opposite them; Melos was in his recliner, watching what was happening. It was Fielding who led the discussion. He informed her that the initial Coroner's inquest had taken place and had determined that an 'open' verdict was appropriate, pending conclusions of the police investigations.

"However, we are working on the theory that Edi was murdered," added the officer.

"Murdered!?" gasped Katya. "But who would want to do that?"

"Well, that's what we're trying to find out. We're pretty certain now she <u>was</u> acting as a prostitute," said Fielding. This confirmed Katya's suspicions. "Unfortunately, we've not been able to trace any of her alleged clients and. without this information, it's going to be difficulty catch her killers.... Did Edi mention any names at all...? Please think hard."

"No, no...she er... she said nothing, nothing at all... She would have been too ashamed. I still can't believe Edi would sell herself like that."

The police had hit a brick wall and after a few more questions, left the flat.

A little later, Clara also dropped by to see how Arjeta was.

Arjeta was sat at the table with her crayons and colouring book. Katya explained that she had become withdrawn again.

"It was like she was when I first saw her... She just sits there at the table, drawing. She calls out for her mother when I put her to bed, and she has... how you say? Er, wet herself, two times."

"Are there any other relatives in Kosovo do you know?"

"No, all her family were killed... It's all I know; it's what Edi said," informed Katya.

"Well, I've spoken to Jenny Wheatley and it's in the hands of the Refugee Council, but we all agree it will be best for Arjeta to stay with you, for now... if you are ok with that... until a more permanent arrangement is found. But she is a Kosovan citizen and as such, she will have to go back to Kosovo at some stage," Clara added.

The thought of a Kosovan orphanage was not an attractive proposition. They were woefully short of supplies, people and materials. Katya told Clara she would look after Arjeta for as long as was necessary.

That evening, Carole invited Katya and Polly around for dinner; Bigsy had agreed to splash out on a takeaway. Carole thought it would distract them for a while. "A good curry and a couple of bottles of wine will do them a world of good."

Alison had agreed to babysit. So, at seven o'clock that evening, Katya and Polly, went around as planned.

It was a great night. Bigsy, after a couple of beers, swapped anecdotes with them and gradually, Katya began to feel relaxed and happy in the company of her friends. She thought back to her time in Kosovo and she realised that she hadn't really had any close friends, certainly none like Bigsy and Carole, and of course Polly who she now considered to be her soul-mate and loved him dearly.

They left Bigsy and Carole's just after eleven o'clock. Alison told them that the children had been good and were sound asleep and, after a short catch up, she returned to her flat.

Polly switched on the TV while Katya made some coffee. She brought in two mugs and snuggled down with Polly and they started talking about the future and what they both wanted. Polly wanted to take up the University offer which looked a formality now, such were his grades. He was also considering some freelance photography assignments. He had already got a very good reputation through his college work which was attracting a lot of admirers, and a couple of agencies had asked him to call them if he decided not to continue with his education.

Katya was holding him tightly. "Do you know, despite everything that has happened, I am so happy. You have made my life complete. I don't think I could have coped with everything if it wasn't for you."

She kissed him. Polly returned the kiss. Katya continued. "I have been thinking a lot about the future and I am going to make some changes. I am going to speak to Clara. I want to try to adopt Arjeta and..." she paused. "I also want to ask her about applying for asylum so I can to stay here."

"Oh that's champion, pet. I can't imagine life without you. I love you; I really do."

"I love you too, Polly."

They soon became distracted and the late film on the TV melted into the background as they made love on the sofa.

Monday morning, Bigsy was on the Hoppa to see his mother. He had spoken to her on the phone over the weekend but wanted to check on how she was coping without Joe. As the bus was driving away from the flats and along the Brompton Road, Bigsy noticed a commotion at the Rankin house. Several police cars were parked outside, and blue tape festooned the walkway to the front door. Bigsy smiled. He felt no pangs of guilt or remorse; it was justice... Heathcote style. It was how things were done.

The headline in the local paper that evening read:

'Couple found dead at house', followed by a narrative. *'Police are investigating the deaths of Trevor Rankin (37) and his wife Pauline (25) at their home in Brompton Road, Heathcote. It is understood that they both died as a result of a heroin overdose.*

They were both known addicts and Mr Rankin had a previous conviction for dealing. Police said they were anxious to locate the source of the heroin as it was a particularly pure batch and without processing, was potentially lethal. Police warned other heroin users in the area to be vigilant... Heathcote's drug problems, see pages 4, 5.'

That evening Bigsy went to the club with Wazza and Chirpie to discuss the recent course of events, nobody was mourning the loss of knob-head Trev and his poxy missus.

Katya, meanwhile, had returned to work at the pre-school club. She, too, had noticed the police cars outside a house as she walked past. The children seemed genuinely pleased to see her back and Mel and Sonia made a bit of a fuss of her. Even Arjeta, after all her trials, seemed happy to be back with the other children.

Following her discussion with Polly on Saturday night, Katya had phoned Clara that morning and arranged a meeting at three o'clock to discuss applying for citizenship and adopting Arjeta.

She was playing with Melos when Clara knocked on the door a couple of minutes early.

"Come in... Would you like a drink?" Katya greeted her warmly.

"I would love a coffee, Katya girl."

"Please... sit down, I won't be long."

She put Melos in his lobster pot and went to the kitchen. Arjeta was drawing at the table. Clara made herself comfortable.

Just then a buzzing sound came from the sofa beside Clara. It was Katya's mobile.

"Your phone's going, Katya," shouted Clara. "Do you want me to answer it?"

"Yes, please," shouted Katya from the kitchen.

Clara pressed the button with the little green telephone.

"Hello."

She listened intently; her face contorted with concentration. She called out.

"Katya, it's a man for you with a strong foreign accent... He says his name is Ibi..."

THE END

Lightning Source UK Ltd.
Milton Keynes UK
UKHW010737051120
372835UK00001B/63

9 781913 170257